**Evernight Publishing**

**www.evernightpublishing.com**

ISBN: 978-1-77130-923-3

Cover Artist: Sour Cherry Designs

Editor: Laurie Temple

FOREVER

# DEDICATION

To my beta readers and authors Lynn Rae and Jennifer Simpkins, both true romantics in their own right, for their tireless support and edits. And to Joyce McGregor, Roberta Graham and Zennia Snider who gave me the pure reader's perspective. I thank you all from the bottom of my heart.

And finally, sincere thanks to my editor Laurie Temple, who held my feet to the fire in the nicest possible way, and used her talents to help create the final labour of love: Forever.

FOREVER

# FOREVER

## *Eternity, 1*

**Allyson Young**



## Chapter One

"Check out that amazing man! Hell, check out *all* those amazing men! Except for the dweeb on the end." At least Lorraine attempted to add the latter sotto voce. "Do you suppose somebody wrote a list titled *Hot Guys,* with some specific parameters, and shouted it out? And they all came here? Like a gorgeous guy convention?"

Amy Copeland smiled behind her hand at the other woman's enthusiastic appraisal. The half dozen men sitting around the big table in the corner were certainly worthy of both the hot and the gorgeous guy labels. Especially the man at the head of the table, the one all the other men deferred to. Not that she'd been looking. Much. He was big for sure, and the time he'd gone to the men's room established he was taller than average too, maybe six-three or four to her five-foot-ten, and he had an easy way of moving—that long limbed stride so many big cats affected. Thick, dark hair with just enough curl, pale eyes, difficult to tell the color in the dim light, but she hadn't missed the hard planes of his handsome face. Or that mouth. Sculpted and sensuous with a hint of cruelty. Sigh.

"Which one?"

"Excuse me?" She turned away from another covert look at the mouth-watering group to stare at Lorraine.

"Pick one. You get first dibs, it being your birthday and all."

Julie, Noreen and even Sandra giggled loudly, giddiness fueled by too many margaritas, and Lorraine tossed back her heavy mane of black hair, a pout twisting her full, carmine lips.

"Amy should get first dibs," she insisted, loudly. "Birthday girl deserves a hot gift and those boys are haawwt."

"Keep your voice down." Amy whispered her plea.

"Why? They're like the best presents ever!"

Jeez. Lorraine's proclamations had attracted the attention of the "presents" and all of them were looking. Amy had just enough to drink to stare back challengingly, while wrestling with a sense of embarrassment. She wasn't interested in a casual hookup. Didn't matter how incredibly hot and sexy Mr. Tall and Muscular was or the way his right eyebrow quirked in such a way as to make her belly hitch when he looked directly into her eyes. She wrenched her gaze away, snatching up her bag. "Potty break."

Giggles erupted behind her as she hustled to the restrooms, an ideal distance from her table and the collection of hunks. Maybe they'd be gone by the time she got back. Lorraine had the attention span of a gnat so at least *she* will have moved on. Hopefully.

The bathroom pretty much reflected the appearance of the rest of the club—basic. No fancy marble-tiled backsplash or stainless sinks. The stained porcelain bowls featured dripping taps, although the hot water was plentiful, and the overhead lighting was dim and tended to throw shadows across the already silvering mirrors. But the drinks were cheap, the music not country, and the bar a marked contrast to the fancy places she'd frequented in Vegas. Sacramento was different, or at least it felt different, and Amy didn't want fancy or the memories similar venues stirred up.

Quickly using the facilities, she washed her hands and pushed her hair off her face, lifting the mass to drop it behind her shoulders. Checked her lip gloss and applied a little more, squinting to compensate for the poor reflective qualities of the mirror. Twenty-seven years old. Footloose and fancy free. Alone in this world, except for Sandra, and wasn't that fucking depressing?

Swivelling on her flats to check the fit of her dark jeans, relieved they hadn't stretched and bagged over her ass, she smoothed the silky stuff of her shirt and straightened the fall of her necklace, centering it over the V of her cleavage. Her index finger lingered on the tiny stylized C. C for change, a gift from Sandra when Amy was released from the hospital. A private, meaningful message. A reminder. Amy stroked it like the talisman it was and reminded herself that hot men, *any* hot men, were off limits. Meeting men in places like this ended in one night stands and she wasn't doing that anymore.

Hopefully, her girls were ready to pack it in. She had no particular place to go, no one to see, but the buzz was gone. Tomorrow would be another day, like yesterday, and while money wasn't so much of an issue anymore, Amy was feeling restless, ready to move on. She'd miss Sandra, a lot. But there was nothing to hold her here, and maybe there would be someplace else. Someone else. Maybe Sandra would want to come with, although her friend really liked the hospital where she now worked.

Exiting into the hall, footsteps deadened by the worn carpet and heavily panelled walls, she checked in her purse for her phone and ran into a wall of warm, solid male. Big, strong hands gripped her shoulders as she rocked back with the impact.

"Easy, sweetheart."

Holy shit. Holy shit. Tall, muscular guy from the hunky crowd. Her pulse kicked up and her face suffused with heat. He was even better looking close up, eyes a darker shade of the silver dollars the tourists fed the slots in Vegas. And as hard. He got her juices flowing, and she struggled against the attraction. So not fitting in with her C for change.

"Excuse me. Sorry." *Oh, good one, Amy. Sophisticated.* Couldn't turn on a little attitude about him blocking the hallway with his awesomeness, a barrier just waiting for an unsuspecting woman to walk right into. She'd become a wuss since leaving Vegas, losing her thin veneer of sophistication. Pasting on a vague smile she made to slip past him, but he shifted, too. She deked the other way. Blocked again. So they weren't doing the supermarket aisle dance, each moving in the same direction while trying to avoid the other. She dared another look at his face and met that quirked brow again, those cruel, sexy lips twitching with apparent amusement. Her eyes dropped down his body in self-preservation. Mistake.

His worn jeans fit him admirably, tightly stretched across his thighs, the solid metal piece of his belt buckle drawing attention to the taut fabric molding his—she swallowed the mouth-watering sensation and pretended to examine the dark material of his shirt while she searched for something to say to conclude the chance meeting.

"What?" Another conversational gem.

"Happy Birthday, Amy."

They hadn't… They had. Her girls actually told this man… Goddamn it. She took a step back and tried another smile. "Thanks."

"Your loud friend—Lorraine—announced the gift idea. I decided who you'd choose."

Can you say arrogant? Confident? Insufferable? Amy knew all her adjectives applied, but damned if he couldn't carry them off. Cautiously, she said, "You thought I'd choose you?"

"Didn't say that. Said I was making your choice."

Okay. She didn't know quite what to make of that. Truthfully, she hadn't really scrutinized the other men at his table, except to note they were mostly all of a type— tall, built, and good looking. She'd really looked at *him*.

"Who are you?" Was that wise? Did she really want to know? She did.

"Dean Chambray. Those guys—we work together."

"They work *for* you."

His eyes narrowed and the sterling in the silver intensified, set off by thick, dark lashes. "Now why would you say that?"

Shrugging, she answered. "They paid attention to you, deferred to you." Probably she hadn't needed to share. Men preferred big, dumb blondes, not ones who obviously paid attention. But she wasn't slipping back into that role again.

He reached out and hooked a piece of her hair, a strand right at that sensitive juncture where neck meets shoulder, pulling it gently until she followed its insistent tugging, moving right back into his space. "Beautiful *and* smart."

Her brain went to mush, the scent of sandalwood and hot male washing over her, the very heat of him tangible. She tipped her head back in order to read his face. "What?"

"You're observant, and interpret what you see accurately. Smart."

Smart. Amy was vigilant and read people and situations out of dire necessity. She'd lived on the edge nearly all her life in a variety of foster homes and one memorable, not in a good way, juvie unit, before being absorbed into the Vegas street life at the tender age of sixteen. Surviving state foster care was a major feat in itself, and to make it off the street and into the high-roller lifestyle, albeit as a bit player … well, good instincts rated right up there with intelligence. Higher. But she possessed her share of the latter, if her history sometimes dumbed it down, made her make poor choices. Her history, and how she confused hot sex with love and affection, was psychology one-oh-one. She mentally thanked Sandra, for the C for change.

Her silence elicited another measured look. "Modest, too. What would you like for your birthday?"

"What? I mean, excuse me?" Another scintillating conversational gambit. Modest? Her? Well, her current job didn't require face-to-face communication, and chatting wasn't high on the list of her past *position.* Discouraged, actually.

"What'd you wish for?"

"Oh. I didn't have a cake or blow out any candles. So no wish."

"What would you like, Amy?" Less patience, more insistence.

Imagining his face if she came right out with it, laid it on him, she felt her lips twitch and fought a derisive snicker, knowing she laughed to cover her wistfulness. *I want a man who'll respect me and trust me, love me and not try to change me, yet take care of me. Someone who won't use me, but will make babies with me and live by my side forever and ever.*

"Nothing, actually." It was true—she wanted the impossible.

"Well, then I'll choose that for you, too. Consider this the bow on top." Dean cradled the back of her head with one big hand, holding her steady with the other placed in the small of her back. He leaned down to take her lips. Startled, she parted them to protest and his tongue instantly surged inside to duel with her own, exploring the recesses of her mouth. Sculpted, sensuous, she'd add sublimely talented to describe those lips. Her eyes closed and she gave herself up to the myriad of sensations. So much for the psych lesson.

Knees weakening, she reached up to push her fingers through Dean's thick hair, holding him close, sealing their mouths ever tighter. The hard bulge at his crotch pressed heatedly into her abdomen and her pussy liquefied, preparing for when this man lifted her so she could wrap her legs around his waist and—holy mother. This was insane! A moan of protest replaced the whimpering sound of her surrender, and he released her lips, although not his grip on her waist or her head. Pulling back, Amy extricated her fingers, awkwardly patting at his hair, fluttering her hands down to attempt to insert them between their bodies. His eyes were mesmerizing, slate grey over silver, churning with arousal. And he was far too close for her to think with anything other than what her weeping pussy wanted.

"Can't wait to unwrap the whole package." His voice was rough and raspy.

Wait—it was *her* birthday. She didn't trust her voice but pushed against rock hard pecs.

Letting her go, he still blocked her retreat, standing in place, waiting, patient again. Amy felt her whole body give a little shudder, actually *felt* the cathartic awareness of something bigger, different, *more* than any of her past experiences with the opposite sex. And it scared the ever-loving shit out of her.

"I have to go." Her voice sounded reed thin and plaintive.

He quirked that brow. "I don't play games, sweetheart. Now or never."

And there it was, spoiling that atavistic awareness. A hookup, a quick fuck, probably not quick and probably great, but she wasn't doing that anymore, not that those hookups in the past had been particularly memorable in the face of what she felt for this man. Chemistry.

The longer-term *positions* weren't anything for her scrap book, either, and something Amy preferred not to think about. It was her birthday, and she supposed she was entitled to a nice present, but she wanted to hang onto it, wanted to keep this particular gift. That desire in itself surprised her, having just met him, but Dean Chambray not only aroused her to the utter max, something deep inside woke up and clamored to be heard, begged to connect with him. No sense in teasing herself. Or it. Because *he* wasn't different. Wrong again.

"Never, then. Thanks for the birthday kiss."

This time he stepped far enough aside to give her room to pass. His face was impassive although his eyes sparked. Thwarted desire or annoyance? Same thing. Amy forced herself to walk slowly back to the table, the age and disrepair of the club more apparent to her heightened senses. The floors dipped from the weight of thousands of feet, the walls marked by countless hands and the faint smell of mildew wasn't totally masked by the crush of bodies emitting both natural and purchased scents. *Don't look back.* Four feminine faces stared her way, three alight with anticipation, Sandra's drawn with worry. Her friend could read her a mile off. Fuck it. It was *her* birthday. "Somebody order another pitcher!"

"Atta girl! You miss the hardbody back there?" Lorraine was as irrepressible as ever and Amy wondered how Sandra had come to include her in the small circle of friends she'd cultivated since relocating. Sandra was a serious, reserved type. But Lorraine was also a nurse, and apparently blew off steam on a regular basis because of the often depressing things she saw on the neonatal unit. As for Julie and Noreen, ward clerks, both of them, and really nice women, they were always up for a party. Amy was just a hanger on. Until Sandra, she didn't spend time with women at all, didn't have girlfriends. But Sandra saved her life.

She decided to answer Lorraine's question with another. "You up for hitting Grand Masters after this?"

"Oh, girl. Nasty. Grand Masters?" Lorraine shrieked it over the sound of the music, then winked comically, her face screwing up, both eyes shutting. She lowered her voice to a dull roar. "You have *those* kind of tendencies? Sure. What the hell? After the pitcher. Somebody order it."

Amy didn't know if she really had those tendencies. But the parody of bondage and titillating sexual acts played out at Grand Masters were intriguing, and even though she'd only attended a few times the entire scene got her fantasies going. Sandra's too, although her friend only grudgingly acknowledged it, saying she preferred her erotic novels. And as far as Amy knew, no man had graced her friend's bed since Sandra's ascent from hell.

Noreen and Julie were game for anything, as always. The jug of margaritas arrived and Amy worked her way through her glass in record time, having resolutely ignored the return of Dean Chambray to his table and the subsequent exit of him and his men after a couple of bottles were drained and a few faint protests died away. It appeared his companions weren't ready to leave, but they kowtowed to him, reinforcing her impression he was very much in charge. The wistful feeling Amy harbored didn't die away at all, and she felt her lips surreptitiously from time to time.

"You okay?" Sandra blinked owlishly. Always a cheap drunk.

"Uh huh. Just decided to live it up. Thirty's just around the corner."

"Hardly. You're not over the hill yet. But okay. You just looked kinda spooked, and I wondered…"

"Nah. It's all good. Drink up. We're missing most of the shows as it is." Amy didn't want to get into a discussion about men with Sandra. That's how they met, because of a man, and Amy knew how protective her friend was with her.

They finished their drinks and her girls headed to the restrooms while Amy went out to find a cab for five intoxicated women, herself included. Guzzling another margarita on an empty stomach … and with no cake. A minivan taxi pulled up, the light on the roof flashing its availability, and she held it until the other women burst through the door, laughing and calling out. Piling inside, she told the driver their destination and sat back to enjoy the ride. She could easily background search Dean Chambray when she got home, or tomorrow even, but decided she wouldn't. No point in tormenting herself.

The crowded conditions of the cab, blended with the various perfumes they wore and the alcohol fumes, made the atmosphere close and she watched as the driver inhaled the intoxicating brew. He attempted to make conversation and Lorraine entertained him with speculation about his "romantic" abilities. God.

****

"Grand Masters? You're shitting me. Andrea'll kick my ass." Randy shook his head. "You're on your own, boss. But take Enrico, and maybe a couple of the other guys'll go."

"I'm not planning to hang around. I just want to see what that big blonde makes of the place." As soon as the description left his mouth, Dean regretted it. He'd made her sound like a floozy from another era and that woman was anything but.

"The birthday girl? You have "words" with her back there?"

"In the hallway, actually. She blew me off."

"No shit. That's a new one for you." Randy's tone wasn't commiserating. There was an undertone of satisfaction Dean understood. He rarely struck out with a woman, and changed them out like his socks. His hunter's instinct was aroused by one blonde Amy, something unfamiliar and very rare indeed.

"I don't play games. They put out or not. Their choice. I don't chase."

"They put out and then you put them out. *No* chase." A hint of censure now colored his lieutenant's tone. Happily married and vocal about it, Randy forgot his own fairly recent man-whore status.

Dean shrugged. "I'm nothing but honest with them, you know it."

"But not all of them were skanks. Some were nice girls."

"They all knew the score. And I'm done talking."

"Uh huh, and that's why you're heading to that tie 'em up and fuck 'em theatre-production-slash-nightclub. The blonde didn't understand the *score*?"

Dean throttled an absurd desire to punch Randy in the head. How could he answer the other man when he didn't understand it himself? He settled for a non committal "curious."

"Take Enrico. If your mind is on Blondie you won't be watching your back. You got that feeling, remember?"

Indeed. He had a feeling. Hence the impromptu meeting at the bar to put a few things into place while the offices were swept for bugs. The whisper of danger was a cold trickle of warning hovering dead between his shoulder blades. He'd totally forgotten the sensation when he kissed Amy. Not a good thing. He nodded to Randy. He'd take Enrico.

"I'll drop you at the complex," he offered.

"I'll grab a ride with Olsen. I want to see what, if anything, was turned up in the sweep anyhow. See you tomorrow." Randy turned away.

Dean motioned to Enrico, who obligingly climbed into the passenger seat. A man of few words, he was silent during the drive to the Masters, and Dean was glad not to have to respond to inane conversation. The serious stuff had already been said and he had a more pressing problem. His cock strained at attention behind the coarse weave of his jeans, imprinting on the zipper if not for the silk fabric of his boxers. The big blonde's absence hadn't mitigated his arousal one iota. He could still taste her, a mixture of tart lime and hints of sugar. And Amy. He could still feel the press of her generous breasts, the poke of her nipples. And her scent. Fuck. His cock tried to nod frantically within its cloth prison and he nearly groaned out loud.

So she liked the Grand Masters. Mind you, lots of people did. Gorgeous bodies of either gender, a little bondage, a hint of kink, lots to tease and tantalize. He wondered if Amy knew of the rooms in the back of the nightclub. He'd gone a couple of times with adventurous women, under the tutelage of a very experienced Dominant, and learned a thing or two about himself and how to pleasure a woman to extreme heights. But he didn't need the trappings or the protocol. Dean enjoyed sex, a lot of it. A good fuck, with nothing to cloud the main event. Long term wasn't in the cards, and while he liked some of the women he fucked, as much as he got to know them, love wasn't in the cards, either. Ever. That Amy puzzled him, or rather, his reaction to her did.

Knowing himself well, he decided to take one more kick at the cat, rather than be distracted by memories of that torrid kiss and the stirring of an unfamiliar ... something. He was uncomfortable, and if an "accidental" run in again with Blondie tonight got her into his bed, well, he'd fuck her right out of it, and life would go back to what passed for normal. It struck him that the woman might not even show up, and he and Enrico would be left sitting in a voyeur's club, hot and bothered, with only each another for company. That didn't sit at all well, although he could admit to finding some humor in the situation. Overhearing Lorraine's enthusiastic agreement about going to the Masters didn't mean they would actually attend. What *was* it about Blondie? He couldn't have even described her friends with accuracy, and that, too, was outside the norm. He couldn't afford to miss any nuance.

The city was hopping tonight, the downtown streets crowded with vehicles and foot traffic, and impatience had him drumming his fingers on the steering wheel as they waited through yet another delayed light.

He checked his mirrors automatically, aware Enrico was doing the same, although all headlights looked pretty much the same in the dark. His weapon was tucked away in a compartment beneath his seat, easy to get to, but he wasn't carrying it into a place like Grand Masters. Amy hadn't missed much with her covert glances, and he had no doubt she'd see the outline of a gun. Her ability to observe and unerringly assess should be telling him to keep his distance—he couldn't afford prescient women—but he felt driven to see her again. However, there was no point in giving her a deeper window into his life when any connection with her was going to be short term, so he'd keep his firepower under the seat.

Pulling into the crowded lot, he found a space big enough to park his truck, and he and Enrico joined the small group outside the club. The pulsing beat emanating from the partially open door had everyone moving to it, some subtly, others blatantly, the scant illumination doing little to hide the excitement and anticipation on the faces of both genders. The doorman looked their way and his casual stance stiffened. The man gestured to Dean and waved them through, past the hopefuls who'd probably been waiting to enter for hours. Sometimes it helped to be known in this city. Or as someone who'd purchased a block of shares in Masters.

Dean slowed beside the doorman and dropped the word in his ear not to delay the entry of five women, spearheaded by a tall, beautiful blonde. He had no doubt Amy would be in the lead, despite her attempt to be self effacing. Intriguing.

They were shown to a table not far from both the stage and the door, one clearly reserved for VIPs, and Dean tipped his chair back up against the wall, relaxing his body while scanning the room. Enrico swivelled his own chair to give him a better vantage point, but of the crowd. The kid knew better than to leave himself open to distractions, however exotic and tempting, obviously taking his assigned role as bodyguard seriously.

The walls were painted a dull, flat black, and absorbed all available light, taking nothing away from the stage lit in various areas to showcase the activity. Heavy, crimson, velvet drapery panels framed faux windows intermittently applied to the walls with lengths of wrought iron tortured into intricate shapes. Dean knew how erotic those shapes were, having scrutinized them while touring the place and doing a deal with the owners. Sconces set at head height flickered ominously, each table boasting the same flickering light in the shape of a candle, the better to add to the mood. Heavy, baroque chandeliers dripped crystals and gave the patrons and serving staff enough light to negotiate the wide planked floors.

The room was full, tables packed with patrons of all ages, from early twenties to early sixties, maybe older, and the atmosphere was heavy with lust. Sultry eyes on the women, and some of the men, seemingly casual gestures actually designed to entice and showcase the bounty of flesh on display. The air seethed with hormones and Dean could see hands tucked under the tables, the black and red cloth providing a barrier to what he assumed were illicit gropings.

A well built fellow, his muscles encased in leather, hovered around a nearly naked woman hanging from a hook in the middle of the stage, her toes barely brushing the floor. He was binding her with red rope, and her spotlit face was beatific in expression, lips parted, eyes closed, relaxed. As the man's hands drifted around her body, Dean could swear he heard her moan despite the pulsing rock music filling the club. Nothing really graphic—he'd seen more of a woman's body in a strip joint—but the intimacy and the trust she showed, the surrender, were incredibly arousing.

Personal exhibitionism wasn't Dean's thing, but he was glad others enjoyed that kink because he got off watching it. He wondered what Amy's private fantasies were and if one night would be enough to explore them. Didn't matter. It would have to be one night, with maybe a casual other time or two, depending on if she understood his expectations. Saying no to him earlier was probably just playing hard to get.

Knowing why he didn't trust women didn't change it. The old lady's ravaged face swam into his vision, unbidden, and he impatiently blinked it away. Why was he thinking about *her*? Maybe this urge to hunt down Blondie was a mistake. He didn't like where his thoughts were going, or the historical shit being stirred up. Dropping the front feet of the chair onto the floor with a thump, Dean made to motion away the waitress heading over to take their order, planning to exit. Then he saw Amy enter the club, hesitating as she did so, body poised to—flee? From his slight vantage point behind the thin body of the waitress, he watched as Amy scanned the room, much the same way he'd done earlier, before stepping aside to allow her friends to pass. Interesting. He forgot all about the fact he'd been about to leave.

The women squeezed around a table offset in a corner, clearly the least appealing of the seating, but the only thing available. "Take two jugs of margaritas to that table in the alcove, the one with the five newcomers," he ordered the still hovering waitress. "And a couple of beers for us."

Nodding, her eyes passing over his face and then obviously dropping to his crotch, the server pushed her breasts out before turning to sashay a nicely curved ass away.

"Asking for it." Enrico missed nothing, although the come-on had been blatant.

Dean shrugged. "Not interested."

"But you *are* interested in the tall rubia who just came in. From the other club."

Give the man a cigar. And maybe a cigar was just a cigar. Shades of fucking Freud. He needed to get this new conquest done. The five heads he scrutinized across the way bobbed in concert, two dark, one red, and two blond. An interesting combination, although Amy's multicolored strands captured his sole attention. What would one call that color? Cream and gold? Whatever—she had masses of it. It framed those purple blue eyes that had so carefully inspected him. Any sounds they made, even Lorraine's, were masked by the music and the crowd response to the scene on stage. He flicked his glance back in that direction.

The female star was totally swaddled in the red rope now with the exception of her breasts, wrapped and cradled, presented for view as they swelled with the constriction. One strand passed between her widespread legs, a knot strategically tied at the apex of her pussy, and as Dean watched the Dom tugged that strand, making the woman shudder and pulsate. He leaned in and kissed her before reaching up to release the binds at the hook. The sub, if that's what she was, or maybe a volunteer from the audience, sagged into his arms and he shifted her weight, carrying her away, stage left. The audience erupted in applause and a few raucous calls and suggestions. Dean's cock protested its lack, suggesting Blondie might welcome some of what was doubtlessly going to take place backstage.

Observing the waitress making her way towards the little table, balancing those jugs of margaritas, he waited for the reaction. Five faces turned in his direction at the server's gesture and he sketched a negligent wave. Lorraine waved back, enthusiastically, followed by the red head and the other blonde. Amy and the brunette looked at each another before nodding his way in tandem. So the brunette was her best friend and the one who'd give her the advice Amy would listen to. Good to know. Enrico was watching them, too.

"The brunette? Beside my blonde? Might need you to run interference, 'Rico."

"She is average, boss. I would wish for the red head. But for you…"

"Not asking you to marry her. Just distract her if need be."

"Okay."

Their beer was set on their table with maybe a little more firmness than necessary, each bottle making a little snapping sound as it hit the polished surface. "They weren't going to accept them, sir. At least not the big girl. But her friends convinced her."

God, women were such bitches. Wasn't enough they sucked men dry with their demands, guilted them out, and fucked them over. They had to take a crack at one another, too. Giving the waitress a disparaging look, Dean nodded and scratched his signature on the check. Little waitress-bitch had presumably found out who he was, probably from the bartender. She smiled her thanks, a brittle, false smile, nothing like the seductive one she'd bestowed on him earlier. His reputation had preceded him. Good.

****

"He came here because he knew you were coming."

Lorraine's complacent comment made Amy want to smack her. Seeing Dean Chambray's handsome visage across the room after the margaritas were delivered had blown her away. Last chance, eh? *I don't play games.* Well, no second chances for him. She accepted and acknowledged the booze when her friends put up a fuss, but didn't have to like it. Sandra got the implication, if they hadn't. But then Sandra knew where Amy was coming from. Recklessly pouring another full glass, she sucked half of it back, hoping the next scene on stage would distract Lorraine. She managed to keep her face inscrutable as the flavor burst over her taste buds—these drinks were far superior to the ones at the previous place. She surreptitiously filled her glass again.

"If you don't want him, I'll be happy to stand in." Lorraine just wouldn't leave it alone.

"He wants a quick fuck, Lorraine, a wham bam, thank you ma'am," she shouted back, past caring if anyone else listened in. "You want that, you go right ahead."

"No, you don't." Red-headed Julie vigorously shook her head and Noreen added her disapproval. "You get drunk and fall into some hot guy's bed 'n never see him again. Then beat yourself up for doing it for weeks. You go home and call Malik if that's what you want. At least he loves you."

Lorraine slumped in her chair and scowled. "Yah, sure. He loves me. That's why he won't introduce me to his family. Because he loves me so much."

Amy shut out Lorraine's continuing complaints, and now, maudlin protests. Julie and Noreen had pulled the bandage off, and they could deal with the outcome. She couldn't let herself think about love and sex and everything in between. It hadn't been, and never would be, for her. Witness what she'd attracted tonight.

"He speak to you at the other club?" Sandra spoke quietly, close to her ear, the alcohol buzz probably burned off some by concern. Shit.

"Speak to me? As in "my name is, and I want to do you, once." That kind of speak?" Her bitter tone nearly masked the sadness.

"Oh, Amy. I'm sorry. What is it with men? Don't any of them want a relationship?"

"Depends on what kind, I guess. You know it's me. I just attract the wrong kind. No surprise." She shrugged and poured another glass, no longer tracking well. Viva the mind numbing agent of alcohol. "Let's just suck these back and enjoy the show. There's always B.O.B. for those one-nighters."

"It's *not* you," Sandra whispered fiercely. "You have to stop thinking that way."

Amy shook her head and Sandra shut up, knowing better than to fight a losing battle at that moment. Not that her friend wouldn't take up the cudgels tomorrow, and the next day… They turned their attention to the stage, ignoring Lorraine's tears and recriminations until Noreen touched Sandra's arm. "Lor's had enough for the night and we have to work tomorrow. We'll take her home. Sorry to put a damper on your birthday, Amy."

"Not to worry. It was nice of you to come." She wondered if she'd see Lorraine again. Tonight had ended in a spate of pain for the other woman, and Amy felt like she'd goaded her. Seeing as Julie and Noreen were tight with her, they might not like Amy, either. But they all smiled sweetly at one another and each took one of Lorraine's elbows to help her up. Weaving a path to the door, they vanished from sight. It occurred to Amy that it might look as if the other women had left to pare down the field—two men, two women. Shit.

Sandra must have thought the same thing. "Wanna go?"

Hell, no. It was her birthday. Besides she was a little afraid to stand, would probably fall on her ass. "In a bit."

The lights flickered and an enormously broad man strode onto the stage. It was constructed in a half circle to allow for the placement of the different apparatus and stage sets. Blood-red draperies, hanging in swathes, created a sensuous backdrop, optimally displaying naked flesh. Two huge television screens flanked either side, allowing patrons in the back a good view of the entertainment, and there were a variety of different lighting systems to be utilized. It reminded Amy of the stages in Vegas, and she fought the nostalgia, because other memories inevitably followed. While able to manage them now, there was no sense in being triggered and totally ruin her evening.

The MC wasn't that tall, maybe up to her shoulder, but obviously fit, with muscles on muscles. His leather pants strained to contain tree trunk legs, and his bare chest shone beneath the spot light. "If all of you are sufficiently loosened up for the evening, it's the volunteer section of the entertainment. Looking for a woman, one who's never been on the stage before. Can't be falling down drunk. Lowered inhibitions is okay because we won't be pushing boundaries—at least not too much."

Laughter coursed through the room, full of anticipation and arousal. Amy shivered. It *was* her birthday and there'd been no cake and no *present.* Fuck Dean Chambray.

"Clothing's optional, but okay for this demonstration. Master Eric is going to restrain the volunteer—" Another man stalked forward to join the MC, also clad in leathers, blond hair caught back in a ponytail, Nordic features reminding Amy of that guy from the Thor movie. He didn't cut as imposing a figure as say, Dean Chambray, but he wasn't bad, oiled and sculpted chest gleaming under the lights. Not bad at all. She swallowed another gulp of her drink.

"—restrain the volunteer on this bed," the MC continued, "and use this interesting implement to sensitize her skin." He held up what appeared to be a pizza cutter, only smaller. Everyone seemed to strain forward to get a good look. Amy missed what he labelled it, but she knew she'd read about it. "Whoever takes her home will be glad she volunteered."

Amy shifted in her chair and Sandra gave her a warning glance. "Don't. Why would you set yourself up?"

"Maybe because it'll be a lesson, Sandra. Teach me not to want what I can't have. I'll be going home tonight alone, and won't forget how I let my hormones get away from me with that man."

"You don't know that you won't have something special someday, Amy! You don't. Give it some time."

"Nope. It's my birthday." She raised her hand when the MC asked again for a volunteer, having rejected all the previous applicants.

"Ah, the blonde in the corner. If you can navigate your way up on stage…"

Amy was up and moving, ignoring Sandra's final plea. Calling on her strong center, the one that saw her through over the years, she made her way to the dais, threading through the tables. She was past tipsy, probably having imbibed close to a pitcher of her favorite tipple in a short period of time, carried forward on a wave of misplaced rebellion. Dumbing her intelligence down. And fuck Dean Chambray again, too. She was still lucid enough to want this.

The MC offered his hand once she mounted the stairs, and she took it, trying hard not to use it for balance and give her altered state away. His hand cupped her chin and he stared up into her eyes searchingly, speaking in a low voice. "I've seen you here before, girl. So you figured to try it this time? But you've had a lot to drink."

"It's my birthday." She pulled her hand from his and waited for him to decide.

"What's your name and who are you here with?"

"My friend, Sandra."

"*Your* name!" She responded to the authority in his voice and her addled wits cleared more than a trifle. God, there was nothing like a self-assured, confident man.

"Amy."

"I'll take her as my volunteer." The other Dom moved in, his blue eyes assessing, cold. Amy shivered and tried to regroup. "It's only sensitizing and I'll avoid the real erogenous zones."

Still, the MC hesitated as the audience murmured and grew restive. "Okay. But I'll be watching, Eric. And you, Amy, if you want it to stop you say red and it's over. Got it?"

"I do." Like, do you take this man to be—Amy swallowed a giggle, now stupidly nervous.

"Will you remove your clothes?"

Clothes. Hadn't thought that through. She hesitated.

"Leave your underwear on." Eric didn't seem to be the type who negotiated, so she figured she would accommodate him. Her bathing suits revealed more than her boy shorts and bra. Wait. Was she wearing pretty underwear? This time a giggle did escape and Eric unexpectedly smiled. "It'll be fine, Amy."

The MC smiled, too, and left them to it. The lights dimmed and Eric had her sit on the bed, tugging off her shoes, then helping her with the tight jeans as she hitched up her hips to pull them down. Her shirt floated away and over her head and the coolness of the fans above the stage made her skin rash out in goosebumps and her nipples bead.

"If you'll just shift up to lie on the bed, Amy. Do you want a blindfold? The live feed will be shown on the screens."

For an instant she panicked. A video. Shit. While she'd been historically able to dissociate from her body—from anything unpalatable happening to her—pictures would make it all too real if they got out there.

Immediately soothing her with his voice and a gentle stroke on her arm, Eric whispered, "We don't make copies for any reason and the lighting makes it pretty hard for anybody to tape it, and there's no cell service in this room. The blindfold will heighten the sensation, though, and provide anonymity."

"Why me?" She whispered back, having puzzled out that the MC would have likely turned her down because he'd recognized how much she had imbibed.

"If you enjoy this, maybe you and I can see where it leads."

Amy liked the sound of it. Eric looked cold and dominant, but he'd already accommodated her boundaries and was suggesting things to her. Not *telling* her. Not suggesting a one off. Not like—she shut it down and nodded. A soft piece of fabric slipped over her face and settled across her eyes as the lights came up again, the elastic resting above and behind her ears to snug it into place. She took a deep breath and began to sink into that space she'd constructed for herself at an early age. Safe, separate and far away.

Vaguely feeling Eric stretch first one arm, then the other out to her sides to be secured in a firm but non constrictive way, she didn't bother to test the restraints.

She'd been at the club often enough to know that utmost care was taken on this stage, the breach of the rules about excessive alcohol consumption notwithstanding. Knowing people were watching would normally have caused her some anxiety, but the blindfold gave the impression of being alone with someone who understood what she needed. Eric certainly knew this gig. When her ankles were restrained in a similar manner, maybe shoulder width apart, her arousal spiked, already awakened by that kiss in the other club. She sighed and drifted, refusing to think about Dean Chambray watching. Refusing to acknowledge it was his attention making her wet.

A disembodied voice described her position, like a starfish, and the alcohol fueled her libido. Maybe being naked wouldn't have been such a bad idea after all… A press of a number of sharp yet painless tiny objects at her left wrist took her focus, pulling her from her musings. Barely audible squeaking sounds accompanied the dragging, pricking sensations as the object worked past the heel of her hand and over her forearm, up her bicep, slowing to make the curve up to her shoulder. Blowing a breath past her lips, she tensed for the next movement, pulled out of her drifting state.

"Shh. Relax and feel." Eric's voice centred her and she sagged again, loose and compliant. The little wheel continued its torturous journey, traversing the length of her collar bone, pausing at the pulse in the hollow of her throat. Her blood began to thrum in response. Down the other arm and back, the sensation trickled over her rib cage. Not a tickle, just firm enough to be sensuous. She moaned as her belly received the attention next, little circles, then figure eights. Able to visualize the path on her skin, entirely in the moment, she arched slightly into the contact and it instantly ceased, returning only when she relaxed and received. Training her.

Amy's eyes fluttered opened behind the blindfold. Eric's voice was immediately at her ear. "Tell me."

"You're training me."

"Of course. That's what I do. Give in to it, Amy. It's just for now."

Not forever. Okay. She could do this. She nodded.

The sensitizing of her legs was indescribable. Even the arches of her feet cried out for more, more of something beyond her ken, but more. As the wheel creaked inexorably up to her breasts, the little teeth snagging the fabric of her bra, the alarm bells rang again and she tensed. Eric retreated, down over her belly to circle her navel, a sweet spot, and she thought everyone could hear her verbal response as it echoed in her ears. Over her hipbone to flirt inside one thigh, the tender flesh quivering, the wheel glancing off her labia, pressing … no.

"Red."

Another press of the teeth, inward and up, her clitoris straining for the touch.

"Red." Louder. No way could Eric miss it.

"You fucking heard her." Not the MC's voice, although his even deeper one joined in, a harsh whisper.

"Goddamn it, Eric! You're pushing her. You had her surrendering, you asshole, but you just had to push it. Couldn't you see it? No wonder subs don't trust you."

Fingers efficiently loosened her wrists while another set worked at her ankles.

"I didn't hurt her. She's submissive." Eric's voice was defensive, if muted.

"You're fired." The rasp in Dean's voice mirrored the one she'd heard after he kissed her. He was stoked.

"Who the fuck do you think you are?"

The MC spoke quietly, but firmly. "Part owner, Eric. Dean Chambray. Pack up your stuff and get out."

The blindfold was eased off and Amy blinked up into a pair of molten silver eyes. She dragged her gaze away and looked at the MC who grimaced apologetically. Eric was nowhere to be seen. She noticed the lights were once again dimmed in her location, brighter towards the front of the stage, and realized no one could see the little tableau playing out. Unless the camera was still on. She sat up quickly and tried to scramble to her feet, foiled by a sense of light-headedness and Dean Chambray's hard hands.

"You'll be on your ass, sweetheart. Give it a minute while Lloyd finds your clothes."

Shit. What on earth had she been thinking? Oh, right. The margaritas had ruled her frontal lobe. She acquiesced and accepted first her shirt, then her jeans from Master Lloyd, the MC. Pulling her top on gave her a better sense of control. She decided not to step into the jeans, but pulled them on past each foot and up her legs, jackknifing her bottom to get them up over her hips and zipped. Buttoned. Dean tracked her every move. She could feel the weight of his eyes and that sense of longing awoke. *No.*

"I'm sorry." She spoke to Master Lloyd.

"What for, girl? I made a bad judgement call and let Eric compound it. Just don't sue."

A tiny laugh bubbled up. "Hardly. A ton of people just saw me splayed out in my underwear on a stage."

"Did you like it? At least until Eric didn't respect your boundaries?" There was clinical curiosity in Master Lloyd's tone.

Shivering, Amy nodded. "Yes. I'm not interested in doing it again, but I guess something like that was on my bucket list."

"Well then, it's not a total fuck up." Master Lloyd nodded to her and walked away, closely resembling that short guy from the Lord of the Rings. The one with the axe. She wished he wouldn't go and leave her alone with Dean.

"I'll take you home." Not a request, not an offer. Telling her.

"S'okay. My friend—"

"I'll take her, too. My man Enrico's already with her, telling her to meet us in the parking lot."

"No! Sandra's not going to take some strange man's word for it, telling her to leave without me." She tried to control her concern for Sandra, and who was this Enrico? If he was anything like Dean…

He made an audible sound of frustration and stepped away. Amy rubbed her arms to counteract the crash of all those endorphins, the waning of the influence of the booze. Lighter steps resonated on the stairs and Sandra hurried to her, reaching to feel her pulse.

"They wouldn't let me up here, just dimmed the goddamn lights and played like it was the natural ending of the demonstration but I knew different. Are you okay?" Sandra stumbled with pronouncing demonstration, and she was swearing, so she was still a little buzzed, but concerned, nonetheless. Amy hurried to reassure her friend.

"I'm okay. Honestly. It was a rush until the jerk pushed me and didn't stop when I asked."

Sandra looked at her searchingly then tried to smile. "And on your birthday, too!"

They laughed together and Amy pulled Sandra into an awkward hug. What a freaking night.

"Ready?" Shit. He hadn't gone away.

"We can get a cab." Beside her, Sandra nodded.

"I'll take you. Think of it as an apology on behalf of the club." Dean's attitude brooked no argument, although his stance was deceptively relaxed. Amy could sense the tension behind it, feel it, and she was too tired to argue, worn down. And something else, something she wasn't going to acknowledge.

"Thanks." The least she could do was be gracious.

A younger, dark-skinned man, intensely attractive in a dark-flashing eyes, white smile kind of way, cupped Sandra's elbow to escort her and her friend immediately pulled away to walk independently. Amy emulated her and carefully avoided any contact with Dean, who gave her a tight, knowing smile. The walk to the parking lot, out the back way, took an eternity and she was intensely aware of Dean's bulk just behind her and to her left. She felt both protected and anxious at the same time.

The night was warm with the promise of rain licking over her senses but she shivered despite the warmth—he was too close. Dean immediately responded and wrapped her up, tucking her into his side, supporting her forward momentum. His misinterpretation of her reaction worsened her weakness. The asphalt felt spongy and yielding beneath her feet, and she tried not to breathe in his scent, reacting to the surfeit of pheromones he exuded. She felt incapable of resisting.

Clambering after Sandra into the large back seat of a big, black truck, with Dean's helping hand far too close to her ass, it occurred to Amy they'd broken the first commandment of personal safety. *Don't get in the vehicle. Once you get into the vehicle, you're toast.* Or something like that. And she'd dragged her friend into this mess. She really wasn't afraid, at least not of what usually happened in those scenarios. She was terrified of her response to the man now cranking the engine over, turning to ask for addresses. The strains of some classic rock had Sandra raising her voice to be heard over the music.

He dropped Enrico first, the other man sketching a farewell, his eyes lingering on Sandra, who didn't acknowledge him. Amy made herself smile her goodbye. The drive to her friend's flew by and she cursed her slow brain for not saying she lived with Sandra. It wasn't too late. She *could* stay with her friend. They lived just a mile or so apart, after all. Amy had needed her space, her own independence but was glad to find a little house to rent so close to Sandra's. Sandra leaned to her, speaking quietly.

"Stay with me tonight."

That was such a good plan, Amy naturally rejected it. The part of her that had made poor choices all her freaking life raised its evil head, shoving her fear aside. Risk taker. Self-fulfilling prophesier. "It's okay, Sandra. I'll call you tomorrow."

"Amy, honey, he's—"

"Dangerous. I know. I do know. I just need to see how this is going to play out. It feels different." Maybe her stupid self was wrong this time. Just like she hoped every other time, although never with such intensity.

Sandra pressed her hand and shrugged, the movement almost lost in the dark interior.

"Ladies." They pulled into Sandra's driveway.

"Thanks." Sandra pressed Amy's hand again and allowed Dean to help her out. He watched until she opened the front door and went inside, before turning and offering Amy his hand.

"Sit up front with me."

She obediently slid over and out of the truck. Shutting the door behind her, he opened up the front passenger side, a hand hovering as she navigated the running board. She knew he recognized margaritas tended to hang around for awhile. The truck smelled of leather and Dean. He went around the hood of the vehicle to vault into his seat.

Turning to her, face lit by the dash lights, he said, "We going to do this at your place or mine?"

Well, cutting right to the chase. No problem choosing the place. No question she wanted this and was going to do it despite all her good intentions to never put herself in this position again. But she wasn't taking the walk of shame in the morning, or immediately afterwards, however he played his casual fucks. *He* could get up and put his pants on and hit the road. And she'd roll over and go to sleep, pretend the night before never happened when she woke up in the morning. But he'd better make it worth her while sexually.

"Mine." She knew her voice reflected both her conflict and determination.

"Okay. And I think it's time I learned your last name, don't you?"

"Oh. Sure. It's Copeland."

"You have protection, Amy Copeland?"

Shit. She didn't. No need for protection when a hookup was something she never intended to do again for the rest of her life. It made for one little additional reminder, an obstacle to stinking thinking. "No."

That garnered her a speculative look. "I only have one with me. We'll stop at a pharmacy."

How many did he think he needed? The question hovered on the tip of her tongue, but she bit it off. Better to focus on how she'd handle things afterwards and try to manage the intense, rising need to do the deed right on these leather seats. Maybe it was the drinking, the kiss, the little scene at Grand Masters, or the combination—but now that it was just the two of them, Amy was champing at the bit. This one off was going to have to do her for an unforeseen period of time and she hoped he was up for it, no pun intended. She thought again that he'd better goddamn well know his stuff, because there was just no room in her night for further disappointment.

Staying in the truck while Dean went into the all-night pharmacy, second thoughts sobered her, and she briefly considered making a run for it. Right, and B.O.B. would assuage this need? Uh huh, sure it would. Dean needed to get a move on. She watched his tall form exit the store, walking a little stiffly, noting his taut features as he neared the vehicle. The well-lit drug store, swirling neon, and bright, wide windows, with vehicles nosing in like suckling kittens to a momma cat, was an interesting backdrop for his imposing form. Handsome enough for a movie star. He strode close enough for a thorough inspection. A long, strong column of throat, wide shoulders, packed with muscle obvious even under his shirt in parking lot lighting. His jeans strained over a massive erection. Oh, boy. No wonder he wasn't walking with his usual prowling gait.

A large plastic sack swung from his hand. Was that a *gross* of condoms? He climbed in, another inscrutable look on his face, and tossed the bag to her. It had too much heft so she peeked inside, reveling in the anticipation, the response of her body to this man. A box of ribbed condoms, little container of aspirin, a bottle of *strawberry lubricant* and a pint of chocolate milk. What?

Switching on the ignition he said, "Nothing like a couple of pain killers washed down with some chocolate milk to stave off a hangover, sweetheart. I don't want you crashing on me before we're done."

Really? His concern was touching, even if it was all about him. "And the lubricant?"

"Didn't know how adventurous you were, Amy, until you took that stage."

Her pussy, already wet, gushed, and she fought to get a full breath. "That was new for me. I've only watched before." Breathless, she still forced the protest out.

"New, but you've been thinking, fantasizing. We'll see how we go."

An experienced man. Hopefully as interested in her pleasure as his own.

"I'll take care of you." A dark, sultry promise in response to the words she hadn't realized she'd spoken out loud.

"Turn into the far side of the drive and get right up to the bumper of my car. The neighbor will have you towed if you put a hint of tire on his side or kiss the sidewalk."

Dean parked where she bade him, coming up nicely short of her beloved Audi Cabriolet, her only extravagance and one she'd paid dearly for in more ways than one. "I'll deal with your neighbor."

She laughed and opened her own door, stepping out with her purse in one hand, the plastic sack hanging from the other. She didn't need a gentleman. He joined her on the sidewalk, catching her arm. "Something funny?"

"When do you suppose you're gonna deal with him?" Slipping his hold, she made her way up the walk and rammed the key inside the lock, knowing she was inviting her own personal sexual vampire inside. He'd drain her dry and move on. Nothing she hadn't known beforehand and nothing she couldn't surmount if she worked hard at it. This was sex—pure fucking—and there was nothing different or special about it. Wishful thinking wasn't a crime, but a dire disappointment.

## Chapter Two

Dean followed her into the brightly lit little house, the solid-wood door shutting firmly behind them. He'd noted it was a square box of a place, wooden siding, turn of the century, with shutters edging the windows at the front. It didn't suit Amy Copeland. She should be surrounded with upscale, clean contemporary lines, a hint of kitsch to speak to that side of her he saw on that stage. The unexpected. And all of this introspective thinking wasn't easing the painful thrust of his cock.

She'd paused at a keypad just inside the entry. Noting the two deadbolts and the security system, his interest was piqued. Women living alone wanted to feel safe, but this spoke of fear, or total awareness of the monsters lurking everywhere. His last words to her played back in his head, that he'd deal with her neighbor. Her warning about the man had woken a protective instinct within him, something he didn't feel unless it involved the job. She was right. He wouldn't be around to intercede on her behalf if the neighbor acted like an asshole. Or around to find out why she took her security so seriously. Funny how that didn't sit right—neither part of it. But he didn't take care of women anymore.

Setting his boots beside her shoes, he took in the surroundings. The place had recently been painted in a soothing shade of green, the hardwood floors refinished. A huge desk took up most of the living space, two of them actually, pushed together, a laptop and a PC on the surface, a pile of paper and a container stuffed with pens and highlighters. The drapes were tightly closed, and there was nothing on the walls to draw the eye. There was only one chair, an armless thing, sort of like a chaise lounge, aside from the one on rollers at the desk. No television. He hoped she at least had a bed.

The open concept kitchen, clearly a recent renovation, appeared spotless, only the bag from the pharmacy cluttering the counter, where she'd placed it. A granite-topped island delineated the area from the living room, but the appliances and cabinets were standard. Amy stood by the island, tossing something into her mouth, chasing it with the chocolate milk straight out of the carton. Taking the aspirin, ensuring her stamina as he planned. He watched her throat work and surreptitiously palmed his crotch. He planned to shove his cock down that throat as deep as she could take him, in very short order.

Tossing the carton into the trash can in the corner, she faced him, tongue hooking out to chase an errant drop of milk. She smiled. One of those powerful, feminine smiles he never allowed his women.

"Come here."

A slow blink, a rise and fall of long lashes over those violet eyes, and the smile softened. She walked to him, long legs scissoring, breasts gently lifting and falling with each breath, and he lost himself in his need. Lost his control, knowing it showed. Her eyes widened, but she kept her smile. Equal. He allowed her that for now. They came together, mouths crashing, lips mashing against teeth, tongues dueling. He fisted one hand in her thick hair to anchor her against his sensual assault until he pulled away to breathe. Her face was flushed, her lips swollen, and when her eyes fluttered open they were dazed with lust and lack of oxygen, the purple hue soft, lighter than the flowers of the same color.

"Do you have a bed?" He hardly recognized his own voice, raspy with lust and dark need.

"Door on the left." Hers was barely above a whisper.

Dean snagged the bag on the way by, dragging her along with him, reluctant to release her for an instant. She pushed open the door she'd indicated and flicked on the light switch. Her hand trembled and he could *feel* the desire rolling off her like a tangible thing.

Two small lamps beside the bed illuminated a room sharply contrasting with the austerity of the rest of the house, very different from the kitchen and the work space. This was a retreat, a cocoon. A queen-sized bed predominated, a tall, brass headboard and foot board anchoring it to the hardwood floor, the thick nap of an area rug squaring off the perimeter. A puffy, white comforter scattered with tiny, white flowers covered the mattress. Several pillows layered the head of it, a small black stuffed animal tucked into their midst. A chair with classic lines filled one corner. He took his surroundings in with the skill of long, necessary practice before his attention was wrenched back to Amy.

Setting her crossed hands at her waist she tugged the bottom of her shirt up and over her head, tossing it across the chair. Busy fingers worked her jeans button and zipper, next pushing them down the long length of her legs. She stepped out and kicked them aside, then advanced on him. The pink lace of her bra didn't cover the darker points of her nipples, and the little briefs clung to her wet apex. The evidence of her need further diminished his control. Dean impatiently yanked his shirt out of his jeans and popped at least one button taking it off. His jeans barely cleared his ass before she was on him, her silken length a sensory explosion against his skin. They tussled for control, falling crossways across the bed, the comforter huffing beneath their combined weight.

He pinned her wrists above her head, feeling the fine bones under his hand. Looming over her to stare into her eyes, searching for something, maybe a reason for his need to pursue her, his physical need superseded it. She panted beneath him, small whimpering sounds emerging on every exhale. Easing the fine chain of her necklace aside, setting his lips on the pulse beating at the base of her throat, he suckled her, then traced a path with his tongue to the point between her breasts where her bra thwarted him. He popped the front clasp with his thumb and her mounds spilled forth, pushing the cups aside, umber nipples beaded into tight points. His mouth closed around one tip, a hand molding the other breast, fingers rolling and pulling the bud. Amy whimpered louder and arched into his touch, her legs writhing to push between his, her heels hooking over his ankles.

He couldn't hold back, and released her hands to slide down her body, kissing and licking a path to her underwear, slipping them down over her hips and off her body as he knelt between her legs. A swollen, pink pussy was unveiled, wet and welcoming, the scent fresh as the sea. Fuck. He wasn't coming in his shorts like a teenager with his first impending lay. The box of condoms resisted his fumbling hands, the cardboard finally tearing, a shower of foil packages spraying to fall over them like confetti at the Super Bowl. Ripping open a package, Dean pushed his boxers down and sheathed himself, wincing at the sensitivity of his begging cock.

Amy spread her legs wider, labia parting in invitation to reveal slick, red, inner lips, and he literally mounted her, a stallion in rut, resting his weight on one hand planted beside her, the other guiding his erection to notch it at her gate.

Incredible, wet heat engulfed his cockhead, sucking at it like a little mouth, and he pushed against the outer ring guarding her entrance, gaining entry with some difficulty. She was soaked, wet and slippery but so very tight, the walls of her sheath grudgingly parting to allow him deeper access, squeezing him, making him pant with the effort to hold off his release. Sweat beaded on his brow and broke out at the base of his spine. At last he was seated to the hilt, balls cradled against the curve of her buttocks. Amy moaned beneath him, her hands fluttering the length of his back, soft, full thighs rising to grip his hips. When her calves locked behind his knees, her hands settling flat against his shoulders, Dean reacted to the way she held him, close, wrapping him up. For a moment he gloried in this feeling so *right*, like coming home, before his brain automatically rejected the intimacy and his lust took command.

Thrusting deeper, withdrawing and pushing back to open her wide to his demands, he fucked her hard, without mercy, dislodging her tender hold on him, taking control, stripping away her power. He pounded her into the mattress, mindless with sexual need, grappling against a greater necessity he couldn't begin to identify. His anus tingled and his balls drew up in preparation to spend themselves. He managed to get a hand between them, seeking the engorged nub of her clit, rubbing it between thumb and forefinger. He forced her climax seconds before he came, her channel clenching around him in a long, slow, flinching kiss of liquid heat, a low cry wrenched from her throat.

Dripping with sweat, he pushed up and struggled to stand, pulling Amy's apparently boneless form with him, holding her up while he stripped the comforter and top sheet back, dislodging the throw pillows to scatter across the floor. He rolled with her onto the mattress lengthwise and laid his head on a pillow with relief. Amy rested beside him, their hips and shoulders touching, skin cooling.

She didn't speak, not a single comment on his performance, no sweet nothings. It irked him, because he didn't want her to be different than all the other women who praised his prowess, yet it soothed him at the same time. She just breathed, in sync with him, as though there was no need to speak about what they'd just shared. And, in truth, he didn't want to try and find the words.

After a few minutes she slipped from the bed, and he watched her tall, curvaceous body cross the room to pass through the doorway, full buttocks flexing, two small dimples resting right above them. He longed to press a kiss on those tender indentations. His cock stirred at both the thought and the sight, and he shut his eyes in mute protest.

He should be thinking about getting up and finding his clothes, or planning round two, not resting comfortably and complacently in this woman's bed. Like he had all the time in the world. He wasn't resistant to change. His business was always changing, and he needed to be flexible, but this was different.

Amy came back, wrapped in a pale pink robe, wiping her hands on a pink towel. She lay back down after tossing him the towel and sighed.

Breaking the silence, he asked, "Bathroom?"

"Right across the hall."

Was she regretting the sex? Wishing she hadn't brought him home? Holy fuck, he was second-guessing himself like a callow youth. Before he kissed her and revealed any more, he took himself off to the bathroom, closing the door behind him. Disposing of the condom, he washed up and struggled not to react to the explosion of color. The bathroom was pink. Really pink. Baby pink walls, bright pink towels, sprays of pink flowers embellished on the shower curtain, fluffy, pink bath mat. Even the soap holder was pink. Who *was* Amy Copeland? And why did he care? This would be over soon, although he was thankfully considering round two, thinking he rushed round one.

The man reflected in the mirror looked the same, if out of place in this pink room. There was no momentous change to note, nothing obvious, and he pushed any thought of her being different far away. The thought of peeling Amy out of that robe strongly appealed, and his cock shifted from its crouching rest against his thigh. Stiff cock, no conscience and all that.

****

Holy shit. *That* wasn't what she'd expected. Somehow she figured the man would rip her clothes off and explore her, do her and be done with her. Amy hadn't missed the fraction of closeness that went past pure carnal interest, like they knew one another from someplace else. She dismissed her fanciful thoughts. He reacted adversely to that weird connection and damn near put her through the mattress with his fucking. Being taken so fiercely by a man, with such determination, yet with a care to her pleasure was a novel experience. But he'd be planning his exit strategy. Hell, he didn't need one of those, having already set the parameters. She knew it and went into this with eyes wide open. Raising her protective barriers against the expected rejection she slipped deeper inside her head and once again drifted.

The bed dipped and her eyes popped open at the touch of his hand on her calf, stroking upward. An enigmatic look drifted across his face as his other hand tugged at the sash on her robe. The tie fell away and the material parted at his urging to reveal her nakedness beneath. Silvery grey eyes darkened and his cock tapped his belly, the broad head nearly purple, glistening with precum. Again? Well, she'd deal with the rejection later, not at all reluctant to fuck this man again. It was just one memorable night to hold against all the anticipated empty ones in her future.

"Get up, sweetheart."

Amy obligingly swung her legs off the mattress as Dean stood to give her room. She squirmed upright and he yanked the sash from the robe as he pulled the garment from her body. He leaned in for a kiss, big hands sliding down her arms to coax them behind her back, the terrycloth sash wrapping around both wrists. Kissing her, tying her hands by feel. The man could multitask, and her former arousal returned in a rush. Her sex drew up and soaked with a renewal of her cream, and her breasts became heavy, nipples hardening, aching.

Dean whispered his tongue over hers and drew away. She opened her eyes to see him crouch to scoop up a throw pillow and plant it at his feet. He gestured and she dropped to her knees, grateful for the softness, appreciating how he held her shoulders to ensure she didn't land without support. His pulsing cock was at the perfect height, aligned with her mouth and Amy made to lean into it. Dean forestalled her, working his hands through her hair, holding her in place.

"I'm clean. I don't fuck without a condom."

She nodded.

"Pool your saliva and then open. Tilt your head back."

His deep, dominant tone had her rubbing her thighs together, the slick surface disconcerting. She was wet nearly to her knees. She did as he asked and the fat head of his cock poked forward to rest on her bottom lip.

"Suck it in as far as you can without moving your head."

Like he gave her any choice, with his hands wrapped so tightly in her hair. Amy sucked and a considerable length of him slid inside her mouth on her saliva, the salty taste of him overlaid with musk.

"Suck more." His voice was strained, the rasp apparent. She sucked harder and wondered if his cock had filled and hardened to its full potential, because the invader was now at the back of her throat, stretching her mouth wide. She couldn't take any more.

"Relax your throat and breathe through your nose, Amy. Suck and swallow me down."

Mind over matter, she chanted in her head, working hard to follow his instructions. The sensation of drowning immediately overtook her and she tensed, remembering to take air her nose, mitigating the overwhelming feeling. His thatch of rough hair tickled her lips, scrotum soft against her chin. Now she'd taken him all.

"Close your lips tightly and don't move." Peering up at him, she saw the clenching of his strong jaw as he struggled for control, and tracked a tiny bead of sweat roll off and drop down to spatter on his forearm. And he began to fuck her face. She held her position and fought her gag reflex, pulling in breaths through her nose, trying to keep her lips closed tightly around him. The crown of his cock slid like velvet against her palate to fill her throat time and again. Her jaw ached and she flickered her tongue on every outstroke in mute defence. Dean growled something above her, the rhythm of his strokes faltering. He erupted and she choked and swallowed, one of his hands loosing her hair to gently stroke along her throat to ease her efforts.

Pulling out against her softening lips, he smoothed a fingertip along her cheek. "You okay?"

She thought so. Her jaw ached, but that would pass. He hadn't hurt her, once again mindful. It had been an experience, one she usually didn't enjoy so much, but her sex ached for attention.

"You looked fucking hot, your hands tied like that. And you did good. Better than—"

Oh no. No, no, no. No, he didn't. Amy glared at him. "Untie my hands."

Dean reached around instantly and tugged and her hands came free. Either a boy scout or lots of practice in his adult life with knots. Probably the latter. Using one hand against the mattress she levered herself up and reached for her robe, giving him her back. Asshole.

"Sorry, sweetheart."

She whirled on him. "You get this time with me, Dean. You get the fuck. What you don't get is to compare me to your other women. That's crass even for someone with your approach to, to…" She wound down like a tired, old spring because she couldn't begin to describe what this man was. A whore? A player? Was it even the sex, or the power, rewarded by the release? Who knew? Who cared? He was an asshole. What he'd given her earlier wasn't even close to what she just gave him and he could put his pants on and hit the road. Before she hit *him* with something really hard and unyielding, like a baseball bat.

"You figure out what it is I am?" Was he a mind reader too? Didn't matter.

"Go."

"Night's not over, sweetheart." One muscular, long arm reached out, the dark hair patterning his forearm, and his big hand caught her wrist.

"Are you insane? It's *over*. And it wasn't that great, FYI" She hadn't meant to say that, really she hadn't. That was crass, too. He just seemed to bring out the worst in her.

"Then I guess I'll have to give you something more to grade me on." The words seemed squeezed out between gritted teeth and his eyes were chips of granite.

She struggled with him as he yanked the robe from her hands and tossed it away, using his size and weight to push her backwards onto the bed. He pinned her hands at her sides, lowering his head to her drenched apex. For a moment she nearly gave in, let him tongue her to orgasm, but she rejected the need. They weren't keeping a balance sheet.

"Red."

His movements ceased as if by magic, his head lifting, eyes narrowing on her own. "Did you just use your *safe word*? With me?"

"You need to go."

She lay sprawled as he moved off of her and then the bed, mouth set and jaw clenching. He dressed without comment, never looking once in her direction as she inched her legs closed and felt furtively for her robe. She didn't think he'd be sexual with her again, but he was most certainly pissed. She wasn't physically afraid of him, but men like Dean Chambray didn't take kindly to being rejected. Especially when he was the one to do the loving and leaving, make that the fucking and leaving. He'd want the last word.

"Keep the condoms and the lube, sweetheart. Wouldn't hurt to get in a little more practice."

Okay, then. There it was. She'd poked the bear in his big, fat ego, and Dean was just a man, after all. Sad. The comment irked her, though, and annoyingly made her wonder what he'd had in mind for the rest of the night's activities. She let the condoms lie, scattered as they were, but snatched up the lube, following him as he worked the locks free and exited her home. Her steps faltered when she realized she hadn't reset the alarm once they were inside. There was that paradox again—feeling both protected and anxious. She shook it off.

The well-lit shared driveway, compliments of her paranoid neighbor, gave her a clear view of his fine ass and oh-so-controlled gait. No massive erection to impede his grace this time—just affronted male. Amy wound up like the pitcher she'd been on the softball team in juvie and let fly. The bottle sailed through the air to smack the windshield of macho man's big black truck dead center, the plastic cap likely popping open, because the liquid sprayed out to scent the night. And to coat the glass and hood.

Amy turned on one bare heel and ran like all the furies of hell were on her tail to make it safely inside her house and throw all the locks, managing to punch in the security code with a trembling finger. She huddled behind the door, breathless at her actions, struggling against impending hysterical laughter. She heard no sound for a really long time, the anticipation nearly killing her, then thought she heard male voices. Listening hard—was that a scuffle? Just as she screwed up the courage to open the door, she heard one slam, and caught the grinding of a starter. He was leaving. She hit the lights and headed for her room, using the glowing square of illumination cast from beyond her bedroom door as her guide.

Hurling herself face down on the mattress, Amy laughed until she cried, the tears flowing with surprising ease, a luxury she rarely allowed herself. They cleansed her somehow, coupled as they were with mirth. It wasn't her birthday any more, the hour well past midnight, but it was one to remember, anyhow. She decided she didn't feel badly used, having shaken up a misogynist womanizer who had a little too much faith in his prowess. And if that something deep inside of her ached and whimpered, well, it was nothing more than she deserved. Secretly hoping for something special was always doomed for failure and disappointment. On that thought she crashed, the events of the night too much for her overloaded system.

****

Dean stood on the neighbor's side of the drive, scowling at the oily residue on his truck, unwillingly smelling strawberries. This was bullshit. The whole evening had been off. He was still unsettled, in fact so unsettled, he was thinking about breaking into a certain blonde's home and spending the rest of the night, or day, or week, or month, as long as it took, to discuss the anointing of his truck, to satisfy his burgeoning need for her, and incidentally, make her *take it back*. Not that great? It had been *sensational*, all of it.

She'd screamed her release. The woman loved blowing him. He had scented her arousal. It was an amazing blow job, none better, and he just had to open his big mouth and fuck it up. Nice afterglow. And she'd used a safe word! What the fuck? He was standing outside a woman's house, his truck lubed, second guessing his sexual performance, having met and kissed a birthday girl and witnessed her amazing submission along with a hundred other people. Dean shook his head. Time to chalk this one up to experience and head home. He was a serious, dangerous *businessman* with a secret that could get him killed, and he couldn't afford to be distracted, not even by a precocious, unpredictable, beautiful, blonde Amazon.

"What are you doing standing out here?" The voice belonged to a thin, bespectacled man wearing a jacket over pajamas, clutching a cell phone. Dean recognized the type. Powerless, so he tried to lord it over others with petty enforcement of so-called rules.

"I was just leaving." Better he let it go and not give little Hitler here any reason to call the cops. Dean had lots of contacts in the department but his street cred would take a hit if they responded to a call and saw—and smelled—the lube. Amy so deserved an ass paddling for that.

"Well, see that you do, and if Mizz Copeland is going to *entertain* this late she'd better watch where people park and ensure they don't hang around. This is a nice neighborhood."

Dean traversed the distance between him and the other man, grabbing the phone and tossing it onto the lawn. He hauled the prick up by the collar and shook him. "Watch your mouth, got me?" When the man's bravado leaked out like air from a pricked balloon and he nodded, Dean shook him again. "You give Miss Copeland any trouble, I'll finish it. Got it?"

He released the asshole, shoving him backwards. Little Hitler's arms flailed to catch his balance. He hustled away around the corner and Dean swung up into his truck. Knowing the wipers would just smear the lube, he turned them on anyway, plying the wiper fluid switch until it cleared enough of a path for him to see through. He drove home immersed in the smell of fruit, wishing he'd put the stuff to better use.

As he parked, a shape flowed out of the shadows, punctuated by the glowing coal of a cigarette. Olsen. The only man in his crew who smoked. Maybe he was grabbing a cigarette outside in deference to Dean's recent threat to make him paint the fucking walls in his unit because of what his habit was doing to them.

The man sniffed. "You hit somethin'?" It was surprising he could smell anything past the nicotine.

"Other way around." Dean left Olsen to puzzle that one out and climbed the steps to his condo, noting with satisfaction the turn that made the property more easily defensible, creating a bottleneck, a choke point, should people want to hit him at home. He had an exit through the bottom level, too, one that few knew about. The rest of his crew lived in the complex, making for additional resources, should he require them. The day would come when he'd put this life behind him, but it was a vague date in the future and he had work to do first. It all came down to one important coup.

Getting himself a beer from his enormous fridge, he pulled his boots off and leaned back on the couch, feet up on the coffee table. He looked around his home, decorated by some firm Randy had chosen, and compared it to the little place he'd just left. He wondered, if *he* had decorated, chosen his own furniture, colors, if it would reflect his personality. It was presently a wickedly expensive, if tasteful, high-end way station, a place to sleep and hole up. He never cooked here, rarely had people over, and his bedroom featured a big comfortable bed and a place to store his clothes. An altogether sad commentary on a home, and a marked contrast to his childhood one, at least physically. Neither nurtured his soul.

Marsha Chambray had no time for her son, pawning him off on *her* mother soon after she pushed him out, unable to spare the time from her pursuit of the drug of her choice. He had a few vague memories of a nice, old gramma, holding him on her lap and reading to him in a broken mixture of English and French, cooking him rich and tasty meals. Kissing him goodnight and making him say his prayers. But she died and his mother came for him, the new family allowance monies the impetus of her newfound maternal drive. She could expand her horizons with the extra cash. As her looks faded, assaulted by the bottle or two of vodka she drank like water every day, supplementing her income with whoring also dried up.

Dean scrambled up on his own from around age four, rejected and rebuffed by the person he needed the most, and he understood it inhibited his emotional expression and made him insistently independent. Once he attended school, he no longer needed her for anything, getting his fix from a constant turnover of strangers and a few regulars.

All the horror stories of Catholic schools aside, Dean had no doubt charity saved him. He got touched a lot, in a good way, the teachers ruffling his hair, some of the women giving him little squeezes, finding him lunches and snacks. Unlike other little boys, he didn't pretend to eschew the attention, soaking it up instead, his size and willingness to use his fists shutting the traps of any kids who remarked on his possible sexual orientation. His quick brain garnered him further consideration, particularly in math and the sciences. It was a wonder his brain developed, considering how much his mother drank, Dean being the exception to that rule about fetal alcohol effects. He supposed he should be grateful she never left the neighborhood because that ensured the consistency of his schooling.

It also meant everyone knew Marsha Chambray's son, fathered by some nameless drifter. The kid who was on the street at all hours, time when some stuff that went down could be attributed to him. Dean lucked out there, too, with the local beat cop taking him in hand, showing him the way. Officer Duncan, unknowingly, was the role model Dean emulated, the profession he decided on the first time the cop caught him acting out and treated him fairly. It wasn't enough to keep him from running errands for the local crime lord, but enough to keep him out of the limelight and line of fire. The money paid their rent and fed him. His mother never seemed to notice she wasn't evicted, and drank her meals, pilfering his hard-earned cash.

That emotional inhibition contributed to his inability to form relationships, too, although it didn't impair his sexual competence. Without the emotional attachment, he could focus his attention on the physicality. Honed sexual skills, coupled with his appearance—he was well aware he was handsome and took good care of his body—meant women were always available, like a never ending supply. It wasn't something he wore like a badge of honor, but he needed the release, one of the few he allowed himself.

Checking his watch, he noted how long he'd been lost in reminiscing. Lots to do in the morning, particularly with an asshole trying to weasel his way into the business. Dean would be a wealthy man in his own right if he cleared his plate of everything but the legitimate side of things, but that wasn't his call. He had a superior to answer to, however vague and tenuous their connection, and there were expectations to be met. He drained the bottle and chucked it into the bin. His housekeeper would be by tomorrow and he made a mental note to leave her a list of things to pick up, then headed to bed, deciding to shower in the morning. And it wasn't because he wanted to savor the scent of Amy still lingering on his skin.

****

The room didn't seem any different at four o'clock. By rights he should be deep in sleep, regenerating, alone in this big, empty bed. Instead he was staring into the dark, senses alert and assimilating any changes in his space as the clock ticked ahead, approaching the time he normally got up. His nose was still full of strawberries, but he could faintly smell Amy. Just a hint of woman and something with grassy overtones. Finally, he got up and hit the shower, scrubbing hard and long, toweling off to fall back into bed and seek that elusive sleep. Nothing doing, so he allowed himself to think about her, resigned to a sleepless night.

He'd had tall, curvy blondes before, being an equal opportunity kind of guy. Hair color, height, and body shape really didn't matter to him. If the woman appealed, he set his terms, and they either went along or they didn't. What was it Randy said so crudely, if accurately? They put out and then he put *them* out. For sure, some of them entertained the idea they would change him, domesticate him. An occasional romp between the sheets, that meant nothing more to him than an intense sexual release, was hardly the basis for what some women anticipated. Those he moved on immediately. The ones who took what he gave them and didn't cling were sometimes invited back for an encore. Dean knew that made him a shit in the eyes of most women, but at least he was honest. He didn't prevaricate. It was all he had to give so they shouldn't expect anything more.

Closing his eyes against what that self-examination led to, he stifled a groan. Good old mom. Say a big thank you to her for your troubles, ladies. Even now, he couldn't shake her, not as an adult, extremely successful by any number of other standards. She wasn't lucid most of the time now anyhow, sparing him to a large extent, but once in awhile the care facility would call and request that he come to visit. And he'd go like a good boy, only to be fucked up for days afterward, yet unable to refuse the summons.

Amy seemed different. He'd been told no before, albeit not in recent memory, and it wasn't a big deal. He didn't chase. So why had he pursued her? Cudgeling his brain didn't formulate an answer so he looked at it from a different perspective. If she wasn't significantly different *physically* than one or two other women he'd had, there had to be something else. He doubted he would have been able to change her mind if it hadn't been for that scene at Grand Masters—he'd capitalized on it—shamelessly.

Dean jackknifed up in his lonely bed, squinting into the darkness. Fuck. She was like *him*. Something as yet indefinable, but very much a part of who he was, recognized something quite similar in her—uncompromising and defined. She probably had some kind of history that precluded building a relationship. He wondered if she felt it, too, and supposed she did, and might be taking a cautious look. Women were better at the nuances than men. Dean had studied enough psychology to know it.

That mystery solved, he decided to leave it to percolate. It would take some consideration before he acted on it, or not. The section of his brain tasked with puzzling out mysteries and solving quandaries relaxed, and he felt the darkness swallow him up. His last thought was that his brief encounter with his Amazon had been *great*.

# FOREVER

## Chapter Three

The faint ringing of her cell pulled Amy from a deep sleep. Struggling upright, she pushed at the hem of her robe, now rucked up around her waist, a lump of the material uncomfortable under one hip. She squinted at the clock. Seven-oh-five. Not fair. The phone began to ring again, and she realized it must be in her purse which was … maybe in the living room. The memory of last night descended like the proverbial ton of bricks and she grimaced. Oh, boy. Not even in her checkered past had she committed such a sheer number of faux pas in a single evening. That would be Sandra calling, holding on until seven before she punched in Amy's number. Well, at least Amy wasn't hung over. She also wasn't ready to talk to Sandra yet.

Staggering into the bathroom, she sank down on the toilet, her nether regions tender and aching dully. The usual morning routine seemed to take a long time. She fumbled the tap on from a sitting position and pushed a face cloth under the stream of hot water pouring into the sink. Squeezing it out one-handed she scrubbed it over her face and neck, daubing beneath her eyes. She winced at the black residue on the pink cloth. Obviously makeup removal hadn't been on the list last night. Standing to wash her hands, she took a cautious look in the mirror. Aside from a classic case of bed head, the familiar face reflected back didn't shout out any revelations, belying the churning inside her chest. Shit. Where were the easy answers when one needed them?

Stripping off the robe, Amy dropped it into the hamper, followed by the washcloth and towel. There was another towel draped over the edge of the hamper and she stared at it, willing it to fall inside so she didn't have to think about the body it had touched. She wandered, nude, back into the bedroom and pulled the pristine white sheets from the bed, rolling the cases off the oversize pillows. She really needed to get the correct size the next time she went shopping—*and* she was thinking inane thoughts to avoid the issue front and center in her head. The linens filled the hamper to bursting and had the added advantage to pulling that towel down inside with them. Only then did she locate her purse and dig through the contents to find her phone.

"Are you okay? I've been calling since seven!"

"I'm fine, Sandra. No harm, no foul. Did the deed, the usual."

Silence. Had she given it away? She thought she'd taken enough time to compose herself… Amy held her breath.

"I'm coming over. We'll go for breakfast. Ten minutes."

"I need to shower first. Make it half an hour."

"Ten. I'm not leaving you alone to think and mess your head up."

"Okay." No point in arguing with an expert. Amy ended the call and took as hot a shower as she could stand.

She could still smell him, and scent triggered people as much, or more, than visual cues. Hence, the laundry pile. What had she been thinking? This felt pretty awful, the morning after syndrome, but awful in a different way. Usually she just felt used. Today she remembered the sexual vampire analogy and involuntarily touched the hollow of her throat, right where he'd—moving on. Had to. She hurriedly rinsed her hair and the residue of soap from her body, resolutely not thinking. She was wrapped in a bath sheet, her hair wound up in a smaller towel, when the door bell rang.

Heart pounding, she checked the security feed. Sandra. Disappointment and relief warred within as she made her way to the door to admit her friend.

Sandra walked right into her and put her arms around Amy's waist, laying her head on her shoulder. Amy reciprocated, although she had to drop her head to do it. It had taken nearly six months before she allowed Sandra to touch her, and now she craved the other woman's caring hugs and little physical contacts like a drug. Sandra's muffled voice reached her ears.

"You got thrown for a loop."

Not yet able to go there, Amy extricated herself from her friend's hold. "I'll get dressed, fix my hair and makeup. We'll talk over breakfast, if I even know what it is we need to talk about."

Sandra sat on the closed toilet seat while Amy applied moisturizer and light makeup, using waterproof mascara, predicting waterworks in her future. Damn. Would she never learn? Pulling her hair up into a clip, she figured it would dry eventually. Sandra may have the day off, but Amy had work to do this afternoon, so they could only spend the morning together. She had no idea what she'd do without Sandra and worried she'd push her friend away at some point with her constant backsliding. So what if it had been months and months since her last stupidness? She'd not only backslid last night—she'd fallen over the proverbial cliff.

The hamper loomed in her peripheral vision while she brushed her teeth. Shoving the toothbrush into the slot in the china holder, Amy leaned to open the folding door shielding the upright laundry unit. It was a simple matter to dump the linens and towels into the washer, adding her bath sheet and the towel from her hair, totally comfortable in her nakedness around Sandra. Her friend had seen her in far more revealing circumstances than this. And in much worse shape. Pouring in detergent with a lavish hand she punched the button and lowered the lid. The comforting sound of flowing water filled the room. Sandra made no comment, her silence eloquent.

Amy had to make a brief trip back to the hamper with her clothes from the night before, searching out her panties and bra, picking up her crumpled shirt and jeans. A fresh outfit was easy enough to pull together, despite the fact she'd put her brain in neutral, and she was good to go. The little dress was perfect for the weather, and the halter tie covered Dean's mark. She lingered over the necklace, but left it in place. *Something* had changed. Sandra hustled her out the door, clearly anxious to get to the debriefing, and after carefully locking up, Amy climbed into her friend's little car.

"Want to go to Zeke's?"

"Sure." The food was good, and the booths big and private in a diner patterned after an old fashioned Italian restaurant. And it wasn't far. Her body clamored for sustenance, but coffee and eggs would have to do. *Stop it.*

Thoughts drifting back to meeting Sandra for the first time. Amy felt her lip curl and looked out the side window until she could relax it. Trust wasn't in her vocabulary back then, and trusting someone paid to take care of her made hardly a blip on her thought process. But Sandra persisted, coming in to see her on her days off, assisting in Amy's recovery, painting the idea of a different lifestyle, a different life. She dragged Amy home with her after being discharged, and Amy went, having nowhere else to go, secretly hopeful Sandra was for real. The thought crossed her mind that the other woman wanted her sexually. They were almost the same age and Sandra had no obvious outside sexual interests, no men or women visiting or calling.

But she soon discovered Sandra's motives were pure, if altruistic. Sandra saw Amy's life as a virtual mirror of her own, if taking place several years later and in a somewhat different context. Sandra had been on the streets as a young teen, running from sexual abuse at home, and ironically having to survive in the same way, before fortune smiled when she drew the attention of a street social worker. Sandra was proof that a person could make something of herself, no matter the history. She went back to school, finishing high school in less than three years, then trained as a nurse. It was no secret Sandra wanted to give back, to rescue people, and Amy was her pet project.

They couldn't be more different physically. Mutt and Jeff, blond and brunette, statuesque and thin, street smart and college-educated. But they shared an intense emotional bond, survivors to the core. Amy knew Sandra had it together in different ways than she did, except her libido was in hibernation, unlike Amy's. Both had been used for their bodies, but while Sandra denied her sexuality, Amy struggled to leash her own. Some people might think that selling one's body on the street didn't compare to being the pussy on the arm of a high roller or an aspiring gambler, but there was scant difference. The men were essentially the same, the sexual acts the same, and the cruelty didn't vary.

The car jolted to a stop, and Amy jerked her thoughts from the past to the present. While unpleasant to recall, the memories no longer traumatized her, and were far easier to pack away. She only wished she could get a better handle on making appallingly poor choices, although she took heart that last night was the first slip since Vegas. Months ago.

Sandra, who always seemed to know when to keep her own counsel, to allow Amy to think her thoughts, led the way into Zeke's. The cool air of the place, perfumed with the smells of frying bacon, baked goods and brewing coffee poured out as the door opened. Amy soaked it in, her stomach growling in response. They were seated by the window, part way down the row of red vinyl-covered booths and chrome tables. Both ignored the interested stares of the primarily male patrons.

"Coffee?" Amy and Sandra each shoved a cup in the direction of the cheerful waitress.

Sandra raised a brow. "Two specials?" At Amy's nod the waitress made a note and hustled away.

Amy arranged all the items on the table, setting the utensils at perfect right angles to one another, squaring off the napkin holder, and placing the salt and pepper precisely in the middle of the table. The ketchup bottle was her final project.

"Are you finished thinking?"

"How'd you know to push me, Sandra?"

"Experience, honey, hard-earned experience. And besides, I know you. I heard something in your voice this morning that scared the crap out of me. I knew if you didn't get moving, you'd perseverate and figure out a way to lie to yourself. You don't have much to compare to."

"What did you hear?" Her voice trembled, and she made an effort to bring it under control.

"I heard an Amy I haven't heard before."

"What?" she scoffed. "You called me after one of my aborted efforts to connect with a guy, like usual, and you heard somebody new? Like a split personality?"

Sandra didn't laugh, didn't crack a smile. She kept her big eyes fixed on Amy's. "What happened, honey?"

"We fucked." There, crude and to the point.

"Here you go, two specials. More coffee?" An enormous plate was set in front of them, filled with pancakes, eggs and sausages, two strips of bacon, toast and hash browns. Amy's stomach roiled in self defense, no longer hungry. Their cups topped up, the waitress moved away, leaving her no choice but to continue the conversation.

"Okay, honey. Whenever you're ready." Sandra carved a small section of her pancakes with the same precision she used when dissecting Amy's pathetic excuses and protests. It was kind of like dealing with your alter ego, albeit without the Id.

Sulking, she shoved a hunk of sausage in her mouth and chewed it down. After doctoring her coffee with cream, she took a sip. Sandra waited her out. Jesus Christ.

"Okay. There *was* something different. You satisfied? I felt different with a jerk who wants sex with no strings. Isn't that just a slap in the face?" She blinked back the tears. "I knew it. He told me, warned me. But I just had to go and get into bed with him, just like old times and…"

"Amy, honey. No crime to want somebody."

"What are you saying?" Other patrons actually turned in their seats to stare. She probably didn't need to scream at Sandra. She didn't want to want that man!

Unperturbed, her friend smiled. "You had sex with somebody who touched you with more than just his body. I'm sorry it didn't end well and upset you, but it's okay. I was afraid he'd hurt you physically. It's progress. Do you see?"

*She did not see.* Breathing heavily, she tried to order her thoughts. "I took a guy home with me you warned me against. We had sex. I felt something different. He was an asshole and I kicked him out. I feel shitty about last night. How is that *progress*?" The acerbic whisper didn't carry as far, but Sandra heard her.

"You always feel shitty about meaningless sex, being used over and over. At least this time around you got past that. So he's not the guy for you. You now have a different measuring stick. A chance at a relationship involving *more* than sex."

Her best friend, her only friend, was certifiable. She decided to share the lube story and was gratified to make Sandra laugh. It made her laugh again, too, and if she wished for a different outcome, wished Dean Chambray was a different kind of man, maybe Sandra was right. She'd be looking for someone with additional qualities from here on in. Once she figured those qualities out. But God, this shit was tough on a person.

Eating a little more of the decadent breakfast, they talked desultorily about their plans for the day, about Sandra cleaning her house, and Amy working on a client's web design request, and they agreed Sandra would make dinner for them both around seven. Amy knew she'd go home and screw the pooch, thinking about what her friend posited instead of getting the job done so she could pay her bills.

They cruised up to her house, Sandra humming along with Adele, something about rumors, Amy wishing she'd eaten more of her breakfast, when she saw it. A big, black truck parked in her driveway, pulled up close behind her Audi, perilously close to old man Zuchinski's invisible line. Her friend hammered on the brakes and they both rocked against the restraint of the seat belts. Dean leaned negligently against the tailgate, eyes obscured by dark glasses, arms folded over his massive chest. Shit. Shit. Shit. Shit. Shit.

"You want to drive away?" Sandra eased her foot off the brake as she spoke.

Having visions of a high speed chase, the winner heavily weighted by the size and power of a vehicle driven by someone who likely practiced NASCAR techniques since childhood, Amy croaked out a negative. It was too soon to see Dean Chambray again. She wasn't ready. The fact that she wasn't surprised to see him flitted through her thoughts with the zip of a hummingbird's wings. This felt different, whatever it was she sensed between them.

"Just drop me off. You said it, Sandra. Something different." It didn't feel too much like an *I told you so* as she warred with a myriad of emotions.

"I'm not so sure I was thinking of *him*, honey, when I went all psychological on you."

"Yah, well, *I* think I'll see what Mr. Fuck 'Em and Leave 'Em wants."

"Amy," Sandra warned. "He's both the same and different than those other men, and in some ways that makes him worse."

Not questioning how Sandra knew that, Amy shrugged. She knew it too, but she was dangerous in her own right. Dean Chambray had no idea. "And I'm self destructive. I know. But I'm going to see what happens. I have to. I'm not afraid of him." *Just of what he makes me feel.*

Her mouth a straight line, visibly containing what was doubtless a lecture filled with sage and wonderful advice, Sandra nodded. "Call me if you aren't coming for dinner."

"I will, Sandra. Love you."

"Love you too, girl. You take care."

****

Watching Amy uncoil her tall, curvaceous form out of the little car was, in itself, foreplay. Her long legs swung out, feet shod in glittery sandals landing side by each on the pavement. His gaze tracked up over her trim ankles and past her defined calves, lingering on the expanse of thigh exposed by the short skirt. The top of her head ducked out from beneath the doorframe, thick hair restrained by one of those clip things women used, and Dean's fingers twitched, wanting to release it and let that mane fall free to frame her face and drift over her shoulders. She straightened up in one lithe movement, her height notable, and he studied the jut of her breasts above the narrow waist swelling into the hips he wanted to set his hands on. Fuck. His cock filled and strained against its confinement and he shifted to accommodate the reminder that it knew her far better than he did. Something he planned to remedy before introducing it to her again. Or maybe the "getting to know you" could wait until after that particular introduction.

That hot, greedy pussy, full breasts with tight, suckable nipples, and her talented mouth were just part of the whole package, though, and while he suspected she was as fucked up as he was, the pull was undeniable.

"You have something you want to say to me?" Seeing her saunter up to him in that confident, loose stride, her features set in an amused mask, challenged his dominance, but he tamped it down, held his stance. The friend's car idled at the curb, then pulled slowly away, and Amy's affect crumbled, infinitesimally, but he caught it. And exploited it.

"You want to take this inside, sweetheart? Or give your neighbor an earful?"

The involuntary flinch was also minute. Dean pushed up and moved into her space, forcing her to walk along with him, their strides close to matching. There was a lot about her in sync with him. She unlocked the door and they stepped inside. Amy pushed buttons on her security panel. Déjà vu. All rational thought of merely talking with her fled as he pinned her against the wall, the thud of her purse hitting the floor counterpoint to the pounding of the blood in his cock.

Amy wound her arms around his neck, hands clutching the back of his head, tugging at his hair. He ravaged her mouth with the same intensity of the previous night, mindless in his desire. The heat of her warmed the center of him as he registered the way she melted against his body, hips flexing beneath his hands. The skirt of the little dress was easy to drag up, removing one barrier to his questing fingers. They found the scrap of silk at her apex, wet with her need, and he slipped them past the elastic, shoving two digits up hard inside her, the ascent eased by her cream. Feeling her rise up on her toes he pulled out and pushed back in again, hooking to search out her Gspot, rewarded with a drench of hot liquid, her sheath pulsing around his digits.

"Put your legs around me."

Responding to his growled command, muffled as it was by her mouth, she hopped up and complied, the strength and flexibility of those limbs apparent right through his clothing. One hand moved to clasp her waist, the other he shoved under her ass. She moaned and ground her pelvis against his cock. He managed to turn and make his legs carry them both to the bedroom, hollow with the anticipation of burying his aching shaft deep, clear up to her throat.

Tumbling them down to the yielding mattress, the springs groaning beneath their combined weight, refusing to release her mouth, Dean planted a knee and reached to free his cock. Amy's hand was already there, scrabbling at the zipper, then gently easing him out, guiding him. He hissed at her touch and she sucked on his tongue. Pulling her panties aside by feel, he felt Amy fit him at her entrance. He thrust forward, fighting to get inside, his body blanketing hers, knees spreading her legs wide. She arched to meet him and whimpered as he fully pierced her, bottoming out at her cervix. Immediately stilling, he lifted his head and studied her face, ignoring the clamor of his cock for more, more, more.

Violet eyes opened and he fell in, willingly. "You okay?"

Her hair, loosened from the clip, drifted in waves around her head, and a fine dew misted her forehead. She shivered and he felt the tiny movement in his balls. "I'm good. God, Dean."

Was this *tenderness* he felt? Possessiveness for sure. He wanted to fuck this woman senseless but wanted to make it mean something more. Jesus.

"Please. Don't hold back. Please."

Pulling back a little, thrusting forward, he established a rhythm that tested the very bounds of his control, the feel of her liquid heat surrounding him nearly too much to bear. She lay, acquiescent beneath him, this time holding on loosely and taking what he gave her, eyes again closed, full lips parted. He worked harder above her, building it, never wanting it to end, not yet knowing what *it* was, seeing to both their pleasure. He insanely wanted her to tighten her hold and assert possession. Feeling her hands tense on his back, he sought her engorged clit, rubbing in concentric circles over the soaked fabric of her panties, holding his own orgasm back.

"Look at me." He needed to see her, right down to her soul.

Lashes fluttering, she focused and stared back into him, then bit her lip, the moan of release escaping anyway. Her pupils dilated and Dean filled her with his seed, the scald of it pushing her eyes wide. He let his weight drop on her, unable to do anything else in the immediate aftermath, their clothing a jumbled barrier between them. Gaining control over his breathing, he lifted up, slipping from her on a gush of fluids. No condom. Fucked her bareback. Jesus Christ.

Flopping over onto his back, tucking his cock back into his jeans, Dean became aware they lay on a stripped mattress, no sheets, no pillows, nothing. He instantly caught the symbolism and smiled to himself. Well, his Amazon hadn't expunged him so easily. As soon as his strength returned they'd be having a talk. A discussion. Something he never had with women, unless they were in the business. He tested a few ideas out in his head, some statements and questions. He should have brought a fucking notepad. The newness, the unfamiliarity of this *thing, it*, was goddamn unsettling but he never backed down from a challenge.

Amy stirred and he got up on one elbow to study her. She stared back solemnly and spoke. "We didn't use a condom."

Shrugging, probably not the best gesture to judge by the way she narrowed her eyes at him, he said, "Didn't seem to be a lot of time, and I told you I was safe. Never been that spontaneous before. You were helping."

Her gaze softened. "I was. I don't remember being that spontaneous, either. And I'm clean, but not on birth control, remember." The soft look was pushed aside by faint anxiety.

"C'mon, let's get you cleaned up." Her dress was rumpled, the skirt folded upon itself and he supposed it, too, would be stained. She let him pull her up and preceded him into the bathroom, casting a glance back over her shoulder and looking startled when he followed. Her eyes widened and she bit down on that full bottom lip.

"What … I mean, there's only one sink."

"Don't need more than one sink." He found the little zipper and released it, gaining enough looseness to tug the dress up and over her head. Amy tensed, then stood passively while he stripped her, unhooking her bra with practised ease, pushing the panties down over her hips where they slithered down her legs. He knelt at her feet, tapping either ankle for her to step out of them, gathering the little pile up to toss them into the hamper. She watched his every move with the intent stare of a cornered animal, a hint of fear darkening the blue-violent of those amazing eyes, but a lot of speculation, too.

Taking a washcloth from the little pile in the basket on the shelf, he dampened it, waiting for the water to run warm, sudsing with a dollop of body wash he located in the shower. He sat on the closed toilet seat.

"I can do it." A hint of panic, or maybe anxiety, tinged her voice.

"I'll take care of you." Dean knew he sounded implacable, and he meant to. He'd fucked this woman without protection, and while washing her wouldn't prevent a pregnancy, he wanted to do it. Part of him regretted knowing her cunt and thighs wouldn't bear his stamp, but he had plans for this pussy.

It was intimate, and something he hadn't done before. He insinuated a hand between her thighs and she grudgingly parted them. Her pussy was swollen and wet with the evidence of their joining. He gently cleaned her with the washcloth, reaching to rinse the material and return to his task. Amy trembled and set a hand on his shoulder to support herself, or maybe just to touch him.

"I like the lack of hair, sweetheart." He leaned in to press a kiss on her mound and she drew away, not responding to his comment.

"Are you done?" Her voice was nearly shrill and he looked up to see the sheen of tears in her eyes.

There it was again, *tenderness,* compressing his chest. He threw the cloth into the sink and stood to pull her tightly against him, one hand stroking the length of her back. "Done, sweetheart. S'okay. Where's your robe?"

A little hiccup. "In the wash."

Well, very real symbolism. Dean released her and shrugged out of his shirt, helping her into it, carefully fastening the buttons from hem to collar. It draped over her full, high breasts enticingly, the manner in which it flirted around the top of her thighs kicking his libido into gear. He throttled it back. "We need to talk."

****

Oh, boy. She was better at the sex stuff. Probably he was, too. Definitely he was good at that. She avoided his stare, still trying to assimilate somebody taking care of her so intimately, let alone that somebody being Dean Chambray. Amy wanted to bawl some more like a baby, crawl onto his lap and let him hug her, soothe her. Scary shit. And it had to be foreign to him too, Mr. Fuck 'Em and Leave 'Em.

"I'll go make coffee. You do have coffee?" At her nod he walked out, clad in those tight, worn jeans, the denim lovingly cupping his ass, that amazing cock tucked away from view. The play of long muscles in his back made her fingers itch to run over them. She opened the door to the laundry and quickly transferred the contents of the washer to the dryer, setting the timer for an hour. Her sun dress joined her underwear from today and last night in the washer, and it occurred to her men always created more laundry. They'd fucked like animals, not taking the time to get their clothes off. That was new for her.

Smoothing Dean's shirt, tugging it down at little further in the back, she went to join him for their little *talk.* The fact she wasn't wearing any panties made her pussy tighten. And wasn't she some kind of slut, hoping for more…

"You drink this shit?" Back to macho Dean. Amy noted the chemical creamer he set by the cups on the countertop.

"I like it." *No need to defend yourself, Amy. He's not the boss of you.* Part of her wished he was her boss. Lord knew, he seemed confident and competent. She'd never had that, ever. Benign neglect, for sure. Ruthless, misguided authority. Reward or punishment without the inherent kindness. But no one had ever given her the sense of simply *knowing* what was best for her, someone she could respect and trust with herself. Sandra tried, and for the most part did a good job, had made solid inroads, but she lacked the *presence.* And she wasn't having sex with Sandra, so that influence was also lacking.

"It's bad for you. I'll see you get some cream, half and half." It was hard to argue with that, and the inference was there, that he'd be around to see to it.

She slipped onto one of the stools at the island, tucking the flap of his shirt under her bottom, feeling the cool faux leather against her thighs. He poured her a cup of coffee, hustling to get the carafe back under the drip before it streamed onto the element. She added some of the creamer under his jaundiced eye.

"So you're not on birth control." His tone reflected nothing other than interest, and she tried really, really hard to detect anything else.

"No."

"You got a reason for that?" Again, mild interest, but she picked up on something else this time around and decided to be brutally honest. A first for her with men.

"Yup. I've got a history of having casual sex with men. Lots of casual sex. It was my lifestyle actually, and

I wanted to change it after … after something happened to make me realize there had to be another way to live." She took a sip of coffee and waited for him to comment. When he didn't, his eyes watchful but giving her nothing to read, she screwed up her courage and continued.

"I haven't been with anyone for coming up to a year. I quit taking birth control to try and tell myself I didn't need it. That I wasn't going to do casual hookups anymore. There has to be more than that. I'm not saying sex isn't important and okay, but the physicality was all that it meant. I wanted to believe I deserved more."

Sipping again, she forced herself to sit quietly, watching Dean process her confession. He let her see him do it, the impassive look falling away, his features still tight but readable.

"First off, if I knocked you up, we'll deal." At her flinch, he raised a hand, lowering it, palm down, in a *wait for it* gesture. "*We'll* deal, Amy. Let it go."

She subsided, once again entertaining that little flicker of hope she'd actually met someone who *would* deal. Competent, not merely arrogant.

"As for you wanting more than the fuck, the sex, can't say where I fit in your plans. I'll meet your honesty, sweetheart. I'm fucked up when it comes to women. Doesn't matter why, although when you tell me your history I'll share mine, maybe. I don't trust women, haven't needed them for more than what we just did. But I'll admit there's something different between us. It remains to be seen if it's enough to make me reconsider."

Okay. Confident, competent and freaking arrogant. But she heard the pain, the emptiness behind the words, being equally familiar with the feelings, even if he wasn't aware the hurt had leaked over. Still, it pissed her off.

"So, you're like, going to test drive me?"

His face suffused with color and a bark of laughter passed his sensuous lips. And she needed to stop looking at that part of his anatomy as well as another so unfortunately hidden by his jeans, and concentrate on his cavalier attitude. The prick.

"I guess that sounded arrogant."

Understatement.

"A touch," she agreed. "We're going to be right back where we ended last night, Dean, if you keep opening your mouth and inserting both of your big feet."

The amusement vanished from his face, replaced by an assessing, dark stare that sent a thrill spiraling through her belly to settle in her sex. Poked the bear again. She just *had* to remind him about the lube incident.

"It took nearly eight dollars to wash my truck, sweetheart, not to mention the cost of the lubricant."

"You gave that to me!" she protested, moving her ass off the stool, abandoning her coffee. She positioned herself directly opposite his big frame, the island a comforting bulwark between them. "I had the right to do anything I wanted with it."

"Except anoint my truck, Amy. You don't mess with a man's woman or his truck."

The strange look washing over his face made her hold her tongue. Interesting choice of words, and he'd obviously realized what he'd said. He shook himself, literally, like a dog shedding water, and fixed that steely stare on her. "How you gonna make it up to me?"

She inched sideways as Dean casually leaned to his left. Sexual excitement thrummed between them, fueled by the sensual intent shading his voice.

"I don't know." Her voice was breathless, husky, and he quirked his brow. She'd see it in her sleep, that trademark expression.

"I do." He lunged and she screamed a little in shock, laughter bubbling up as she navigated the corner of the island, bare feet slipping for purchase on the planked floor, losing momentum. And he was on her, his long arms making it no contest. He turned her body into the countertop, hard body pressing against her back, burgeoning erection against her buttocks. Grasping first one hand, then the other, he lifted her arms to lay them on the tiled surface, folding her fingertips under the opposite edge, the length stretching her out. A hand on the back of her next urged her torso to lie prone, the position putting her on the balls of her feet. Her breasts mashed flat, nipples beading harder at the hard, cool façade and her cheek rested just outside the ring made by his coffee cup.

"Hold this position. Don't let go."

*Or what?* Amy desperately wanted to ask it, wanted to know what he would do. But she didn't. A tiny voice in her head soothed her choice, *s'okay*, somehow louder than that rebellious one shouting *go to hell*.

The shirt rode up and she could feel the air on her exposed ass. Dean pulled it higher and tucked in around her waist. "My hand or the wooden spoon."

Managing not to laugh out loud, the absolute ridiculousness of the moment stunning her, Amy tried to answer. He was giving her another choice, bizarre as those choices were. "Hand." The suppressed mirth was audible despite her best efforts.

She'd never been spanked before. Slapped, kicked, punched, locked in her room, the cellar, denied the basics for days, beaten, but never spanked. Did he think he'd punish her this way? Ha. Think again. A big hand smoothed over the curve of her buttocks and a big foot gently kicked her ankles apart. Knowing what was now open for Dean to view triggered an aroused response, and she fought not to close her thighs. She was so wet, she could feel the moisture coating them.

The first smack caught her by surprise. It echoed around the room. The next few stung a little, but did more to heat her skin, an interesting sensation, particularly when he rubbed the affected area with his palm. But, like the little wheel wielded by Eric had done, when the whole surface of her ass was heated, as well as the tops of her thighs and the crease where buttocks and thighs met, she was sensitized beyond reason. Her pussy throbbed and she reached back to try and get a hand under her to ease the need.

Dean forestalled her, grabbing her fingers and flipping her onto her back, one of his big hands protecting her spine as he lifted her higher onto the counter. The pressure and instant temperature change against the tops of her buttocks elicited a gasp. She panted in reaction. He pushed between her legs and leaned over her, dropping a kiss on her forehead. "I told you not to let go."

"Sorry. I couldn't, I mean…" Amy tried to quit babbling, amazed at her response to the spanking. Dean placed a hand under each of her knees and slid her even further up, bending her legs, placing her feet flat on the cool surface. He again grabbed the hand she tried to pleasure herself with and sucked the fingers into his mouth, soaking them with his saliva. Setting them between her folds he sat back on a stool.

"Do it, then. Get yourself off."

This was intimate. She was splayed on her own kitchen island, Dean's shirt up around her waist, one breast partially displayed as her struggles loosened the top buttons. As if reading her mind he reached out and flicked the rest of them open, pulling the material aside to totally bare her to his gaze. His eyes were molten silver with lust, features tight. She could see the pulse hammering at the base of his neck, muscled chest rising and falling with the intensity of his breaths. She took a deep breath of her own and closed her eyes.

"Keep your eyes open, Amy. I want to see all of you."

Prying her lids up, she focused just above his right shoulder, inserting her middle finger deeper between her labia as she did so. She was drenched and hadn't needed need him wetting her fingers but it made the act hotter, even more intimate. He stared down at her apex, and she got on with it. Truth to be told, she was so close it was no real effort. Her clit was swollen, poking out from its protective hood, and she circled it, dipping down to gather more of her juices, anointing it, rubbing those tiny circles ever faster. The far off tingle in the soles of her feet and in the small of her back announced her impending orgasm. And Dean pulled her hand away.

"Noooo," she moaned. "Please…"

He blew across her begging flesh, pulling her back from the edge, then pushed what felt like two fingers up inside her. Her cream, redistributed, ran down her cleft, and she could feel it, hot and sticky at her buttocks. He pulled his fingers out and followed the wet trail, pausing suggestively at her anus, pressing lightly. When his mouth descended to press an open mouthed kiss on her pussy, Amy simply begged.

"Dean, please. Please."

Skilful nibbles and licks were the response to her pleas, and the pressure at her bottom hole increased. A digit pushed past the tight muscle just as Dean's tongue lanced into her channel. She chanted nonsensically in her head, hands fisting at her sides, longing to push into his hair. Another finger joined the first and stretched her back entrance, his tongue now circling her pussy opening.

When he sucked her clit between his teeth and bit down lightly she screamed her release, arching into his hold. Her pussy clenched on air, the invaders in her ass feeling impossibly huge.

Heart rate and pulse slowing, she blinked up into Dean's eyes, his mouth and chin wet from her orgasm. He smiled at her, not one of those smug male smiles saying he knew how hard he'd made her come, although she had no doubt he was fully aware. It was a diffident smile, cautious, and it made her reach a hand out to him, fingers catching in the hair on his chest, tugging him down to her. She kissed him, tasting herself on his lips.

"Even Steven?" She used a term she barely remembered from her childhood.

He squinted. And smiled a real smile. Teasing had just been added to whatever it was they had going on, and it felt fine. Turning from her, she watched his nice ass disappear down the hallway, heard water running, and then he was back. Back with a cloth to clean her up. Jeez.

"I have to go." Back to confident, competent Dean. It was disconcerting.

"Okay." She knew she sounded puzzled, didn't try to hide it.

"I have a meeting at six and shit to do before. Business. You want me to come back after?"

*Did* she? Do bears crap in the woods? "Yes."

"It'll be late."

"I'm going to dinner at Sandra's. I won't be back until maybe nine."

"Late, sweetheart, for me, means maybe two in the morning."

"Oh. What is it that you do?"

"That's a conversation for another day. I need my shirt."

Amy squirmed off the counter and pulled it off. Totally at home in her own skin—Vegas show girls tended to get that way—she didn't miss the way Dean's eyes tracked the movement of her breasts or the way his gaze dropped down her body. The crotch of his jeans bulged—the man had incredible recovery time. She gestured to him. "That can't be comfortable."

"It isn't. But you'll make it up to me tonight."

No way should her pussy get wet again. She decided to ignore it. "Ring the buzzer, two shorts, one long."

"You could give me a key."

"I could, but Sandra has my spare."

"Those are pretty good locks, but I could show you my lock picking skills."

"You could, but then I might shoot you."

Obviously, that wasn't the right kind of teasing for him. He stepped into her, tense and scary. "You have a weapon?"

"Yes. Both Sandra and I do. We're licensed and we trained."

Some of the tension relaxed from his big body. "Where do you keep it?"

"Where I can get to it in a hurry, Dean. And *that's* a discussion for another time. Don't you have to go?"

"I can't believe I'm standing in the kitchen, having an argument about a gun with a naked woman." He flashed her another pussy-wetting smile and struggled into his shirt. She was getting addicted to those smiles. The kiss he laid on her was added to her list of addictions. Gently pushing her in the direction of the bedroom, he patted her bottom.

"I'll lock up. I don't want anyone catching a glimpse of you when I leave."

She walked down the hall, hearing the front door open then shut firmly, the lock engaging. Well. She hustled back and armed the system again. She had enough time to make up the bed, get dressed again and get some work done. Then she'd buy a dessert for dinner. It would be a long time before she could make anything on that island without remembering how she'd been Dean's dessert.

****

"After that breakfast, neither one of us needed caramel crumble, Amy," Sandra chided as she set dishes in the sink and rinsed them.

"I felt like one, and you're so freaking thin, and in such good shape, you intimidate me."

"I ate my share of cholesterol this morning, probably enough for the week. I don't want to be in some hospital bed with an illness I could have prevented with good diet and exercise." The, *and with no one around to visit me,* was unspoken but audible anyhow.

"I've gained a few pounds," Amy allowed. "But I still swim a couple of times a week and I walk. I mostly eat healthy except for Zeke's. And caramel crumble."

"I don't care about a few pounds, Amy. It's your heart you need to worry about, and your knees in later life."

"So I'll swim a few extra laps."

"Although you burn calories doing the horizontal bop, too."

She stared at Sandra's back.

The other woman still busy at the sink.

There was amused acceptance in Amy's voice. "Sandra?"

"The new Amy came for dinner. A hint of happy and fun. I worry he's not the right guy, but for sure he's bringing something out in you. I hope you get to know him beyond the sex."

Sitting back in her chair, considering, she scraped up a little piece of caramel crumble with the tine of a fork, sucking the morsel into her mouth. Was she happy? She was happy when she saw a beautiful sunset, or saw a baby with a loving mom. Happy when she saw an animal loved and cared for. Happy to spend time with Sandra. Did Dean make her happy? The sex fulfilled her, nothing to fear, skilled and satisfying. It was fun to tease a little, be taken care of so intimately. And she was looking forward to seeing him later. But that was maybe just the sex.

"Quit thinking so hard, damn it. Quit analyzing. Just feel for once."

Wowza, Sandra was pissed. And correct. Amy was, behind the scenes and away from her conscious thought, minimizing what had transpired with Dean. On the heels of that revelation came the shit-scared feeling he was doing the same thing and might not show up later. This considering a relationship thing wasn't just tough. It sucked. Before she'd kinda moved right in with the guy, all casual and no second thoughts. No thinking period.

"It doesn't suck. It's just new," Amy protested. And talking out loud to one's best friend tended to get answers that were food for thought. She got up and gathered the rest of the dirty dishes to carry them over to Sandra.

"What time's your shift tomorrow?"

"Seven. So I'm kicking you out by nine. I hate getting up so early."

"Tell that to someone who believes you. You called me at seven this morning." Amy gave her friend a little hug. "Make some tea, then and we'll sip like old grannies and leave my sex life out of it for awhile."

# FOREVER

## Chapter Four

Jeez. The buzzer pulled her from a deep sleep. She'd laid awake a long time since going to bed at eleven, having again worked haphazardly on the pending web design after coming home from Sandra's, thinking about Dean. It was also curious how Mr. Zuchinski hustled into his house, abandoning his front lawn vigil, when she pulled in earlier. But she must have gone under the veil of slumber after checking the clock around one, and now was cranky from being interrupted in REM sleep.

The buzzer went again and she staggered into one wall in the hallway, feeling her way through the darkened living room to the front door. Reaching for the handle, it occurred to her the person with his goddamn finger on the buzzer might not be Dean.

"Who is it?" she croaked, wishing she'd thought to check the feed.

"Jesus, Amy." No mistaking that voice. Or that tone. She disarmed the alarm and fumbled the door open and was nearly mowed down by a fast-moving male. The door slammed shut and her feet barely skimmed the floor as Dean hustled her into the bedroom. He stripped before her fascinated eyes, hopping on one foot to yank the laces open on his boots, shoving his jeans off, dragging his boxers along with them. He wore the same shirt as earlier and a couple of its buttons pinged against the floor as he tore it off.

"Fucking smelled you the whole goddamn time. Had a hard-on the whole goddamn time. Kept making people repeat themselves." He muttered some more but she couldn't hear him past the roaring of her arousal as her nightgown was peeled off and his weight bore her down onto the bed.

****

He had her on her knees, his arm looped around her waist, holding her close to his chest as he powered in and out of her from behind. His free hand pinched and rolled her nipples. He reached a different place in her from that angle, and was pushing her higher with every stroke. He could feel it, the little rippling sensation within her sheath. Their bodies slippery with sweat, the sounds of their coupling blending with the panting breaths sawing in and out of their chests.

"Get yourself off, sweetheart," he gritted.

Feeling her reach to work her clit, knowing she was working it hard by the way her channel responded, her release still blindsided him and she shuddered with the intensity of it, taking him with her. Setting his teeth in the point of her shoulder he groaned through the pleasure. The fine links of the chain she wore caught in the stubble on his jaw and he vaguely wondered about the significance of that stylized C.

Pulling out to deal with the condom, he watched as she burrowed into the bedding, snuffling into her pillow. He drifted the sheet over her cooling body; she was out like a light. It felt strange to be smiling as he cleaned up in the bathroom, then returned to take the side of the bed he usually slept on. Bonus.

Lying beside the woman who just rocked his world, Dean forced himself to stay awake. Amy breathed sonorously, clearly exhausted. He'd lost track of how many times he got her off, after the hard, urgent fuck as soon as he crossed the threshold. He delighted in her responsiveness, the resilient strength of her incredible body. Rarely did he sleep with the women he hooked up with unless he was inclined for more in the morning.

After the past twenty-four hours he doubted he'd have any inclination for sex in the morning, probably not until the afternoon, but he wasn't going anywhere. He rolled to spoon against the satiny feel of Amy, his cock daring to make a distant, lewd objection about waiting until the afternoon.

****

"Are you going to tell me what you do?" Amy bit into a piece of toast, the tip of her pink tongue flicking out to snag the tiny bead of jam from the corner of her mouth. Dean wanted to feel that tongue anywhere on his body again in the very near future.

"I own a variety of businesses around the city. I own some of them as sole proprietorship, some as part owner. I'm a silent partner in others. I don't run any of them. I have people for that."

"Uh huh." She hopped up to get the coffee pot, topping his cup without asking. It felt domestic, although how he even recognized that feeling… But she was giving him a look he recognized as disbelief.

"What?"

"And you hold court with … who? Other investors? Your partners? They looked like muscle to me, the ones at the club."

Fuck. He *knew* she was smart and didn't miss anything. He answered a question with a request. "Tell me what you do."

"I thought I had. I design and build websites, monitor them. I have a small client base, enough to pay the bills."

"You have a considerable chunk in savings and investments too, sweetheart."

Her cup crashed to the counter and her eyes narrowed on him, the pure violet darkening to gentian. "Have you done a background check on me?"

There was no sense in sugar coating it. “Had Randy do it when I decided to come over yesterday. He’s my right hand man.”

The ominous silence was abruptly broken. “And whatever it is you do, you need to know who you’re fucking?”

“No, Amy. I need to know who I’m spending more than one night with. Don’t push me.”

She worked a hand through her mass of hair and sighed. “I got money from a settlement. From my life back in Vegas. He settled out of court.”

Dean’s chest constricted. Amy’s voice had softened, becoming distant. He recognized a defence mechanism. “Randy didn’t say anything about a settlement.”

Shrugging, the movement causing her breasts to shift under her pink robe, she answered. “The record is sealed. I signed a non-disclosure. Rich boys with rich fathers can get away with murder. Didn’t get that far, lucky for me.”

Fuck. His vision darkened and narrowed, fists clenching. He hardly recognized his voice. “Who?’

“Can’t tell you. I’ll get sued and as you know from having *Randy* check on me, I don’t have much more than my car, the nest egg and the income from my web design business. I rent this place.”

“You can tell me who he is, Amy.” He strove to keep his voice calm.

Staring at him, she rested her chin on steepled hands. “No.”

Dean dropped it. She’d have her reasons aside from a non-disclosure agreement. He’d put Randy on it and ferret the information out. He wasn’t sure he wanted to know what the asshole had done to his woman that stopped short of murder, but also necessitated a fair chunk of change as a settlement. Her beautiful face showed no signs of violence, and he didn't recall any scars on her body, aside from a few tiny marks. One marring the smooth expanse of her belly, another near her left breast, one at her navel. He conveniently ignored the fact he'd just called her his woman. If she could tell him what happened, he'd listen.

"He ruptured my spleen, fractured my left cheekbone, gave me a concussion when my head hit the wall, broke my left wrist, my jaw, three ribs, and apparently raped and sodomized me afterwards. I don't remember that." She spoke as though it happened to someone else.

"Fuck!" He'd never felt so furiously impotent. "Why?"

"Because he wanted to, and because he could. He paid for me, and I suppose he saw me as a disposable toy. Boys play with and break their toys."

Dean went to her, wondering that he could even make his body move without exploding in violence against a faceless enemy. Her eyes were dry, calm and untroubled–unnaturally so. She willingly went into his arms however, huddling against him as if for comfort. A wave of possessiveness left him feeling hollow, and he rocked with her in place, resting his lips against her temple. His eyes closed against the picture she'd painted. A brave, hopeful survivor, and he'd thought to treat her like the other women he fucked—he'd never allowed himself to get to know any of their stories. But this was Amy. Rich boy was going to meet someone, or two someones, in a dark alley a time in the future, and whether he lived or died depended upon how nicely he begged for his miserable life.

"Go put some clothes on, Amy. I want to sit and talk with you somewhere besides these uncomfortable stools. Not your bed. It makes me think of other things."

She stepped out of the circle of his arms and reached up to touch his cheek, a drifting gentle contact that tugged at the middle of his chest. At his heart. She went.

****

The lounge featured some comfortable privacy booths and a fully stocked bar. Music played softly. It was early afternoon—they'd both required several hours of sleep to recharge. Amy refused a drink, accepting some water with lemon, and curled into his side. He was relieved that booze wasn't something she used on a customary basis. A few regulars passed by and nodded to him, their eyes drifting to Amy. He knew they attracted attention; anything he did out of the ordinary would be whispered about. It didn't matter to him at that moment, he wanted to talk with Amy and not drag her off to fuck her in new and enticing positions. At least not until they talked.

"You were a call girl?" He didn't want to think of her in that profession.

She laughed, but the sound was devoid of humor. "No. I hadn't quite gotten to that level, but close. My parents died in a car crash when I was just over two. Both were only children, with few surviving relatives, and I guess with no life insurance the initially interested ones decided sixteen years of parenthood, after raising their own kids, went beyond family loyalty." There was no bitterness in her voice, simply acceptance, and Dean knew she'd dealt, because he'd done the same thing.

"I grew up in the System, foster homes at first, a scrawny, miserable, little kid crying all the time for her mommy, or so I recall being told when I got older.

Wouldn't bond with any of the foster moms, so got shuffled around. My file was like a horror show to read, but it was as if it happened to someone else, you know?"

Dean *didn't* know. He hadn't dissociated his experiences, and he wondered which approach was better, or if people just did what worked for them. He made a noncommittal sound.

"Then group care, which was really juvie, because of a youthful mistake. Mistakes. I tended to accept dares and the judge frowned on several counts of public mischief. I got out and was on the street at sixteen. Don't know how I stayed clean, away from drugs. Booze never really appealed. Until I discovered margaritas."

The look she slanted his way had his cock stirring. He'd make sure to have the ingredients for her favorite tipple available from time to time. Drunk sex with Amy promised to be a lot of fun.

"It wasn't a stellar life, but fortunately, I was a late bloomer and really lucky no one bothered the gangly, skinny kid. I panhandled, worked as a waitress, lucked out with a government sponsored computer course for the homeless, such a joke, but I took advantage and excelled. Problem is you can't find that kind of job without money to start with. You have to have a place to live and the right clothes to be interviewed.

"Then I woke up one day and discovered my best asset. I had bloomed, so to speak, and was starting to attract unwelcome attention. So I walked into a casino, took my clothes off and got a job as a show girl. Once I got comfortable with wearing something on my head and nothing on my ass or boobs I was good with it."

She laughed again, this time for real, tilting her head to the side, eyes looking up and to the left, clearly remembering those experiences. He'd never thought about it, never considered how it might be for a woman to present herself to the public like that. Mostly to men.

"They had a spa on tap for waxing, lasering, all that kind of stuff, and every girl wants to learn makeup. It was fine, because I discovered I'm a girly girl. I strutted with the rest. It wasn't until I got older that management gave me the option of going to the parties. The guy who hired me knew my age. Nineteen isn't exactly a big number in Vegas. He took a chance but wasn't going to risk the law, so he waited. I might get away with it as a show girl at the actual performances, but not the parties. He was a good guy."

Dean doubted she met many good guys. He was just relieved for her sake she hadn't prostituted herself, that her issues with quick hookups were a result of poor personal choices. Although that might not say much about him, he thought wryly. They were indeed a fucked up pair. "But not like a call girl."

"Nope. You could hang out, have a good time, sometimes the guys would leave you money. I won't say I didn't sleep with some of them, but nobody had any expectations, or if they did I wasn't pushed. But show girls who can't sing and dance, who just strut, get replaced by fresher stock."

It was an altogether depressing comment on the vagaries of men and societal expectations. Dean dreaded what was coming next, but he needed to know. And he was going to have to share something, too. He wasn't certain which was worse.

"I became an escort. I didn't have much else to fall back on, although I kept up my computer skills. Again, my choice if I slept with the client. They weren't actually looking for that, if you can believe it. They needed camouflage or distraction from what they were up to. It was me looking." The painful chuckle belied the composed way she now talked about her past. She was getting close to the difficult stuff. Her face had lost some color and he could feel her beginning to tense.

"They wanted somebody on their arm to pull the eye while they worked the tables or did their deals in the rooms. I went out on countless calls for a few years. I made lots of bad choices in men when I wasn't working, some who used me for sex, lived off me, smacked me around when their lives weren't going well. Those I lost in a hurry. Not much different than the way I was treated in foster care. But I took the emotional shit they slung my way to heart, for some stupid reason. I've learned I don't have to take that anymore." Was there a warning to be detected in that last statement? Dean replayed it in his head and decided to take it at face value.

"You ever go to the cops about the domestic violence?"

"No. For all the obvious reasons. Women like me don't get a lot of sympathy from the men in blue."

He shoved his fingers into her wealth of hair and dragged her head back, forcing her to meet his eyes. "Don't. Don't demean yourself. Ever. Or sell yourself short. I won't allow it."

Staring back assessingly, she finally nodded. "Do my best, babe. Old habits and all."

Settling back against his shoulder as he sifted through the strands of her hair, she continued, swirling the straw in the glass of water. "I went out on one last call, although I didn't know it was a last call at the time. Rich kid from … another state, asked for a big blonde. He dragged me from casino to casino, lost a ton of cash, tried a whole lot of fondling to establish his man-about-town status. I avoided most of it without making him look bad, and when it got time to shut it down, and we were back at his hotel, he asked me to stay the night. I refused and he let it go. Just like that. Disarmed me, really, because I sensed he was pure asshole.

"He sucked back a couple more drinks, said he'd walk me to a cab. But he was unsteady on his feet, seemed really drunk, so I took him up to his room. Thought I'd just dump him on the bed and leave, you know? I'm not stupid. I enlisted the help of one of the guys who scan for people using the elevators without cards and we went up together. But once we got to the room, just opened the door, the security guy's radio went and he had to go."

Dean tried to control the tremors of rage permeating his control. Amy looked up at him and ran her fingers across his cheek, easing the tightening there, soothing his jaw. She was still tense, but it seemed to dissipate as she reached out to him, violet eyes soft.

"It's done, babe. But you wanted to know. Do you still want to hear it all? I mean, you already know the worst of it."

He nodded, turning his head to press a kiss on the palm of her hand, a gesture he had never made in his living memory. "I want to know, even as I don't."

After a moment, she continued, leaning away slightly as if to avoid the heat he could feel emanating from his gut. "I let my guard down for an instant, and rich boy took advantage. He dragged me inside and as they say, the rest is history. The maid found me in the morning and called 911. I nearly bought it, but laparoscopic surgery removed my spleen, the ribs didn't puncture my lungs, and the rest healed. It took time for the bones to knit, but they did, although the jaw was the worst of it. And the visits to the dentist. Stay away from me with needles. Sandra was one of my nurses and she saved my head, most importantly. We're now best friends."

Sandra, as he'd already figured out, was going to be the wild card in what appeared to be a *dating* relationship. But he couldn't let that distract him now. He wanted more information about rich boy and hoped Amy would let something slip. "How did you get him charged?"

"The cops did. I was out of it. But it was his room, registered in his name, the security guy verified I wasn't interested in staying—that man felt so bad. He wrote a deposition and that counted for a lot. Rich boy's DNA was everywhere and when they caught up with him—his flight hadn't even left—his knuckles were still covered in my blood. Daddy swooped in and paid me off."

"So *he* didn't pay."

Amy gave him a startled glance, leaning into him again, this time absorbing his angst with her whole body. "I don't think a night in lockup was much fun for such a pretty boy, and a trial wasn't something I wanted, believe me. It might have gone against me. I took the money and ran. Like the John Cougar song, but it was for the best."

"And you don't want payback?" The word sounded venomous even in his own ears.

"Dean. I don't want him to hurt other women, if that's what you mean. It tortures me, that he thinks he got away with it, but there's no real impetus by the courts to prosecute rich men. Not when the victim isn't pure and innocent. Not when the woman asked for it, working in a risky profession. And don't get all pissy. You know how escorts are perceived."

Rich boy wouldn't be hurting any other women. He wouldn't be able to lift his hands high enough. There were some things worse than death and Dean knew a fair number of them. He quit pressing her. Being powerless and defenseless was a foreign feeling for him, one he'd left behind when he was about ten. But Amy's experience was fresh, and she was still at risk, by virtue of her gender.

"Your turn." Dean heard the expectation in her voice and went for broke.

"I have legitimate business interests. I also run street protection and illegal gambling. I launder money."

Her body tensed and she drew away slightly, then sat up to put an arms' length between them, scooting along on the fake leather seat. Her violet eyes were enormous, teeth tugging at her bottom lip. "Holy shit."

He waited.

And Amy processed. "Do you pimp women? Sell drugs?"

"No. Never will."

"Do you, uh … hurt people?"

"Only the competition, and then in self-defense." He wasn't going to tell her what he was capable of and who he really was. At least not yet and maybe never. It could get him killed.

"Is anyone going to hurt me to get to you?"

Fuck. He should have thought of it, as she had good reason to ask, was still feeling vulnerable, and probably always would in some regard. He'd just heard her describe her life on the arm of scumbags in a volatile city. "We've never had an issue with any of my crew's women being used that way, sweetheart. But I've never had a woman, so can't promise you."

"It scares me, Dean. I was on the fringe of shit in Vegas, for sure. I could have been worked over before, or put down. But I moved here to get away from all that."

"Let's find our way, Amy. We have a time frame, anyhow."

"Time frame?"

"Until, if, you're on your period. That dictates how fast this relationship moves. You carrying my kid changes things." And he'd used the R word. So fucked. Still, it didn't feel too bad.

"You romantic man." Amy's tone wasn't close to matching her words and she shoved further away from him.

He couldn't help but laugh, reaching out to pull her close, ignoring how stiff with umbrage she was. "I have limited experience, sweetheart, but give me points for trying. Okay?"

Softening, she agreed. "But it's gonna be a trial. We're two damaged people, babe. There'll be a lot of insanity ahead. And I don't want to have to be watching my back."

"I'll have someone on you when I'm not around."

"Uh, uh. No. I'll feel like some wiseguy's piece."

He waited. If she couldn't accept the additional risk of being with him then they should probably end this now. The panicked sense of dread boiling up from his belly, the disparate sense of outright refusal to even consider that practical response took him by surprise. He cast around in his head for something to make it work.

"You could move in with me, have a safe place to live and work, if you're concerned." Holy shit. Fuck. When he lost his head, or thought with his smaller head, or whatever part was now dictating to him, he fucking lost it to the max. But he'd never had a woman before, past the casual night or two, and he'd never fucked without a condom before. Life was spiralling out of control, and it was a curiously thrilling sensation. Just not one he was familiar with.

Amy curled away from him again and set her mouth in a gesture he wondered if he'd be seeing a fair number of times—if she accepted his offer. It spoke volumes to him; a mixture of surprise, caution and amusement, laced with a little fear. Her words confirmed his increasing ability to read her.

"You *are* spontaneous, babe. I wouldn't have thought it, but first forgetting protection and now making such a cozy suggestion?" The fear surfaced, outweighing the other emotions. Her eyes shone a purple midnight-blue. She might want something more than casual sex, but it scared her, too.

Shrugging, he explained, finding the words as he spoke. "You could still keep your place, kind of a safety net, if you want. Be with me, have it known, and be safe. Until we figure things out."

Unprepared for her response, he found himself wondering what planet he woke up on that morning.

"Still stacking the deck, Dean. There's always a qualifier with you. When I get my period. Live together until and *if* we figure things out. I'm no expert on relationships, but you've already set us up to fail. You see an ending. I don't know why you hold women in such low regard, but I'm not interested in being the poster girl for failure. I've got work to do. Take me home or I'll get a cab." She slid away, across the bench seat and got to her feet, making her way to the exit.

Thinking fast, once again overcome with that unfamiliar panic, Dean scrawled his name across the check and followed her. He stared down the men looking at her as she passed, varying degrees of interest and lust on their faces. The women looked disdainful or aloof, studiously ignoring Amy or their lips curling, clearly envious. He decided he wasn't letting her go. And when he made a decision he went with it—unless something significant proved him wrong.

Already outside and yanking on the passenger door handle, she turned to give him an imperious stare, violet eyes unreadable, but her features were taut. He remoted the locks open and moved to help her inside. Shaking him off, she was buckled in and leaning back against the leather seat, eyes closed, when he got in behind the wheel. He cranked the key and drove out of the lot, letting the silence build. In his experience, however limited on the emotional front, women broke it first. No surprise, Amy didn't. Fuck. He put his foot down and drove to his home.

"We're here." He wondered if she might be sleeping, or if she'd dissociated. It didn't matter to him. She could be angry, maybe even hurt, but she was comfortable enough to relax her guard around him.

Looking around, she blinked. "Where?"

"My place. C'mon in and we'll talk some more."

"I have work to do."

Dean gritted his teeth and went around to her door. "Amy. Get out of the goddamn truck."

"Bossy pants."

Relieved at being teased, he yanked her out and kissed her, delighted when she kissed him back. "I'm going to fuck up regularly, sweetheart. Be glad I figured it out."

"That's like number four, babe. Okay, we'll talk and then I *have* to get my work done. No contest."

Dean urged her up the stairs to his condo, mentally sorting through the ways he'd screwed up that day. Or was she counting from that kiss in the hall? Four? Four?

****

"So that's my life story. In a nutshell." He was sweating, and had to get up a couple of times to get a beer to keep his mouth lubricated. He'd told her pretty much everything, from his birth, to his whore of a mother, the struggle to get out of Dodge and make something of himself, to his return to running the business. He skimmed over his college degree and didn't share his ultimate secret, although he thought it might seal the deal between them in a good way. But he couldn't make himself share that and didn't care to examine all the reasons, beyond basic survival. He told himself it was too big a risk to share so soon. So instead, he promised himself he'd set a fluid deadline. A time to tell her if they happened to be established as a couple, some time down the road.

Amy hadn't interrupted very often, other than to ask about sibs and other family. Seemed they were both alone in the world. The other sounds she made weren't out of pity, but of understanding and acceptance, acknowledging his confession. Something he hadn't even done in Catholic school. Confession. It felt good, whether for his soul or not remained to be seen.

"Wow. Ever wonder how we're here and not buried somewhere? Or in jail?" Her face was solemn, those remarkable eyes petal soft.

He shrugged. "I don't think about it much. Like you said, it's past. I move forward. What?" Amy's tiny snort made him look.

"You move forward like I do. Influenced and sometimes burdened by the past." She laughed, a pure musical sound. "Listen to us. Probably the most I've talked to anybody about this shit aside from Sandra. You?"

"I took some courses in the military, psychology stuff. I figured some things out. But I don't talk about it. And I'm done talking about it."

Amy stretched from her curled-up position on his couch, taking up little space for such a tall woman with definite curves. His eyes tracked the movement of her breasts and traced a line up to her mouth, tilted deliciously in a smile.

"Okay. I didn't know the military offered psychology courses, thought the recruits weren't encouraged to think, but hey. And I'm done talking, too. For now. It made me tired."

"Would you like to take a nap?" His cock hoped so. It would rock her to sleep. And he hadn't missed her quiet challenge. For now. He wondered if he could keep opening up to her.

"Nope. Work. I'm disciplined."

"I work different hours, so your job will fit in well with mine, I think. Especially if you work here. I can show you the den." *And the bedroom.* She hadn't shown any interest in his place and he wondered how she viewed it. Impersonal? Cold?

"I'll take the guided tour another time, babe. We need to keep finding our way."

Were those *his* words of caution coming back to bite him on the ass? They were. "I'll take you home. I'll be by tonight. Not as late."

"Sure. You come on by. *Whenever*." That snark was back in her tone.

"Old habits, sweetheart. Like yours. I say something you don't like, you say so and we'll talk. Otherwise, I cut to the chase and don't play games. The soft shit, my history, just got said and I'm over it." For now.

Bottom lip again caught between her teeth, Amy looked up at him through her lashes and nodded. He could see how she must have looked as a kid and that thing in his chest swelled and his throat tightened. This was way more than lust, and it was both exhilarating and frightening. Dean Chambray didn't do scared. He tore his eyes away and grabbed his keys.

Randy exited his SUV, parked at the curb a couple of units down, and looked their way as they descended the stairs. He threw a casual wave.

"Randy." Dean raised his voice a little. His lieutenant ambled over, shambling, loose stride deceptive, as was his size. Randy could move like a cat if he chose.

"Amy Copeland, this is Randy, my right hand. Randy—"

"Blondie. I remember." The other man cut him off, offering a big hand to Amy, enveloping hers. "Nice to meet you."

"And you, Randy. I understand you know far more about me than I do about you."

Well, shit. Dean froze at the subtle threat in Amy's tone, remembering she had some skill with computers, too. Randy heard it as well and carefully let go of her hand.

Amy smiled brightly, nodded, and stepped around his lieutenant to make her way to the truck. Randy held his eyes for a moment and Dean shrugged. "Later."

Amy was once again impatiently waiting for him to open the damn door locks. He helped her inside, and this time she allowed it. As they drove to her place he put it out there. "Don't put your nose into the business, Amy. You won't find much about me because Randy takes most of the attention off me. But he's private."

When she didn't reply, he tried again. "Part of what we need to agree on, sweetheart. A trust thing."

Her head turned his way, and he took advantage of the red light to study her face, violet eyes enigmatic, features pensive. "I don't betray my friends, Dean. Or my enemies. You'll learn that about me."

Thinking on that statement all the way to her place, Dean wondered if was possible to take her at face value, tell her everything. But he couldn't do it, at least not yet. He knew it was a fault, but trusting someone wasn't an intrinsic part of his makeup, and Randy was the only one he truly trusted, and then only with the business and his real identity. Randy didn't know the shit that made Dean. The package felt evenly split between his right-hand man and his woman, and was all he could manage at this point. He was feeling fucking overwhelmed, to tell the truth.

The sun was shining and the city bore up well under it, considering the summer heat would soon suck all the life out of it. They skirted downtown, and the sidewalks were full of pedestrians, most of them women, dressed in a variety of outfits cut to beat the heat. He would normally be evaluating each one and enjoying the sight, but his attention was taken by the quiet, statuesque blonde sitting beside him. Wishing he knew her thoughts, but content to just be with her, another chapter in his life obviously opening, Dean took her home.

Kissing her goodbye, hearing the locks snick into place behind her, made him gloomy and he stood, staring at the door until he collected himself. He wanted her in his home, available, easy access, yes, but also to spend time together. He wanted her to make his home their home, a real home, and wrestled with the notion, certain the long-put-to-rest little boy within had suddenly awoken, uncertain if it would make him a better person, or weaken him. In the end he got back in his truck and went to his main office. There was always work to be done, even if it wasn't always what most businessmen pursued. And it would distract him from this bizarre need to consider domestication … what the fuck was that, anyhow?

## Chapter Five

Well, that had been interesting. Interesting? Amy wasn't certain what words described her day with Dean Chambray. Run over by a steamroller might be closer to the description. So he knew much of what made her tick, and she knew some of what made him. There was one huge difference, at least she believed there was. Casting an eye at the clock, Amy called Sandra's number. Time for a confab.

"On my way home now. And you can bring Thai here. I'm too tired to come to your place and leave again later."

That was Sandra. No questions asked. Amy wanted to talk, she'd listen, but on her terms, being aware one needed to look after oneself in order to help others. Amy sometimes felt the gauche teenager around her friend. She called in the order and checked to see if she had the cash or needed to stop at the bank. She didn't have credit cards, and rarely used her bank card. She hated the thought of being out there as a byte in the unseen storage units of information compiled by Big Brother and God knew who else. By the time she drove to Sandra's her friend was home, changed out of her uniform and making ice tea.

"Long day?"

"Pretty much the same. Too many patients, not enough staff. But that new obstetrics surgeon does wonderful work, and his patients heal quicker, get to go home earlier. I like the hospital, overall. Glad we moved here."

Amy couldn't resist. "What's his name?"

Sandra paused, in the process of placing a spicy shrimp in her mouth. "Who? Dr. Wyatt? I don't know his first name."

Dropping it, because Sandra really didn't know, wasn't playing it coy, they talked a little about upcoming events—a one-man theatre production in Sandra's case, a new movie release in Amy's. They sat on little bistro chairs at a small, round table, inset with colorful tiles outlining a fantastical bird shape. Their plates covered its wildly beating wings and the takeout boxes nearly obscured the body, but she'd seen it enough times to know what it looked like. She carefully set her sweating glass down exactly between the bird's head and shoulder.

"You still seeing him?" The casual question didn't hide Sandra's muted anxiety.

"I think so."

"You think so?"

"Yah, well, we've been together pretty much except for dinner with you. And we've been talking."

Silence. Even the real birds in the miniscule yard Sandra's home boasted, the manicured beds of flowers and lovingly tended trees making it an oasis, didn't break the quiet. Amy hurried to fill it.

"I told him. Everything."

"Okaaay. That's out of your comfort zone. Trying to chase him away?"

"No, Dr. Freud," Amy retorted. "The opposite. He's fucked up, too, and I wasn't going into this, whatever it is, without putting it out there. It felt right."

Sandra drank her tea, a tremor visible in her hand. She wiped her mouth with a napkin featuring the logo of the Thai House. "Felt right, as in you trusted your instincts?"

"Okay, I know my instincts with lovers can be shit. But I read people pretty good. You know that. Even guys. Hell, especially guys, at least the ones I don't fall into bed with. That's where I screw up."

"And this is different how?"

"He hasn't used it against me."

"Early days, Amy." Her friend's big brown eyes were narrowed, full of concern, and Amy winced. Early days indeed. And if he used it against her it was going to hurt like a mother.

Gathering up her courage and organizing her thoughts, she continued. "I trust him with it. With my stuff. And he shared, too."

That had Sandra looking, eyes widening and her mouth opening to close with a snap. "Shared what?"

"I'm not gonna say all his stuff. But his childhood wasn't any better than mine and he got out with a little help from strangers—sound familiar? He enlisted, and when he got out he, uh, got into business."

"What kind of business?"

Okay, here it came. Amy didn't want to say, didn't know how much she *could* say, so she repeated what Dean said.

"Holy mother! You're dating another criminal? You know what he does and you're still seeing him?"

"That's the least of my worries."

"I can't wait."

Amy didn't think she'd heard sarcastic Sandra before, at least not with her. She didn't know what to share first. "We didn't use protection once."

Her friend stared, and to Amy's amazement, laughed. But there wasn't an ounce of mirth in that sound. "What are you? Twelve? For God's sake." Sandra got up and began to clear the table.

This was probably what having a real mom would feel like, but it was bizarre, Amy decided. They were peers. Nuts. She picked up the remaining evidence of their meal and followed Sandra into the kitchen. They worked in silence for a few minutes, tossing the dregs of the food, wrapping up the good leftovers, stacking the dishwasher.

"There's more."

"I don't doubt it. When you do something, you do it big, honey. Is he twelve, too? Or just one of those macho men who leave it up to the woman? Hasn't he heard about sexually transmitted infections?"

Amy had thought about those and hastened to tell Sandra Dean had reassured her on that count. She *was* twelve. She knew she was clean and believed Dean was, too. But if he fucked *her* without a condom … her belly clenched right along with her jaw and jealousy coursed through her veins. Had he lied to her? She didn't know who she was angriest with at that moment.

"So, want to tell me the more part?" Sandra sounded resigned and disappointed and Amy's heart sank. She forgot to be jealous about all the other women.

"I'm sorry, Sandra. When are you going to get tired of picking up my pieces?" She heard the fear of rejection in her voice, and it clogged her throat.

"Never. Now tell me."

"This is new to him, you know? New to me, too, but I want it. I want to try it. And I'm pretty sure I want it with him. I feel it, and you said it at breakfast. It's different. I know there's more and I want it."

"With a criminal? A man who 'forgot' to use protection." Sandra's air quotes looked ridiculous and Amy inexplicably wanted to laugh.

She crossed into the living area and folded herself into a tub chair upholstered in a paisley fabric of warm earth tones. She really needed to decorate her own living room, but all it did was contain her work.

Sandra took a seat on the couch, pulling her legs beneath her, regarding Amy with interest. So she quit stalling.

"I do pick 'em. I know. But he's up front and real. And he's competent."

At her friend's hitch of breath, Amy knew she'd coined it, so she continued with thinking out loud. "I'm good with him taking charge. It's a relief. And if I slow down enough to listen and not react, he makes sense. If I don't like it, he wants to know, so we can talk. No games."

"Okay. So what's the catch?"

"I want it all. I want to be optimistic. He keeps thinking in time limits. I called him on it, but I get the sense he's thinking I'll fuck up, and he'll be proven right. It's a big freaking worry."

"As far as I know, honey, relationships evolve. They develop and strengthen and weather the bad times. We all have our breaking points and sometimes relationships suffer. But maybe you're rushing." Sandra was clearly dialing it back.

"Exactly! Different paces. But it's weird. He wants me to move in—"

"Whoa. He's thinking time limited but wants you to move in? I don't understand."

Amy hesitated. Sandra wasn't going to like hearing this part, and she was surprised her friend hadn't already picked up on it. Probably the possible pregnancy and definitely the criminal part distracted her. Funny how *she'd* honed in on the safety piece, maybe because she could be pregnant, but certainly because of her history, her awareness of the increased risk posed to people who hung out with other people who broke the law.

"I don't want anyone going through me to get to him."

"Fuck." Sandra's usually pristine language deteriorated badly. "So living with him keeps you safe. While you build this relationship, at least until you find out if you're pregnant, or until he finds a reason to shut it down."

"Yup. And it's insane but I'm going for it."

"Glad I could clarify it for you. And you *are* insane. Step back, build some space until you can think with your head, Amy. Give it two weeks *away* from Dean. Or at least until you get your period. Or not. Be objective. Don't keep repeating the pattern."

Sandra's plea made total sense. Her friend knew her and understood her. But she'd also said Amy was happy, different. She felt conflicted, desperately wanting to go with her gut yet listen to Sandra too.

"I'll call Dean. I'll take a little time." She didn't know how long she'd hold out against the need for him, but she'd try.

"Okay, Amy. And just so you know? Whatever your choice, I'm always here for you. Although he might not allow it."

"That won't happen, Sandra. He's arrogant and certain, sure of himself. That's the appeal, well, part of it." She couldn't tell her friend any more about the sex and the incredible pull between them. It felt so personal between her and Dean. "But he won't control me that way, cut off my friends."

Sandra didn't look convinced, yet nodded and offered more tea. But Amy needed to go home and make the call without Sandra overhearing. *And* get that website finished. There were others to update, too, if she ever sat down and booted up her computer.

"I'll call you."

"See that you do!"

Momma Sandra.

****

"What's wrong?" Dean's voice was sharp, and she could hear the rumble of male voices in the background. No glasses clinking, or music, so he likely wasn't in the bar.

"Nothing. Sorry. I didn't plan to call you, really." And she hadn't, when he programmed his numbers into her phone, and stored hers in his fancier one. "I just wanted to let you know I'm having an early night, so I'd catch you tomorrow." In truth, she hoped to get his voicemail, but this was probably better. Grab the bull by the horns and all that.

"What's going on, Amy?" Even the sound of his voice, intense and full of appeal, had her pussy dampening.

"I need a little time, Dean."

"You've been talking with Sandra."

Thinking he was maybe too astute for her own good, she hesitated. If he was going to give her grief over Sandra… "Not about your stuff."

A beat of silence. "I believe you," he said quietly. A door closed in the background, but close, and she realized he'd taken the conversation private. "Talk to me."

"I need a little time, Dean. We met three days ago and you're talking about me moving in."

"Because you're worried about safety. As am I."

So he was thinking about her, appreciating the shadow he cast might throw over her. Amy wavered. "I should think on this some more. This is my style, jumping in without looking, and drowning."

"I won't let you drown."

No, he'd haul her out and leave her on shore, shipwrecked, desolate. "I'll see you tomorrow."

"I don't chase and I don't beg, sweetheart."

"Not asking you to," she retorted. "Pick me up at eight and we'll get breakfast."

Silence. He was going to refuse. Over before it really began. Maybe Sandra was right but she was so scared of losing him, never seeing him again, she thought she'd go to her knees, and clung to the edge of the desk.

"Eight. And I'll bring the fixings, make you breakfast. But Amy? This is once. Once."

Okay, so he was bending for her. She didn't want him to change, didn't want him to break, but neither did she. She was already rethinking her request, the idea of sleeping alone in her bed vaguely repugnant.

"Amy?"

"Oh, shit. I'm so bad at this."

Rich, rolling laughter, making her press the cell harder against the shell of her ear, wanting to absorb the mesmerizing sound. Something new about Dean. She'd be learning all kinds of things about him, if she didn't screw it up. Or if he didn't.

"Whatever we have going on, sweetheart, this, uh, relationship, isn't going to follow tradition. I'll see you at eight."

The irritating beep of the phone, signaling the call was ended, had her pulling the damn thing from her ear, punching the off button before setting it carefully on the desk. Well, she had her slice of time, to *think* on this *thing* they had, and was now struggling with a wave of arousal and hardly inclined to work, let along think. Was her gut reaction to be trusted? Or maybe the reaction of an organ situated a little higher, in her chest? Romantic love. Who would have thunk it? Her eyes filled and one tear escaped to meander over the curve of her cheek, streaking its salty path across her jaw line to lose its integrity and smudge on her throat. Amy sniffed and blinked back the flood. Scary as shit. Maybe work would help—and pay the bills.

****

Building the website took a lot of concentration, anchored by some decaf coffee—information page, pics, catalogue entries, buy links. Amy eschewed chemical creamer, pretty sure she wasn't pregnant, but no sense in taking any chances. Everyone knew the risks to the unborn, and that meant no alcohol, no unnecessary chemicals and probably no vast amounts of sugar. Her sweet tooth would have to suffer for the next week or so. She avoided thinking about having a baby, other than in the hypothetical sense, because it terrified her. Amy wasn't sure if you could study to be a good parent or if it would just come to you when the kid arrived, but she dreaded the work ahead. She wasn't ready, and Dean, well, he would probably either excel at the parenting stuff or be horrible at it. There were just no shades of gray with that man. He hovered in the back of her mind as the hours crept past and she alternately cursed and blessed Sandra for asking her to take this step back.

Hitting *save* for the final time and running through the various components of the site as a test run, she sent the proof to the client who lived in … Regina, Saskatchewan, Canada. Loosely translated, it meant the Queen, swift flowing river, settlement or village. Strange, but true. The woman was selling knitted calf ear covers. Also strange, but true. Anyone who would want to protect tender little newborn calf ears from the apparently frigid temperatures up there in Regina, Saskatchewan, Canada, was all right by her.

"Shit." Okay, talking to oneself wasn't uncommon, but thinking about B.O.B., just a few steps away in the bedroom despite the diversion of calf ear covers, was kind of lacking when she had an amazing stud to meet those needs. Except he wouldn't be there until breakfast. Eight o'clock to be precise, and that was a long time. She tossed the pencil in the general direction of the cool wire holder she'd found at the stationary store and reached up to let her hair down from the clip. Maybe she should think about watching a movie, or take a nice long soak. The idea of water surrounding and easing her appealed the most.

****

The grassy bath salts foamed under the pounding of water pouring from the tap. Amy eased into the steaming bath and set her head on the little blown up pillow hanging over the lip of the tub, her hair caught back up on the top of her head. When the water level crept up to the edge, she pushed the taps closed with her toes. Bliss. She soaked for some time ,thinking about Sandra's advice, comparing and contrasting several scenarios, but knew her mind was already made up. She was going to move in with Dean, take the dual risk. She might never have another opportunity at her forever, and anything worthwhile having required effort. Dean appeared willing, and if he used that uncompromising attitude in a good way, she figured it might be okay. Besides, she suspected she loved him, as insane as that might sound. Not that she knew what love felt like, but this thing they had going on wasn't just about the great sex.

The cell phone sitting beside the tub beckoned. It was a woman's prerogative to change her mind, right? And he worked late, he said so. She punched the key for his number.

"Amy."

"I'm hungry now."

Was that a weighted beat of silence? "Half hour."

Pouring a healthy dollop of the same scented body soap onto her sponge, she washed up before standing to rinse beneath the shower, the foamy water swirling down the drain at her feet. She ran her razor over the soft stubble on her legs—lasering her pussy and armpits had been all she could afford before being so rudely cut from the herd of tits and ass—shaving her legs was simple enough. Wrapping a towel around her, she moved to the bedroom, pulling the clip from her hair as she went. The throw pillows were easily piled on the chair, and Bogs was set on the dresser. The little bear was in sad condition, and deserved better than being tossed to the floor. The buzzer sounded in the prearranged sequence, filling the silence and like the proverbial Pavlovian dog, Amy's mouth watered. She raced to open up. No time for pretending, no time to waste.

Dean strode past her, eyes darkening when she turned from locking up behind him as he took in her state of dress, or undress as the case might be. He had a cardboard tray holding two tall plastic cups, and a large paper bag, grease stains decorating its white exterior. Leather jacket open over a black tee shirt, same worn jeans with the hint of threads showing through the pocket right about where he'd stashed his keys. Which drew her eyes to the bulge beneath his belt buckle. Pausing only to toe off his boots, the tray and bag thumped onto the counter and his index finger hooked into the towel, right between her breasts.

Amy willingly let herself be drawn tight against him. Leather creaked and his scent enveloped her. She wreathed her arms around his shoulders, fingers linking behind his neck, and relished the feel of his big hands settling on her ass.

"I brought you some food. For later." He stared down at her, and she lost all perspective. Food? She went on tiptoe and brushed her lips across his. As if it was a signal, Dean was galvanized into action. Her towel crumpled to the floor before they made the hallway, his leather jacket discarded at the bedroom door. She frantically worked the belt buckle and went to her knees, opening the button, pulling at the zipper, dragging the denim down, taking his boxers along with them. His cock sprang free, up to slap his firm belly, mushroom head purple and wet for her, male musk rousing her senses. This time, her way.

Nuzzling the soft skin of his shaft, she traced each of the veins with the tip of her tongue, whisper soft, before laving the one pulsing hard, all the way from the base to the cockhead. His thighs tightened and Amy ran her hands up and over the play of the long, powerful muscles, then dipped her head to lick the crease of each thigh near his scrotum. The crinkle of crisp hair met her tongue and she cupped his sac, rolling each testicle with reverent care.

"Fuck, sweetheart. Put me in your mouth."

Ignoring him, she nibbled and licked, weighing his sac with one hand, stroking upwards with her other to drift her fingers over his shaft. Dean's hands fisted in her hair and tugged her head back. Eyes churning with lust, the skin tight across his high cheekbones, he growled his displeasure. "Quit teasing."

Hiding a smile, she leaned back in and rapidly whiffled up his cock, lips suctioning in tiny increments until she reached the V whereby, without warning, she sucked him inside on a breath. Dean stiffened and a groan reverberated around the room. Carefully shielding her teeth with her lips, she worked hard at taking him deeper with every bob of her head, salty precum lubricating her mouth with every pass. She circled the base of his cock with her hand, pressing just hard enough to delay his release, tormenting him, wanting to pleasure him senseless. He pulled away, breaking her grip and hauled her to her feet to spin and shove her onto the bed. She loved the way he handled her, forcefully but without doing any real harm. The faint bruising from his mouth and strong fingers were badges of honor she would gladly bear.

Chest heaving, cock straining, shiny wet from her efforts and his own, he folded her legs up and pushed her knees wide apart, positioning them near her shoulders. He stared down at her spread pussy while sheathing his cock, kneeling to guide it into her. Pressing past the initial resistance, their collective breath hitched, and she watched as his eyes closed, cock fighting for territory. Planted to her cervix, he slung her legs over his shoulders and unleashed his power again, his big cock prodding high in her channel, making her pant.

Working above her, sweat darkening along his hair line, jaw ticking with strain, Dean pumped harder and harder, swiveling his hips, grinding against that spot and pressing the top of her apex. Pinned beneath him, all she could do was arch up and hang onto his muscled forearms. Her orgasm shuddered outwards from deep inside her sheath and she screamed with it, jerking helplessly as he pushed her up again with measured strokes. The second climax made her bear down hard and she felt his erection break within her, wishing for the sensation of his scalding seed. As he pulled out, her legs slipped bonelessly from his shoulders to sprawl wide. He dealt with the condom, yanked his pants up, and stood looking at her. She couldn't read him, unfamiliar with the look on his face, but thought it boded well. She realized she hadn't said a word since he'd walked in the door.

"Hello, babe."

"Thought maybe cat got your tongue." That infernal brow rose.

"Nope, but something else did, at least until you went all caveman on me."

"Worked for me. And you."

Having no smart ass response to that truth, she contented herself with a smile and closed her eyes. When she opened them, Dean wasn't in the room. She could hear him, paper rustling and cupboard doors opening and closing. He appeared in the doorway, carrying a plate and that cardboard tray. Pushing up to one elbow she spied donuts. Donuts! If she had any doubt before, it was gone. The man brought her *donuts*.

Setting the plate on the closest nightstand, Dean pierced each lid of the cups with a straw and offered her a choice. "Chocolate or strawberry."

Milkshakes *and* donuts. Oh, my God. "Chocolate."

The cold bottom of the plastic cup placed on her belly made her shriek, but he distracted her with a donut, and she fumbled to hold the shake steady while getting a grip on the sour cream glazed confection. Pure decadence, and she'd have to swim a mile of laps to wear it off, although the recent sex might count for something against those calories. Sandra's voice sounded far back in her head and she pushed it away.

Dean stripped and climbed into bed beside her as she wiggled up to a semi-sitting position, almost too intent on her treat to take in his amazing body. Almost. They ate in relative silence, broken only by the sounds of the straws grating on the plastic lids, and soft slurping. The latter kind of reminded her of the noises she made sucking his dick, but she didn't say it out loud.

"I was gonna stop and pick up the ingredients for a real breakfast, sweetheart. But you probably have them here."

Languidly reaching over, she pressed a fingertip against a krueller crumb caught in his chest hair, lifting it away from his skin to tuck it inside her lips. He watched her with the eyes of a predator, like the wolf she saw in the zoo as a child. She shivered and he snagged the sheet pulling it up to cover them, careless of the crumbs. Men definitely made more laundry.

"I love donuts and shakes. I like food, period. Which means I have to counteract the intake with exercise." She felt her mouth twist into a miserable moue.

"You work out?"

"More swim and walk. Sometimes I'll go to the gym if there's a specific body part requiring attention."

Big hand pressing the sheet against her body, outlining her curves, he shrugged. "Nothing here requiring attention."

Laughing, enjoying the way Dean's eyes tracked the movement of her breasts under the sheet, Amy replied. "And I want to keep it that way. Stay healthy, anyhow. So the donuts and shakes gotta be a treat."

"Okay. Don't eat them regular, anyhow."

Noting how his speech sometimes segued into down home patter, then into educated patterns, she speculated, then dismissed it. Part of his appeal and probably not important right that moment. Lots to learn.

She casually said, "I've got my own exercise machine by the look of things, anyhow."

Dean froze, straw half way to his mouth, and his head inched around until he could look at her. She gave him her best smile and was rewarded with one of his. She put her empty shake container on the side table and turned off the light, settling on her side. He followed suit and wrapped an arm around her, spooning, sated cock pressing against her ass. The press of his lips against her hair didn't go unnoticed and she managed to say it, striving to hold back the intense pull of sleep.

"I'll move in whenever you want."

There was no hesitation in his reply. "Next weekend. I'll take care of your lease, store your stuff."

"'Kay."

## Chapter Six

"But I like my bed!"

"My bed is bigger, Amy. You can choose a different headboard, new bedding. Not pink."

"I like pink."

"Then buy pink underwear, sweaters or something. I'm not having pink towels or sheets."

"Any other directives?"

She was already over it. Dean could tell. There were some things he wasn't going to bend on, and pink shit was one of them; otherwise she could redecorate to her heart's content. She was on her period, too, so he counted himself lucky to avoid a major battle, because he'd heard women could be unpredictable when their hormones were out of whack. Lucky, too, that she wasn't pregnant, because it was too soon, and would have pushed his hand. His job was too dangerous for a child to be brought into the mix, forcing him to shut things down before he'd accomplished everything that he had to do. Not that he hadn't entertained some thoughts about having made a baby inside Amy, finding the idea attractive. If he was going to have kids, and at thirty four he should be thinking about it while he still had energy for them, then Amy would be his first choice to bear his babies. The only choice, if he was honest. He flinched at the idea of giving her that kind of power over him. It was probably good she'd be going on birth control immediately.

"Dean?" She was staring at him, all sensuous curves in dark tight jeans and form fitting purple tank that matched her eyes almost exactly, and that mass of hair spilling to catch the light. Beautiful.

Pushing back his uncertainty, he answered. "What?"

"I said, I'll pick up some groceries this afternoon. Anything you'd prefer for dinner?"

Dinner. Babies. Someone living in his home—there when he got back from whatever his business demanded of him. The uncertain feeling vanished, replaced by an unfamiliar sense of contentment laced with anticipation. "Not real fond of salad, none of those jellied things with vegetables."

"I have no idea what those are, babe. I cook basic, but maybe now I have someone to test things on I'll experiment a little."

Manufacturing a shudder at the idea of being a guinea pig, he watched her laugh and was ridiculously delighted to have coaxed the reaction. "I'll drive you."

"S'okay. I heard you tell Randy you'd meet him in about ten from now. Will you be home around seven?"

"That'll work." And how had he forgotten telling his lieutenant they would meet? As if he didn't know the reason for his distraction. He didn't like her driving that import, no matter the fact the Germans made a good product. It wasn't that big a vehicle and she drove it like it was made to be driven, making him worry—and it was a convertible.

"I'll do some shopping for here, too. No pink. Just some stuff to soften the edges, make it less so totally freaking male."

Wrapping a hand around her wrist, pulling her close for a kiss, he spoke against her temple. "I am freaking male, sweetheart. But decorate at will. Leave me the bills."

"No. I want to do this on my dime."

Well, shit. He'd almost made it out the door on a high note. Making himself nod, he kissed her again and hustled. Randy would deposit the money directly back into her account. She didn't need to spend her cash. He had plenty for both of them.

As he got behind the wheel, his cell buzzed. Amy. "I know that look, babe. I'm decorating on my dime. You want me to see this place as my home too, you let it be."

Busted. "Steak, potatoes for dinner, sweetheart. See you at seven." Last word.

****

The high end furniture boutique wasn't a place she'd normally go to purchase items for her home but this was Dean's home. Hers and Dean's. She couldn't put just anything into that designer pad.

"Things going okay?" Sandra idly fingered a drapery panel as Amy tried to decide between black slubbed silk or a fine charcoal wool for the living room windows. The area rug was a mix of gray and black with cream. Maybe the wool, but in cream, and she could paint that feature wall dove-gray. Closer to the vision in her head. Steel blue accents and the occasional hit of red.

"Amy?"

"Uh huh. Things are fine. Hardly any bumps, actually. For the most part we like the same things, and aside from him hating pink, Dean doesn't care about what I do with the place. How about a damask comforter in stripes? Taupe, cream and blue?"

"Different than your usual taste, honey."

True. The pink in her bathroom was over the top, but Amy had never been allowed girly. She wished she could have brought her comforter, but his bed was a king. "I feel more grown up."

"Well, choose or wait for another day. My feet hurt and I need coffee." Her friend smiled, and nudged her.

"I'll come back. I don't want to rush. Besides, I'm having too much fun."

"Suzy homemaker?"

Shrugging, she replied, "I like it so far. Dean doesn't expect it. He'd take me out for every meal or we could order in, but I like it. I have time. It's easy to work around my business, although I'm getting busier. And then there's Lois. She cleans the place and I'll tell you I *really* like that."

"Your place was always spotless."

"Didn't mean I liked it. Cleaning. I don't mind the day-to-day things like dishes and laundry, but having Lois take care of the major stuff makes me feel relieved."

They strolled a few stores down and found a place to sit in the food court. Sandra dumped her bags and went to get a couple of coffees while Amy held their spot. She stretched out her legs and thought a little about her current living situation. It felt … fine. Great? That too. Like it was meant for her. She'd lived briefly with other men, but never felt settled or welcome, and the expectations irked her. The initial pleasure in doing things for them soon paled, probably because they took it for granted, and it was one sided. Dean wasn't like that. He gave back.

"The stuff looks like it's been on the element for hours," Sandra grumbled, putting the cups down on the plastic table. "Everybody's drinking those fancy coffees, and you can't get real java anymore."

The coffee was indeed terrible, and Amy managed only a few sips, longing for her chemical creamer. But the fridge held half and half at home. She opened another container from the dish on the table and dumped it in, stirring with the little plastic stick.

"You're happy?" There was a wealth of emotion in the question, although Sandra was concentrating on her cup, tipping it from side to side, peering into the depths.

"I can't imagine being anywhere else, Sandra."

"You're not wearing the necklace anymore." There was no judgement in the comment, but considerable interest.

"C for change, Sandra. Biggest change in my life. And for the better. I know it's still early days, but I don't need the necklace to remind me."

"I hear the hope, honey."

"I hate it when he's away for more than a few hours. I want to be with him and talk, learn more about him. I'm figuring him out, reading past the superficial stuff. And the sex isn't bad."

Their laughter, Sandra's startled and likely unwilling, Amy's smug and satisfied, caught the attention of those around them and a few people smiled back, caught up in the infectiousness of the sound. A handsome visage caught her eye and she stared, the laughter subsiding. She literally felt the smile drop from her face. Enrico. Just *happening* to be here? In the Mall? What the fuck?

Her friend flinched back as Amy shoved to her feet, coffee sloshing with the movement. She marched over to where he sat. Pushing away her need to snap at him, she manufactured another smile, a very different one, and had the satisfaction of seeing Enrico's eyes become wary. "Don't skulk, 'Rico. Join us. Must have been a long, boring afternoon."

"Miss Amy. I couldn't intrude."

"Amy. I'm nobody's miss. And you've already intruded. Don't make it worse."

Standing, his lean frame covered by a perfectly pressed shirt tucked into dark trousers, he could have stepped out of a GQ shoot. Not as tall as Dean, about her height, and not as muscled as Dean, Enrico still had that predatory male thing going on, sexy and sleek. Hotness rolled off him. Nodding gravely, he gestured for her to precede him and she strode back to Sandra. Her friend's face was pale, eyes huge, her little teeth marking her bottom lip.

"You remember Sandra. Sandra? Enrico. Seems we have a guardian angel."

Sandra narrowed her eyes. "Angel? I doubt it."

Okay then. Amy was pissed that Dean ignored her refusal to have one of his men on her when she wasn't home or with him. She liked Enrico, found him quiet but intensely aware and intelligent the few times they'd spoken. He'd lugged her boxes of shoes and clothes up the stairs into Dean's condo without complaint, too, and didn't comment on her un-American choice in cars, like Randy and Olsen. The other men in the complex were polite and kept their distance, but she'd only just arrived, so it was to be expected. Their women were more welcoming, and Amy looked forward to introducing Sandra to them. However, at this moment she wanted to figure out the enmity between her friend and Enrico. More on Sandra's side, because Enrico wasn't giving off any vibes he didn't like her…

"Enrico's gonna join us and then follow me home. Right?"

Nodding, but never taking his eyes from Sandra's face, he answered. "I do my job, Miss Amy. Amy."

Sandra found her coffee very interesting again and said nothing further.

"I can't say I like being a job, Enrico, but that's between your boss and me. Sit. Please."

As he pulled out a chair and dropped into it, Sandra picked up her purse. "Restroom."

Enrico tracked her movements, and then gave Amy a look before glancing around the area, clearly vigilant. "I regret making you uncomfortable."

Caught speculating on the obvious *something* between him and Sandra, Amy regrouped. "Not uncomfortable, Enrico. It'll be uncomfortable now, because I'll be thinking about all the stuff Sandra and I did today, and the fact you were there, too. Sure you weren't bored?"

A Gallic shrug. "Dean wants you safe. He has never had a woman before, full time, and of late there have been … there are always instances for concern."

"What do you mean by instances?"

"That is for Dean to share."

"And if I ask him?"

"Then he will tell you what he wishes for you to know."

Male chauvinist pigs, the lot of them—Amy bit the words back, fueled more by a niggle of fear. She hated not having information if it meant looking out for herself. Although, she had Dean assuming that task…

Where the hell was Sandra? Enrico must be wondering, too, because his attention again diverted to the area where the restrooms were advertised with not only the words but cute little signs of stick people, one dressed in an outline of a skirt. The noise in the food court felt dampening, oppressive, and Amy looked around her with increasing paranoia.

"I'll go get Sandra."

"No."

Holy shit. Another arrogant male. She wondered what the meetings were like, the ones Dean presided over so regularly. Almost without exception, his crew moved and acted like they knew their stuff, confident and aware. Testosterone must pervade the very walls. He'd chosen men like himself and managed to lead them. Pride and lust warred for supremacy in her belly, nudging aside her initial annoyance with her man for protecting her. But it didn't totally conquer her fear.

"Is something going on?" She lowered her voice and asked again.

"I am to watch over you." Avoiding her question, the bugger. "Your friend will be back. She doesn't like me, and she doesn't approve of your connection with Dean. It makes her conflicted."

Arrogant, intelligent, *and* perceptive. She was surrounded. The appearance of Sandra, normally smooth stride jerky, distracted her.

Sandra spoke upon gaining the table. "I need to go. I'm working five days straight starting tomorrow, Amy. I need to get a few things done at home."

Amy decided not to out her. If Sandra wanted to flee, go home and hunker down, she'd respect that, although it would have been interesting to see how Enrico managed the spa appointments set for the day after tomorrow. That she'd now have to cancel. She and her friend would have had a chat by then, so it still might be on, but right now, Amy was willing to hunker down, too. Enrico's scant sharing had reminded her of her choice—to be with a man who was in the business of acquiring enemies. They picked up their purchases and filed through the tables, the handsome man a silent shadow behind them.

****

The meat was perfect. Charred on the outside, bloody within. Dean cut a chunk and speared a piece of potato on the end of the tines before putting in it in his mouth. Amy hadn't said anything about Enrico, who had given him the heads up as soon as he saw Amy home safely. Waiting for her reaction was impacting a great meal. Chewing and swallowing, marking the subtle spices she used on the food, he broached the subject.

"You made Enrico today."

A cool violet stare, accompanied by a slightly raised brow was all he got. She forked salad into her mouth, full lips closing around the greens, tongue licking a tiny dot of dressing from the bottom one. He considered setting the meal aside and eating her instead but wanted to address the elephant in the room.

"Nothing to say about it?"

Pushing her nearly empty plate away, Amy blotted her lips with a napkin. A real napkin, thick, cream linen to match the pattern on the heavy new place settings. It was like eating in a high class restaurant but better, and damned if he didn't appreciate it. He hadn't missed the surplus of shopping bags set against the far wall either. She tilted her head and looked at him again.

"I *had* plenty to say. I told you I didn't want somebody shadowing me because it reminded me not only of Vegas, but of what you do. And it scares me to think I might need that kind of protection. No, Dean, don't make that imperious gesture—it doesn't reassure me. You obviously are concerned. Let me finish.

"After thinking about it, I decided that if you're worried, I should be, too. And if I'm going to be with you, then I'll have to accept your assessment and the steps you take. I don't want to know details, but I'll accept your actions. Doesn't mean I'm happy about them. And you'd better be forthcoming in the future about any such "arrangements" that concern me, or you'll find I won't be so understanding." She leaned forward to top up his water glass. "Dinner okay?"

What? Fuck, but she humbled him, no matter that not-so-subtle threat she'd tacked on. She trusted him, and wasn't that a kick in the ass? He set his utensils down, lest he make another *imperious* gesture and took her hand. “Don’t know how much there is to worry about, Amy, but I can’t be too careful where you’re concerned.”

Hand lying lax and compliant in his, she smiled and inclined her head. “Eat your dinner, babe. I made dessert, and then later I’ll need to work the calories off. Sex in a pan, for my sweet tooth.”

He didn’t eat dessert, donuts being the one exception, but would try the confection and eat her later. Take his caloric reducing role seriously. His cock muttered and protested at the delay.

“There’s something awkward between Sandra and Enrico.”

Mouth full, he settled on raising his brows in a “continue” gesture.

“She pulls inward and won’t engage with him. He doesn’t like it and hates to take his eyes off her.”

Unable to eat another bite, pretending not to see the pile of salad greens on his plate, he nodded. “I need him for another job, anyhow. Mike can replace him.”

“I didn’t mean for you to—”

“Sweetheart. Babysitting women shouldn’t be hard work, but it is. The men will be okay with switching off.”

“Babysitting? Hard work?” Carefully neutral tone of voice yet with a thread of venom.

When would he ever learn? Never. She’d deal—he hoped.

“Trailing along behind in a mall, watching you pick out underwear and lace things, take forever to choose. It’s torture. Or so I hear.”

“Too bad you won’t see the lace thing, then, babe. I bought it with you in mind.”

“Leave the dishes, Amy. Dessert later. Get your ass to the bedroom.”

The mischievous smile and snort of laughter made him lightheaded, but probably because all the blood in his body had gone south.

****

A bottle of strawberry lubricant reposed smugly, dead centre on her pillow, the coverlet stripped back to the foot of the bed. Dean had disappeared into the bedroom while she put the finishing touches on their meal, but she hadn't noticed the lube, not a bag or a bulge in a pocket. Probably too busy checking out his ass. She came to a dead stop and his big hard body blanketed her, arms encircling her waist. A press of his lips at her ear and a deep, sexy rumble, "Been thinking about your ass all day, sweetheart. More, since Enrico reported back about the lingerie store."

She hadn't planned to make it that easy for him, had decided in fact, to eschew the sexy nightwear for another time when she wasn't feeling so annoyed with him and his less-than-tactful comments. But the heat of him and the sight of that lubricant had her thoughts tumbling with arousal and need.

Core soaking with wet heat, her belly feeling that sharp little zing of excitement arrowing straight to her clit, she leaned into him, the solid evidence of his erection pressing back. He was *asking*. She stepped forward, out of his arms as he released her. Her choice. Anal wasn't her preference, at least not with the men she'd fucked before, but with Dean … she pulled her clothes off, sensing his approval. And maybe some relief.

Clambering onto the bed, knees actually a bit weak with anticipation, she crouched on them, pressing her breasts into the mattress. She offered her ass, hands stretched out in front of her.

"Fuck me, sweetheart." That raspy tone was back in his voice, perhaps at the evidence of her compliance.

Clothing rustled and his belt hit the floor with a clank of metal on wood. The thrill of arousal built when he knelt beside her and gently looped soft rope around both wrists to secure her hands to the headboard. The feeling of being helpless and at his sensual mercy had her pussy spasming, and she closed her eyes to add to the sensation.

The sound of the lid of the lube popping open was crisp against his heavy breaths and the pounding of her heart. Cool liquid drizzled and flowed between her buttocks and she squeezed and gasped simultaneously.

Dean immediately stroked her ass, first one side then the other and a finger insinuated itself between her cheeks to swirl the lube over her puckered opening. Amy relaxed and breathed, slow, deep pulls of air, while her sex quivered and clenched independently, ignoring the commands from her brain to run from that finger. He pressed insistently and slid inside, and she fought the inclination to push him out. His murmur of approval warmed her even as he added another finger. In and out, ever deeper, spreading the digits to stretch her, the lube facilitating his efforts. Another finger and she whimpered. So full.

"Shhh. Breathe through it, sweetheart. You are so fucking hot and tight."

The invaders withdrew and more lube coated her, dripping down to join the juices flowing from her pussy. A snap of latex. She panted.

"Knees apart, Amy. Wide as you can."

Hot flesh covered in silky hair slid along the inside of her thighs as he knelt between them. Hard hands gripped her hips to raise her to a sharper angle, then the poke of his hard cock, seeking a portal. A hand disappeared and left a cooling imprint on her hip. She could visualize it, the spatulate shape of fingers, the wide palm. The press at her back entrance steadied and advanced. Fuck, he was too big.

"Push back. Amy, I've got you. Push back."

His plea steadied her, the desperate need in his voice drew her. She pushed and he slid past the ring of muscle guarding her anus, bringing tears to her eyes. Panting harder, she prayed for it to be over. This was Dean and it still didn't make it better.

"You gotta breathe slower and deeper, sweetheart."

Okay. Oxygen. She adjusted her breathing and he pushed in further. A splinter of pleasure pierced the discomfort and she cautiously explored it. The heat pouring off him made her hotter, and she panted.

A pained chuckle above her. "You ready for a little more, sweetheart?"

Managing a muffled agreement, she felt him inch his way forward, deeper, stretching her and awakening her with jangles of sensation. The velvety feel of his sac bumped gently against her labia and Dean leaned over her to nuzzle the back of her neck.

"You're soaked, Amy. I feel you on my balls. You okay? Need more time?"

Not knowing what she needed, she blindly grasped the head board slats harder, the rope around her wrists tethering her to the earth. This was different than the impersonal shove and painful thrust of ass-fucking. Something primitive uncoiled deep within her, rising to meet him. "No more time," she gritted out.

Taking her at her word, he took her, hard. Reaming her, the stiff length of his cock dragging and pulling along nerve endings she didn't know she owned, the friction indescribable. He was claiming her, making her his in such an intimate way. His sweat coated her back, the harsh soughing of their collective breathing filling the room, and she strained, reaching for a release she hadn't believed possible. Dean withdrew, and then shoved back in to seat to the hilt, invading her with such controlled dominance. He orchestrated a pinch of her clit with his fingers, and she flew. The sound bursting from her throat would have brought the whole complex running if not for the fact he dropped his full weight on her, cock pulsing perceptibly to her heightened senses, pressing her face into the pillow to muffle her scream of completion.

Struggling to breathe, trying to cope with what had just transpired, Amy hitched against the two hundred plus pounds draping over her. Dean raised up, his skin separating from hers with an audible slick-and-slide, and pulled out, leaving her curiously empty. Holy shit. She couldn't make herself move, although her thighs and knees were protesting the position. Her eyes leaked. Overwhelmed.

A warm cloth slipped between her legs to gently wipe her pussy, then up to cleanse her between her buttocks. A kiss on either ass cheek, and one on the base of her spine. "Used you hard, sweetheart. Sorry. You might be a little sore."

How did one respond to that observation? She remained mute.

"Hey." Dean eased her legs together then coaxed them straight and the rush of blood returning to cramped muscles made her eyes leak some more.

Amy winced.

He rubbed the long muscles before releasing the binds at her wrists, then took hold of one shoulder and her hip to gently flip her over onto her back.

Her hands, fingers numb, reluctantly released the headboard as her weight transferred. He set a knee on either side of her, lacing his fingers with his own and stared down into her eyes.

"Did I hurt you? I'm sorry. Are you okay?"

Registering the soft weight of his scrotum against her mound, the concern radiating from his eyes, she wondered how often Dean apologized.

"You didn't hurt me, not really. I'll be sore. Hell, I am sore. But that was something."

Relief loosened his features until she thought they would melt and run together. He leaned in to lick at the tears prevalent at the corners of her eyes and she closed them in self defense against the tenderness.

The intimate surrender of the act swelled her heart. She loved him. In for a penny…whatever that trite old saying one of her foster mothers used to say. "Love you, babe."

Stiffening, his hands nearly crushed her own, and his knees locked at her hips, making her eyes pop wide, seeking to read him. He relaxed almost instantly, but wariness chased the tenderness away. A brief kiss and he swung his body to lie beside her. If he got up and left their bed—she wasn't sure what she'd do, but it wouldn't be pretty. He didn't have to repeat the sentiment, but if he left her, disregarded it…

"Like a punch in the gut, sweetheart. I have no idea what to say. Don't know what I'm feeling, either."

Okay. She could deal with the honesty. "Nothing to say, Dean. It'll fall out of your mouth or it won't. But I'm not taking it back. Now go cut me a piece of dessert. It's in the glass pan, second shelf from the bottom in the fridge."

A beat of silence, during which she steadfastly refused to look at him, staring instead at the ceiling, awash in emotions, trying to contain the leak that was back in her eyes. The bed frame creaked and she bounced a little as his weight lifted, and she was again treated to a great backside view as he presumably went to do her bidding. Her hand felt blindly for the box of tissues on the nightstand and she yanked several loose to mop at her tears.

****

The dessert was exactly where she said it was, and Dean lifted the long pan out to set it on the counter. Peeling back the clear wrap he noted the amount of whipped cream and chocolate sprinkles mounding the surface.

Amy's proclamation of love rocked his world, shit, blew it up. His knees actually felt weak, like they did after a very long run. She'd moved right on past the intense physical attraction and labeled the *thing* between them, present right from the get go, and now stretching and unfurling itself. Growing to cement their relationship. Jesus. His heart pounded and his gut lodged somewhere near his throat. Trying to catalogue his emotions, he shuffled through the utensil drawer for something to cut the gooey confection and serve it up.

A tall ceramic container near the stove snagged his attention, all manner of cooking objects protruding from the wide mouth. Made sense to have big spoons, rubber spatulas, egg flippers and the like, close to the action, but it was unfamiliar. A change. Just like his life was undergoing, hell, his head. And his heart. He debated, then cut a big slice. One plate. He'd feed his woman and maybe eat some of that cream off her nipples. Fucking her ass wasn't something he could even think about right then. Aside from coming harder than he'd ever come, red splotches and black spirals clouding his vision, his cock exploding like a powder keg, it felt like he'd made her his, forever. *Forever and ever, you'll stay in my heart and I will love you, together, forever…* shit, that fucking Randy and his insistence on that sixties channel. Fucking maudlin stuff.

Toting the dessert, a fork and a handful of napkins, he traipsed back to where Amy waited for her sweet treat. Only fair. He'd had his.

**FOREVER**

## Chapter Seven

What a piece of work. If Amy didn't have to lay eyes on that woman again in this life, or any others, she would count herself lucky. But Monica was her man's mother, and if he could make himself see her when her health took another turn for the worse, then Amy would support him. Did drunks develop that kind of mean personality because of the alcohol abuse or did the booze refine it, knock all the boundaries aside? Had Monica always been like that? Dean's childhood was probably worse than he described. He had minimized it, or maybe was in denial just to survive the memories. Amy supposed the care facility staff were paid well enough to put up with the stuff the woman spewed, maybe slipped her an extra shot of vodka or whatever her favorite toxin was, but holy shit. Monica still tried to drip her bitter poison into her son's veins, and while he appeared impervious, Amy knew it had to make an impact.

Well, that painful visit was over and she hoped the next one was far, far in the future, or never. Dean told her they'd become more infrequent and sporadic as his mother's periods of lucidness diminished. He'd talked with the doctors. The drive there took longer than the brief contact, but the twenty minutes or so felt like an eternity of venomous accusations, insane insinuations and bizarre comments, delivered in a sprightly, carefree voice more suited to a kindergarten teacher. Twilight zone.

Mother Chambray took one look at Amy and took flight into la-la land. Witch? Please. Dean shut the visit down instantly then, protective of her. It didn't erase memory of the lined and worn countenance of the middle aged woman who stared at her out of Dean's eyes, but it went a long way in reminding her that he was willing to make the effort to be with her, Amy. To try a relationship with a *woman*.

After dropping her off, with a hard kiss that had her wishing she'd enticed him into the condo for another, different kind of attempt at erasing the memory, Dean headed downtown on "business." Amy didn't think about that—she mostly liked his crew, and quite liked their women, now that she'd spent more and more time with them. Nobody talked shop, at least not around her, and working on the emotional components of this relationship took most of her energy and interest. She didn't want to know anything further. She decided to get some work done before she started dinner. This whole housewife thing, although the actual wife part wasn't yet in the cards, if ever, was surprisingly still comfortable, even after several months. She *liked* taking care of Dean. Her laptop glowed as it powered up and she entered her password, thinking she might invest in one of those big dough mixers and start making her own bread. A giggle escaped her and she shimmied in place. Despite the earlier visit to the bitch from hell, she actually felt *happy*.

Absently scrolling through the news feeds, a name leaped out at her. The rest of the stories flowed effortlessly across the screen beneath her frozen fingertip until she yanked it from the cursor. It took forever to find the correct feed again, so long Amy wondered if she'd actually seen it. *Brent Whittaker*. Locating the name, she skimmed the article, her belly filling with ice. *Tourist in Vegas. High roller. Mugged and severely beaten. Police searching for leads.*

Up from her chair, across the room with no memory of making a move, Amy set her back against the bookcase and stared at her laptop, breath stuttering in and out of her lungs. Gone was her cautious realization of happiness. Brent had gone back to Vegas, clearly ignoring the condition she stipulated in the settlement, because she thought she would still be living there and didn't want to lay eyes on him again. The prick. But the fact he'd returned to Vegas wasn't the issue.

A mugging and beating wasn't that unusual. Brent being in that particular part of Vegas was. He liked the high profile casinos. Unless he went with a woman, or… Amy quit puzzling and returned to her laptop, concentrating on finding and collating information until she thought she had a clearer picture. You couldn't always believe what the newspapers reported, but her brain put the idea forward. Her belly thawed and ached in agreement. She thought hard and picked up her phone.

"Amy?" Randy's mellow voice soothed her. "What's up?"

"Got a question for you," she burbled—the stereotypical blonde. She hoped it would soften Randy's typical vigilance.

"Sure, kiddo."

"Brent Whittaker?"

Randy was good, but he hesitated, just enough of a pause to confirm it. Holy fuck.

"Thanks, Randy."

No hesitation then, as he tried to retrieve it before she terminated the call. "Not familiar, Amy. Somebody I should know?"

"You can drop the act, Randy. My God. Where is he? Never mind. I'll call him."

"He's right here, kiddo, looking at me. Wanna talk to him?"

The decision was taken out of her hands. Dean's deep voice filled her ear. "Sweetheart?"

Maybe this was better than face-to-face because she had absolutely no idea what she was feeling and was terrified to explore it. "Brent Whittaker."

"That douche bag."

"Why did you do it?"

"Because he hurt you, could have killed you."

"You didn't even know me, then!"

"I know you now, and he wasn't getting away with it. He won't raise his hand to another woman again."

Deciding she didn't want to know what *that* meant, Amy didn't respond. Instead, she picked something mundane to try to right her world. "I'll see you at dinner."

Silence. Then, "That's it? See me at dinner?"

"Don't know what else to say, babe." She punched the end-call button and hunkered down on the floor. The cell immediately shrilled. Dean.

"You okay?"

"I don't know."

"Coming home."

"No. I'll make dinner. It won't be ready for awhile."

"Amy, I'm on my fucking way. Don't you leave or call Sandra. This is for you and me to talk about."

"You didn't talk to me about it before!" Her voice climbed the higher registers and she concentrated on her balance, her thigh muscles beginning to ache from the position.

"It wasn't something I thought you'd find out." The sound of traffic in the background didn't mitigate his blatant honesty, although why he'd withheld this from her...

Speechless, she gulped in air. "I'll be here."

"Will I need to watch that throwing arm of yours?"

Ah, humor. Amy supposed she should recognize how their way of relating had progressed. Pity she wasn't feeling in the mood to joke. She clicked off again, and dragged herself to her feet to go make a pitcher of margaritas, taking her time, forcing herself to calm down as she measured and double checked every ingredient. Maybe Mother Monica had something right after all.

The first swallow tasted wonderful against her tight throat. She figured she'd wait until Dean got home before sorting through her jumbled reaction. Knowing him, he'd be flying along in that truck of his.

Scrutinizing the frosty glass didn't make things any clearer, and her outrage hadn't been calmed by either concocting the drink, or drinking some of it. She took another swig.

"Crack me a beer, sweetheart." Dean came through the door, a man on a mission. Amy halted the next lift of the frosty glass to her lips, the anticipation of more of the sugar-rimmed edge, followed by the tart taste thwarted.

Despite the shock of what she'd learned, the sight of him in those tight, faded jeans, leather jacket swinging loosely to reveal another fitted, black tee stirred her senses.

Gray eyes watchful, he leaned down to pull his boots off. She got him a beer and set it on the coffee table. She made to sit in the leather chair but Dean forestalled her.

"Ass on the couch, sweetheart. You're not pulling away from me."

Well, shit. "You aren't going to soften me up, Dean," she warned, and defiantly took the far corner of the couch.

"Didn't think you'd find out, like I said, sweetheart, but I'll say my piece."

She interrupted him. "Randy figured it out. You told him what you learned from me and he put it together, found out who Brent was. I asked you to leave it alone."

"And I considered it, for half a second. That kind of man, preying on women, he wasn't going to stop, Amy. And the fucker hurt you." The intensity in his voice made her flinch, and she took another drink before putting the glass down beside Dean's beer. She'd lost the taste for it.

"When did you find him?"

"Couple of weeks after you told me—we had some other stuff going on or it would've been quicker. Randy can find anyone. He's got contacts everywhere."

"Why Vegas?"

Dean shrugged and reached out a long arm to snag her wrist, pulling her up against him. She didn't resist, wondering why she didn't. Maybe she was one of those people who secretly lusted for revenge and didn't want to admit it? Maybe she was secretly thrilled that Brent had got his. "That was one of those things. Got word he was going, I know people there."

"And if it gets traced back to you?"

"Never happen."

"And if it does? Just supposing? What if they connect the dots?" She could hear the bitter sarcasm in her tone and he pushed a hand through her hair to tip her head back. Instead of the icy glare she expected, the tenderness reflected in his gray eyes shut her up, until his next words.

"Sweetheart, nothing's going to happen to you."

Tearing herself out of his arms, she bumped the table, and her drink slopped every which way. Dean's beer tipped over and she snatched at it, and then gave into her spiralling emotions. She hurled the bottle across the room, where it shattered with a gratifying smash and clatter, and tinkle of glass. Dean's shocked face nearly drew laughter from her overworked brain, and she bit down against it, aware of how insane she would sound.

Taking advantage of his apparent immobility, she jumped to her feet and set both hands on her hips, knowing she must look the quintessential fishwife.

"Goddamn it, Dean! Are you so thick? It's not *me* I'm worried about!"

His big frame tensed, and his eyes went molten, and then he was on his feet, prowling to her. Yanking her against him, his mouth came down on hers, stealing anything else she thought she might spout in her indignation. His tongue worked against her own as he held her head steady for his kiss. All of the tension quite suddenly drained from her, and she sagged in his embrace.

Pulling back, he stared down into her eyes. "Sweetheart. I'm sorry. I should have known you'd be worried about that, about me. But I promise you it'll be fine."

Amy went with it, abdicating her stance, whatever it had been, bowing to the inevitable. It was done, and Dean would do what he believed to be right.

He pressed her down on the couch cushion, never breaking the kiss. His hands smoothed down her arms and sides to slip beneath her shirt, branding her belly with heat and roughness, finding her bra clasp and popping it open. Her clothing was pushed up between them to bracket her throat, and Dean tore his mouth from hers to transfer his clever tongue to an exposed nipple, sliding down her body as he did so. A splinter of pain pierced the pleasure as his teeth nipped, then the two morphed and bloomed as he suckled and pinched the tender bud, rolling and tugging her other tip between a calloused forefinger and thumb. She arched into the sensation and spread her legs to the insistent nudge of his knee between hers, her pussy already creaming and soaking her underwear. He seamlessly switched breasts and Amy adjusted, wishing he had two mouths.

Kissing his way down the center of her belly, wet, abandoned nipples aching and mourning, he worked the button and fly of her jeans and traced the exposed flesh above her panties with his tongue.

"You smell so fucking sexy, sweetheart. Lift up."

One leg of her jeans slipped down and off, the other hung from an ankle as Dean tore the scrap of lace covering her crotch free. "Soaked." He stared at her. "I freak you out, I think you're scared and you are, but it's for me. And still you're drenched."

Hooking one of her legs over the back of the couch, the other bent at the knee to set her foot on the floor, Dean ran a finger between her folds. Peering up at him over the rucked up fabric below her chin, she met his gaze.

"Want my mouth or my cock, Amy?"

The long finger pushing up inside distracted her, as did the second one that joined it. He pressed his thumb on her sweet spot, a gentle pressure, just enough to hint at even better things to come. "Sweetheart?"

"Cock." She needed the closeness, the full body contact.

His other hand went to his belt to free it as he continued to work between her legs. A moan built in her chest and worked its way up to spill over her lips. So close.

"Hurry, babe."

Eyes darkening with his need, he opened his jeans and reached in to pull his cock free, the head glistening with precum, thick vein pulsing. His fingers left her wetness and painted a path over her mound and up to either breast before retreating to assist in the divesting of his jeans, shoving them down to his knees. He nearly fell onto her, a splayed palm on the cushion beside her head catching his weight. His cockhead slid into her, hitching at the initial stricture, then opening and stretching her sheath to accommodate his girth as he plunged deep to come up hard against her cervix.

They both moaned and her eyes met his, falling into him.

God, she loved his man.

Her arousal plateaued with her thought. The sex was slow and unhurried. He thrust and retreated, looking deep into her eyes. She could feel her release build from a slow simmer to an aching need to burst, and as the skin over Dean's cheekbones tautened, she clenched hard around him. He ground his pelvis at the top of her apex and it was the touch she needed. Her climax peaked, sweet and full. He thrust twice more, and the heat of his cum, coupled with the prod of his cock deep within her channel, pushed her over again, hard on the heels of the first release, making her shudder.

Dean shoved his arms under her to hold her through it and then lifted her and rolled to flatten her against the back of the couch, his softening cock still inside her, skin to skin.

She tucked her chin into his throat and breathed in his scent, feeling his heart beat. After a time he stirred. "Okay?"

"They could have killed him. I couldn't stomach it thinking you—"

"They knew not to, sweetheart. He just won't raise a hand to a woman again. Literally."

She digested that and didn't press for details. Dean dropped a kiss on her temple. "Dinner?"

"I'll get on it." She supposed it was the least she could do after two orgasms, but really didn't want to get up for the next decade or so.

"Ordering in, sweetheart. What do you want?"

****

As he consulted his phone for the number of the restaurant, and referred to the menu he'd unearthed from the drawer beside the stove, Dean wondered if he'd missed an opportunity to share all of the truth with Amy. It might have been too much for her to reconcile, right on the heels of learning he'd taken care of the asshole who'd hurt her. Still, he wondered if he'd fucked up.

He thought back on his adult life. There hadn't been any money for college, so Dean enlisted. He tested high, and after basic training got kicked into intelligence. That was an oxymoron in many cases, but he thrived in the military, on the routine, appreciating the cause and effect, despite the often resulting chaos. He became known for his ability to piece situations together, think outside the box, and excelled at interrogation, emotionally detached but skilled at faking it. He didn't need to use his size and strength either, or at least, not often, because it was obvious what he was capable of to anyone with eyes in their head and working brain.

The military-provided college education got him a degree in criminology and he was heading home after discharge, planning to apply at the police academy. An intense, solemn man, exuding power, approached him in the airport, had a quiet word, and Dean's life changed forever. High stress, a demanding life on the edge and the money and lifestyle that came with it was offered and he took it, well aware of the danger. Hell, he jumped at it. He replaced the crime lord of his youth seamlessly; all of his bonafides, to fit with his new situation, polished and prepared and put in place by the man who became his handler.

Dean weeded out the losers in the loosely knit organization and recruited others who were more competent. He led effortlessly, and his crew followed, people accepting that the kid from the old neighborhood got himself some good training in the military and used it well. If anyone noticed that street crime dropped in his territory, and the head of the competition, as well as his replacements, were incarcerated on a regular basis, it wasn't traced back to him. The necessary violence was credited, however, and he used it to his advantage. He wasn't an undercover cop—hell, he'd go to prison if the authorities caught him—although he was doing the work of one, without the rules and regulations.

But all of it was with one long term goal in mind. There was a man who had managed to keep his identity secret, yet who was slowly building an empire of criminal enterprises on the west coast. It was a tantalising mystery to solve, a challenge Dean couldn't resist, although it had taken far longer than he'd thought for that man to sniff around his enterprise. And now the time was coming…

"Dean? When's the food going to be here?"

He yanked his thoughts to the present and hurriedly dialled and placed their order. Amy's appetite sometimes rivalled his, and he'd kept his word insofar as helping her work off any unnecessary calories.

# FOREVER

## Chapter Eight

"I don't get it. That's the second place that's pulled out of our action." Dean shoved back from the desk and pushed out of his chair. Pacing sometimes helped.

Randy lifted one shoulder. "I don't even know how they were made, even, to be contacted. Burnett is chipping away at the fringes of the operation, buddy. And he's ruthless. More'n you. Those little people are scared and it figures he'll have convinced them they should fear him more than you."

Lowering his voice, although the place had been swept, and the rest of the crew were out "encouraging" the folks Dean had his thumb on, he had to ask. "You think Burnett smells something?"

The man was like a ghost. Dean knew he existed, but few people ever saw him, and Randy had unearthed only one photo. A nebbish, unremarkable man, the kind you'd pass by on the street or lose in a crowd. But Dean would know him.

"Don't know how he would," Randy said. "Just you and me are aware. Andrea thinks it's me who crossed over, that I'm walking some kind of fine line. She's okay with it and keeps quiet. And who would she tell without getting me killed?"

"It must be interesting when Andrea and Amy get together then."

"She says Amy doesn't bring up work, ever. Andi dropped a couple of thoughts one time, and she changed the subject."

Dean advanced on Randy. "Your woman playing some kind of game with mine?"

"Hell, no. I think she was looking for any sign Amy knew about me, that you'd figured it out. It's a fucking convoluted mess, Dean. Only I know you're not really a career criminal. Andrea thinks I'm staying clear of the bad shit somehow, despite being an informant. I don't like keeping the secret even though I know the reasoning behind it. Why won't you tell Amy?"

Jamming a hand through his hair, Dean turned on his heel and went to the coffee maker. "I've asked myself that. At first I couldn't because we were new and she could have blown my cover. That's why my previous connection with women was so perfect. No need to share. Now I feel I can trust her, and I don't know how to tell her because she'll be upset I withheld, didn't trust her. It's a big fucking secret for her to carry, as well.

Randy muttered something and shook his head. He met Dean's eyes. "I worry about Andi's safety, too. Not a good plan to drag women into this."

"Can you imagine life without these two particular women?" Dean could hardly believe those words emerged, but he couldn't imagine being without Amy.

His woman was a never ending stream of surprises and pleasure. Nearly a year, and the sex never got old, the rush never dwindled. He wondered that he had the strength some days to get out of bed and tend to his business. Birth control early on made fucking her even better, seeing as he could ditch the condoms.

But it was far more than the sex. She accommodated him, regardless of how autocratic he acted, as long as he was reasonable and she could make sense of it. Shit, she even took his old lady in stride. They never talked about his business despite the fact she found out his reach and power after the Whittaker deal. Aside from a couple remarkable displays of her temper, they rarely argued and her sweet, loving side was a soothing balm to his pocked soul.

She told him, snuggled up to him in the dark, how he eased her burden of always having to take care, look out for herself. It humbled him even as he took fierce pride in providing for her, in meeting her needs and being a bulwark between her and the shit that could befall her. She loved him for who he was. Not only did she say it, it shone through her actions. Dean figured he'd soon come to say it back, allow it to fall from his mouth instead of biting it back, withholding that last part of him, a festering reminder of his past. *Don't love, don't trust.*

"She's something, your woman." Randy was scrolling through a screen on his computer, multitasking. "Olsen snarked about you getting soft, whipped, at our July fourth party—drunk, the asshole—and she cut him a new one, cold as ice. Never raised her voice and he nearly kissed her feet apologizing."

"What the fuck?" That was news to Dean. Not that he was surprised about Amy dealing with Olsen on her own.

"You went to get more beer. Helping out. You never helped out like that before, and people took notice. You do things differently because of her. In a good way, Dean, so quit with that fucking look."

"I'm fine with different, Randy. I'm not fine with Olsen." And he'd be chatting with the man, only because Olsen bothered Amy.

"She dealt, Dean. Double jeopardy, remember? Not something you support? And it'll make others speculate if you intervene."

It didn't take long for him to regain his senses. He didn't always need to protect Amy. She had the tools and it would be good to remember that she chose her battles, like she did with him. An uncomfortable feeling of dread flitted through his gut as he recalled how sick she'd been several weeks ago. Some kind of flu. He'd driven her to the hospital himself, over her objections, calling Sandra to meet them there. Seeing her hooked up to IV bags freaked him. He held her while they shoved the needles she hated in, her silent tears chipping away at his control, wanting to punch the male nurse on her behalf.

Sandra softened towards him that day, seeing his concern for her friend, but he'd have gladly forgone that change in attitude, rather than have his woman suffer like she did.

They sent her home, rehydrated, the high fever broken, with a prescription for antibiotics to help with the chest infection, and she recovered quickly. Dean took turns taking care of her with Sandra, both of them ignoring Amy's protests. Sandra had even attended the Fourth of July party, although she left early and avoided Enrico like the plague. The youngest member of his crew didn't seem affected one way or the other, the tall, red headed piece of ass on his arm a standout among the other more conservatively dressed women. But Dean couldn't help but note the way Enrico watched Sandra leave.

"Hey! You wanna look at this demographic?"

Pushing the distracting memories aside, he focused on the task at hand. At the end of an hour, the territorial lines were redrawn and they'd put a plan together to replace the two mom-and-pop enterprises they'd lost, at least until he could bring them back into the fold. They were leaking information from somewhere. Randy had encrypted Dean's laptop again, as well as his own, and background-checked the crew. Nothing.

Dean had taken to working at home sometimes, making his schedule unpredictable, he and Amy working shoulder to shoulder in his den. No one knew where he'd be on any given day so it was unlikely anyone was eavesdropping at opportune moments. He liked spending time with Amy, sometimes just watching her efficiently build those sites, subtly encouraging her clients to accept ideas often quite different from their own, but better. She really didn't need to work, but she liked it, and her schedule was totally flexible, suiting him.

"Any ideas who's fucking with us?"

"Nothing so far, Dean. Whoever it is, they're subtle. I can't tell if they pick up on a comment, steal information or what. But for sure, it's getting passed to Burnett. He zeroes in on the weaknesses, like the undefended outposts in Star Trek's planetary system."

"Still watching that old shit?" He punched Randy's shoulder.

"Me and Andi have all the movies and the TV series. Even the first one. The acting's painful but we're addicted."

"Uh huh. Well, spare me. I think Burnett's the front man for the guy I've been waiting all these years for."

The enveloping silence could have been one of those cloaking devices from that old sci-fi space show his lieutenant was hooked on. Dean waited while Randy processed, the man's quick brain so at odds with his defensive tackle's body.

"You're sure?" Caution underscoring the words, along with a touch of elation. Knowing they could both get clear if it was so and they got it done. Randy's cropped blond hair threw his broad features into stark relief, dark blue eyes boring into Dean's.

"Had a brief meet with my handler last night. Put everything together and it looks that way. All the intel from different sources is paying off. Burnett gets sent in first and chips away, softens operations. Recruits and turns crew members."

"You've been doing this nearly six years. It fucking well took long enough."

"You're in it close to that." And Randy wasn't yet thirty. Dean wondered idly if they'd keep in contact when, if, this got over.

"I know. What'll I do after?"

Laughing, although not with real mirth, Dean replied, "We're getting ahead of ourselves. Have to decide whether to let Burnett in a little closer without showing our hand, or push back and make him show his. I'm thinking we push. Patience apparently is running thin for his boss."

"Then let's take our former "clients" back and expand a little more."

"Call in the crew."

****

Shoving her hair back, hand searching blindly for a clip, Amy studied her latest design request. She decided not to take it. Selling tasteless nude photos might be someone's interest but she didn't have to collude. Porn wasn't her thing. She had her own fantasies played out in the bedroom. And the kitchen, the living room, the dining room, the—the front door opened and closed, shutting those prurient thoughts down.

"Hey, sweetheart." His voice sounded blurred. Drunk? Strange, Dean rarely drank more than a few beers. After that meeting with his mother some months ago, Amy could understand why. He didn't drink much, didn't smoke, no drugs except for an occasional aspirin, ate healthy. He was a paragon, if you could overlook his arrogance and supremely male attitude. Which she did. Mostly.

Hopping up from her chair, she hurried out to greet him. And stumbled to a halt. Dean's bottom lip was split, dark, dried blood crusting over, right eye swollen. Blood speckled the front of his torn shirt, too much to be the result of his lip injury. Her eyes dropped to his hands, the knuckles bruised and cut, puffy. Heaven help her. No stranger to faces damaged by hard objects and thrown fists, a wave of dizziness still engulfed her, swiftly dispelled by a rush of fury. Fucking men.

Ignoring him, she crossed to the kitchen, yanking open a drawer full of clean dishtowels. She threw one in the sink and turned on the hot water, squirting in some antibacterial dish soap. Grabbing another, she turned to the fridge, noting the dark expression on Dean's face. Did he think she'd welcome him? Like coming home from the war? The past months of quiet, shielded from his actual *job,* had lulled her. Her anger turned inward. She *knew* the business he was in, but damn it all—she kept her head buried in the sand until things like this kicked up the sandstorm. Damn it.

"Sit at the counter, Dean."

He didn't move immediately but she kept her focus on filling the towel with ice, and at last, he settled on one of the fabric topped stools, swinging to face her. Turning off the tap, she wrung the fabric dry, hissing under her breath at the sting of the hot water. He watched her approach with wary intensity, but submitted to the press of the towel on his lip, a flicker in his eyes the only indication of how much it had to hurt. The dried blood slowly came away and with it a slow trickle of crimson. She examined it carefully but thought he wouldn't need stitches. Eating and smiling were going to be a bitch though, and kissing… She could smack him.

"Hold the ice pack to your eye while I wash this out. I'll clean your knuckles and then get some peroxide for them. Human teeth are filthy."

His hand encircled her wrist and held her in place. "Part of the job, sweetheart."

"And again, I don't have to like it. If you come home with a knife wound, or shot, I'll…" Tears spilled to short circuit her ultimatum. How could she even give voice to such things? What the hell was wrong with her?

Yanking her hand loose she stomped to the sink. "Put the goddamned ice pack on your eye." She swore he chuckled, but when she whirled on him, all she could see was his hand holding the towel, shrouding his features.

Cleaning his knuckles with a little more fervor than likely required didn't give her any satisfaction, and the peroxide foamed nicely to reassure her he'd be fine, no infection. But when he pulled her onto his lap, wedging her between the countertop and his muscled chest, she wept like a child, noisily and unabashedly. She'd cried more since she met Dean Chambray…

"S'okay, sweetheart. It's all right."

It didn't feel like it would ever be all right. She was a mess and the suspicion nibbling around the edges of her consciousness, the one she shooed away by resolutely thinking of other things, made her sad. Dean was in a dangerous business and there wasn't room for her and her suspicion. Apparently antibiotics and birth control really weren't a good mix, but maybe her cycle was just screwed up.

After a time she clambered off his lap, taking the ice pack with her to empty the melt into the sink. She rinsed it, then used the fabric to wash her face clean of tears and makeup, fumbling a tissue from the box on the window sill to blow her nose. Behind her, Dean stood and pushed the stool back under the counter, the feet grating over the tile.

"I'll go change."

Nodding, not trusting her voice, she closed her eyes and pulled herself together. Dinner.

She was gazing into the freezer, trying to think about the bag of frozen shrimp and a creole sauce she'd sourced on the 'Net when he called her. He was in the den, staring at her computer screen.

"This is shit, Amy."

"I know. I won't take the work. I was in the process of drafting a polite rejection when you brought your damaged self home."

"Good." He moved to his laptop and cocked his head.

"What?"

"It's on. I thought I'd turned it off."

"I didn't notice. You'd better plug it in, babe. If it's been on all day your battery will be down."

Nodding, he secured the cord and made the necessary connections, then powered down.

"I'll make dinner."

"We'll go out. Join a few of the crew at Remingtons. They're expecting us." There was a strange echo in his voice and she examined his face for a clue. Got it.

"You want your world to know, right? Who won the skirmish. Jesus."

"Wear something sexy, sweetheart. That way *my world* can look at you."

A dull clang registered in the back of her mind and she shivered. Her head shook from side to side in an involuntary reaction.

Dean was on her in an instant, so in tune. He wrapped her up. "What's wrong?"

"If it's all the same to you, I don't want people looking, babe." She said the words as lightly as she could, but knew he heard the dread when his eyes filled with tenderness.

"Poor choice of words, Amy. But you could turn up in a sack and they'd still look at you. I only meant it that way."

"Okay. I won't take long." Resolutely pushing her anxiety down she hurried to the bedroom. Dean followed her, heading into the bathroom to shower, taking a clean pair of boxers with him. After slipping in behind him to grab her makeup kit, she returned to the bedroom. Pulling a clean button down shirt and a pair of dark jeans out from his rapidly diminishing side of the closet she laid them on the bed, then dug a pair of socks from the top drawer of the bureau, before considering her own outfit for the evening.

Choosing a little black dress, deceptively modest until she zipped it, she reapplied her makeup a little heavier than usual, paying attention to her eyes, squinting in the less than ideal lighting above the dresser. The heavy white-gold earrings anchored the look, with her hair swept off her face and secured by a silver comb. Black stilettos with a silver heel to match her bag pulled the whole thing together. Dean's sure gait actually faltered when he emerged from the bathroom.

"Fuck me, sweetheart. You look amazing." He crossed to the closet and extracted a casual suit jacket. His hand went to the pocket and delved inside, emerging with a shimmer drifting between his fingers. Crossing to her he reached for her hand and clasped a stunning white gold chain around her wrist, pads of his fingertips pressing down firmly on the clasp.

"Seems a good time for you to wear this. Replace that necklace you took off."

Bereft of words, her heart pounding, Amy stared at the gift. He wouldn't give it to her to placate her, or for any other reason other than because he wanted to. He had noticed that she took the C for change necklace off, of course he had, although said nothing. His timing sucked—or did it? But his gesture meant the world and she would try not to think about the cold shard of terror embedded in her gut. She had made her choice and was just going to have to get used to it, keep an eye out for him, herself and her suspicion.

After giving her an assessing glance, he yanked his clothes on, slightly battered features giving him a rakishly handsome look, and gestured for her to precede him.

At last she found her voice. "It's beautiful, Dean. I love it. Thank you."

"No more beautiful than you, sweetheart. Now let's go and celebrate."

She wondered if she'd missed an opportunity to have a serious conversation with him, or at the very least clarify what they were truly celebrating.

****

The impromptu dinner party was raucous, Dean's crew clearly riding an adrenaline high, although she saw a few surreptitious movements to ease sore ribs, so her man wasn't the only one with overt injuries. Enrico sported a broken nose, taped and splinted, and he squinted at her through nearly crossed eyes. He was without feminine company and looked a trifle lost. Andrea gave her one of those, *they're idiots but what can you do* looks, and patiently cut Randy's steak for him, since one of his hands was bandaged. Two other men showed cuts above opposite eyebrows, bookends of war, and their women visibly compressed their mouths, whether with concern or annoyance, Amy couldn't tell.

Lee sat passively beside Delores, a dark bruise, darker than his mocha skin, covering a cheekbone. Delores had a little muscle ticking beneath her eye. Only Olsen appeared unscathed.

Amy supposed Dean led his troops—he would hardly hang back and direct their movements. She wondered if the rest of his crew were so damaged they stayed at home or if they were doing other things, part of the job. She made a very real effort not to grind her teeth.

The meal was finally consumed and the conversation dwindled. She could follow Dean from the restaurant, relieved to leave the false gaiety behind.

****

"You didn't partake of the margaritas, sweetheart." The beer and a couple of unusual shots of tequila with Enrico slurred Dean's speech a little. She'd driven home, handling his precious truck beneath his jaundiced eye.

"Somebody had to drive."

"You do me different when you drink."

Uh huh. She most certainly did. And she wasn't doing him in any form tonight.

"Talk to me." No sign of having imbibed alcohol now, just that steady determination.

"I already talked to you. I'm not going to dwell on it, but neither am I going to be happy and cheerful."

"Punishing me? No sex?"

Pulling into the drive, she stomped on the brakes, the seatbelts catching hard. The gearshift in park she pulled the keys from the ignition and managed not to throw them at him, setting them down gently instead on the console between them. "If I'm punishing you that way, Dean, then I'm punishing myself. I'm still freaked. And scared. I love you and seeing you come home like that, seeing your face over the next few days is going to remind me of just how scared I am. Now, please, let it go. I'm tired and just want to sleep. I'll be okay in the morning."

When he didn't respond she threw open the heavy door and struggled down to the pavement. Tight, short dresses and heels weren't meant for riding in trucks.

His door slammed and he was there to help, steadying her, closing her door. His split lip pressed on her shoulder. She knew it had to hurt, but he persisted for another moment, then drew her to the stairs. They ascended in silence and Amy punched in the code, the green light signalling an all clear.

Once again the thin veneer of civilization became apparent to her—locks and security systems a way of life, particularly in the one she'd willing chosen. She'd just have to deal.

Kicking off her heels, she trod off to the bedroom, exhaustion dictating her movements. She was tired all the freaking time. Stripping off her dress, she tossed it over the chair she'd brought with her from her place, the only piece of furniture she thought might fit the design. She should really hang the dress up, but was so done in, she wasn't certain she could even take her underwear off. Dean knelt at her feet, pulling her against him so she could allow first one foot then the other to lift and lose her stilettos, and then he slipped the lace thong over her hips, letting it to slither to her ankles. She stepped out and he stood, already stripped to the waist.

Reaching to unhook her strapless bra, gently pressing a fingertip to each nipple when it fell away to reveal her breasts, he spoke quietly. "I can't change things yet, Amy."

Yet. Did that mean… She searched his face, finding it open, although detected no immediate answer to her silent hope. But it was enough he hinted it.

"Go to bed, sweetheart." He left her to walk into the bathroom, and after pulling the hair jewellery off, putting the earrings beside it on the bedside table, she dropped onto the mattress like a stone.

Sucked dry. The shimmering links of his bracelet around her wrist not an inch from her eyes hypnotized her. It would be fine. She'd trust him with everything, her life, her well being, her heart.

****

It hurt like fucking hell to brush his teeth and Dean saw blood in the sink when he spit. Chewing his food had been an exercise in both pain and frustration, although he hadn't let on, both to spare Amy more worry and to set the example for his men. That shot to the face would be a reminder for awhile. The other man had been determined and as equally reticent. None of the bruisers would say who hired them or if they even belonged to another organization. He'd let them go, bloody and bowed, as an example, a reminder, that Dean Chambray wasn't to be fucked with. With any luck, he'd have pushed somebody's buttons. The somebody he most wanted to lure in.

Losing himself in his woman tonight would have been optimum, but she'd been strung so tight he was afraid she'd shatter. Having seen soldiers stretched to that limit, there was no way he'd push Amy past it. He had to tell her who he really was. It would probably make her worry even more, part of the jumble of reasons he'd avoided sharing in the first place. Fuck. She would see him as even more vulnerable, guarding such a secret. Never mind the competition—his whole crew would turn on him, and her, if they found out, with the exception of Randy. And Randy would need to protect his own ass and his own woman.

He also needed to tell her he loved her. But in what order? Would she see a proclamation of love as softening her for the revelation he was actually sort of undercover but had withheld that gem? That he hadn't really trusted her? It wasn't just his past getting in the way. He had other loyalties, too, including the promise he'd made to his handler and the unspoken one to Randy. But he needed to tell her.

The rest of his clothes hit the hamper and he paused to make sure his boxers stayed on the rim instead of falling to the floor. Amy had muttered about so much laundry and he suspected he was the cause, not that she nagged him. She put up with him and then some. He didn't think there was anything he could pinpoint that she did to drive him crazy, except maybe her retail habit. She was encroaching on his half of the second closet and she insisted on buying him shit he resisted wearing. Though she did have great taste.

He was distracting himself, delaying the inevitable. He should talk to her tonight, tell her how he felt and promise to talk at length once they were both rested.

Sliding into bed beside her, spooning tightly against her back, ignoring how his cock surged in eager anticipation at the press of her soft buttocks, he said it. "Love you, Amy. And we need to talk seriously in the morning."

Not a hint of movement, no change in her breathing greeted what he considered to be a particularly momentous proclamation, and Dean fought a smile despite his chagrin. Great timing. Shit. She was in deep sleep, breath puffing out in those short exhalations, making him smile wider.

His ribs ached from a couple of punches, and there was one really tender spot on his right thigh from a steel-toed boot. Amy would no doubt react to those black and blue marks in the morning.

He thought about the unexpected melee that afternoon. They'd clawed back their territory and feathered out a couple of blocks, certain to get some attention. It had been like sending up a flare. He was impatient for the next move, additionally frustrated by the inability or refusal of those they'd battled to share the whereabouts of Saul Burnett, despite the message he'd sent.

## Chapter Nine

The combination of the booze and physical exertion the day before, and probably his emotional outburst, albeit to deaf ears, made Dean sleep in. He ached dully and tentatively touched his lip. Shit. The condo felt empty and he impatiently shoved the covers back. Amy's side was cool to the touch, although her scent lingered. He hitched over a little and buried his face in her pillow, then willed his body upright.

There was coffee in the carafe on the counter, a note held in place under his favorite cup. Well, he didn't have a favorite cup but Amy bought him one, and it was a cup and a half, nicely weighted to fit his big hand, fingers never trapped by the oversize handle. She noticed everything. Amy's childish sprawl advised him she had some shopping to do and to let her know if he'd be home for dinner if he had to leave before she got back. He poured a coffee and took it with him into the bathroom.

Standing under water as hot as he could stand, soaking out the residual stiffness and forcing the bruises to better manifest themselves, Dean considered his day. Probably best to show his face at the office later, drive around a little, pick up something to eat, maybe brunch, as it was close to mid morning. He was shaving, cautiously sipping his coffee around his puffy lip when his cell shrilled. Randy.

"You need to get down here. Now." He knew better than to ask questions after hearing his lieutenant's tone.

"Leaving in five." He dropped the razor beside the soap dish and rinsed his face quickly. Boxers, jeans, shirt. He sat to pull his socks on and hustled to step into his boots. It had taken a bit of convincing for Amy to leave them by the door instead of tucked out of sight in the closet. He hustled back to scrawl on her note, confirming dinner. That was hours away and he figured he'd deal with whatever Randy had uncovered by then. He called her too, on the way out to the truck, not surprised when it went to voice mail. Amy was smart enough not to use her phone while driving. He just wanted to hear her voice so listened to it asking him to please leave a message then told her he wanted lots of meat for dinner, forget the green stuff she always prepared, ever hopeful.

Randy called again, telling him to drop the truck and come in through the back. What the fuck? The conversation was cryptic and short. Not a good sign.

Leaving his vehicle on the street a couple of blocks over, Dean worked his way through a maze of alleyways, ducking in the back of buildings, many of which he either owned or rented space in. It was then a simple matter to use the side door of the storage unit attached to the back of his office and make his way inside. Randy hunkered over his computer, using both hands, the bandage discarded, although it had to fucking well hurt.

Speaking over his shoulder, he said, "Saw you coming on the feed. Didn't see anyone else. I've been fielding calls all morning. Seems you struck a nerve, buddy."

"You should have called me earlier," Dean groused.

"No sense in both of us getting our shit in a knot. And you took a pretty good shot to the temple, too. Your eye is fucked up."

"Amy iced it, cleaned me up. I'm good. No vision problems, not even a headache. Catch me up."

"The last place we convinced to join the parade closed up this morning, early, burned to the ground. No word on anyone inside."

"Fuck, I hope not. I didn't think he'd retaliate so quick."

"At least we know we got his attention." Randy's voice was devoid of humor. "We need to be prepared. Burnett's obviously gonna pull out all the stops."

"Agreed. Put a guy in our new ventures and in the ones we took back."

"That'll leave us spread thin," his lieutenant warned.

"We'll ask the police for support, warn them anonymously about some hot spots." And he'd give his handler a call too.

He didn't relish that idea. The man would question him about his long term relationship with Amy and put additional pressure on him to keep things quiet. She was a distraction, but one he couldn't imagine living without.

They strategized a few more scenarios, trying to predict the push, after Randy called and assigned the crew, telling Olsen to come to the office. The man's lock-picking skills were beyond the pale, and he could assess a building's weaknesses in a heartbeat, but he was useless in shoring up confidence, and even more useless with his fists. He was a social isolate, by choice. Dean's stomach complained, and he called Olsen back, asking the man to pick up some breakfast burritos and good coffee on the way, eschewing Randy's bitter brew.

Now, there was nothing to do but wait and wonder as time crawled.

The front door creaked open and Olsen's hands pushed into view, although he hesitated just out of sight. Dean moved to grab the precariously leaning tray of java, and the grease stained bag perched on top. The smell of eggs and spices had him ripping open the sack and extricating a burrito, wrenching off a huge bite while forcing the lid off a black coffee. Not as good as Amy's but close. He ignored the sting in his lip. Another bite of the combination of eggs, beans, cheese and soft tortilla calmed his gut and he chased it with another swig of coffee. Randy fished a burrito out and slowly unwrapped it. Olsen shut the door and dropped a big envelope on the desk, reaching for a cup. His nicotine-stained fingers were repellent and the stink of second-hand smoke made Dean lean back.

Gesturing to the envelope, he asked around a final mouthful of breakfast. "What'd you bring?"

"It was on the step. Figured it was too big for the mailbox, got dropped there."

"We get our mail down the block, Frank."

Olsen shrugged and dug a cigarette out of the package, heading back to the door to smoke on the sidewalk. Dean had an edict of no smoking in any of their offices and he was glad to see the man followed it.

Randy wiped his hand, the bruised fingers still swollen, and pulled the envelope over. Slitting the end with his pocket knife, he stowed the lethal weapon back in his pocket before spilling out the contents. His eyes popped and his face suffused with color. "What the fuck?"

Dean leaned over to look and blinked. He snatched the top photo out of Randy's suddenly lax grasp and stared at it. Blind, intense rage snuffed out the initial incredulous reaction and he barely suppressed the urge to choke the messenger. The burrito surged up his throat to gag him and preclude any thoughts he might have expressed.

Olsen poked his head in the door and coughed.

Randy forestalled him from coming in. "Enrico needs you over on Dundas, Frank. Thanks for bringing breakfast. I'll return the favor."

Forehead a mass of furrows, Olsen looked at them both, then shrugged. "No problem. Dundas?"

"Yah. 'Rico's nose is making things tough to concentrate. Needs another guy." Randy prevaricated with the ease of long practice as he excluded Olsen from Dean's revelation.

"Sure. I'll catch you later."

The door shut and Dean pitched his cup against the far wall, the dregs dripping pathetically, the cardboard making an insufficient sound to express his rage as it fell to the floor. Hollow, like his gut. "I fucking near told her I was—"

"Shut it." Randy glared him into silence. "None of us were here last night. I checked the security feed but who the fuck knows if the place is clean?

"What does it matter? It could have been Saul fucking Burnett himself delivered that envelope. Making himself invisible. He's pushing and letting it all out. He's been getting his info from *my* woman. Nothing he doesn't know if he's listening right now."

Randy gestured again and punched a number on his cell. "If she doesn't know about your…thing, then he doesn't—'Rico? Olsen coming your way. Needed him gone for a bit."

They set the pictures on the desk, side by each, all six of them. Amy was predominately featured, smiling in all but one, her head close to Burnett's—good buddies. Different outfits each time. Dean closed his eyes. Her ability to read people, noticing everything. Hearing everything. His laptop open and vulnerable, especially to someone with her skills. He wondered when Burnett had gotten to her, or if she'd been a plant in the bar that night.

If that loud-mouthed Lorraine was part of it, had set him up deliberately. Nothing seemed impossible to imagine.

And he'd nearly told her about being, if not exactly undercover, certainly not a real crime boss. *Had* told her he loved her. Did she hear? Pretended to sleep? Did she laugh? Fuck. If he hadn't decided to wait until morning to drop the rest of it. If she hadn't gone shopping. If. Wishes and horses. Beggars. Bullshit luck, because she could have been cozying up to Burnett right fucking now with the priceless information that Dean Chambray was some sort of undercover agent looking to pull in the shadow man Saul represented.

He hurt so hard he couldn't get a breath against it. Fuck. All of her sweetness, even her attitude. Taking care of him, *loving* him. Right. Fucking him over. Well, he'd been well and truly fucked, blinded by sweet pussy. His cover still held by some quirk of fate, that bullshit luck.

"He's giving her something in every shot, Dean. You can't see it clearly but it's rectangular, wrapped in paper. Money?"

What the fuck did it matter? She'd betrayed him, could have brought down years of careful work. Could have got him killed. Randy too. Played him.

"You can't make out what she hands over in any of the shots. Weird."

"Probably a thumb drive. I worked from home some, remember? We shared an office and I wasn't with her all the time. Making her coffee and bringing her shit. And I either left the laptop on or she cracked the password. She knows her way around computers." He was flat now, controlled, the rage banked.

"Might explain things. Too much for a coincidence anyhow. But who sent the pictures? Burnett wouldn't out his source."

"I don't give a fuck who sent them. We'll figure it out later. Call everyone and make sure they know to expect a push. I'm gonna go and have a chat with Amy."

"Time for that later, Dean, when you've cooled down."

"I want her gone, Randy. Gone. And that's *my* job. Then I can turn my attention fully to Burnett. And whoever pulls his strings. Shadow man. He's coming and I want Amy dealt with before I deal with *him*."

"I'm coming along with you. You're too close to doing something stupid. I can call everyone on the way. We need to shut this office down for now anyhow, seeing as somebody got that close to deliver the goods without anyone seeing him."

Dean didn't care. He'd given Randy organizational orders and the man would back off on the drive to the complex. The time would help him stay cool. No way was he letting Amy see how she'd gotten to him. Randy could serve as witness, and a constant reminder, of how stupid he'd been to trust a woman. Or love one.

****

Amy was in the kitchen when she heard the feet on the stairs. Loud, stomping feet. Smiling to herself she shut the oven door on the prime rib she was preparing for their evening meal, a celebratory dinner. She'd slipped out to the pharmacy while her man slept, unable to hide behind denial any longer. She had confirmed the news for Dean, and while her belly fluttered in anxious anticipation, deep down she believed he'd be okay with it.

He had truly settled over the past several months, no longer as tightly drawn, maybe not expecting their relationship to have an ending. Seemed to be cautiously accepting the possibility she wasn't going to fuck him over or try to manipulate him. Not that Dean had any say in how that very first relationship in his life affected him; the piece of work who'd birthed him set the sure-fire-failure option in motion for each subsequent one.

Amy shook her head, setting the oven mitts to rest on the counter. Dean might have cut his mom out of his life, but Marsha, in death, would once again cast her evil pall. Still, Amy would be right there, by Dean's side, and they'd see it through. She had lots of experience in seeing things through to the other side, and this time it meant everything to her. So this time there would be a positive outcome no matter what it took. Because it was Dean.

They would need to have a really serious discussion now that her suspicion was confirmed. He'd hinted at getting shut of the business, and maybe her news would have an impact. He'd do what was right and she'd trust him with it.

The prime rib was her only other purchase of the morning as she tried to get home before he left, but she missed him, his coffee cup on the bathroom sink, towel carelessly tossed on the floor. He'd obviously left in a hurry, but had taken the time to answer her note. Left a voice mail too, which inspired her to buy the beef.

The door flew open with such enthusiasm it rocked back on its hinges to meet the flat of Dean's hand. The look on his face sucked the air out of her chest. Not enthusiasm. Nearly uncontrolled violence. Forcing her flight response down, hoping to help soothe, Amy made to go to him, only to be forestalled by the imperious upswing of his other hand. The Terminator couldn't have done it with more terror-inspiring authority, the manila envelope he clutched—a weapon.

His grey eyes locked with hers and the glitter of rage then colored over with the sheen of scorn and hatred until they were shards of crystal. Being adept at reading looks and gazes, she knew this did not bode well for her, and she was always the master of understatement, the empress of hope since meeting Dean. Her hand drifted to rest on her belly, an automatic, protective gesture.

His tall, muscular form froze in the doorway, filling the space. She could hear his deep, heaving breaths. The faint ticking of the clock, the drip of the sink and all the other usual noises in their condo faded away before the sounds he was making, and her vision narrowed to focus on him. She was vaguely aware another large body flanked him, and saw an equally large hand clamp down on his shoulder in an attempt to fix him in place when he leaned forward threateningly. The nails of that hand were clean, with the exception of badly bruised fingers, the nail beds purple and blue. Randy, his hand injured in the fight—was it only the day before? Her anxious mind seized on the details while quailing from the symbolism. It knew pain was in the offing, just not the form it would take.

"Get your shit and get out." Her man's handsome face was set in granite, offset only by the unsuppressed fury churning in his eyes.

"What's wrong?" Was that her voice? That tiny, tentative whispering thread of sound?

Dean never turned his temper on her. Amy saw him angry, pissed, furious even. He didn't hide his emotions. He acted many of them out, but she liked that about him because she didn't have to watch so carefully and ensure the accuracy of what she was reading in order to protect herself. It had been a huge burden Amy had been glad, no, supremely grateful, to relinquish.

"Shut up, Amy. Did you think I wouldn't find out? Did you think I'd be blinded forever by you spreading your legs for me and sucking me off each and every fucking day? Did you think you'd distract me?"

Shrinking back at the vitriol in his voice, a nugget of humiliation taking root and unfurling way down inside, Amy worked hard at masking her pain. She gave Dean everything sexually. Willingly. He'd never spoken to her with such disgust, aired their personal lives. He knew how ashamed she was of her past. She couldn't think of anything to say, couldn't respond in light of the fury he exuded. Snatching up a jar of spices from the cabinet he hurled it at the opposite wall where it smashed and shattered into slivers to emulate her crumbling life.

"Find out what?" She finally managed to croak the query past the tightening in her throat.

The envelope sailed across the short distance, windmilling, catching her thigh with an edge, a surprisingly solid blow. It settled at her feet. She stared down at it, lifting her other hand to link fingers with the one at her belly, to refrain from reaching for it. The innocuous yellow brown of the packet didn't shed any light of explanation yet pulsed with dark warning. Squinting, she could make out Dean's name, written in bold, black strokes, but no return address, at least not on the side she could see. Amy raised her eyes once again to his.

"Out. You've got a half hour. And you don't show your face anywhere I do. You see me in the distance, you turn and walk the other way. I come into a place you're at—you haul your ass out. Or I won't be responsible. Clear?"

It hit her then. She'd been wrong. She'd been wrong a whole lot of times when younger, but she was so certain she and Dean had it right. *Wrong.* And it gutted her, left her without an ounce of energy. She had no clue what it was she'd done, but it didn't matter. Dean wasn't going to give her a chance to explain, even if she could. His shit was deep and while knowing it well, she truly hadn't believed it would drown what they had. Had. Past tense. She'd allowed herself to hope, been lulled by the apparent growth of their relationship, and was suddenly transported back in time to her expected reality.

*Get over it, Amy, wrap it up. No time for tender reminiscences.* Making herself nod she looked away from his beloved face. The familiar numbness from all past mistakes flooded over her, the comforting shield of shock easing the wrenching pain. His boots hammered out the door and down the steps.

Amy became aware of the clearing rasp of a masculine throat and raised her gaze to meet Randy's. Randy liked her and she liked him, and she and Andrea were cautiously developing a friendship. Past tense. He was staring at her with scorn, his upper lip ever so slightly curled, big body radiating disgust. He'd picked a side and that too was no surprise. Why would anyone pick hers? Amy thought she was making other friends within Dean's circle, but loyalties being what they were, well, she was naturally on the losing end. She ignored Randy with not-so-surprising ease. It didn't matter. Only her news mattered. She had to get gone and somehow regroup. If not for that news she would probably have opened her throat with the big knife set perpendicular to the carving board. Anything to end this. *Drama. Not the time.*

Remembering the roast, she slipped for an instant into the banality of everyday life. Turning off the oven, she grabbed the oven mitts to lift out the partially cooked meat, carefully setting it on top of the stove. The rich scent made her nauseous now and she doubted she would ever be able to smell roasting beef again without an olfactory stab of painful remembrance.

Randy passed behind her and from the corner of her eye saw him dip his knees. He snagged the envelope and shook the contents onto the granite countertop. The glossy papers slithered like a snake and one came to rest directly within her sight line. Staring at it in confusion, Amy could feel her eyes narrow and her brow furrow. Why had someone taken pictures of her talking to Saul Burrows? She looked the question at Randy.

"Dean got them in the mail, Amy. Imagine his surprise, bitch."

Involuntarily flinching back at the epithet, she still had to ask. "Why would anyone take a picture of me and Mr. Burrows?"

"Mr. *Burrows*?" Randy's tone was almost comically high pitched.

"Yes, Saul Burrows. He works in the deli I found. He saves me stuff and arranges for me to get different ingredients I can't get other places. Orders it special. I bought the prime rib from him this morning."

"That's Saul *Burnett*, Amy. And he doesn't work in a deli. He's moving to control street betting as well as our other interests and is pushing Dean hard. And he knows a lot about Dean's business."

Shaking her head, glancing at the clock, she was unable to process and had no time for mysteries. Dean's ultimatum rang in her ears. Now twenty minutes and counting. She had to go. Turning on her heel, she hurried into the bedroom, the one she'd shared with Dean and would no longer. Nearly a year of carefully working out the bumps along the way, sweetly balanced by need. The moving in after such a short time made it formal, a day she'd remember forever as a turning point in her life—to hell.

Standing there for a few moments staring blindly around, brain not registering what it was she needed. It came to her. Nothing. Her clothes filled one of the closets, and part of another, not to mention her shoes.

Amy's weakness was shoes and Dean indulged her, but they meant nothing to her now. She needed him and he wasn't hers to have, if he ever was. It was like she was a different person, all hint of the past year with Dean extinguished like time travel. Her purse sat on the dresser and she grabbed it up.

Dropping the strap over her head, settling it on her shoulder, ignoring Randy's speculative look she crossed to the bed, carefully picking up the little black bear from its nest on the throw pillows. Her one and only tie with the best part of her life, even if she couldn't really remember her parents. Moving to the den where her laptop lay, she hefted it. It fit into the wide mouth of her bag, and accommodated the cord too.

Her heart wasn't so numb anymore. It was hurting like a mother, and Amy wondered if it might fail before she got out the door. *How can you mend a broken heart?* The line from a juke box oldie pounded behind her temples.

"Uh, Amy? Maybe I should talk with Dean for a minute before you leave."

Randy was a smart guy. Amy knew that. He was also Dean's best friend and trusted right hand, his lieutenant. Maybe he saw something Dean missed, because Randy wasn't blinded by her sucking *him* off each and every day. That bitter thought came out of nowhere and gave her strength. Managing a final grand gesture, as hollow as it was, she unhooked the delicate gold bracelet from her wrist and let it curl onto the dresser, a slender shower of symbolism. That bracelet had meant as much to her as any wedding band. She answered Randy, avoiding his eyes.

"Wouldn't matter, Randy. He was just looking for an excuse. Always has been. I knew it for the truth, but I hoped and fooled myself. I thought I was enough for him, that he actually trusted me… Anyhow, wrong again. So more fool me."

A shard of defensive memory pierced her single-minded purpose to get clear. Amy detoured into the dining room, carefully keeping her body between Randy's sharp eyes and a place setting at the head of the table, her hand drifting over it. Sleight of hand, learned at the tables in Vegas in another life. The little paper stick with its proud plus sign, tucked into the little plastic bag, like a party treat for the aborted dinner, fit right into the crease of her palm. A no brainer.

"You need to wait, Amy. Something stinks here." She could very nearly see his clever brain ticking over. But Dean had crossed the line. Betrayal, only not on her part. She couldn't expose her secret—Amy shoved the thought away, afraid Randy might read her.

Brushing past the man, pausing at the coat closet to snag her jacket, she shoved the baggie into the pocket, and was out the door after toeing into her flats. He said something, but Amy couldn't hear the words past the increasing sound of those lyrics and their accompanying melody filling her head. *How do you mend those broken dreams? How does a loser ever win?* She fumbled the keys out of her purse and stabbed them into the lock on the driver's door of her car. The close call in Vegas allowed her to buy that vehicle. It was only five years old, had low mileage and was in good shape. It would get her where she needed to go.

She had two stops to make before she really got gone. One at the bank and the second at Sandra's. Sandra wouldn't say she told her so, although Amy would feel it all the same, getting involved with such a dangerous man. Sandra would tell Amy she loved her and cared about her and for Amy to call when she got where she was going. She owed it to her friend to say goodbye face to face.

****

"What?" Dean's voice shook the rafters. Randy actually stepped back half a pace, so he could only imagine what his face looked like. His guts roiled.

"It was a set up. Something to tie you in knots and have you looking the wrong direction while his minions swept in. And it would have worked except for your refusal to let Amy cloud your thinking. I don't know how you did it."

A hint of the other man's regret got through and rubbed salt in Dean's mortal emotional wound. He sourly reflected on how past dire necessity taught him how to wrap up his angst over Amy and shove it away.

"I saw your woman's shock 'cause it wasn't as personal for me. She looked so fucking bewildered. She actually asked me why someone would want to take a picture of her and the deli guy. It took me the rest of yesterday and half the night but I found the asshole who took the pics. He said he had to work real hard to get the right angle to make it look like Amy was more than just a customer. Burnett was selling her fucking meat and other grocery crap, Dean. Pretending to work the deli. I've already had a word with the owner."

The words pushed past the stricture in Dean's chest. He felt blindly for his chair and nearly fell into it, peering up at Randy. "Fuck me, no. And I fell for it. So we've got somebody else sharing my shit with Burnett and I dealt harsh with Amy. Didn't even question it. Didn't even give her the benefit of the doubt or ask her. Fuck. Where is she?"

Randy shrugged. "Dunno. She took you at your word and got gone. Grabbed her purse and jacket, her computer, drove her car away. I called Mike but he couldn't make it across town in time to track her and I had to look into this as a priority. She moved right along, Dean."

Dean sucked in air and struggled to control himself. "She didn't pack her shit?"

"You didn't give her time to do much of anything, buddy."

Randy's practicality rubbed Dean the wrong way, a sure sign he'd fucked up royally. He relied on Randy's realism. But if she didn't take her stuff, then she'd have to come back for it. Wouldn't she?

"I didn't go home," he muttered. "Didn't want to smell her, feel her there. Stayed at Crystal's. Thought I'd give it a couple of days." And thought to erase the pain by turning to Crystal, a woman who knew the score, one who'd fuck him and hardly notice when he'd gone. Except he couldn't make himself go through with it, and slept in her spare room. Seemed one part of him knew Amy better than his stupid fucking pride did, contaminated as it was by his fucking past.

Randy nodded sagely as though he totally understood, and maybe he did. Randy goddamn near pushed Andrea away with his own brand of shit. Dean focused. Amy would go to Sandra. She had slowly been building a posse amongst the crew's women, but not one of them meant what Sandra did.

"I'll go see Sandra."

"Mike missed her there, too, and Sandra sent him packing with some choice words. Amy wasn't in real good shape, Dean, just so you know. I asked her to give me some time with you, but she said it didn't matter."

Dean fought the unfamiliar panic blooming in his chest, dissolving that earlier tightness, but it felt worse, it that was possible. "What else did she say?"

"Something about you looking for any excuse."

Dean wouldn't be surprised to look down and see the handle of a blade protruding from his gut, the slice of agony so real it made him sag back into his chair. The truth fucking hurt. He *had* been looking, no matter how certain he was that he hadn't been. And his woman blinded herself with her love for him, accepted him, trusted him, took the chance, believing he returned it. He *did* return it. He just hadn't trusted it. Fuck. He had let his shit bite him on the ass once again and driven Amy away. And at a time when Burnett would be closing in for the anticipated, easy kill, having so cleverly set Dean up, finding Amy and fixing it with her would have to wait. Waiting could be the death knoll. He knew it, but it was bigger than both of them. He had to deal with Burnett and make it safe for Amy to return if he possibly could. Dean clenched his eyes shut for a couple of seconds and decided.

"Get Enrico to Sandra's and tell him to drain her. I want to know everything she knows. Enrico can charm a snake, and he's familiar with Sandra. They had something going on. Meantime we'll surprise Saul with a preemptive strike, not just shore up the resistance. Call in our markers with local law enforcement and shout out to Minor—he's the only cop we've got in our pocket who'll be able to act quickly on this. I'm finishing it and not doing it again with that asshole Burnett. And find the informant. Clear?"

Randy clearly ran the percentages, his dark blue eyes getting that far away look, then nodded. "That'll work. Minor just got that promotion within the department and will be looking for anything to make it look like he deserved it." Randy's thin contempt for the crooked cops shone through. "As for the informant … that'll take time. And Amy'll be a project."

"Amy will be coming back, Randy. No worries."

## Chapter Ten

"You're such a find, sweetie, I so mean it!" Francine's expressive, pixie-like face beamed up at Amy. "I was a bit leery when Harold told me about you, but as usual he was right." The little woman waved her hands about and hustled to the door, then turned and rushed back, silvery gray hair flying about her head.

"We'll be back in a week. You're sure it's not too long?"

"I'll be fine, Francine," Amy replied patiently. Francine was like a butterfly, in perpetual motion, and she wondered what Francine had been like as a child. For sure, she'd get an attention deficit disorder label today. Amy involuntarily looked down at her belly. Getting her stress under control was important. Babies didn't need stress.

"Well, you can always call, now Harold has that phone getting service anywhere. If he remembers to turn it on. And Joyce is a good 'un. Her husband'll pitch in, too."

"Joyce and I will manage just fine. And Bob said he was just a call away."

Francine's face brightened again. "Then I'll go before Harold comes to get me. You know how he fusses."

Amy put her arm around Francine's narrow shoulders, feeling their fragility beneath the pink polyester of her cardigan, and guided the older woman to the door. Harold's big, old, blue Mercury sat at the curb, idling, and Amy could see his head tipped forward, resting on the steering wheel. Probably counting to a hundred. Francine could indeed be trying.

Her boss, well, one of them, went up on tiptoes and Amy obligingly leaned in for a kiss and a hug. Another one. Francine exited in a swirl of fabric and floral perfume. Harold was out of the car like he had eyes in the back of his head, opening the passenger door for his beloved wife. She remonstrated loudly with him for letting the cold air out. Amy smiled, watching from the motel entrance. She'd known better than to walk Francine to the car, unwilling to risk another lengthy discussion and reminders. A solid *clunk* signalled the start of a new chapter in all of their lives, the car door closing behind Francine, and a moment later, the car pulled out into traffic, stately as an ocean liner. Amy sighed with relief and returned to the desk.

No reservations that day, but there was usually a certain amount of drive-up traffic because of the motel's location and well tended exterior. As soon as her employment had been secured, the next thing Amy did was design a web page with the ability to make online reservations. Harold caught on quickly, and even Francine figured it out. There weren't a lot of people reserving rooms, but every bit would help. The larger chains made for really stiff competition, and The Restaway Inn hardly featured a lot of amenities.

But it was scrupulously clean, and the beds were excellent; Harold and Francine knew the hotel business even if they didn't have the money for swimming pools and water slides. Nor the space. They were slowly updating the television packages, with only three rooms to go—Amy stayed in one of those and cared less—the bathrooms featured big tubs and rain showerheads. Francine had seen them in a magazine and apparently scoured the salvage yards, locating twenty claw foot tubs in good shape and easily refurbished with recoating and expensive fixtures. Amy loved her tub and suspected many of the other guests did, too.

The old subway tiles lent a certain charm and had been grouted again to sparkle like new. Maintenance was key and her bosses had it down pat. Amy was supervising the installation of wireless internet, and she figured the next step would be carpet to replace the clean, but faded floor coverings. The diner right next door was a huge bonus, featuring excellent home-cooked fare for a reasonable price. Price. The reasonable rates brought people in, the easy access from the highway notwithstanding.

With only twenty units, one maid was sufficient, also taking care of the laundry, the facility built onto the owners' suite out back. Harold took care of the maintenance, hiring only when the job was too big for one man, Francine did the books and managed the front desk. Neither wanted to retire and so it was a sweet deal. Amy loved them both and kept counting her blessings to have stumbled upon such people.

Her mind went back to how she'd walked into the motel that horrible day, exhausted, to beg a phone, her cell dead, the charger left behind.

That day had unfolded the way she'd planned after Dean threw her out. First the bank to close out her account, then to say goodbye to her best friend. Sandra had hugged her, made her a cup of tea to go, along with a sandwich, let her cry. Great, gulping sobs of agony, rivers of tears accompanied by belly cramping angst. Her friend offered her the spare room, urged her to stay, but Amy had needed to put distance between her and Dean. She'd start to show in a few weeks and someone would tell him, take great delight in putting the needle in. And Amy knew how Dean would respond. His pride would demand he provide for his bastard, and subsequently her. No way was she going to allow that and be doused with his vitriol again. No way would she expose a child to the animosity between them. Her baby deserved better. Better than what either of his or her parents got.

So she had hugged Sandra fiercely and promised to call within the month, adamantly refusing to be in touch earlier. Certainly not via email. "Randy knows something's not right, Sandra. He's like a dog with a bone, especially when it concerns his best friend. And you can't tell a lie to save your soul so I won't put you in the position. Dean would have to respond if the truth came out, in order to be the *man*, and I'm not allowing it."

"But, honey. You love him and you're knocked up." Sandra's earthy practicality wasn't particularly welcome, and then she really messed up. "And it's his baby, too."

"Fuck that, Sandra." She would have taken it back if she could, but her friend was changing horses in midstream. Amy knew her friend, and Dean had mended some fences over the past while, so Sandra had come to like the man. But Amy needed loyalty now. Sandra flinched against the bitterness spewing from Amy's mouth. She apologized, patting Amy's hand as she did so.

"He messed up, Amy. Badly. I'm just worried about you and the child."

"Sorry to snap at you. But Sandra, he didn't trust me. Nearly a year. Nearly a whole year of lots of good times, lots of intense history with me to balance out the shit. And he didn't even give me a chance."

"A year against thirty odd years," Sandra murmured sagely.

Amy paused. What the fuck? She'd thought Sandra was waiting for things to go south, worried and anxious despite coming to like Dean a little. Maybe…

No, she couldn't take the risk. How many times would he find an excuse and gut her? How many times before she was destroyed totally? Who'd raise the baby right then, if she was fried emotionally?

Shaking her head she said, "I know it, Sandra. But I've got my own history, and I've run out of resilience. And trust. A rare commodity and I find I can't live without it. And Dean can't seem to afford it."

The memory of his face, twisted with rage—and pain. Amy pushed it away, hard. She hurt, too, and he hadn't let her explain, wouldn't let her close, hadn't even given her a tiny benefit of the doubt. And then there was the fact, just beginning to penetrate, that a rival, a criminal rival, had used her to get to Dean. All her old fears and memories of Vegas surged back, and ice filled her veins. Amy rubbed her hands together against the cold. She no longer had just her to worry about.

Sandra sighed and blinked back the tears shining in her big brown eyes. "I'll miss you, honey. It won't be the same."

"I'll call you, and you can let me know when you get some time off. We'll meet somewhere and catch up. Okay?"

"What about when you, uh, deliver?"

Amy dissolved into tears again and impatiently wiped them away with the backs of her hands, her cheeks already sore from the scalding salt. "We'll see what we can work out." She was terrified about that day in the future, but there was too much else to do first, and a long time to get there. She hefted her purse, her savings tucked inside with the laptop, and moved to the door.

Sandra wrapped her arms over her chest, hands cupping her elbows. Her thin, pleasant face was drawn with anxiety, and not a little fear, the dark hair such contrast to her pallor. Her eyes were full of tears.

"I'll be fine, Sandra. Know it. Amy Copeland survives. And I have another life to take care of—find a doctor, take vitamins, all that stuff."

Sandra attempted a watery smile and Amy returned it.

"I'll call you."

The drive to the next city over had been made on autopilot. As silly as it was, Amy would miss her car. Buying foreign hadn't won her any new friends, and Dean didn't like the fact the Audi was a convertible, but she loved it. And she could drive it to capacity too, as well as any man. But it was too distinctive and she needed the money. The piece of shit the dealer graced her with was more suitable for a mother-to-be, nondescript, unmemorable, but he assured her it met all safety ratings. And it died half a block from the Restaway Inn, ominous warnings flashing on the dash, shimmers of heated air rising from the engine to curl over the windshield. Amy pulled to the curb and went to find a working phone.

Fate? Karma? She didn't know. Didn't care, although she wouldn't ignore the possibility. She had walked into the lobby and hadn't looked back. Harold reposed behind the counter, an older man wearing a neatly pressed, white shirt tucked into dark trousers. His greying hair cut close to his head, a little goatee adding spice to his look. Calm blue-gray eyes surveyed her, but in a "are you a customer or somebody else" manner. Assessing but with no intent. A little name tag, gold letters etched on a white background announced his name.

"How can I help you?" A kind voice, baritone, still full of strength despite his age. She could recall those kindly words even now, if she didn't realize their import at the time.

Amy explained her phone dilemma and Harold stepped up, unbidden. He called somebody named Chaske, and a tall, skinny black man arrived before Amy had time to drink the water Harold pressed on her. She'd struggled up from the depths of a comfortable chair to reach a hand across the coffee table to Chaske. He declined her accompanying him, citing the heat as a deterrent, so she and Harold watched in air-conditioned comfort as Chaske climbed into her new-to-her wheels, then out again to pop the hood. The man didn't need to mime the bad news. Amy could tell by his stance. Nothing good was under that cloud of black. Shit.

Ridiculous tears threatened. It was nearly dark and she was exhausted. Only a hundred miles from home and no way to increase that distance unless she took a bus.

"Don't you fret, Amy." Harold knew her full name. She hadn't dissembled. How could she in the face of his kindness? "Chaske will take the beast away and let you know what's wrong, give you a quote. You can stay here."

Chaske backed his wrecker up to the van and efficiently hooked it up. The vehicle looked sad, discouraged. Much like Amy felt. Being taken in by a used-car salesman was the icing on the cake.

"Do you have much luggage?"

Startled, Amy focused on Harold. "None. I was just … passing through."

"Where you going?" The first intrusive question, but it was okay. Flight wasn't a lot of fun, and unless Harold and Chaske had some kind of racket going whereby they bilked people out of shitty old vehicles and rented them a room to murder them later, or worse … she could use some support.

"I don't know." Kind of sounded pathetic, put out there like that. Amy's breath hitched in her throat. Surely she'd cried enough tears at Sandra's. Apparently not.

"Well, how if we have some dinner and talk awhile? I have a phone call to make but that's pretty much it for the night unless we have people stopping. We still have a couple of open units."

"I don't want to impose." Amy lifted her purse.

"You aren't, Amy. And you're not okay. My daughter, Louise, would have been about your age when we lost her. Have dinner with an old man."

And so it went. Harold ordered dinner from the dinner after ascertaining her favorites—the diner's limited menu didn't detract from the fact the food was excellent. While they waited for delivery—Harold had an arrangement with the proprietor, small businesses supporting one another—he placed his call. Amy couldn't help but overhear and realized he was talking to his wife, Francine, recovering from a surgical procedure. The affection overshadowed the worry in Harold's voice and his obvious relief that Francine was feeling better even in the short time since he'd visited over lunch was inspiring. It spoke to hope for relationships everywhere, except for Amy's. Harold regaled Francine with her story and assured his wife Amy was a nice young woman. Like Louise.

"Francine is worried you're a scam artist, Amy. But my explanation was sufficient. She can't wait to meet you."

"Uh, I don't know how long I'll be here." In truth, she had been planning to revisit the dealership and have a chat with the little weasel who had not only taken her on the van, but stiffed her insofar as the cash on the Cabriolet went, too. Hindsight. She worried about the hours passing, though, running through her fingers like the sands of proverbial time. And she was so tired.

"Well, you can't go anywhere without a vehicle. If you can't afford a room we'll work something out."

"I can afford a room, Harold." Boy, who said there were no kind people around anymore? "I just need to travel, put some miles on."

Their food arrived, clearly forestalling some curious questions on the tip of Harold's tongue. The boy bringing in the bags was polite and respectful of Harold who called the kid Beanpole, but introduced him as Sean. Sean was maybe five foot two and kind of square, like a solid box of flesh. But he seemed okay with the nickname, and Amy smiled as cheerfully as she could, calling him Sean.

Harold didn't share hers, which was interesting and very discreet.

"You'll forgive a curious old man, Amy, but are you in trouble?"

Taking a deep breath, she closed her eyes. "I'm running away from a relationship, Harold. I'm not in trouble. I promise." She might *be* trouble though, might attract it here. Dean balanced both sides of his business, and she rarely was exposed to the less savory one. Like so many women who fancied themselves in love with a bad guy, she'd come to pretend it didn't matter. But her plan had been to leave as soon as that damn van was repaired.

"Okay." And that was it. Harold had left it alone. Amy wanted to explain further but decided to let it lie. The whole experience that day had been surreal and maybe her instincts were playing tricks on her.

They sat at the coffee table in the welcoming lobby and ate the meatloaf and mashed potatoes with the green beans and gravy on the side in quiet appreciation.

The cherry pie with the flaky pastry was like ambrosia and Harold's quiet moan had Amy smiling around a mouthful, just managing not to emulate him.

"I'll give you the key to the unit next to the office. Maybe not as quiet, but we live right behind, so if you need me…" Harold didn't look at her, packing up the detritus of their meal. "Want one of Francine's night things?"

"That's okay. I'll manage." God. So freaking kind.

"There's coffee in those single makers in the room, Amy, and if you're up by seven we'll have breakfast."

"Done."

Amy had been up by six-thirty that following morning. Always a light sleeper, she started at each and every unfamiliar sound, automatically reaching for a large, hard body that wasn't beside her. Her loneliness and despair caught up to her at some point, her fingers finding the apex of her thighs to search out her clit, seeking something, anything, to help her sleep. It was a lonely, shallow release, nothing like what Dean gave her, and only made things worse. When dawn pushed its pale light around the edges of the curtains, Amy was grateful for the excuse to get out of bed.

Donning the underwear washed out in the sink and hung to dry from the shower rod, she sniffed her shirt. Her nose wrinkled. It smelled like defunct van air freshener and of emotional angst, but it was all she had. The bath in the incredible tub the night before had eased her stiffness but didn't work any miracles on her state of mind. She strove to wall off her memories of Dean, surround them with a moat full of resolution to have a future without his bullshit, and raise a healthy, happy child. She decided to believe that fat lie for now and turn it into the truth when she was stronger. Her jeans were okay, but she eschewed her socks, toeing into her shoes barefoot. Running her tongue experimentally over her teeth, Amy decided the first order of the day was a little shopping, toothbrush first on the list. Her stomach rebelled at the very thought of toothpaste, an interesting detail to process.

Harold was already behind the polished counter in the lobby, now wearing a shirt in a pale shade of blue, with charcoal grey pants. He smiled, and Amy beamed back, fully aware of the pretense, but determined to try. Her lips trembled with the strain and his face sobered.

"Pancakes and bacon okay?"

"Sounds great."

Harold nodded as if her reply hadn't sounded thin and shrill. "I asked for a carafe of coffee and some tea."

She sat in the same chair and leafed through a newspaper and a few magazines while Harold busied himself behind the desk. Breakfast arrived, courtesy of a young girl, clearly getting ready for school, backpack weighing her small frame down. She, too, greeted Harold with respect and looked at her curiously. Amy nodded and got up to take the bag of food and lay the items out on the coffee table.

"We normally eat in our suite, Amy, so if you'd prefer ... "

"No, this is fine." No way was she presuming any further. She had to get moving, and this man was too good to be true. Convincing herself that her emotional walls were partially rebuilt, Amy wasn't taking any chances, adding things like the kindness of strangers to the load. There was nothing left in her for payback.

The food was every bit as good as the meal the day before, the pancakes made from scratch, the bacon crisp. Coffee, laced with cream and a little sugar was wonderful for about half a cup before Amy rethought it, both because of the caffeine and because her stomach hitched little warnings. She supposed it was time to revamp her diet.

"What kind of work do you do?"

She swallowed the last of her pancakes to answer Harold. "I design websites and I can do tech support. Pretty much self-employed, but I contract out." It was the perfect job. She could work from anywhere, anyplace, anytime. It had fit around Dean's erratic schedule, not that she'd needed to work. Good thing she kept up her skills, considering.

"So you're good with the public, can follow a system, routine?"

"Uh huh." Where was this going?

"Want a job?"

Amy sat straight and blinked. She could feel her lashes fluttering wildly as she tried to process. "Job?"

"I need someone to keep an eye on the desk while I go visit Francine. And she's gonna need some time to recuperate, maybe two weeks or so, once she's home in a few days. I can't find anyone to spell me except for a little time here and there."

"But you seem to have contacts all over," Amy protested.

Harold nodded. "And they all have small businesses, too, or are taking care of grandkids and don't have a lot of time to spare. You can live here until Francine is on her feet and by then the coast should be clear."

"Coast?" Amy heard herself inanely repeating after him. "Harold. I'm not running from the police or even an abusive boyfriend. I'm not. And if you think that, why on earth would you want me to work here?"

"I believe you about not being in trouble, at least not the kind you're saying. But you're in trouble, anyhow. You hurt, I can see it, and I trust my instincts."

Blowing out a breath, Amy sank back into the comfortable chair. Working as a desk clerk for a couple of weeks. Maybe a month. She could probably do it, and get her head straight, too. If Harold had read her so easily, she was a mess. Maybe she could use the time to regroup and plan. Besides, she had no wheels, and it was now too late to backtrack to the dealership. Her instincts were sharpening, maybe just from paranoia, but Dean had a long reach considering his resources and contacts.

"Point me in the direction of a store where I can pick up some clothes and essentials."

"So you'll do it?" Harold sounded ecstatic.

"I'll be back as soon as I can and you can show me the ropes. Make some notes about anything complicated while I'm gone." Having a purpose felt kind of invigorating, not to mention distracting. She certainly had no time to wallow in the what-ifs.

Harold made her take his car, a big boat, meticulously maintained, and Amy bought enough clothes to carry her for awhile, using some cash from the sale of her Audi. Nothing extravagant, but two pairs of serviceable black pants with elastic waistbands, something she didn't realize were available for purchase. Tailored shirts in white, blue and pink, all with darts to open later for extra stomach space, would serve as a desk clerk uniform. Basic toiletries, underwear, socks, a pair of sneakers and a loose jacket. A cell phone charger for when she was ready to call Sandra, and she was set. The little mall had everything and she made a mental note of the location.

A tall, red-haired woman wheeled a cart from the room Amy decided to consider her own when she returned. She parked the Mercury in the closest visitor's slot so Harold could back out with ease. Upon closer inspection, the red hair most definitely came out of a box, and the face it surrounded was lined and tired. However, bright green eyes twinkled her way. "Hi. You'll be the new desk clerk! I'm Joyce. Nice thing you're doing for Harold. I couldn't get it all done by myself."

"I'm Amy. Nice to meet you. Glad to help."

"I have a couple more units. See you later."

Amy put her purchases in her room, pausing only to change into one of her new shirts and a pair of those black pants, before making her way to the lobby to be trained as motel desk clerk extraordinaire.

True to his word, Harold left her in charge the same day while he was at the hospital, and upon Francine's return home, Amy stepped in until Francine was back on her feet. Their vacation came hard on the heels of that, and by then, Amy was well established in Harold and Francine's little community of friends. The van wasn't beyond repair, but would take considerable time, because Chaske refused to take her money, simply saying he would work on it in his spare moments. Amy suspected he was eking things out, timing it until his friends were back from holidays, but she would have stayed anyhow.

****

*Amy will be coming back. No worries.* Famous fucking last words. Dean pushed both hands through his hair and vaguely registered he needed a haircut before he looked the wild man he was struggling with internally. His business had survived Burnett's attempted takeover, and the defense had been bloodless, thanks to the careful planning. Everyone executed their deal flawlessly over the intervening weeks. Except the man he'd sought for years hadn't shown his hand and it appeared Saul Burnett had moved on to a different city, let alone a different neighborhood. Dean couldn't figure it out—either total failure or Burnett's boss had fallen back to wait for a better opportunity. It was getting fucking tiresome.

But, far worse, Enrico was certain he got everything from Sandra, yet there wasn't anything to get, really. Amy had gone to say goodbye, said she'd call, and hadn't yet done so. She just vanished. Any number of calls to her phone had gone to voicemail, until the box was full. Nothing. It was turned off, the battery pulled or Dean could have traced the GPS.

Her car turned up one city over, in a used car lot, and the junker she bought with a small part of the proceeds had never been registered. She paid attention. Amy knew the dealer plates would get her some distance before she needed to register the van and get insurance. But she didn't. Or, if she had, she didn't use her own name, and dropped right below the radar. Dean couldn't find her, anywhere. At first he hadn't understood why she was hiding so carefully from him. Until today.

She'd emptied her bank account, not a princely sum, but enough to move clear across the country if she chose. She'd need a job—even doing web design meant paperwork, and the government had no record of her, either. It was insane. He put his best man on it and hired a better tracker from the outside but the days went by, followed by weeks. It was eating him up inside. He bought the damn car back. Amy loved her Audi and it was least he could do. It was parked in the garage, waiting for her to come home.

The place still faintly smelled like her, fresh and grassy, and Randy hadn't lied. Amy left everything but her purse and laptop. And Bogs. If that stupid little, moth-eaten, battered stuffed toy had remained, he might not feel so hopeless, believing she'd return. It felt so fucking final. Finding the bracelet was just the icing on his cake of pain. Dean was haunted by *stuff* at every turn. Her clothes still hung in the closet beside his own, a drawer in his dresser dedicated solely to her underwear and those nightgowns he wouldn't let her wear to his bed. He didn't let her wear anything to his bed. He'd have given her the whole goddamn dresser in retrospect, both closets, because that one drawer was jammed tight with lace and satin.

He would put out the eyes of anyone who witnessed it, but he fondled those articles of clothing and slept with one of her favorites under his pillow every night. The deep purple gossamer thing with the little straps that set off her warm, tanned skin and matched her amazing, expressive eyes before he took it off her. Witch eyes, his mother called them, all seeing, his bitch mother even then trying to foul what he and Amy were building. Well, Amy hadn't seen *his* shit coming, so couldn't guard against it. Goddamn it.

He itched to feel her thick blond hair beneath his hands, itched to push his fingers into it and hold her head steady, the better to plunder her lips and feel them around his cock. He missed his woman, with curves and some heft to her. A woman to lie on and lose oneself in. And she took everything he had to give her then gave it back. Loved him. She said it, didn't hold back, didn't play those games. Dean only ever said it to her that once, and she'd been asleep. He told her he didn't know what love was before, though, and what a message he'd given.

But it was the stuff in the bathroom trash making him crazy. He'd told Lois to stay away, not wanting anyone to touch Amy's things or interfere with her essence. So the garbage had piled up over the weeks and he hadn't noticed, wouldn't have picked up on it except he booted the can sideways in a fit of pique when he dropped his razor and it fell behind it. The contents spilled across the floor, tissues, an empty toothpaste tube, floss, the usual detritus. Amy hadn't managed to empty it before she left. Correction. Amy hadn't left, he'd thrown her out.

The home pregnancy test stood out like a beacon. He cursed and shovelled all the other crap away from it, his fingers snatching up the box, the label burning its message into his brain. Dean didn't know how long he crouched over the mess on the floor, staring at the innocuous box for further enlightenment. He'd crushed it in his hand and found himself wandering the condo, casting about for further sign. He didn't find any little white stick but he knew the truth anyhow.

Dean never ate in the dining room before Amy came into his life, and certainly not after he threw her out of it, so had no occasion to enter the damn space. He remembered staring at the place settings, and now knew Amy was going to share something momentous that fateful day. An announcement to be served up with that prime rib she'd prepared for him, left to moulder on the counter.

The revelation took his breath away. They'd made a baby together. He could have made her pregnant that first irresponsible, but oh-so-spontaneous time when he forgot to use protection for the first time in his life, and had thought to do by right by her. Taking her into his home, telling her they'd deal. Such a fucking cavalier attitude, because he really hadn't allowed himself to go there. But now she was indeed carrying his baby. It was no longer a case of if—and an unfathomable sense of utter delight, tempered by sheer terror, nearly put him on his knees.

Amy was God knew where, with little money and no job, a junker car, and his baby growing inside her. His personal punishment wasn't swift and just. It was slow, torturous and just. And nothing compared to what Amy had suffered, he was certain.

Cudgeling his brain and memory for any sign about her pregnancy came up empty. Maybe her breasts had been a little fuller, the nipples more sensitive, but he could be grasping at straws. She'd been really tired, and he had heard somewhere that was a sign. How could he have not noticed? *Because you never concerned yourself with her cycle, trusting her to take care of protection against pregnancy, lost in your lust and desire for her all the fucking time. Fucking irresponsible again.*

The idea of a baby in their lives, his son or daughter growing inside Amy, terrified him, while creating such excitement and anticipation he was vaguely nauseated with the mix of emotions. He decided he could approach it like he did everything else, with determination and great will. He'd do the job right, rise about his past and upbringing, be the best father possible. He didn't even stop to wonder if Amy would make a great mom. Nothing to wonder about. He'd never let her know he was anxious about being a good dad. He'd given her enough to worry about.

It hovered in the back of his mind, that brutally salient fact of why she was hiding from him. Amy was *afraid* he'd come looking for her, so she covered her tracks. Afraid he would find out her secret and come for her, not out of love but obligation. God help him. He'd progressed enough in this affair of the heart to understand that nuance.

Shoving his feet into his boots, Dean yanked the laces tight with barely suppressed violence. He couldn't just sit at home and do nothing no matter how exhausted he was. He needed to do something, anything. Fuck taking a day to regroup. He was going to rattle some cages. What he had just learned made it even more imperative. Calling Randy, he first confided the news, to his lieutenant's low whistle, muttered regret, and cautious congratulations. Then Dean told the man to pull in the trackers.

****

"There's no sign!" Forrest's attitude was actually tinged with a hint of resentment and Dean recognized he'd pushed too hard. The other man never failed to track his quarry and he was taking this loss with less than good grace. "I can't even find the fucking car she bought. She drove it off the lot and went north, or maybe northwest, depending on the day that shithead dealer is asked. The road splits just beyond his property and the only reason he even thinks Amy turned right is because he thought she was hot and paid attention."

Dean growled audibly and Forrest shut up. Dean pinned him with his eyes and asked, again, "And she didn't tell him anything? Not a slight, fucking idea about where she was headed?"

"She didn't seem to know. Seriously, Chambray. That little worm tried to hit on her and she wasn't evasive, or he'd be covering to save his pride. He said it was like she was sick or something, spacy, and just wanted to get it done. I told you."

Turning to Enrico, Dean fixed him with a stare, trying to ignore the sick reference. Amy had good reason to be sick. "You get anything else from Sandra?"

The slight, handsome young man shrugged with Latin grace, his dark eyes heating. "That one is formidable, sir. She cannot be read unless she chooses. But I do sense something, as of today."

"And you fucking well kept it to yourself?" Dean was on his feet, gripping the edge of his desk to suppress his need to vault over it and throttle Enrico.

Another shrug. “I have been trying, boss, but you have been interrogating us in order, it would appear.”

True. He had started with the trackers. Getting soft, because he’d heard that women who truly connected managed to keep that connection. Amy taught him that, with her intense loyalty to Sandra that was fully returned. “Tell me.”

“I have nothing but a feeling.”

“How long since you asked?”

“I stayed away for a week. Told her I was working.” A look twisted Enrico’s lips, almost too quick for Dean to read, but he intuited it. His best interrogator was fucking the source, and Dean’s conscience flickered. Sandra was a good person, a good friend to Amy, and neither would take kindly to Enrico using her. He quashed his guilt. Means to an end.

“So you got back into her bed and had this feeling?” He noted how Enrico’s eyes narrowed. Maybe something more going on there, than a means to an end.

“I asked her how her best friend was after a … a moment when she was more likely to … share.” A shift in the air surrounding Enrico made Dean choose his words carefully. He gestured for the other men to leave and Randy took Forrest away with a hand on his arm, talking about reimbursement and other jobs. He hadn’t lost sight of Dean’s position and the need to project confidence and stability. Brooks followed along.

“I’ll go see Sandra personally.”

Enrico nodded, his right fist clenching at his side, although he instantly loosened it. Dean studied him. The other man’s position should be reassessed. Lots of potential there. He balanced loyalty to Dean against an asunto del corazón with Sandra and Dean wouldn’t fuck him over. He stepped around the desk and spoke close to Enrico’s ear.

"An affair of the heart?"

"Si."

"She won't know from me."

"My thanks, sir."

Dean hustled after Forrest and Brooks. "Both of you stay close. If I get a hint, a direction, I want you both on it. Understand?"

Cautious nods. He wondered what his face looked like to garner such caution and if it reflected the molten anguish he battled within. He didn't give a shit. But then no one but he and Randy knew Amy was pregnant. And probably Sandra. *If* she was still pregnant. His gait stuttered, and the horrific pain in his chest took his breath, thinking that he might have lost their yet unborn child.

Dean couldn't imagine Amy terminating their baby, but he supposed she couldn't have imagined he'd kick her to the curb either. Shit. Just another self-administered form of torment for him to endure until he found her. Not when. Until. He had a clue and was putting every single fucking one of his eggs in this particular basket because there seemed no other leads.

"Randy."

His lieutenant materialized at the door. "I'll get the truck. It's in the lot. All the construction for the new curbs."

Dean snapped his attention to the faint sounds of pavement shattering beneath the pile drivers. "*I'll* get the truck. You call the city. This block was done last year."

"Fuck me." Randy narrowed his eyes. "Glad you came down today."

Of late, the mostly legal businesses he ran in this corner of the city were doing really well, despite the economy, but his other services remained unfavorably looked upon by either the law or the competition. The police were usually predictable despite the distance he had to keep, and the competition varied with every coup. Right now, his rivals were a loose cabal of wannabe wiseguys trying to move in where Burnett had failed. Dean's sources kept him abreast of their efforts and he'd need to step on a couple in a while, but they weren't yet a real threat. He wondered if that shadowy head man was still circling.

But no way did the city replace curbs twice in two years, so it was the law putting its nose in. Shit. He didn't have time for this. He thought he'd sorted things when he moved Burnett along. Pulling his cell out of his pocket he found Minor's contact and pressed it, heading back into his office, shutting the door.

"Yeah."

"No name, don't talk. I doubt they've had time to set up to snoop, but somebody reneged."

Silence. Two beats. Dean continued. "I have something to take care of, but my second's here. Text him when you know." There was no question Minor wouldn't do as he was asked. He owed Dean big, forever, and Dean didn't ask much of him. The bigger worry was if the other man had been cut out of the loop, or was being set up. Well, Minor was smart and wouldn't get caught easily, witnessed by his rise through the ranks. And if he'd been burned, then they'd soon know. Dean severed the connection and went to collect the truck keys. Randy was already on the phone, complaining to some clerk about the noise and inconvenience, demanding to be shuttled to a supervisor. He nodded and went out the door, leaving his lieutenant to sort it out.

Was it his imagination or did the hard hats pause in their tasks to survey him? Did the cacophony of noise ease a trifle? Dean dismissed the thoughts. If they put someone on him he'd know. The truck locks clicked open in blind obedience to the remote and he swung into the sun warmed interior, the hot leather seat cradling him, the cold, empty feeling deep inside his gut such a marked contrast. No. He was going to find her. Nobody stayed hidden forever.

****

The motel was like a way station in her life. While the nagging pain in her heart was omnipresent and the burgeoning life in her belly, with all its impact on her day-to-day living, an inescapable reminder of her recent past, Amy put her head in the sand of kindness and acceptance and got on with it. She took great pains with her diet and took prenatal vitamins after seeing a doctor at a walk-in clinic. He was kind, if harried, and after confirming the pregnancy, offered to refer her to an OB-GYN. She'd declined the referral for the moment, not knowing where she hoped to be in the next while, and took a handful of pamphlets outlining prenatal care.

She remembered calling Sandra before the full month's timeline was up, maybe a week ago. Playing chauffeur for Francine, first to the doctor for a follow up visit, and then to a lunch date with a small group of friends, Amy was overcome with the intense need to check in. Francine and her cronies laughed and talked and giggled, drank and ate with joy and abandon, the camaraderie of the sisterhood. It was too much for Amy to bear.

Sitting in the car, she'd placed the call, desperate for the connection, closing her eyes with happiness at the sound of her friend's voice. She had caught Sandra going out the door to work, but the five minutes of catching up a little was worth its weight in gold, and the risk of using her cell minimal. They were miles from the motel.

"I'm so relieved to hear from you, Amy! I've been worried sick. Are you sure you're okay? And the baby?"

"I'm good, Sandra, honestly. Landed on my feet for sure. This little critter is doing some stuff to me, but according to the information out there, it's to be expected. All normal. I'm taking good care. Diet, vitamins, lots of rest. I have to see a baby doctor, I know it. Are you okay?"

"Fine. Just missing you. Work is good." Sandra hesitated and Amy waited.

"Dean is looking for you, honey. He apparently figured out he screwed up and wants to talk to you."

Choosing her words carefully, not wanting to ask Sandra how Dean looked, if he was okay, Amy replied. "Can't go there, Sandra. I won't be able to trust him again and now there's more than just me to consider. I might let him use me as an emotional punching bag, but not the baby."

"You think he'd be cruel to the baby?"

"No. But he'd lash out against me and shit rolls down hill. I'm not allowing it. Somebody has to consider the vulnerable." Unlike what both she and Dean had experienced in childhood.

"Well, you'll have to make that decision, honey. Better you than me. He's apparently anxious, though. And he doesn't know you're pregnant so…"

Amy believed she'd convinced her friend she was well and content, coping with life, and she daren't rip the gossamer bandage off her broken heart. She avoided giving any hint of her whereabouts to spare Sandra further subterfuge, promising to call again. She was homesick, and admitted to feeling some relief that Dean was anxious, that his memory of her wasn't besmirched by betrayal. Unlike hers of him. And she'd taken the battery out of her phone again, successfully managing not to check her voice mail.

Running the hotel, engaging in the routine while Harold and Francine were away, soothed her. Up early to fix a non stomach-upsetting breakfast, checking for reservations, helping Joyce if the need arose, welcoming and checking in guests, ensuring the lobby was tidy and appealing. She ate her other meals whenever it made sense, and when she was hungry, in between the parts of the job, like ordering supplies and taking phone calls. It was steady work, not onerous, and wasn't really boring with the exception of the long periods of time between guests arriving and departing. People watching became her thing, from behind the boundary of the counter. There were a few late calls, fewer in the night, and for minor things, like batteries for the remote.

Her bosses called every day, but Amy didn't get the sense they were checking up on her. Their brief holiday was marred by inclement weather, but Harold was determined Francine rest and use the time away wisely. She found herself missing them, like the family she didn't remember. Joyce didn't have much time to chat, but sometimes they'd have a coffee, tea for Amy now. The other woman was overtly curious, but not in a malicious way and was easily diverted. All in all, it was a wonderful opportunity to regroup.

The ping of the bell over the door jarred her from her reverie, yanking her into the present. A young man in a dark uniform pushed through into the lobby, hefting a toolbox. "Tom, from Western Cable and Ethernet."

It didn't seem possible so much time had passed while she was off in her head. Amy showed him the rough map she'd drawn of the motel property, complete with measurements obtained from Harold before he left. It was an easy install, so Tom assured her, and set to work. Amy organized the paperwork and entered it into the old computer. She hoped to encourage her bosses to invest in a new one after the carpet installation, but attempted to throttle back on her involvement. It hadn't escaped her notice that Harold and Francine saw her as a pseudo-daughter, seeing as their only child, Louise, died of cancer years ago. You should never outlive your children, she mused, feeling badly for the pair. She was honored to have them as adoptive parents, albeit for a short time.

Her own child wasn't yet really noticeable, at least not to people who hadn't known her before. Amy noticed her waist thickening a trifle, her breasts a bit larger, the nipples certainly more sensitive, and her stomach often dipped and roiled in reaction to certain foods and teeth brushing, but she wasn't quite three months along. Close though. The purchased prenatal vitamins were tucked out of sight in a drawer, as she wasn't yet ready to share with Harold and Francine. And Joyce would shriek the news to the heavens. In any event, she soon needed to find a place to live more permanently in order to find a doctor. Lots of things to consider. She was cautiously examining the combined fear and elation of impending motherhood. Alone.

"Miss? Want to test signal strength? I've tied in with the phone service."

Amy logged on and was pleased with the result. "Hang on a second." Poking her head out the lobby door, she spied Joyce's cart two units down. It took barely a minute to rap on the door and for Joyce to pull it open.

"Hey, Amy!"

"Keep an eye on the desk, Joyce, please. I'm going to take my laptop to the last unit and test signal strength. It's empty right?"

"Sure is. I'll head straight to the office. You're sure yanking The Restaway into this century. Not sure our guests will value wireless but—"

Joyce was still talking when she disappeared into the office. Amy grabbed her laptop, locking her room door behind her, heading to number twenty. Another couple of minutes and she was satisfied. She badly wanted to check her email account, having dispatched explanatory notices to present clients, refunding their money where appropriate. But she didn't want to be tempted into opening one that would give her whereabouts away. She knew Randy's skills. The FBI couldn't track her down as quickly.

All of her hours alone in the queen sized bed in Unit One, the ones when she wasn't actually sleeping, were fraught with memories of Dean. Oh, she fought them, and usually managed to banish them behind that mythical wall she built, for a time. Then his face would pop up and display on the back of her eyelids, yanking her out of preparation for sleep. The memory of his hands on her, inside her, his mouth … and his cock, driving her over the edge. The most disconcerting thing was waking in front of the door, hands pressed flat, forehead resting between them against the cool surface. Wanting to go to Dean. Looking for him. It happened time and again, interrupting her fitful rest.

And she was so tired all the time, anyhow. It was a good thing her job wasn't onerous, and afternoon naps were sometimes possible. Amy missed Dean fiercely, at least the man who didn't wear that murderous expression the last time she saw him. She missed being with him, missed the sex. Amy tried not to pleasure herself to fantasies about Dean, but she did, coming hard, shuddering against her release, but without any joy. She hated him, too.

"I think it's good, Tom." She set her laptop down on the counter and nodded to the tech. Joyce hurried out, calling her farewells.

"I'll leave my card. Be sure to call if anything needs adjusting." He chuckled. "That lady thinks it's magic and incantations."

Amy smiled, too. Tom packed up and headed out and she turned her attention back to the never ending paperwork.

## Chapter Eleven

"So she called me." Sandra stomped past Dean and dumped her coffee into the sink, turning the tap on full to rinse it. She was wrapped in a robe, and he supposed she'd worked the night shift, so that meant he'd woken her. Certainly she looked tired, as anyone would after just a couple hours of sleep. "How did you know?"

"I didn't. But I guessed she'd call you at some point so I planned to keep checking." He didn't want to drop Enrico in the shit. He chose to stand in the middle of her kitchen, forcing her to find a way around him as she moved. "How is she, Sandra?"

"Okay."

"I know she's pregnant."

Silence reigned, broken only by the soft gurgle of the remainder of the water as it swirled down the drain, and the humming of the fridge. Sandra stared at him, a myriad of emotions flashing in her eyes. "Who told you?"

"I found the test. I didn't know if it was positive or not, although I hoped…So thanks for confirming it."

Unable to pretend anymore, he slumped into the nearest chair, and passed a hand over his face. "I've been going insane."

Dean didn't give a shit about macho male posturing at that moment, wasn't afraid to show his feelings. If he thought he could shake the information out of Sandra he would, but he knew better. And Enrico wasn't a man to cross, despite his youth. Sandra was young too, about Amy's age, maybe a couple of years older, and surely, he could appeal to her soft side.

"She's fine. She didn't want you to know because you'd pull this."

"Pull what?" He worked hard to keep the threat from his voice.

"Hunt her down because you knocked her up. Your kid and all. Male pride." Sandra's voice was derisive, but Dean detected a plea buried beneath the snark. A plea for him to dispute her.

"I'm looking for her because I fucked up, Sandra. I was searching before I knew about the baby. You fucking know that. I didn't trust Amy and that was fucking stupid. I kicked her out. I kicked my pregnant woman out of our home."

"And you took this long to come and tell me this? You sent your boy instead?"

Dean shook his head. "I just found out. Home pregnancy test in the garbage. I've been looking for her since the day after I threw her out, Sandra. A baby just ups the ante. Help me."

Sinking down at the kitchen table, Sandra dropped her face into the cradle of her hands. Dean sat opposite her and waited. He knew a battle of conscience when he saw one. Despite his history, he, too, struggled from time to time, moreso since his relationship with Amy had developed into something serious. She was so earnest in her belief of the golden rule. Without the *eye for an eye* part, unless he was mixing his parables.

The words, when they came, were muffled. "I don't know where she is, but I know she's not living. She's in some kind of twilight state. She sounded like a freaking cheerleader, all fake happy. Desperate." Sandra raised her head and locked eyes with him. "Amy loves you, Dean. She was the making of you. And you completed her."

Nothing he didn't know. Nothing he hadn't tortured himself with, but the additional flagellation by Sandra's wasp tongue was expected. She loved Amy, too, and hadn't betrayed her. Dean heard her out, holding onto his temper, being as patient as he knew. "I know it,

Sandra. All of it. I need to find her. She needs me, especially now."

"I'll try, when she calls again. Maybe she'll listen."

"Tell me about the call." He wasn't leaving until he heard everything.

"She called, said she was fine. Bullshit. I told you. She's working and the people are kind."

"What kind of work?" Dean asked every question occurring to him, dissected every word Sandra remembered, to no avail. He froze. "Did she call you on her cell?"

"I don't know. Maybe. Why?"

Damn it. Amy's phone had been offline for weeks. Dean believed she'd either tossed it, lost it, or hadn't bought another charger, the one for her little cell still plugged in by the nightstand. He pulled out his own.

"Randy? Get Lee to do the GPS search again. Use his contacts with the provider. Amy called Sandra and might have used her cell." He confirmed the date with Sandra and passed it on. Amy hadn't cracked her computer that they'd been able to tell—certainly she hadn't opened even one of the emails he'd sent and asked Randy and Andrea send, not that Andrea wasn't already reaching out.

"Will do. And Dean? You were right about the city not doing those fucking curbs. I'll meet you at the usual place and we'll talk."

Fuck. It never rained, but it poured. "I'll be there. Pull someone in to sweep the place." He turned to Sandra, watching him with a peculiar expression on her face. Dean raised a brow as he shut the call down.

"You're a ruthless son of a bitch, Dean Chambray. You think you're able to juggle your various lives right now, but at some point it'll come down to the job or Amy again. You think on that. And tell that Enrico not to come around. He's got your stamp on him. I'm not going down that path."

Dean nodded. Sandra was nothing if not clear, and her assessment of his lifestyle right on the money. Maybe not so young after all, and as world-weary as Amy. But he couldn't sort it out until he knew what was going down, and Amy was his priority.

"You'll have to tell Enrico yourself, Sandra," he said as gently as he could, marking the twist of pain on her face. "I'll have her call when I find her."

****

Randy was already waiting for him at the bar. Dean had picked up a tail about four blocks from the place, so they were cruising, looking for him. He slid into the booth and the waitress brought him a beer.

"Minor says it's some joker in the district attorney's office looking to climb the ladder. The guy's related to some police official and they're stroking him, letting him mount an investigation. Lord knows where he got your name in his sights. The asshole's creative." Randy rolled the bottom of the bottle across the coaster, the condensation marking the paper in little half circles.

Dean nodded. "How long?"

"Maybe another three days. There's no will behind the asshole and the money and personnel will soon run out. The sweep found nothing, but Olsen turned an electrician away the day before yesterday. Wrong address. He remarked on it. I didn't pay attention. My fault."

"Enough fucking blame to go around, Randy. Let it go. We'll let the asshole's party play out, maybe point him at Unez. He thinks he's my latest up-and-coming competition. The two of them can dance."

Randy nodded. "Should be easy enough. I'll have a couple of the guys draw them a map to Unez' place when he's meeting with his crew." A bark of a laugh. "With any luck there'll be some stupid who acts out and the cops will have something to train on. Now I can get back to looking for our leak. Whoever it is, I'm not even getting a hint, but he'll crawl out of his hole at some point."

Dean nodded. If anyone could track that dead man down, Randy could. He asked his lieutenant the pressing question. "Amy?"

"She used her cell. Got a placement. Not an exact location but a block spread. Might need to wait for her to call again."

"No. I'll canvass myself once I lose my tail. She might have already moved on, but Sandra said she's working so that speaks to her living there. I'm not waiting." He only hoped she hadn't driven far away from her new home to place the call.

"Well, good hunting, buddy." His right hand man looked pensive for a moment, and furrowed his brow. "Amy might not be interested in coming back."

"I won't be giving her the choice, Randy. I'll put fucking locks on the apartment if I have too."

"Oh, man. This isn't like when we held those guys until the siege broke."

Dean nodded. "No, this is about bringing my woman home and spending time until she forgives me. I'm bringing her home, and I'm not letting her go."

Silence. Dean didn't think his plan was unsound. Finally, Randy spoke. "Okay, then. But if you fail, and from the way Amy reacted that day, you just might, it could bring you down. You'll leave the business open to a coup because you'll be with her to keep her calmed down, or you'll be in jail on kidnapping charges."

"Noted." Dean took the coordinates and went home to pack a bag.

Trading his ride for an SUV at a prearranged point, he ditched the half-hearted efforts of the tail. One of his crew, similar in size and coloring, swerved the truck into traffic, following orders to return to the office after a lengthy scenic trip. Dean sat behind the wheel of the black SUV and watched his vehicle, and the blue sedan, convoy down the street before turning in the opposite direction, the GPS programmed. He thought about Randy's warning. His second in command was right and Dean knew it. He could ill afford to take a lengthy time period away from the business given the recent interest by the bureaucrat, and kidnapping Amy might not be the best plan in the long run.

But he knew his woman. She'd have talked herself out of them as a couple to protect herself—and their baby—from what he'd done, and Amy was stubborn. Stubborn in her refusal to give up on him, insisting he was a good person, a man she had total faith in to make the right choices in life, do the right things in the end. She didn't approve of his shadier business activities, yet didn't nag him or dwell over much on that side of his life because she had faith and accepted what she couldn't change without considerable consequences, aware of the balance in life. He regretted, more than ever, never finding the right time to tell her the whole story. She'd simply accepted his edict to get gone, delivered as it had been. That stubbornness alone might defeat a lesser man.

The miles flew by, and not just because of his heavy foot. Dean thought of the scenarios he might be faced with, would have to address, deal with. Worse case was that Amy found a protector, and Dean might be forced to do something drastic, something she would definitely object to. He decided not to consider that scenario, because it was his possessiveness talking, his crippling need for her. It was too early in the game for Amy to be with anyone else, if he deserved any luck at all.

Best case, she was working a job, living hand to mouth, and could be extricated without much fuss. The people she worked for might be kind, but kindness was no obstacle or consideration for him when it came to bringing her home.

The pretty city streets of Santa Rosa soon enveloped the SUV. He saw the coordinates coming up and slowed his speed, spirits sinking when the strip mall came into view. Shit. Fuck. At least thirty stores, a couple of restaurants, a bowling alley and some office space. Not to mention a few decrepit houses on the edge of the mall property and across the street. The good news was, it wasn't all private housing; sometimes it was difficult to persuade a homeowner to allow access. Dean decided Amy must have called Sandra while at work, just to be optimistic. He parked the vehicle and pulled up a Google map to reconnoiter from overhead, noting the relative compactness of his search area. He'd start with a restaurant, feed the inner man and work his way from there. Maybe he *should have* brought a few of his crew.

****

"More coffee?" The waitress smiled at him, an obvious come on. Dean didn't have time for it, although could have charmed the information out of her. He shook his head and reached for his wallet.

"I'll just bring your bill." A hint of snip in her tone.

Sighing inwardly, Dean gave her his best *get on your knees* look. It never failed, except sometimes with Amy. The waitress blinked and tried another smile. He pulled the picture of Amy out and showed it, pulling one up on his phone, too.

"Private investigator. Looking for this woman." He'd decided to play it as it felt right, and looking for his *wife* wouldn't work with Susie the waitress. Amy wasn't his wife yet, but she would be.

Susie took the little square of celluloid with fastidious care, scanning it. "Is she in trouble?"

Trouble? Or maybe needed to be found because of an inheritance? Amnesia? Trouble, he decided. Amy was too beautiful for this woman to feel kindness toward. "Took off with something that didn't belong to her."

"Oh. And *you're* looking for her? Not the police?" Well, there was that. Susie apparently wasn't stupid.

"The owner is impatient." True.

"I see. Well, she doesn't eat here, or at least not as a regular. I'd remember."

"Can you check with the other staff?' Dean hinted about a reward. Susie obligingly took the picture to the other waitresses and even showed it to the cook.

"Nobody remembers her." A trace of sadness in her voice, but over the money, Dean was certain. "Do you want to leave your number?"

He dropped a business card into her outstretched hand, along with the money for the food and a fair sized tip. She squinted at the card in an unattractive manner. "Dean Chambray? Investment and Insurance services? I thought you said—"

"This *is* about an investment, Susie. Call me if you see her and I'll make it worth your while."

Dean tossed his napkin on the table and pushed up from his chair, aware of the woman's assessing gaze. He could only imagine the number of acquaintances he'd make before the day was out. A wave of worry leached his strength for an instant. What if he couldn't locate her? He couldn't stand to think of waiting much longer, couldn't bear the idea of not seeing his child grow beneath her heart. His concern for her, always present, had soared exponentially since learning she was pregnant and dealing with it herself. Squaring his shoulders he made his way out the door, back on an even keel. If he couldn't find her, she'd eventually call Sandra again, and her friend would do the right thing. Talk Amy into coming home or tell him so he could make it so.

****

The hotel bed groaned beneath his weight as Dean fell back onto the cushioned surface, droplets of water still beading on his skin. He'd pulled a pair of boxers on after his shower and thought to rest his sore feet before going out for a late dinner. He then considered ordering room service, but there were only two more restaurants to canvass at that fucking strip mall and it was still relatively early. Who knew the number of stores that could be shoved into each nook and cranny of the concrete structure? Who knew the amount of *stuff* available for sale in this great country? And the people working in them… Dean thought dealing with the criminal element was a shit job. But sales had to be the worst.

Staff either ignored him or were on him like white on rice. The shoe stores and women's apparel were a dark hell. The good news was it didn't take very long to ask and he doggedly persevered, adjusting his approach accordingly, showing Amy's picture. With no hits. Not even a hint of recognition. The guy in the gags and costume place nailed it.

"She's something, buddy. I'd be looking for her, too. You think anything happened to her for sure? I hope not. She in love with the person taking that picture, maybe?"

Dean hadn't taken the picture, but she'd been looking at him when the camera caught the expression on her beautiful face. He rubbed his eyes with his knuckles and rolled off the bed onto his feet, resigned to staying the night and resuming his search in the morning if necessary. It was unlikely anyone at the remaining restaurants would know Amy—were other people in the restaurant business kinder than Susie? Was his woman waiting tables, or cooking? She'd taken to the happy housewife role like a duck to water, surprising herself, but confiding how much she liked it. Keeping his home, taking care of him, serving him because she trusted him never to abuse it, and to give back what she needed, to take care of her. And he had, right until he'd fucked it up royally. Time to move and quit berating himself. People might be home in those houses by now. She might even live in one.

Pulling a fresh shirt on, he yanked up his jeans and sat to slide a pair of socks over his aching feet before lacing up his boots. He made a quick call to Randy to check on the status of events back home.

"Same old, buddy. But I got word the pressure is lifting. You?"

"Haven't got a hint, Randy. Nothing. She might have just stopped around here to call Sandra." Dean heard the desperation leaking over in his own voice.

"There's always Sandra, Dean. It's been a month. Those two won't stay quiet for too much longer. A day never passed without contact, right?"

Dean supposed Randy was correct. It spoke to Amy's stubbornness and determination to avoid him though, that she hadn't called Sandra before. She was protecting her friend, ever loyal. Loyalty. Right. He should take a course. Although loyalty was earned, not learned.

"I'm heading back to eat at the mall where she called from. I've caught all the stores, but I want to try a couple restaurants and the housing across the street after dinner."

"Want a crew to help? They can be there in a few."

"I have to do this myself, Randy. It's not about sending my men to bring Amy home. She's not part of the business." And she'd hate him worse. "And Randy? Give some thought that shit keeps descending whenever I'm distracted by my woman. First Burnett pulls that shit, then I'm taking some time away to fucking rejuvenate and the law takes notice."

Silence. "Fuck. I'll think on it, Dean. Later." Randy hung up.

Dean contemplated the stereotypical hotel carpet for a couple of minutes. Like any cop, he didn't like the smell of coincidences. But he would finish the search before heading back. If he couldn't get this done he'd blanket the area next time she called, and they locked down her location. Maybe he should have a crew on standby. And just how desperate was he? That desperate. He'd make it happen.

****

"Sure. Tall, built, blonde, right? Sweet girl, too." The skinny bartender polished another glass and slid it into the rack above his head, apparently oblivious to Dean coming to attention like a bird-dog on point. A lethal bird-dog. "She looked after Francine real good. The old girl'd been sick for awhile and wanted to kick lose, drink too much. Blondie wouldn't let her, but in a really nice way."

Tiny black spots swirled in Dean's vision as he forgot to breathe. Not possible. Couldn't be this easy. He focused. Casually, he said, "So she took good care of Francine?" Dean tried the name out on his tongue. Francine.

"Yup. Fran and her girls come in about once a month for lunch. They raise a little hell but it's kinda mild, ya know what I mean. Blondie's first time. Think she drove Francine in that old Merc."

"Know where I might find Francine?" Dean knew he wasn't doing casual well any longer, and the bartender really looked at him.

"What'd you say you wanted Blondie for?"

Dean could feel the attention they were drawing, a couple of wait staff looking their way, the few other patrons becoming interested, wanting their beverages. He hurried to explain, lowering his voice. He had no clout here and finesse was part of who he could be anyhow. "Blondie's name is Amy. She went missing a few weeks ago and her family and friends got worried."

"ID." Not a request, the bartender's brow furrowing with apparent disbelief.

Dean worked a card out of his wallet, having yet to pay for his beer. He pushed it across the bar.

"Investment and Insurance Services. What you do?"

"Real estate and consulting, business opportunities and research." Not a lie, really not even stretching the truth. "Amy was part of the organization." Again, not a lie. Dean strove to look reputable and harmless, no small feat for a six-foot-four, two hundred and twenty pound man with lean muscle and a face that told a story of never backing down from the hard knocks of life. He worked hard at not clenching his fists.

"She looked okay to me. Maybe she's making a different life. Doesn't want to be found."

Suppressing the urge to throttle the other man, Dean leaned back on the stool. "If she's okay, that's good to know. She doesn't want to return to her old life, I'll take the message back and leave it alone." Fat chance. "But I need to see her in person to be certain. In case someone is influencing her."

After an eternity of polishing, the man spoke, thin face thoughtful. "I don't know where Francine is at just now." He raised the cloth at Dean's instant protest. "I know Martha though, and I'll give her a call."

Dean suffered through the stereotypical greetings of the phone call to Martha, and the social drivel that followed. Apparently Martha knew her way around a wine bottle or two. Shades of his mother. The receiver was shoved his way as the bartender went to serve someone else, and a querulous voice spoke loudly in his ear. "Francine went on a holiday. She'll be back tomorrow. Can't leave the motel too long, even if she's got good help and the weather's the pits where they're at. So they're on the road. Tell Bobby your number and he'll pass it along to me tomorrow." A hollow click signalled Martha's unavailability.

Gritting his teeth, Dean considered his options. He could probably persuade Bobby to give him Martha's address and find out where this Francine lived, but that would draw more attention and waste time. A patient man when it suited him, Dean had reached his limit, what with the possibility of finding Amy so close. He pulled the phone closer, straining the long cord to its limit, and punched in the numbers to retrieve Martha's number while Bobby's attention was elsewhere. When the bartender returned, Dean decided not to leave his card, sliding it across the polished surface of the bar, flicking it into a pocket. No point in giving anyone a direction to look if he found Amy tonight and returned her home. A rescue attempt by a bunch of old ladies was just bizarre enough to attract the wrong kind of attention and bring down trouble. He was just relieved Amy was all right and had obviously fallen in with *kind* people, to quote her in absentia.

A reverse directory check on his phone found Martha Clarke almost instantly. Dean hustled out to the SUV, his dinner order forgotten. His strides slowed as he considered cutting out the middleman. He called Randy.

"Do a search for mom-and-pop motels, hotels in Santa Rosa. Look for the name Francine." Randy had access to a variety of computers and search engines simultaneously and Dean wanted his expertise. He forced himself to sit stoically, drumming his fingers on the wheel, staring at nothing in particular, marshalling his strength. His cell rang.

"Francine Bower nee Cavers and Harold Bower. Co-owners of The Restaway Inn on Provencher and LaValle, phone number 707-555-7378. You found her?"

"Think so. I'm heading over there right now."

"Dean?"

"What, Randy?"

"Watch your step with that girl."

Dean clicked off without comment. Randy didn't need to worry. Dean would do right by Amy, do what was in her best interest. She might not agree with him, but he wasn't leaving her to cope, alone. His bag was back in the hotel, but there was nothing in it he needed, and the credit card he used to guarantee the room would be charged and that would be the end of it. He programmed the GPS and pulled out of the lot to go get his woman.

## Chapter Twelve

Amy sat tall and stretched, easing off the stool Harold thoughtfully provided for her behind the counter. All expected guests had already checked in and the motel was full up. No special requests, and lots of approving comments about the wireless. Check out was eleven, with no one asking for a late one, and tomorrow's reservations were light anyhow. She frowned, then remembered it was mid-week and there might be a few drive-ups. Reaching over to the switch on the wall, Amy flicked the No Vacancy sign on and looked to ensure the old neon lit up. A dark SUV pulled up to the curb and idled, but no one got out. Probably somebody making a phone call.

She'd been staying in her boss's suite since they left, in order to respond to any guest calls or arrivals later in the evenings and right now she wanted her dinner, leftover lasagne from lunch with a spinach salad. And a tall glass of milk.

Hopefully, everyone was buttoned down for the night. She expected Harold and Francine back tomorrow afternoon, the couple cutting their vacation a little bit short because of the weather. Francine apparently took the incessant rain personally, and Harold's muttered imprecations were audible in the background when the older woman called.

The old computer was in sleep mode and Amy opened the little drawer holding the keys to the front door. She tended to lock up around this time. Guests could use the buzzer or call the desk if they needed anything. Both could be heard in the living quarters, and there was a phone extension available in their kitchen. Tired beyond belief, she turned, making her way around the counter to the door when it opened, the bell announcing the arrival of someone who hadn't read the no vacancy sign. Damn it. Now she'd have to point them in the direction of other lodging. She pasted a smile on her face and saw him.

Amy's breath caught in her throat, her sex drew up, her belly clenched and her head swam. She quit cataloguing her reaction to Dean as his tall, muscular form filled the doorway, shades of that fateful day. But his face was quite different. A certain watchfulness layered his features but his eyes were that calm, clear gray of tenderness, something he showed only her. Amy backed up, slowly, as if from an unpredictable wild animal until her back came up against the wall.

"Amy." Dean crossed the room toward her, moving slowly, but with purpose. It rolled off him in waves. She shook her head against an overwhelming sense of powerlessness before he was on her, pulling her tightly against him, fisting one of his big hands in her hair. Pulling her head back, he stared deeply into her eyes, face descending until his mouth took hers.

She resisted with the passivity projected by shock, her thoughts swirling to finally coalesce into a moment of clarity. *No!* She couldn't get away from the embrace. Dean was too strong, and he held her so tightly the button on his jacket imprinted her skin right through the fabric of her shirt. His cock swelled against her pelvis, that long, hard length a pressing reminder of his potent possession, the proof residing beneath her heart.

Pulling his lips from hers he stepped back a short pace, her lack of response apparently making his eyes narrow, the silver shade of annoyance encroaching on the tenderness. Then it disappeared with the placement of his big right palm on her abdomen. Amy bit back a moan. He knew. How could Sandra have done this to her? The betrayal made her faintly nauseous.

"What do you need to pack, sweetheart?"

"What?" His familiar scent was surrounding her, lulling her, his proximity dismantling her pathetic barriers.

"We're going home."

Okay. Enough. Amy drew both hands up to chest height and pushed with every bit of strength she possessed. Dean actually stepped back, enough to give her space to breathe and regroup.

"I'm not going anywhere."

"Get your shit, Amy. I'm not going to argue with you about this."

She supposed her language would be something to throttle back on when her baby was born. Children tended to repeat what they overheard, but that was a long time off. "Fuck you, Dean. You aren't the big man here."

His face tightened, lips firming. Amy tore her eyes away from the seductive promise of that mouth and tried to push past him. His long arms came up and caged her against the wall.

"Don't need to be the big man, Amy. I came to take you home and that's what I'm doing. As for the other, we'll get to that."

She lost it. No excuse. She simply lost it, reacting to his arrogance and to her own impending weakness. Dean manacled her right wrist but not before her nails sliced into his cheek. He blocked the frantic lift of her knee with his thigh, using the bulk of his body to restrain her until the furious rage fueling her brief outburst subsided. Amy sagged, drained, and Dean turned with her in his arms to perch her on the stool. The furrows she'd dug on his face welled with blood and she willed nausea back, wondering how she'd ever come to do him harm. He snatched a tissue from the box on the desk and pressed it against his face to staunch the blood, but his concern was for her.

"Where can I get you something to drink?"

Shaking her head, "I don't want anything to drink. I want you to leave me alone."

"Not going to happen, sweetheart. We'll pick up something on the road."

"I. Am. Not. Going. Any. Where. With. You."

She felt him take a deep breath, and his shoulders straightened. "You want to leave your shit behind, I guess that's your call."

Amy struggled to contain herself and reason with an unreasonable man. "I have a job. I can't just walk out on people who *trust* me."

She had the pleasure of seeing Dean wince, although she took no real enjoyment in wielding the word like a weapon. But it was all she had.

"Francine's coming back tomorrow or close to it. Don't deny it. I heard it from a reliable source. Call someone to hold the fort. Or don't. But we're leaving. You don't want me or any of my crew around these nice folks."

Her breath sawed in and out of her lungs at the not so subtle threat. This was not happening. For sure Harold and Francine didn't need the shit Dean could bring just with his presence. She tried to waylay him. "We should talk about this."

"No dice, sweetheart. We'll talk when you're home, where you can't run."

"That's not your call, Dean. You threw me out. Threatened me. You didn't stop to consider—"

"And I regret that, more than you'll ever know. I'll make it up to you. Now, last chance, Amy."

"Did I stutter? Maybe I did, because you aren't hearing me. I am not going back with you. Don't you fucking push me."

His big body tensed further, and far different emotions cracked the arrogant façade. "Amy. Please. I'm not going to go away. If you know anything, you know I'm telling you where I stand."

And

She did know. He'd be in her face—and Francine and Harold's—day in and out. She read his intent and couldn't stand against it. She accepted the immediate reality. There would be another opportunity, and she'd take care not to involve anyone else like the Bowers.

Harold and Francine would be home tomorrow, and she should stay to tell them, give her notice, but she couldn't face them. What could she say? That her … boyfriend … no, that felt too simple a label for Dean. That her former … lover and man of her dreams could cause them grief by his very presence if she didn't leave?

"All right. Let go of me. I have to make some arrangements in order to leave." She tried not to believe that there was relief and … happiness … softening on his features.

Picking up the phone she called Joyce, aware of Dean watching her intently, listening hard, as his hand drifted over her back in a curiously comforting manner.

She steeled her body against his touch.

"A family emergency? Oh, honey. I'll come straight over. You just put a sign up on the door telling people it'll be about thirty minutes and get yourself going. I'll stay and see if my niece will help with the rooms—oh, listen to me carrying on, thinking out loud. I'll tell Francine tomorrow and you come back as soon as you can. Drive safe."

Amy numbly set the receiver back in the charger, wondering when she'd become such a facile liar, and looked at Dean's handsome face, the scoring of her fingernails marring his cheek.

"Done? Where's your stuff?" Impatience colored his tone, but she could feel the tension, as though he was questioning himself.

"I'm in Unit One." He was once again an insurmountable force, like the tide, inflexible, wearing. Amy wanted to surrender, let him take charge and carry her along with him, take care of her and their child. It seemed she had no will and that infuriated her, stiffening her spine. *He didn't trust you! And he won't trust you again.* He shadowed her while she locked up and turned off lights, attaching the little sign Joyce suggested to the door, right above where the hours of operation were indicated. His action made her angrier. They met no one during the short walk to her room but she continued to catalogue possible opportunities to circumvent him. None readily occurred.

Emptying the closet and dresser, folding her paltry belongings into a small pile on the bed, setting her toiletries on top, took such little time. Dean pulled the empty bag from the trash can and held it while she placed her belongings inside. Bogs' glass eyes blinked up at her from the depths. And wasn't that a reminder of the fact of her transitory existence? Every move brought her closer to hopeless despair but she refused to cry. The weak part of her, her heart, urged her to let go but her pride shrieked in outrage. Pretty hard to have a relationship without trust. She shoved her laptop into her purse and made to put the strap over her head.

"I'll carry that, Amy. And the bag."

Goddamn him. He wasn't leaving her an out. Even if she managed to run, she'd have nothing to fall back on. She passed her purse over, mute with outrage and he put it beside the bag of clothes.

"Use the facilities, sweetheart. We won't be making any rest stops." His voice was gentle, probably because he was getting his own way. She couldn't let herself soften.

Stepping into the bathroom, Amy closed the door, forcing herself to shut it quietly, without fanfare. She wasn't wasting an ounce of precious energy. She'd need it all. After washing her hands, she placed her hands on the counter and stared into the mirror. A flushed face reflected back, the purple iris of her eyes nearly eclipsed by the wide pupils. She saw resolve and swallowed hard, pushing everything else aside. A survivor. Dean had no idea, although she once thought he had understood. She pushed off and turned to open the door, stepping through, avoiding his sharp stare. Fuck him.

"Give me your hand, sweetheart." Oh, the endearments. Trying to make his dominance more palatable. Fuck him. She hid her hands behind her back, a childish gesture and as futile.

"I'm not going to risk you acting out on the way to the vehicle. Give me your hand."

The feel of his big, calloused palm wrapping around her much smaller one was sufficient enough for her body to awaken yet again, remembering his touch. She hated her response.

"Don't disappoint me, Amy. You walk with me and get in the car." The silken threat caused her nipples to bead painfully behind her practical bra, purchased to support the enlarging future sustenance of her child. *Her* child.

As if he read her mind, Dean said. "I'm still fucked up over the fact you're pregnant and weren't planning to tell me. Who in hell has been taking care of you?"

Was he fucking insane? His behavior just underscored her reluctance, the prick. Amy breathed against energy sucking rage. She stared at him, not trusting herself to answer without bursting into impotent tears.

His voice gentled. "My ass nearly hit the ground when I found the test box in the trash, sweetheart. I'm sorry I wasn't there. Let it go. Please. Let me make it up to you."

She said nothing, bound by necessity, the skeins of love notwithstanding. Those, she was sure, would soon permanently turn to the chains of hate. She'd been right in telling Sandra that Dean would see this child as his duty, his particular call to honor. At least her friend hadn't gone over to the enemy. How could she have forgotten about the package in the garbage? Dean shrugged and draped her jacket over her shoulders. He picked up her stuff, correction, her *shit*, and tugged her out the door.

Helping her into that SUV parked closest to the entrance, naturally in a loading zone, Dean buckled her in. Amy heard him put her things in the back before he rounded the front of the vehicle to climb into the driver's seat. She felt him looking at her, but it was easy to ignore him in the darkness. Staring straight ahead she concentrated on her breathing, slow and steady, tired unto death. Dean cranked the engine over and pulled out into traffic, then onto the freeway, and Amy didn't dare to look back at the little motel she thought might be the fresh start of her life. Leaving tore at her. Would he ever lose the ability to hurt her?

****

Dean drove steadily into the deepening night, the road's middle line ratcheting out in increments within the scope of his lights. He pushed the vehicle right along, but not too far over the speed limit to attract the attention of the police. He wondered if Amy would turn him in, and he'd be forced to look for her all over again. The overwhelming relief flooding him when he walked into that crappy little motel and saw her rounding the counter, alive and well, still left some residual weakness in his knees. He thought she was coming to him, and his heart beat insanely in his chest. But the look on her face instantly crushed his hope, and despite his attempt to hug her right inside his body, express his love and need through the kiss of a starving man, Amy resisted. Her stubbornness was indeed profound. Dean knew he'd been correct in overwhelming her, not giving her time to think or plot, instead pushing her into returning with him. He blessed the darkness. It was his friend. He'd get Amy home under its cover.

Amy looked beautiful. Tired, but beautiful. Her hair was the same bountiful mass, her lips pink and soft, despite her fury. There was a little more fullness to her sweet breasts and he'd felt the slight swell of her belly where his baby grew. He longed to press his lips there before kissing down to her apex, pushing her thighs wide to lick and explore his pussy, finding that little nub to nibble and suck until she closed those full thighs around his head to prolong the sensation, her cries stifled by her fists or a pillow. His cock thickened again and Dean shifted his position, the leather seat squeaking beneath him. He risked a glance at Amy, wondering if she was recognizing the strength of his will and coming to accept it. She was still his woman, would always be his woman, and he was going to take the best care of her from here on in.

She was asleep, slumped slightly against the door, her profile softened, reflected in the glass, hair in drifting tendrils catching the intermittent light from oncoming traffic and from the dash lights. His possessiveness and the need to protect her, have her close by and take care of her, outstripped his own desire and he turned his attention back to the road. He'd do well to cultivate those emotions because he doubted Amy was going to welcome his carnal attentions, at least not immediately. Dean forecast some personal time in the shower, and cold showers at that. He debated making a stop for food, but they'd be home in under an hour. Fumbling with his cell, he called Randy.

"I'm an hour out. Is there food in the condo? Amy will be hungry."

A low chuckle filled his ear. "So she agreed to come back. Must say I'm surprised, buddy. You always did have the power of persuasion."

"There was no need for discussion, Randy. Amy agreed." *Because she didn't want you around her new friends.* For once he was overtly grateful for the shadow he cast.

"Holy shit. Okay. Maybe you'll give me the goods later. There's food. And I'll ask Andrea to drop off some milk for your *pregnant* hostage right away. You take care."

"Hardly a hostage. Although it's gonna take some convincing for her to stay."

Rather than considering the possibility that convincing Amy might prove to be impossible, Dean smiled at the note of envy in Randy's voice. His friend wanted a baseball team of kids and Andrea wasn't convinced. He'd told Randy about his true identity when the shit with Andrea went down. Randy had planned to give up the life for her, and Dean jumped at the opportunity to tell his lieutenant. Despite his decision to go straight, Randy was pissed with Dean's actual job—no one liked to be taken in—but soon came around. The other man shone in his position in the business, a schemer at heart, and willingly stayed as Dean's right hand. Dean decided he'd be sharing a fundamentally important piece of information with Amy in the near future, that of his undercover status. He'd blown her trust because he hadn't trusted *her*, a vicious cycle, and now he couldn't think of anything more important to trust her with. He would willingly put his life in her hands, although probably not right away. He wasn't blind to how furious she was with him, and while he didn't believe she'd out him, their present relationship would hardly withstand another body blow.

The exit loomed in the darkness and Dean followed it, navigating the streets to his home. The entire complex housing him and his crew, like a medieval fortress, interspersed with a few naïve young couples, came into view. No families, no children. It gave him pause. His child wasn't going to be raised there. But that was a ways down the road. He had a woman to placate and gentle.

Pulling into his drive he shoved the gearshift into park. The lack of motion likely woke Amy, because she jerked upright and he could see her hair flow around her shoulders as she looked around.

"Home, sweetheart. Wait until I come and get you."

She didn't respond, and Dean sighed inwardly as he exited the vehicle. He was tired, worn out from the pressure and exertions of the past weeks. However, she would expect him to act out. He was going to do the exact opposite and kill her rage and hurt with kindness. Grabbing her purse and the garbage bag, he opened her door, reaching in to click open her seatbelt, not really concerned Amy would try anything. She knew who lived in the complex and that she wouldn't find any support here. His men, and their women, would follow his orders, not matter the friendships Amy had forged. He took her elbow once she swivelled her legs out, and held her in place until she was steady on her feet. She was probably exhausted despite her nap.

Guiding her to the stairs, he felt her steps hesitating, but he urged her forward, wondering what was going through her head, but well aware it wasn't anything he really wanted to hear. As she approached the door, her lithe body stiffened and she yanked her elbow from his grip. Dean punched in the door code and turned the handle, ushering her inside. She stopped in the middle of the room and looked at him, one golden brown brow arched. Dean closed and locked the door behind him, and Amy's eyes tracked the movements but remained blank and aloof.

He took a step toward her and she wheeled away, heading toward the bedroom. Dean beat her to it with two lengthening strides and held out his hand appeasingly. Amy brushed past and went into the bathroom, closing the door against him. After a time he could hear water running in the shower. Blowing out a breath of relief, he sagged to a seat on the bed, setting her belongings beside him. That had gone far easier than even he'd expected. He dared hope she still felt enough for him that they could build on it, move past his utter stupidity.

Then he heard it. It was hard to discern above the beat and hiss of the water and through the closed door, but the faint sounds of his woman crying, sobbing in despair, permeated his head. He scrubbed his face with his hands, then hardened his heart. He'd done what he had to do. He got up and went to put together something to feed her.

The shower shut off but Amy didn't emerge from the bathroom. Dean rapped on the door, reluctant to invade that slight privacy despite the total openness they'd shared previously. When she didn't answer his worry spiked and he opened the door. Amy sat on the closed toilet seat, wrapped in a bath sheet, drying her hair with a smaller towel. She didn't look his way and Dean tamped down his annoyance, aware it was a more palatable emotion than what he was really feeling—worry that he wasn't going to be able to fix this.

"I've made a meal."

"Okay."

He couldn't stop the words. "So your attitude doesn't extend to refusing to eat?"

Her hands didn't stop plying the towel. "I'm pregnant, Dean. I wouldn't do that to my baby."

Fuck. He deserved that. "Our baby, Amy, and I'm sorry. Will you come and eat?"

"I want my nightgown and a robe, some panties."

Gesturing behind him, Dean nodded. "All your things are here. Help yourself."

When she didn't move, he got it. "I'll be in the kitchen."

Amy joined him a few minutes later, bundled into her pink terry towel robe, her scrubbed face and damp hair making her look about sixteen instead of the twenty-eight years old she was. He'd fucking well missed her birthday and had that to make up to her, too. She settled on the stool as far from him as she could get and reached to fill her plate with fruit and cheese, adding a slice of buttered bread. She deigned to accept the glass of milk he poured and ate quickly.

"We need to talk," he began.

"I'm tired, Dean. Babies do that to a woman. I worked a long day and lunch was a long time ago. I don't have the energy to hear anything you plan to share."

He decided not to say all the things that immediately leapt to mind. Like how she could have called him when Sandra told her he was looking for her, wanted her back. She didn't have to work. She was *his* responsibility. A few other things came up, but he bit them all back and nodded. He was being an ass, retreating behind selfishness because her comments cut him to the quick. He knew this side of Amy existed, heard it invoked on his behalf, but never dreamed to see it erected against him. Even in those first few days of butting heads, early in their relationship, she hadn't been so cold. But then the stakes hadn't been so high. Shit. This was *his* fault and *he* had to fix it.

When she got up to carry her dishes to the sink he forestalled her. "I'll do that. Go to bed. I'll be there shortly."

At last she faced him, looked him in the eye and Dean rejoiced inwardly, although took care to shutter his own, a feat, because he hadn't had to do that with Amy, not since their first time together. "I'm not sleeping with you."

"You are, Amy. I'm not sleeping anywhere you're not from here on in. I'm going to be there for you."

She studied him, those violet eyes now impassive, resolute. "I have no doubt you can seduce me, arouse me. We have history and you owned my body. But it'll be force for all of that, Dean. Rape. You take what you want but you won't get *me*. You think on that. And you think on what your *child* will think of his father."

Fuck him. Fucked. He didn't want just her body. He wanted all of her. And he couldn't let himself ignore the last part of her statement, because he was determined to set a fine example. "We'll sleep in the same bed. I'm not letting you build any more distance between us."

Shoulders back, she walked away, but not before he saw the sheen in her eyes. It killed him to make her cry.

Dean cleaned up, listening to the sounds of Amy getting ready in the bedroom. He then made his way to the second bath to clean up, stripping to his boxers. For some reason, perhaps because of the enormity of the day's events, he checked the coin in his right boot heel that identified him as more than Dean Chambray, the criminal. The one thing he could use to certify the real reason he headed up his small organization—if his handler was even available at such a time as he was forced to reveal it.

Their bedroom was in darkness, Amy's shape under the blankets delineated in the ambient light filtering in from the street above the window coverings and through the tiny cracks between the slats of the blinds. He climbed in beside her and wrapped his arm around her waist, hauling her into him, tucking her fine ass against his pelvis. He rested his chin on the top of her head, scenting her shampoo, relishing the silken feel of her against him, selfishly resenting the fabric barrier of her night apparel. His cock hardened, instantly, knowing how close it was to his heart's desire, uncaring of ultimatums and ethics and values, and he willed it into submission. He desperately wanted to touch and explore her whole body, see the changes his child had wrought, to love her, bring her pleasure.

Amy held herself rigid for a very long time, but at last, Dean felt her relax into slumber. He tried to ignore the tiny voice suggesting not only were the battle lines joined, Amy was in possession of some weapons he had never trained in, nor ever expected to wield. She'd be quite the better loser. A frission of unfamiliar anxiety kept him awake considerably longer, and at one point he carefully exited their bed to ease his lonely cock in the bathroom, like a truculent teenager. But not before double checking that the front door was locked, and hiding her purse in his gun safe.

## Chapter Thirteen

"So I can't leave, can't call Sandra or anyone else, not even my bosses at the hotel, and you're staying here with me until I give in?" The venom in Amy's voice made Dean want to check for acid burns. But it was nothing less than he expected—or deserved. He thought back to the previous hour, an equally tense experience, while he waited for her to calm down and process what he'd said, not just react.

Waking later than usual, his body probably recharging after the momentous events of yesterday, Dean immediately noted the lack of warm woman beside him. He'd rolled to his feet in one quick movement, his ears registering no sound in the space other than the hum of the appliances and a drip in the adjoining bathroom. Moving quickly and silently on the balls of his feet, he gained the living area. Amy was curled into a corner of the couch, staring out the window, once again wrapped in her robe. Probably sensing him as his movements disturbed the air, she glanced his way then resumed her perusal out the window. Dean broke the silence.

"Good morning, sweetheart. Give me a minute and I'll make breakfast."

"Don't worry about it." No intonation, nothing. He supposed the flat affect was her chosen tactic of the moment, although her lack of spirit was alarming.

"You need to eat. The baby—"

"How about if you let me worry about the baby, Dean? I know what my body is telling me, and it's suggesting I not put anything in my stomach at this time."

He forced himself to shrug, ignoring the stab of pain resulting from the insinuation he would hardly know what she was experiencing because he hadn't seen her for weeks. Precious weeks wasted because of his actions. Moving on.

"I'll shower and dress. You might feel better by then."

A hint of surprise drifted across her beloved features. Amy clearly expected him to respond in kind, familiar with his refusal to be disrespected. Well, she would learn he could be flexible where she was concerned. Especially when their relationship had suffered a setback. Dean preferred to think of it that way. A setback sounded manageable.

As he quickly showered, he wondered that Amy hadn't smothered him in his sleep. She'd been angry enough, although this aloof, resigned posture worried him more. The scratches on his face were scabbed over, but still very much evident. But she loved him too—he prayed she did—and surely it hadn't turned to hatred. It was up to him to deal with the *setback* and bring all of that glorious caring back so he could bask in it and return it with interest. He'd tell her he loved her when he thought she wouldn't throw it back in his face. Deciding not to shave, in deference to the furrows on his cheek, he considered his next step. Probably setting the ground rules after breakfast was best. Amy might revolt, but better to start out as he meant to finish, and she might listen better on a settled stomach. Tossing the towel over the rod, Dean strode into the bedroom to dress, coming to an immediate halt.

Amy clutched a scrap of fabric to her chest, eyes wide and startled. She'd been dressing, presumably taking advantage of his morning ablutions to do so in private. The shirt she held did little to conceal the lace of her bra, and the expanse of skin above her navel glowed in the early morning light. He noted the convex curve of her belly before his gaze travelled to the tiny panties covering her sex, down the long, lovely length of her legs. When he looked back into her face, Amy was pulling her gaze away from his lower half and Dean struggled to hide both his jubilation and response. She might be pissed, and trying to remain distant, but definitely not immune.

Giving him her back, she slipped on the shirt, yanking it around her. He could tell by the way her head tilted and the way her hands worked out of his line of vision she was buttoning it. The conservative cut and color didn't reflect his Amy. She then sidestepped to the bed where a pair of black pants lay. Dean frowned, while devouring the sight of Amy's ass, her full buttocks partially cupped in satin. Was she eschewing all the clothes she left behind? Making yet another statement?

"Something wrong with your jeans, Amy?" He wasn't able to totally hide the little bite in his tone, feeling he was fighting a battle on all fronts, wondering if his plan to be kind and understanding was the best one after all. Fuck, he was never stymied like this.

She stepped into the pants before answering him. "I probably can't zip my jeans and my self esteem is challenged enough as it is."

He ate up the physical distance between them in one stride, whirling her to face him, gripping her shoulders, giving her a little shake, grimly pleased with the real emotion filling her eyes that caused her lips to part invitingly.

"Stop the bullshit, Amy. You're pregnant and beautiful. You'll embrace it!" His cock swelled and filled, and he ground his pelvis against her, pulling her close. "Does that feel like you've lost your appeal?"

It killed him to see her blank her expressive features again, veiling her eyes, visibly pulling away emotionally, doing her level best to ignore his arousal.

Just as she ignored her own, her nipples hardening against his bare chest. "Telling me how to *feel* now, Dean? That's beyond even *your* control."

He carefully released her, holding onto his temper and his desire, smoothing the rumpled fabric down over her arms. "Go sit at the counter. I'll make breakfast as soon as I get dressed. Go now, Amy, before I paddle your ass and fuck you senseless."

She pushed past him, dropping her head, but not before he saw the tears standing in her eyes. Fuck. Was he driving her further away? He grimaced when he replayed his words in his head. Ass. Yanking his clothes on, he hustled out to the kitchen. Amy sat obediently at the counter, hands folded like a student in detention, staring downward. Dean went to make coffee.

"Can you eat now? Eggs? Toast? Cereal?"

A delicate shudder but she wouldn't look at him. "Toast is fine."

Cracking a couple of eggs into the pan heating on the stove, he depressed the toaster button on four slices of brown bread and put out some butter and jam. He poured Amy a cup of coffee and set the cream beside the cup. When she made no move to touch it he sucked in air and forced a question. "Not drinking coffee?"

"No." Goddamn it. His palm itched to smack her ass and he rubbed it on his jeans, turning back to his eggs. Sliding them onto a plate he grabbed the toast and put two slices on a separate plate for her. She probably didn't eat butter anymore either.

"What can you drink?" There, that sounded civil. How had he thought this was going to be easy? *Because where Amy's concerned, your brain turns to mush.*

"Milk or tea, water, some juices." Flat, distant comment.

"I'll make tea."

"Don't bother."

"Do you want to pour some milk?"

"You told me to sit. I'm sitting."

This was fucking insane. Holding onto his temper with his fingernails, Dean stalked to the fridge, retrieved the milk and poured his woman a tall glass. The clacking sound it made when it hit the counter in front of her belied his control. He returned to his breakfast and ate without further comment, aware of Amy breaking small pieces of toast off, chasing them with milk.

He tried again with the sweet talk, desperate to connect with her, make her see reason. *His* reason, he accepted, reluctantly. "I'll clean up, sweetheart. You do whatever and when I'm done, we're going to talk."

She gave him a measured look before standing to head back to the bedroom. He heard the bathroom door shut with more force than necessary and breathed a sigh of relief. He could cope with anger better than her distant, exacting responses. The clean up complete, he made tea, an unfamiliar process, but one he hoped Amy might give him brownie points for. No surprise, she refused it when he called her into the living room, aware she'd exited the bathroom and was sulking in the bedroom.

Dean waited for her to curl up in a chair, again as far away from him as she could manage before taking his own seat on the couch, and laid out the ground rules. Gone was the controlled, distant Amy. She'd framed his edicts pretty well. Nothing doing until they got through this rough patch. No Sandra. No Harold and Francine. Just them.

"We're going to hash this out, sweetheart. Without outside interference. Just you and me." He thought that sounded fair and reasonable.

"What's the end game, Dean? Spell it out. You're not my father." She was back to distant Amy.

"Ultimately? I see us married, preferably before you have the baby, with some changes in my business."

"You want to marry me? Marry someone you believed betrayed you, tried to take your *business* away. Someone who used sex to try and fool you?" Bitterness, underpinned with pain echoed in Amy's voice. "Because of the child?"

"Not just because of the child, sweetheart, although I want him. I'm thrilled about him. I want to marry you because I want you beside me for the rest of our lives." The words echoed in the room, a passionate statement and a plea.

"Until the next time." Her words were nearly whispered but so full of pain and acceptance they filled the room.

Dean wearily pushed a hand through his hair, again noting the unruly length. "I didn't expect you to take me at my word, Amy." Although he'd stupidly hoped. "But I've put it out there. It's up to you now to learn to accept it, because you're mine, and we're going to be parents not too far in the future."

"I'm to accept it. Just like that." Her eyes were nearly black with rage and indignation, lips tight, face flushed.

"I'll be doing my best to convince you, sweetheart. We're gonna spend time together, talk. I'm making time for this because you're important to me. I'll make it up to you."

"Good of you to take time out of your busy schedule, Dean. Good of you to tell me how my life is going to play out. Well, you can think again, rethink your plan. Last I checked you can't marry someone without their consent. And keeping me here is going to get old fast.

"There's doctor's appointments to consider, never mind the fact that I'll go stir crazy and my emotional state will affect my baby. And you aren't enough for me, boyo. Not nearly. I need *friends*, people I enjoy spending time with." It went without saying Amy was furious, vibrating with her rage. And she stabbed him with her words in precisely the right places, too. She was indeed the better loser.

"Fuck, Amy. I didn't mean it like that. I have to make sure the business runs okay because it impacts on us. You. You come first. I'll make arrangements for you to see a physician, and you'll come to find I'll meet your needs. Your emotional state is your choice."

****

Amy got up and went into the bedroom wishing she had the strength to throw something heavy and hard right at Dean's fucking head. But she was drained once again, exhausted and worn down. He'd thought of everything, her jailer and the love of her life. He said he *wanted* her, regretted his behavior that day, wanted her forever and was happy about the child. The complete package. But he didn't love her, didn't voice it, and there *would* be a next time. Maybe not right away, but it would happen, and Dean would turn on her. Well, so be it. He wasn't going to let her go, would find her if she left again, and running while pregnant wasn't a plan. The baby deserved better.

Lying down on the unmade bed, curling onto her side, hands tucked beneath her cheek, Amy worked out some ground rules of her own. She'd stay, and take care of herself, deliver Junior—Dean was probably right about the gender. When wasn't he right? Then return to her old life. With one exception. She wasn't having sex with him. He wasn't going to use her sexuality to undermine her intention to fall out of love with him. Surely, if she built enough physical distance, the emotional attachment would fade or morph into something different. Maybe a kind of friendship. For Junior's sake.

Tears spilled out, pouring over the bridge of her nose, to join the deluge on the opposite cheek, slipping across her temple to soak her hair, dampen the pillow. The bed dipped and a big hand gently rubbed her back. "Sorry, Amy. But that's the way it has to be."

Pulling one hand out from under her head, Amy scrubbed at the tears, using her knuckles. She rolled to her back and squirmed up to sit against the headboard, locking gazes with Dean, not three feet away. His face was tender, the skin over his cheekbones no longer so tightly stretched, sculpted mouth softened, his eyes luminous. The damage her nails had caused to his face was scabbed over but she tried not to look at the scratches—she regretted lapsing into such stupid violence. She decided.

"I'll stay willingly. I won't give you any trouble. We'll try for a new relationship for the baby's sake. But I won't marry you and I won't have sex with you."

He studied her, not missing a nuance, typical Dean, and nodded. "We should marry for the baby's sake, but that's your choice. He'll have my name regardless. As for the sex, time will tell."

"You aren't listening, Dean. *Listen* for once in your arrogant life. Force me and I'll hate you. It won't be good. Take it to other women. All I ask is that you be discreet, for your child's sake."

Moving with that deceptive speed he had, he gripped her biceps and hauled her so their faces almost touched. "There won't be other women, Amy. And no other men for you, either. *We are going to work this out*."

She said nothing, forcing her eyes to stay open when he took her mouth, insistently, his tongue tracing the seam of her lips until she opened for him. But she somehow remained aloof and he finally released her, his face now dark with suppressed emotion. "I'm going to see Randy, arrange a few things. You'll forgive me if I ask you to stay in the condo today. Until we test out this *new relationship*."

"Trust, Dean," she managed. "Remember? This will be a little test. I'm going to see Sandra. I'll be sure to keep you apprised of my every move."

His movements jerky, Dean tucked his shirt into his pants, then crossed to the dresser. A set of keys sailed to land beside her, and he walked from the room. She heard him in the den, and he returned with her purse. "Your Audi is in the garage. We'll be finding you a safer mode of transportation. But if you are so determined to see Sandra…"

"There's a van in Santa Rosa. Paid for. I'll—"

"*I'll* send someone if you're intent on having the fucking thing. Leave the address. Be back for dinner." The front door slammed. Amy slumped back and sighed. Now there was nothing but to get on with it. Except another storm of tears overtook her, this time, curiously, because Dean gave in so easily. God save her from the vagaries of pregnancy hormones.

Rising from the bed, she went into the bathroom to wash her face, applying some concealer to mask the dark flags beneath her eyes. Mascara would probably be a bust today, although some blush was in order—her pallor was marked. All of her things were exactly where she had left them. She drew the brush through her hair and tossed it on the counter. She'd drive straight to Sandra's, she decided, wouldn't call first. If Sandra wasn't home, at least she'd be out in the world and could cope with the disappointment there, instead of in this place she was again to call home. The one Dean threw her out of, and would again, no matter how he protested. The acidic taste of acrimony assailed her once again, but she pushed it down. Made her bed. Time to lie in it. She pulled Bogs from the garbage bag and carefully set him on the corner of the night stand by her side of the bed, the one true thing in her life besides Sandra.

****

"Amy! Oh my God, girl! Get in here!" Sandra dragged her into the house, pausing only to close and lock the door behind her. "Are you okay? Are you back to stay?"

Thanking her foresight not to wear eye makeup, Amy sobbed into her friend's arms, the grief and confusion pouring out in veritable rivers. Sandra led her to the kitchen and got her settled on a chair, ripping a wad of tissues from the box on the counter. Amy grabbed them and mopped at her face. She had to quit doing this to Sandra.

"Hey. It's okay. It's all right, honey. Please, Amy." Sandra's soothing utterances slowly penetrated, and Amy began to calm down. The other woman patted her hand and got up to pull a couple of bottles of water out of the fridge, offering one after twisting off the cap.

"He found out I was pregnant and tracked me down."

"I didn't tell him, Amy. He knew when he came to see me."

"I know, Sandra. I left the damn test box in the trash and old eagle-eye ferreted it out. Probably had to take the garbage out himself." Okay, that sounded petty, but still… Where the hell was Lois? Amy decided she wasn't picking up after Dean, or cleaning his house. If he'd fired Lois then he'd need to find a replacement.

"He was looking for you long before he found out about the baby."

"Uh huh. Dean never has a problem in admitting he was wrong and then fixes it. Or does his version of fixing. He *made* me come home with him. I felt like I had no choice because of how it could turn out for Harold and Francine." *And because he said please, and that he was sorry, and wanted to make amends, and I'm still a pushover where he's concerned because I love him.* No, she wasn't going there.

Sandra regarded her, features marked with worry.

Amy continued, "And what if he doesn't learn from this particular mistake? What if I don't trust him making amends?"

"So that's it. You figure he'll—"

"Look at his track record. We had it good, better than anything either of us dreamed of. But he turned on me anyhow."

"And you're not into giving second chances."

Amy slammed the bottle down on the table, the plastic sides flexing under her clenched fingers. The water gushed up and over the top, running down over her hand, soaking the fabric at her wrist. Sandra jumped up for a towel.

"I'm sorry, Amy. I warned him about getting caught between you and his business, being forced to make a choice."

"What are you talking about? Whose side are you on?"

"Yours, honey. Yours. Dean is everything to you and you know it. I understand you're scared but I've been thinking about it." Sandra hardly looked her age, just two years older than Amy, her face wise with wisdom belying her years, gained from experiences Amy could only guess at. "You love him, and he loves you, whether he can tell you or not. And there's the baby to think about. You might want to consider grabbing onto this new opportunity with both hands, Amy. For however long it lasts. Nothing lasts forever. We both know that. Live it. Or follow your path and live half a life. I know he forced you to come home, and that sucks, but it's what the man knows, imposing his will. And he thought he was doing the right thing."

"I don't know, Sandra. It hurt so much. I can't take it again."

"You can. If you have to, you can. But you need to make your choice. All I'm asking is that you consider everything very carefully. Make the right choice." Sandra got up and threw the rag into the sink. "I have to get ready for work. Evening shift. I'll call you tomorrow. I'm so happy you're back."

Amy couldn't stand the undecipherable emotions coloring her friend's words. Shit. "Sandra? You all right?"

"Yup. Just need some time and I have to work. I'll call you."

Amy initiated the hug this time around, and went out to her car. No place to go, no one she really wanted to see, although at some point she'd have to face Andrea and the other women, who would all know she'd run away, and then come home with her tail between her legs. Kind of.

She decided to go shopping and postpone that inevitable meeting for as long as she could. If Dean was going to keep her, then she'd spend a little of the money from the sale of the car she was presently driving. The curious irony made her laugh, and then want to cry again, but first she needed to make a call.

"Restaway Inn."

"Harold?"

"Amy! Honey, are you okay? Joyce told us you had a family emergency."

"Uh, about that, Harold. My boyfriend paid a visit and—"

"Do you need the police? Where are you? Give me an address." Harold sounded freaking scary.

"I'm fine, Harold. Really." As fine as a woman could be who agreed to live with a man who'd fucked her over, to have his baby, while forgoing the fringe benefits of amazing sex. All while she tried to fall out of love with the father of her baby and the giver of said amazing sex. "I'll come back to visit in awhile. I promise. I'm so sorry I left before you came home."

"S'okay, Amy. As long as you're okay. You sound shaky."

"I'm safe and fine. Maybe not my ideal hope in life, but neither was running away."

"How's the baby?"

"Uh..."

"Can't live so close and work together without us noticing, honey. Although Francine put it together first. Still not feeling great, first thing?"

"No, but that will pass soon, apparently. At least according to informed sources on the 'Net."

"The wireless deal was inspired, Amy. You come see us whenever you want. And you call."

She promised, tucking her phone back into her bag. The closest mall was only a few blocks away, and retail therapy would keep her from thinking too much.

****

Dean slouched on the couch, feet on the coffee table, nursing a beer, ostensibly watching the game, but his attention was fixed on the door. When he got home, he knew Amy was out because the car was gone. He was still disappointed to find the condo empty, although her grassy scent permeated every room, refreshing the bouquet of a month ago. He heard the slamming of car doors and vaguely, male and female voices. He was at the door with no memory of setting his boots on the floor or pulling his ass off the couch.

"Thanks, Enrico. 'Preciate it." The sound of Amy's voice floated through the open door, followed by the rush of light footsteps on the stairs. The little smile playing around her lips vanished the instant she laid eyes on him, and she slowed her pace. He reached out a hand for the numerous bags dangling from either wrist.

He wouldn't say it, but the last hour had been hell, wondering if she was coming home or once again fleeing from him. *Trust.* The meeting with Randy had been barely a distraction, and Dean had little memory of what transpired, the decisions made, but assumed one of them did. Thank God for Randy. "You run into Enrico?"

"We pulled in at the same time. He unloaded my parcels." She didn't look at him.

"Enrico got with Sandra." Dean had no fucking idea why he had to say that, except it was true and maybe he didn't want her to hear it from anyone else. Unless Sandra had already told her.

His comment was enough to make Amy give him her eyes. "You sicced him on her, Dean? To ask about me and he used her? Tell me you didn't do that."

Not willing to fight with her on the landing where everyone inclined might listen in, he drew her inside. "I asked him to check with her. I wanted to find you."

"And you couldn't ask her yourself?" Amy tossed her purse on the coffee table and wrapped her arms tightly across her chest. Her breasts plumped and rested on that makeshift cradle and Dean tore his eyes away from the enticing sight. He was in the shit. Again.

"I was putting out the fire Burnett ignited, Amy. I couldn't be in two places at once, and Sandra wouldn't have given me the time of day. Her loyalty is to you."

She muttered something sounding like, "You might be surprised." And walked back to that one person chair to drop into it and stare out the window. Dean stood awkwardly for another moment then set the sacks down beside Amy's purse.

"You buy some new clothes?"

"With your money."

He dug deep for patience. "Good, that's what it's for." And was rewarded with a glare. He wondered if this was how she acted when she was a teenager and if an ass whupping then had worked to correct her attitude. He was becoming obsessed with that ass. Not that he'd really raise a hand to her given her condition. Any ass paddling would have to wait until it could be doled out as an erotic spanking—she liked those.

"Do you want to eat here or go out?"

"Doesn't matter."

"Goddamn it!" His voice thundered and echoed in the space and Amy flinched. He modulated his tone as best as he could. "Respect, Amy. Being civil. You might remember how, if you cast your mind back. I'm trusting you. Hold up your end."

He tugged off his boots and they hit the floor by the door with a satisfying thud. He stalked into the bedroom to change. "Put something on you'll want to wear to the steak house."

Bags rustled in the living room and Amy passed through his line of sight to shut herself in the bathroom. Dean sighed. His temper had always been close to the surface, sometimes useful in his line of work, but he could control it, too. Except around his woman, apparently. At least, not when she was displaying this side of herself. He chose a tailored pair of pants and a long sleeved dark shirt, toeing into a pair of comfortable shoes, one eye on the bathroom. Was she crying in there again? Plotting? Shit. He was going to expire with need, but seducing Amy would be highly counterproductive and Dean was a good strategist. Except for losing his temper. But goddamn it to hell, she pushed his buttons. He missed his mostly sweet Amy and had to accept it was his own doing.

"I'm sorry for being rude. I'm ready." Amy emerged from the bathroom, wearing an amazing dress, the blue patterned material clinging to her high breasts to fall away around her waist before fitting snugly around her hips and thighs. It skimmed her knees, detracting a trifle from the incredibly sexy look. Probably all that saved it from being inappropriate wear outside of the condo. The blue kitten-heels raised her to nearly eye level, if only she'd tip her head back and give him her eyes.

Dean forgot what she said and sifted through his memory bank to ensure he made the correct response, determined to say nothing that could be misinterpreted. "Apology accepted. I'm sincerely offering mine. We should go."

****

Dinner was an extremely polite, civilized affair. Dean felt like he was on a blind date, or at least what he assumed a blind date felt like. The only animation Amy displayed was related to the couple she worked for in Santa Rosa, and she blithely asserted her intention to visit them in the near future.

"I'll take you. We'll find a time."

Visibly struggling with her response, Amy gave him a grimace he supposed might pass for a smile and nodded.

"Not good enough, Amy. Words." He didn't allow non-verbal communication in any important walk of his life.

"Yes, Dean."

"You can introduce me, sweetheart. Especially if these people are going to be part of your life." There. He could be flexible.

Amy rolled her eyes. "They don't need the kind of trouble you can cause."

"Then we'll get together someplace neutral. But I want to meet them."

"Fine." Dean, like every other man on the face of the earth, knew what that word, spoken by a woman in that particular inflection, meant. But he chose to take it at face value.

The rest of the meal passed with him carrying the conversation. Amy displayed no interest in his comments about the legal side of his business and he avoided any mention of the other part. He figured he should broach the baby issue.

"When are you due?"

"Middle of March. Around St. Paddy's Day. I saw a GP but I need an OB-GYN soon."

"I want to go to those appointments with you. All of them. And I'll take those coaching classes with you for the delivery." He heard his words ring true, to mirror the feelings in his heart, and Amy's startled gaze turned to wary acceptance.

"Okay."

"And you keep me apprised. How you're doing, feeling, everything. Let me help you, be there for you."

"As long as you respect my boundaries."

His inner caveman surged. The urge to put her under him, show her how insane it was for her to deny them both, was so strong, the other diners faded away, the sounds of china and utensils dissipating. Dean breathed through the need and nodded. Absolutely no verbal confirmation was passing his lips, but Amy appeared satisfied. Know thine opponent, sweetheart.

## Chapter Fourteen

The next several weeks passed in an interesting mixture of pleasure and torment for Dean. Amy slipped back into her housewife role almost without a ripple, picking up her web design contracting with equal aplomb. It felt eerily normal with the exception of the fact Amy refused to have sex with him. She didn't refuse the reinstatement of Lois, and he recognized how tired she was such a lot of the time.

Sleeping with Amy, and being in close proximity in the condo, was sometimes excruciating, he wanted her so badly. He took care of himself in the shower, determined to wait until she came around, although the hold on his restraint became more tenuous every day. It helped to accompany her to the excellent doctor he found at Sandra's hospital, following along with the growth and development of their child, especially at the ultrasound. His possessiveness, coupled with a sense of tenderness he didn't know he was capable of, cooled his jets. A little. Their baby was cagey, refusing to give up its sexual identity to the ultrasound technician, but everything else was proceeding well. Dean tried to pretend he didn't tear up at the sight of that little creature curled up within Amy's womb.

Any morning sickness was confined to the morning, thank God, with the exception of certain smells and foods her stomach objected to. Her occasional retching and suffering because of the fruition of his seed left Dean feeling helpless and wishing he could change places with her. She let him hold her head and wipe her face with wet cloths, and press one on the back of her neck. Caring for her was intimate and gave him hope she would come to trust him again—and let him have access to her body once more, although that was truly secondary.

Amy grew more beautiful with each passing day of her pregnancy, any stomach upset notwithstanding. Her skin glowed and she radiated an inner serenity Dean envied, believing she had fallen into dissociating the sexual part of their history, using the skills honed by earlier survival. He was eternally grateful to have her back in his life, making meals, keeping his house, being there when he came home, her burgeoning belly living evidence of his legacy, and hoped he was doing enough to assure her of his sincere concern for her well being. True to his word they slept in the same bed, and therein lay the rub. Once asleep, Amy snuggled with him just like she used to, but it was simply that. Snuggling. Grinding his teeth and jerking off in the shower was his lot, for now.

They didn't argue, Amy's sweet side moved fully to the fore, and he thought he was successful in shielding her from the continuing evidence that all hell was going to break loose, certainly before their child was born. All his meetings with Randy, and the forays into his territory, tracked rumors and other slight indications that someone was sniffing around the perimeter, nibbling on the fringes. His experience taught him that a big push to take over could be imminent.

He soon had to tell Amy the truth and make plans for their future, and include her in that planning. But he wanted all of her before he did so, uncertain if it was because he thought their renewed sexual connection would mitigate the fact he'd withheld some important information, or if he thought she'd withhold forever. She definitely wasn't getting a prize, but he wasn't ever letting her go.

His life seethed with uncertainty despite Amy's serene and apparent acceptance of hers, and it was taking its toll. Dean was becoming increasingly concerned, anticipating the move from that shadowy crime lord, but he was unable to do anything further to guard against it. He worried about Amy, and he worried she would pick up on his anxiety.

They went to have dinner with Francine and Harold, and Dean made an immediate attempt to disarm their cautious and slightly hostile attitude by expressing his earnest appreciation for taking care of Amy during their temporary separation. After fielding a variety of arch comments from Francine, he made good progress as the older woman dissolved into giggles and flirtation.

Harold was a tougher nut to crack. The man listened and withheld his judgement and Dean was concerned he hadn't made his intentions clear, but after one particularly piercing stare, apparently accepted Dean's sincerity. However, he didn't miss Amy's wistfulness when they bade the couple farewell and resolved to keep in contact with his woman's saviors. They might well play that role again in the near future. He'd send her to stay with them if he thought it in her best interest, depending on what happened in the next while with the shadow man.

****

Amy wasn't certain she liked this state she was living in, kind of a floaty, beatific frame of mind. It was like she was drifting, and nothing really made an impact. She suspected it was primarily because she was pregnant, the soup of hormones simmering and making her calm and acquiescent. It helped that she was living with a man who took very good care of her without any expectations other than wanting to spend time with her. Oh, she knew he wanted to have sex with her. The evidence of that poked her backside each and every morning and each and every night when they were in bed. And she caught him looking at her like she was lunch. Of late, Amy battled a resurgence of physical need she could only combat by thinking loving and sweet thoughts about her baby, and sometimes morosely wondered at the veracity of her thinking—that a relationship without hot sex with Dean was indeed what she wanted. Her painful memory of his treatment of her that day had begun to fade in the face of his caring and respect of her wishes, and that damned feeling of hope had set roots in her heart again, wanting to believe he wouldn't pull the same shit.

"Everything going okay, Amy?"

She pulled herself from her musings and smiled at Sandra. "I'm good. Really good. Hardly any more morning sickness and I feel—content. Best way I can describe it."

"You look it, too, like a Madonna or something." Sandra smiled back and Amy was struck by how pretty her friend looked. Her skin wasn't so pale, and she moved with more confidence somehow… Amy couldn't put her finger on it.

"Are you seeing Enrico?" She had no idea where that came from.

"Off and on."

Well, shit. What was that about? She thought they were friends. "Nice that you thought you could share." Amy heard the hint of tears in her own voice. Damn hormones.

"Oh, honey. Sorry. It's just that … well, Enrico and I…"

Amy shook her head. "It's okay, Sandra. I'm hardly someone you want to ask for relationship advice."

Her friend pushed up from the couch and went to the fridge, returning with the pitcher of lemonade. She topped up their glasses, then set the jug down with a thump on the coffee table. She didn't use a coaster, totally *not* Sandra.

"I thought he was fucking me to get information on your whereabouts. And he's a criminal."

"Holy shit." Amy had absolutely no idea what more to say. Sandra's brown eyes were downcast, and her hair fell forward to mask her face.

Her next words were muffled. "I was attracted to him that night at Grand Masters, but dismissed it. Blamed it on the booze. I was determined not to go there. Determined not to feel any kind of attraction. And then he was assigned to follow you and just seeing him was like … it made my heart beat faster and it was hard to breathe."

"Oh, Sandra. That's chemistry."

"How am I supposed to know what chemistry is, Amy? There was no *chemistry* in my experiences on the street. Just a lot of abuse and being used. Disgusting. Men were pigs. But Enrico is so assertive yet polite, and he's so good-looking. And I'm not."

It was Amy's turn to be fierce. "Don't say that. Looks aren't everything, but you play yours down. You know you do."

Sandra raised her eyes at that slightly convoluted piece of reasoning. She laughed a little. "You're biased. Anyhow, when you took off, Dean sent Enrico. I didn't know anything and thought that was the last I'd see of him, but he kept coming around, and one thing led to another." She paused, clearly out of breath.

"He didn't force you."

"God, no, Amy. Does he look like a man who has to force a woman?"

"How a man looks doesn't necessarily determine the kind of sex he wants," Amy said darkly. "Dean told me you and 'Rico had something going on, but I didn't want to think it."

"Why?"

"Because I thought you would have told me. And because he's a criminal, too."

Pushing her fingers through her hair, Sandra sighed deeply. "I put him out when Dean came to see me right after you called. I knew Enrico told him. His first loyalty is to his boss, and I didn't want that, and I didn't want the risk. I wanted to be someone you could come to if it all goes bad with Dean's business."

"You broke off a relationship with Enrico in order to be a safe haven for me?" Amy burst into noisy sobs, the first emotional outburst since she'd accepted some of Dean's terms, and he'd agreed to hers. "You can't do that."

"I can't," Sandra agreed, scooting over to put her arm around Amy's shoulder. "He wouldn't give up, and sometimes I'm weak."

Drying her tears on her sleeve, Amy touched Sandra's face. "Do you love him?"

Sandra turned away, pulling her arm back to her side, shaking her head. "Don't know what love for a man is, either, honey. Enrico can get any pussy he wants at any time and probably does when I won't open the door to him. I'm going to move as soon as your baby is born and I know you're okay. But I took my own advice to you when Dean brought you back—I'm going to take anything Enrico will give me until I leave. There's no happily ever after for the likes of me but I'll pretend awhile."

Despite the shock and the penetrating sense of loss, Amy made herself nod. Sandra's fear of intimacy was such a big part of her, and if her instincts were telling her to run, Amy wouldn't argue. She was terrified for her friend. She asked one last question.

"Does he love you?"

"He says he does, which makes me question his sanity and his motives."

They sat quietly, lost in their thoughts for a long time, and Amy wondered if Sandra's sadness was a profound as her own. Her cell rang, Dean's ringtone, and she answered.

"Where are you, sweetheart?" Was there a hint of something other than loving interest in his tone? Annoyance? Concern? She couldn't detect any, and part of her, a part asleep for some weeks, woke up and flexed.

"At Sandra's."

"We have reservations for six."

"Oh, shit. I'll be right home."

"Do *not* rush, Amy. If we're late, it's no big deal."

He was allowing her to drive the Audi, despite grave misgivings, making her promise to drive sedately. Given her hormonally regulated state, it wasn't an issue, and she definitely didn't want to drive the now repaired mommy's van. At least, not until after the baby was born. She wished she hadn't made such a big deal about it.

On the one hand, she recognized the fact Dean was worried about her driving the sporty convertible, concerned about her safety. On the other hand it ticked her off that he didn't think she'd be sensible.

"I'll be home in twenty."

Hugging Sandra, who looked back to normal, Amy grabbed her purse. "We'll talk again soon, Sandra. Who knows what the next few months will bring?"

Giving a tiny shake of her head, Sandra pursed her lips and didn't respond. She walked her to the door and hugged her back, hard. "See you soon, honey."

****

Amy drove home with care and caution. She had no doubt one of Dean's men was in the traffic behind her and knew Dean would do something like take away her keys if he got a report she wasn't being sensible. He met her at the door, pulling her inside, bending to kiss her cheek.

"I put that new dress out for you. Do you need to shower first?"

Amy never dreamed that Dean would become a lady's maid and nearly giggled. "Nope. Had one before I went to Sandra's. I'll hurry."

She hustled out of her maternity pants and loose shirt. Baby was really making an appearance now, all out in front. She looked like she'd swallowed a watermelon. As she smoothed her hands over the bulge, she saw Dean watching from the doorway. The look on his face made her heart ache, all tenderness and caring. He crossed to her and gently rubbed her belly.

"Okay? Do you want to stay home?"

"I'm starved. When aren't I? Are you sure twins don't run in your family?"

He blanched before her eyes. "Pretty sure. Why? The ultrasound—"

"I was just teasing, Dean," she said quietly. "It's just that I want to eat all the time."

"Then get the dress on and I'll feed you." He picked up the article in question and dropped it over her head, awkwardly, the buttons at the back ending up under her chin. "I'm better at taking things off," he muttered.

Amy fought the shiver of awareness, wondering if her conversation with Sandra about thwarted love and her most recent thoughts about unwanted celibacy were contributing to awakening the beast of arousal. Dean finally got the fabric sorted out with her help and fastened the buttons. His big hand closed around something shimmering on the coverlet and lifted it to show her. It was the white gold bracelet she'd left behind.

"Will you wear this tonight, sweetheart?" His face was calm but his eyes were full of hesitancy.

Taking a deep breath, she replied. "Why?"

"Because if you won't marry me, at least I'll feel that you've forgiven me a little."

Had she forgiven him? Maybe a little. It was hard to hold a grudge in the face of how he now treated her. She nodded and his smile touched her heart. He carefully fastened it around her left wrist, and pressed a kiss on the clasp. God.

"We should get there in time if we leave now. C'mon, let's feed you."

Ignoring the sudden chaos of her emotions, she allowed him to walk her out to the truck. "Pretty soon, you won't be able to make it up inside, Amy."

It was true. Stepping up on the running board and clambering into the front seat was becoming difficult, even with a gentle boost from Dean.

"I'll bring the SUV home tomorrow."

*He* wouldn't drive the mommy van, she found herself thinking sourly, but he'd expect *her* to. Although the fact he hadn't replaced it with a vehicle more … Dean … ridding himself of another reminder of her flight from him, said something. Besides her request for it. She knew in her heart it was because he respected how the people in Dominion City helped her when she was in need, and all the work Chaske had done on it to make it safe and reliable.

"What?" He looked into her face after ensuring her seat belt was fastened.

"I don't want to drive the mommy van."

"You won't have to for awhile yet."

"*You* can drive it."

Dean began to laugh. He shut the passenger door and went around to get in on his side. She could see his shoulders shaking with mirth. He was still laughing when he swung into the seat and cranked over the engine. "I was wondering where feisty Amy went," he finally choked out. "I thought earth mother had totally replaced her."

She wanted to be angry but couldn't. She laughed a little too. So he had noticed her calm, relaxed state, even more vegged-out than previously sweet Amy. Of course he had. He didn't miss anything. She wondered if he'd noticed her reaction to him when he was helping her dress, though … she just had to accept it. He'd been patient and given her lots of time to come to it. She belonged to Dean Chambray. Now it was a question if she could open herself up to giving him everything once again.

****

Amy ate her steak with obvious relish and devoured the potato and side dishes. She declined dessert and coffee, and Dean realized she was still trying to avoid too much sugar and caffeine. She looked the picture of motherhood in her dark blue dress, the silky fabric fitted sweetly over her breasts to fall in folds around her swelling belly. He knew, without looking, that she wore heels for the evening, because she'd surreptitiously kicked off the little ballet flats just before they went out the door and toed into the fancy shoes. He'd given her that small rebellion, the little danger to her well being, because he wouldn't let her fall.

Her hair drifted around her shoulders, the white gold of her earrings glinting through the thick strands. He was pleased beyond belief she had agreed to wear the matching bracelet, feeling it symbolized a closer move to resolving the biggest issue. She smiled at him, hopefully full and content. He wanted her relaxed because he'd decided to tell her everything. Life as they knew it would soon change. He could feel it in his bones, and Amy needed to be prepared. A movement in his peripheral vision took his immediate attention.

"'Lo, Dean. How you keeping?" Crystal's timing couldn't have been worse. Her slender figure was wrapped in a form-fitting revealing scarlet dress, and she teetered on extremely high heels as she leaned over their table. Was the woman fucking blind? Dean decided to see it through, although he could feel Amy's immediate interest and her tension.

"Good, Crystal. You?"

"Not complaining. Haven't seen you in awhile. Not since—"

Dean cut the woman off. "Crystal, busy here."

"Hiyah, honey." Crystal's cold, blue eyes were vacant as they turned to Amy, ignoring his not so subtle reminder. "This the same woman? When you came to me after—"

Well, shit. "That would be none of your business, Crystal."

This time his tone was *crystal* clear, and Crystal wasn't a stupid woman. Dean wondered why she had even said it in the first place, then realized she was altered. Her pretty face twisted for a split second before smoothing out, and her painted lids dropped over her eyes before she blinked them open.

Amy shifted, and the timbre of her voice spelled huge trouble. For him. All her sweetness had soured. "Nice to meet you, Crystal."

A tall, thin man materialized to Crystal's right, his arm snaking around her waist. He nodded in Dean's direction, and Dean recognized him as one of the owners of the restaurant. "C'mon, honey. They're waiting for us."

Dean waited for her to start something, but she relaxed into the guy and managed a little wave. The silence following their departure weighed heavily.

"Amy—"

"Don't. I'm not talking about it here. Take me home."

At least she called it home. Fuck. Dean stood and offered his hand. Amy ignored it, no surprise, and clambered to her feet, her usual grace and balance impaired by the swelling of her belly. He inwardly cursed both Crystal and his stupid reactive foolishness and resigned himself to an interesting discussion. Amy's icy silence in the truck reminded him of the day he brought her back home and he longed for the time before he'd been a fool, although the return of the attitude was getting old.

Back rigid, shoulders set, she climbed the stairs ahead of him and he restrained himself from smacking that lush ass. Instead, he gave her space and waited patiently while she entered the code on the door, taking two tries to get it right. This did not bode well.

"You eased my so called betrayal with that skank?" Amy threw her purse in the general direction of the couch, and tossed her light sweater after it. Her breasts heaved beneath the fabric of her dress as furious color welled up from its neckline to paint her cheeks. Her eyes matched the color of her dress, but were absolutely livid.

Well, right into it. Dean decided not to mention that Crystal really wasn't a skank, although considering the fact she was obviously using, he might be wrong about that. And he was actually elated at Amy's jealousy. Gone was the calm, sedate earth mother.

"No."

The quiet denial appeared to take the wind out of Amy's sails. She stared at him for a long moment, an eternity, and then visibly accepted it. Whatever his actions that fateful day had done to their relationship, she obviously remembered he never lied to her. He might refuse to answer, withheld things he didn't think it in her best interest to know, but he never lied. The fire went out and with it, her spirit. The high color in her cheeks faded before his eyes, her shoulders slumped and tears beaded on her shuttering lashes, spilling over to course in rivulets down her cheeks. What the fuck? He loved sweet Amy, but he liked to see her feistiness, too.

Gathering her unresisting body into his arms, Dean crooned into her ear. "S'okay, sweetheart. It's all right. I've got you."

"That's the problem," she wailed, burrowing her face into his shoulder. She sobbed and hiccupped. "You've got me and it's so fucked."

"Shhh. Amy, it's okay," he insisted, and went with his gut.

Easing her away from his body, he wrapped an arm around her and walked her into the bedroom. The late evening sun poured gold through the slats in the blinds. Amy stood like a child, passive under his touch as he worked the buttons open on her dress and slipped it from her shoulders. It drifted to the floor to float around her ankles on a wisp of sound, barely audible over her stuttering breaths. Disposing of her bra next, Dean pressed a kiss on the top of each slope of creamy breast, seeing nothing but woman—his woman. He shrugged out of his jacket and frantically yanked his shirt over his head, fumbling with his belt and fly, all the while pushing into her space, forcing her to move backwards to the bed.

As her legs came up against the mattress, she sat, abruptly, and he shoved his jeans and boxers down. His cock sprang free, towards its woman. He hadn't taken off his boots, and his clothing hobbled him, stuck around his ankles. Dean didn't dare take the time to remedy the situation, afraid Amy would collect herself. He had to believe he'd interpreted her anguished proclamation correctly and was going to capitalize on it and bind her to him while soothing her angst.

Kneeling at her feet, he gently pushed her legs apart and hitched between them, feeling very much the supplicant. The crotch of her panties was damp and he pressed an open mouthed kiss against it, huffing his breath as he did so. Amy moaned above him and he chanced a glance. She was leaning back, weight supported on outstretched hands, her eyes closed.

"Lie back," he urged, gratified when she did so, flopping back like a rag doll. The growing swell of her belly obscured his sight line to her face and Dean's heart swelled in reaction to the evidence of his child until he could barely get a breath against it.

Insinuating both hands under her buttocks, he grasped her underwear and pulled it to the tops of her thighs, then reached to pull it away from her mound, the view of the full, pink lips of her labia taking what breath he had left. He fought against the light-headed sensation and stretched the material ruthlessly to work it over her thighs and down over her feet. Folding her legs, he set each foot on the edge of the mattress, splaying her wide. God how he'd missed this, the sight and smell of her!

He fell on her, hands returning to fit beneath the globes of her ass, lifting her cunt to his mouth. He feasted, relearning all her crevices and sensitive spots, stiffening his tongue to thrust up inside her channel, ignoring her clit. Amy whimpered and writhed, but his shoulders kept her knees wide, and her position didn't allow her to sit up or retreat. Her honey lubricated her folds and he lapped it up as fast as she made it.

"Please, Dean." A whispered choke of begging sound. At last.

Whirling his tongue over the knot of nerves at her apex, he exerted more pressure, then sucked it against his palate, hard. Amy screamed and arched high from the bed, feet battering against his upper arms, a flood of cream drenching his chin. Dean released her clit and lapped gently, bringing her down. His cock was doing its own form of whimpering and weeping but he ignored it. He straightened and lifted his head, looking at her over the proof of their passion all those months ago, a curved, sweet bulge covered in silky skin. Amy's tearstained face rose up and gentian eyes met his own. Was there forgiveness and acceptance mirrored there?

****

Pussy still clenching on emptiness, Amy fought the languor brought about by the amazing orgasm. Dean knelt at her feet, the lower part of his face covered in the evidence of her release, watching and waiting. In that instant, she surrendered. She loved him past sanity, and needed all of him, not just the caring, involved father of her child. Withholding, avoiding sexual intimacy, hadn't protected her heart, hadn't allowed her to build a wall between them. If anything, it had forced her to recognize everything Dean was without the sex. And she wanted it all. Ignoring the nervous little voice way back in her mind, the one reminding her of his perfidy and asking why she'd think he wouldn't fall again, she smiled and reached out for him. He smiled back, and there was no triumph or smugness, simply joy mixed with relief.

As he got to his feet, she wiggled her body sideways and up towards the headboard, finding a pillow to set her head on. Dean wavered, big body swaying, and he grunted, an annoyed sound, swivelling to sit beside her. He bent over, and she admired the long, strong lines of his back and the way his tightly muscled ass barely compressed against the mattress.

"Forgot to take my boots off."

Laughter burbled up from her belly, and his head came around, silvery gray eyes fixing her with a glare that couldn't hold its integrity as his sense of humor asserted itself. He returned to his task, and she heard each boot hit the floor with a thump followed by the clank of his belt buckle.

As he turned and worked his way to her, carefully slinging a leg over the swell of her belly, planting a hand on either side of her head, she noted the amazing length and thickness of his cock, before it nuzzled her mound, precum anointing her skin. Dean dropped his mouth over her own and she gave over, opening to allow his tongue entrance, his chest hair gently abrading her sensitive nipples. She pushed up with her hips to press against his cock, reveling in how he shuddered. In an instant, he levered his weight up and set his knees between her widening legs, pushing them wider, the immediate sense of welcome vulnerability making her pussy cream.

"Can't wait," he muttered, and his cock pushed between her folds, lancing unerringly to find her gate. A surprising pressure, familiar yet distant, assailed her as he jerked his hips forward and thrust inside, fighting his way past tender, swollen tissues. It had been such a long time. He finally seated himself as deep as he could push, and it made her eyes water with pleasure, her sheath stretched, that certain place high up near her cervix prodded by the wide mushroom head of his shaft.

"Are you okay? Is this alright for you? And the baby?" His desperate question touched her.

"It's fine. The doctor said so."

Beginning to thrust, to withdraw and retreat, each time with a little twist to torment her G-spot, Dean worked above her, now twining his fingers with her own, a sweet imprisonment, looking deep into her eyes. The storm brewing in his gray gaze mesmerized her, coupled with the talented plunging of his cock. Amy's release again built, impossibly, and she closed her eyes against it. After such a drought…

"Look at me, sweetheart. Please." Forcing her lids open in response to his agonized plea she once again connected on an emotional level … and flew. Dean's eyes dilated, the pupils swallowing the gray of the iris, and she saw not only her own anguished pleasure but the depth of his, backed by tenderness and something even deeper.

"Love you."

Unsure if he actually voiced it, or telegraphed the pledge in the intensity of the moment, she nevertheless believed him with all that she was. Tugging one hand free, she raised it to cup his cheek, accepting his weight as he collapsed upon her, noting how he kept the bulk of him from where their child rested.

After a time he moved away, their skin grudgingly separating. Settling on his side, raised up on one elbow, he cupped first one of her breasts, then the other, sweetly pinching the nipples. His big hand coasted down to her belly, fingers spread wide to rest with a gentle pressure. Baby awoke abruptly and a little bump visibly pressed between Dean's forefinger and thumb. Their collective breath seized as his hand froze in place. The bump disappeared and the smoothness of the curve reasserted itself.

"Think that was a comment?" Dean's tone was wryly amused.

Laughing, enjoying the fact she'd expressed mirth twice in one day after the careful monitoring of her emotions with him over the past months, Amy nodded.

"I'm sure it was. Probably don't want to know what she said, though."

"He."

"Unless you can read ultrasounds, babe, don't be so sure."

Dean kissed her, a hard, possessive press of lips. "It doesn't matter, although the idea of two of you scares the living shit out of me."

"It should." And that was all she would ever say, a fitting final comment about his actions that awful day.

Dean watched her, eyes narrowing, that familiar silver hue quite evident. And smiled. "The next one can be a boy. He'll have a big sister to look up to. And Amy? I'm sorry. For everything, but mostly how I didn't trust you. I promise it'll never happen again. I'll be sure to fuck up, but never about that."

Searching his eyes and face, believing in the veracity of his assertion, Amy allowed herself a tiny smile, then snuggled into him, suddenly exhausted. She felt him drop his head to the pillow before she went under.

****

Lying beside Amy, his future wife, and their unborn child, in the now waning sunlight, Dean catalogued his options. The big shark was circling. He didn't know how he knew it, other than the renewed little hints of careful probing of the outlying businesses, but he was certain. His intuition rarely failed him, despite that one spectacular failure he wasn't going to think about anymore, seeing as Amy had shut that door. Idly drifting his fingertips down the length of her, over her shoulder, down her arm, feeling each delineated bone of her ribs, the baby taking most of her caloric intake, he drew a deep breath. He'd tell her over a late dinner tomorrow, one he'd put together with his own hands. It might stir up a pile of crap, but she had to know, because a shitstorm was coming and Amy needed to be prepared.

## Chapter Fifteen

"You're a good cook, Dean." Amy nibbled the potatoes au gratin he'd fixed to go along with the thick pork chops. "I'd forgotten."

"Hard to fuck anything up when there's cheese." He wondered if he should tell her before dessert, a thick slab of chocolate cake loaded with fudge icing. He'd unearthed it from the depths of the freezer, probably secreted there by Amy in the throes of her sweet tooth.

"Good point." He caught her staring and realized he hadn't responded to her little jibe.

"I need to share something, sweetheart." The hint of wariness in her eyes, the former happiness beginning to fade, made him spill it.

"I'm not who I told you I am. Not a crime boss, not really. I'm undercover. In a way." He waited for her to ask questions, suddenly uncertain what else to say.

A slow blink, followed by another, violet eyes again darkening to gentian, but this time with an emotion he couldn't read. The blood drained from her face and he was glad she was sitting down. Her lips parted and then shut tightly, only to open again as she sucked in an audible gulp of air in order to breathe some words out.

"Holy fuck."

"I'll get you a piece of cake." Avoiding her face, he pushed up from the table and moved to the counter, choosing a steak knife to saw through the partially frozen dessert. He set a large piece on the plate and carried it to her.

Staring at the hunk of chocolate, then up at him, Amy appeared totally bemused. She broke eye contact, picked up her fork and sliced off a piece of cake, placed it in her mouth and chewed. She swallowed and put another piece of the sweet on the utensil, pausing only to take a drink of milk.

"Amy?"

One single negative shake. She made steady inroads on the dessert until only crumbs remained. Those she mashed with the tines of the fork, and Dean picked up on the restraint she was displaying. It was evident in the way her fingers pinched the fork and in the tenseness of her body. Standing abruptly, she picked up her plate and carried it to the sink. Dean jumped despite himself when she hurled the inoffensive piece of china against the unforgiving stainless steel where it shattered.

"Jesus H. Christ, Dean! Any other surprises? Any other *minor* freaking things I should be apprised of?" She was incredibly beautiful, cheeks now flushed with hectic color, eyes glowing, breasts heaving with indignation above the curve of her pregnant belly. He'd upset her two days in a row, damn it.

"That'd be it."

"Uh huh. Okay, then." Throwing her hands in the air she turned and stormed into their bedroom and the bathroom door slammed. He followed slowly and stood outside it, resting his forehead in his palm. Maybe he should have waited a little longer. He just didn't know how much time they had before he and his crew were up against it.

Water thundered into the tub and he distinctly heard the metal lid of Amy's bath salts rattle, envisioning her slamming the container back into place after tipping a generous amount into the bath water. When the taps were turned off, he quietly entered.

Amy lay amidst a foaming sea of bubbles, the taut buds of her nipples coated in the froth, her long legs bent to accommodate her height. Head tipped back on a folded towel, long length of hair spilling over the edge of the tub, she kept her eyes closed, although he had no doubt she'd heard him come in. He perched beside her and picked up her pink bath sponge, squeezing on some body wash. Amy's eyes flew open at the sound and he just knew she was remembering the first time he'd taken care of her. It had been the first time he'd taken care of *any* woman he'd had in his bed and he wished he'd told her that piece of information. It seemed really important now.

Wordlessly, she sat up and leaned forward, lifting that abundance of hair and piling it up on her head, holding it in place with both hands, resting her forehead on her knees. Dean washed her shoulders and the nape of her neck, then drifted the sponge down the velvety length of her back. After rinsing her, he eased her back with a gentle pressure on one shoulder and reached to wash her throat and upper chest.

"I was recruited fresh out of the service. Put in to replace a guy I'd done some work for as a kid, after he went up on a bunch of charges. He died in prison, so it was easy to stay on. It was a long-term plan, sweetheart, and perfect for me. I had no ties, no family I cared about, and my whole life to wait."

"For what?" At least she was speaking to him.

"To take down somebody who's been moving out from LA in ever widening circles, annexing all the bigger cities."

"Like what you do? Protection? Betting? Laundering money?"

"More. But he's highly structured and wants it all. He wants to absorb the drug trade and all the whore stables, too. We figure it's just him, well-insulated from the people he employs, but he's organized and smart, has one hell of a set-up. Law enforcement apparently can't figure out who he is, but Burnett is always the forerunner. I pushed Burnett out, figuring it would get an immediate reaction, force the head guy's hand. I was wrong." He set the sponge down and rolled his sleeves up, then felt for her ankle, cradling it in his hand to lift it out of the water. Paying close attention to washing her long, narrow foot, he waited.

"So what does that mean? You have to start again?" Amy lifted her other leg without any encouragement, crossing it over the opposite knee as he lowered her foot back into the tub beneath the diminishing bubbles.

Circling the sponge over the curve of her calf, "I think he's making a move, or will be shortly."

"So it could hit the fan, then."

"Yes. C'mon, get up."

It took her a second to process, nose wrinkling, brow furrowing, but she struggled upright with his aid. He efficiently washed the rest of her, noting how she went up on her toes when he ran the sponge between her legs and up the cleft of her buttocks, and his cock took notice too, but he subdued his carnal interest despite the past hiatus in their sexual congress. They had to talk, not fuck. He helped her out of the tub.

Standing on the bath mat, Amy wound a large towel around herself while he released the water, then allowed him to lead her into the bedroom. She sat on the bed and Dean pulled the chair close.

"I wanted to tell you for a long time. Even before I was an asshole. And then afterwards…"

"So you tell me you love me *and* share your secret identity all in two days." She cut him off with an impatient wave of her hand.

"Would you have believed me before?"

"That you loved me? Maybe. Yes. I don't know." She knuckled her eyes. "Yes. I think I've always known."

It took her a few minutes to continue, but that was probably because his weight took her backwards on the bed, and his mouth forestalled any further sharing. When he released her lips, she blinked up at him, eyes dazed and her full mouth swollen.

"Just thought I'd confirm your last assumption, Amy," he told her, hearing the rasp in his throat as he did so. He returned to sit in the chair, after pulling her back up to her former position, and tucking the ends of the towel into place.

"Oh. Uh huh." She stared back earnestly. "But, Dean, the undercover thing … didn't you think it was something I should know?"

"Yes. But it wasn't just me, us, to consider."

Tilting her head, Amy obviously worked things through, her intelligence evident. "Randy?"

"Randy. And Andrea." Dean ran a fingertip down her forearm.

After a few moments, she nodded thoughtfully. "You withhold from me again, Dean Chambray, and I'll poison your food. No bullshit excuses about your dear old mom fucking you up, or your cynicism from the *work* you do. You either trust me or you don't."

Dean had a satisfying vision of smacking a curved ass bright pink before fucking it, but recognized it for the red herring it was, and solemnly nodded back.

Amy stood and unwound the bath sheet, dumping it unceremoniously on his lap. Her skin glowed from the heat of her bath and he felt his mouth water as she slipped beneath the covers. "Going to bed. I'm done like toast."

He hung her towel up and headed back to the kitchen to put the food away and stack the dishwasher, trying not to think about that sweet ass. Domesticated. Whipped. Fine.

****

"It makes sense now."

Dean knew she wasn't asleep, could tell by the remaining tension in her body when he finally climbed into bed, reaching to pull her against him as always. He'd figured she was thinking.

"What?" He was a little anxious to even ask, but she hadn't had very long to assimilate the revelation.

"You talk like a lowlife at times, then slip into a college dialect. I thought it was because you chose to fit in with whomever."

"The military paid for my education and also educated me in ways I'd never learn from books. I'm more comfortable speaking *lowlife*. I grew up lowlife." He punctuated his statement with a sly pinch of her nipple.

"Ouch! Jeez, babe. They're sensitive."

"And I didn't pay them any attention today at all. That'll change tomorrow."

The tiny shiver she made suggested he didn't have to wait, but there was so much more to discuss, because he knew her quick brain would come to all of it. He wasn't disappointed.

Amy pulled away, scrambling towards the edge of the bed and there was a click. Light flooded the room and she lurched to a sitting position, one shoulder against the headboard, holding the sheet to her breasts. He could see how wide her eyes were.

"You sent someone after Brent. What kind of cop does that?"

"This kind," he returned implacably. "I'm not actually a cop. I have no status. If things go sour, I'm fucked. But it gives me leeway I might not have otherwise. And I couldn't deal with that asshole myself, unfortunately, so had to arrange it."

"But—"

"No one hurts you, Amy. Well, except for me when I'm being an asshole, and those days are past. But you're mine and I protect what's mine."

"But—"

"I've been in this business for over six years, sweetheart. I've crossed plenty of lines during that time. Nature of the game. I've had to live with those decisions, supported, by the way, by my handler. Taking care of Whittaker is something I'm happy to live with, and I made that decision without checking with anyone first. Having said that, I want out of this gig and if what I believe is coming materializes, that'll be sooner than later."

Biting down on her full bottom lip, Amy studied him, her hair now a wild, tangled mane. Dean felt a cold hit of fear in the base of his belly. Remembering her concern about someone going through her to get to him, he knew she'd be worrying about their baby. What if she thought it too big a risk?

"You scared?" He needed to get her talking.

Nodding, she worried her lip some more.

"I want you to move in with Sandra."

"No."

"Jesus, Amy. I just told you I expect a shitstorm, and you're scared, justifiably so. If you live with Sandra for the next while you'll be safer, and—"

"No."

"Then go to Harold and Francine, just for the next—"

"Uh uh."

"Why the hell not?"

Flouncing flat, Amy yanked the sheet up around her shoulders and reached to shut the light.

"Amy!"

"Go to sleep, Dean. I need some time to process all of this."

*Give me strength.* He reached to haul her close again.

She spoke so softly, her voice muffled by a drift of hair, he had to strain to hear her.

"Nobody ever cared enough to protect me before, except for Sandra. It's part of my forever."

He felt her slip away into sleep shortly afterwards, leaving him to ponder her statement. Once again, she humbled him, especially when he'd failed her so badly before. He'd have to put another man on her, probably Olsen. Amy didn't like the man much, but he was the guy who willingly moved wherever he was needed, and had a mean streak a mile wide. Dean could wind him up and put him in defense mode.

****

Amy wouldn't talk to him about the previous day's revelation. He woke to a hot, wet mouth enveloping the head of his cock, a questing tongue tantalizing the sensitive notch. Nearly embarrassing himself with the insanely quick build to his release when she deep throated him, moaning, the vibrations scrambling both his balls and his brains. Dean felt his cum jet out in hard, unrelenting spurts, and Amy took it all, releasing him with a smug, pleased look on her face. She bounced from their bed, all round curves and silky skin and he caught up with her brushing her teeth, scrubbing with enthusiasm. She spit and rinsed, her morning sickness well past. He pressed her up against the vanity and fisted a hand in her hair, pulling her head back, bowing her body to lift her breasts. Admiring their additional heft and darker nipples, he used his free hand to roll each bud into a hard, thrusting point. Amy watched his movements in the mirror, and he, in turn, watched her watch. Her violet eyes glazed a little and her lips parted as he increased the pressure.

Releasing her hair, he slid his hand beneath her buttocks to find her pussy lips already slick and wet. He lubricated his fingers and drew her cream back to her anus, pressing insistently against the puckered star. As he popped through the outer ring of muscle, she gasped and her head lolled back against his shoulder. The mirror reflected the split of her folds as she adjusted her stance and he fucked his finger in and out of her back entrance, adding another to stretch her ever wider. With a judicious hitch of his hips he manoeuvred her cunt against the cool edge of the vanity top. Eyes popping wide she ground her pelvis against the granite as he increased the invasion of her anus and tormented her nipples. One of her hands came up to weave into his hair and she came, jerking against the counter, the scent of aroused woman wafting up around them. Dean carefully withdrew his fingers and eased her to the side in order to wash his hands.

In a disembodied voice, she asked, "Scrambled okay?"

Meeting her slumberous eyes in the mirror, Dean nodded, hiding a smile. "I'll take a quick shower."

Breakfast was ready as soon as he made it to the kitchen, stopping only to towel off and pull on a pair of boxers. He sat opposite her, prepared to enjoy his meal and continue their conversation, but Amy wouldn't go there. She was wrapped in her robe, and had brushed her hair, her skin glowing without any cosmetics.

"You've said it all, right? No more surprises?"

"Right."

"Then we wait and see if this guy shows his face. You deal with it, and then we move on. I don't see any point in talking about it any further."

That was his Amy. She'd put her faith in him, and all he could do was try to ensure her safety to the very best of his ability. "Mike will be assigned to you when you're out and Olsen while you're at home."

As expected, Amy's mouth indicated her opinion of Olsen, like she'd bitten into something sour, but unexpectedly, she didn't balk. So she *was* scared, probably terrified, but in true Amy fashion she'd puzzled it out and accepted what she couldn't change. Unless she moved in with Sandra or the Bowers, which she refused to do, he had to admire her *savoir faire*. And seeing as he was part of her *forever*, Dean really didn't want her to live away from him. He'd just *have* to ensure her safety. Hers and their child's.

## Chapter Sixteen

"I'm all lopsided." Amy stood sideways in front of the long mirror, one hand resting on the top of her bulge, the other beneath, pressing the material of her shirt against her shape. Her breasts, restrained behind a "sensible" bra, jutted proudly above the baby belly. She twisted slightly to look at her ass and frowned.

"You look beautiful." It was easy to say, because it was true. Dean stepped into her back, looping his arms around her to hug her close, setting a hand on either side of her belly.

"I'm getting tired of being pregnant," she confided, relaxing against him. "Baby is not cooperating. She wakes up when I want to sleep. We can't seem to get coordinated. And my back aches."

He'd stuffed his brain with information on pregnancy, and understood the last trimester to be significantly different than the first two. He'd pretty much missed the first one, and the middle months were like the Twilight zone, what with Amy's retreat into serenity, at least until her sexuality asserted itself. Life seemed balanced, with the exception of his fucking business, something he didn't want to think too much about because all was quiet on that front, mocking his intuition. She wouldn't marry him until the baby was born, and he gave her that, understanding she didn't want to look pregnant in the pictures, although she looked so beautiful, all round and glowing, he wished she'd reconsider.

"Not even two more months, sweetheart. The doctor says you're doing great, gained just enough weight and your blood pressure is not too bad."

"Uh huh. And he doesn't have to pee all the time and have to have sex on top or sideways."

Dean couldn't stop his snort of laughter. Junior indeed came between them, if in a good way. But they'd figured it out and Amy couldn't say she didn't get taken care of. And she took care of him. But he tried to look serious. "We'll try it from behind, later."

"Pig." She extricated himself from his hold and wandered to the closet. "I need to go shopping. And I don't want to take the mommy van."

Trying not to groan, Dean smiled instead. "Sandra working today?"

"You don't want to take me?" She matched his smile and arched a golden brow.

Suckered. "What are we buying?"

"Lingerie. I want to feel feminine. And maybe a couple of dresses. Some shoes."

"I'll take you for the underwear."

"But—" She pouted.

"Underwear." It didn't take much of an effort to be firm. Retail therapy was not his thing, but he'd do underwear. It was partly for him, after all.

"Okay." A trace of poutiness colored her tone, but she was smiling. "And Dean? We need to start looking for a crib and changing table and stuff."

Shit. He didn't want to be living here when the baby came, but he had to wait for whatever was coming down to actually come down. His home was defensible, surrounded by his crew, and no way was he leaving Amy unattended in some house in suburbia. She might be going to Francine and Harold whether she agreed or not. Sandra was a bit too close for comfort and there was a chance someone might look for her there. And Enrico was still chasing that dream, inadvertently painting an arrow to Sandra's.

It was a bit soon to push Amy again, hard on the heels of losing her car, but he'd do what he had to do. As she searched for an appropriate pair of shoes to wear with her outfit while shopping, out of the dozens she had to choose from, his memory drifted to a couple of weeks previously when Mike turned her in…

"I wasn't. He's wrong. He drives like an old man." Amy drew herself up to her full height and glared at him. Pregnant or not, she pulled him like no other and he instantly wanted to fuck her into submission, knowing how strong she had to be to surrender to him.

"Look at me and convince me you weren't making like you were at Indianapolis."

"Hardly Indianapolis," she muttered, avoiding his eyes. "I was in a hurry and I was being careful."

"Keys." He held out his hand.

"No. C'mon, Dean. Mike over reacted."

"Keys. You scare the shit out of me driving that car in the first place, let alone when you're going to have a baby."

"Jesus." She dug them out of her purse and tossed them over. "You must think you're my dad."

Watching her stomp into the kitchen to open the fridge and peer inside made him want to feed her or take some of the sting of him being so autocratic away. He'd decided to do both.

"What are you thinking about?" Amy came back with her shoes and he pulled his mind from that prurient memory and smiled at her question.

"Nothing."

"*Nothing* wouldn't give you that smile. Tell me."

"I just was thinking about how I made it up to you over the Audi."

"Oh." Amy's face flushed and her lips parted a little."It seemed a waste of perfectly good toffee ice cream to me! And I had to change the bed!"

"*We* changed the bed, sweetheart. And Lois did the laundry. *I've* never eaten ice cream from such interesting—surfaces before."

"It was damn cold. And sticky."

"I didn't noticed. Other than it was tasty."

She gave him an arch look and sashayed past him towards the front door. "I might just dip something of yours in something equally tasty, Dean Chambray. Once I have *you* tied down. You give some thought to that."

"Never gonna happen, sweetheart." All the same, he might be interested in pursuing that train of thought—without the restraints. He hurried to hold the door for her and drove them to the mall, willingly putting himself through the torture of shopping, although he set a mental time limit.

****

She was getting tired again, just like in the first trimester. Her back ached and she'd have bursts of energy and then become lacklustre. It was the same with her head—at one moment all of her vigilance would surface, her senses acute, like an animal scenting danger and protecting its young, and in the next she'd become complacent and uninvolved in anything taking place outside of her immediate sphere.

Dean had suffered through an hour or so of choosing scraps of silk and lace underwear. Granny panties might have been a better choice, but Amy wanted sexy. Her bras had become garments stitched with panels of unforgiving fabric to support her burgeoning breasts—the attempts to cover the industrial construction with pretty lace and colors and trim failing miserably in her opinion. So she bought hot panties that barely covered her sex and ass. Dean liked them, too, if the molten look in his eyes was anything to go by.

He acted as usual no matter her mood, adapting and coping with her advancing pregnancy, seeming to manage his "business" and assuming the dual role of father-to-be and lover with amazing aplomb. Amy thought he was probably doing better at building their relationship than she was, although she had the excuse of the little creature growing by leaps and bounds inside of her. The child certainly affected her moods and her general well-being and governed what Dean would allow her to do—or not do. She prayed every day that she would be a good mother, having no example to follow. Dean's approach was simple—don't pull the same shit his mother did. That woman lingered on, but Dean didn't visit her anymore, a choice Amy wholeheartedly supported. Good old Marsha didn't know anybody anyhow, and Amy didn't want Dean to see his mother like that.

It went without saying their child would lack for nothing money could buy, but Amy was determined to meet Junior's emotional needs, too. She decided parenting courses wouldn't be amiss and was considering how she might broach the subject with Dean because she wasn't going by herself. It would have helped if she had some friends with kids but none of Dean's crew had any, most of them young men, with even younger women. Andrea was coy on the subject. She appeared to want children on the one hand, but insisted she wasn't ready on the other.

Reconnecting with Andrea and the other women hadn't been as uncomfortable as Amy had originally envisioned. She had no idea what they knew—or didn't know—and because they respected her silence on the matter, she spent more time in their company, when she wasn't with Dean, or doing for Dean. They were excited about her pregnancy and were talking about baby showers and stuff, although she insisted they wait until after her child was born. She didn't want to jinx anything.

Amy occasionally allowed herself to think about D-day—delivery day. Intellectually she understood the process, having read more than was probably healthy on the subject. Dean was going to be with her, and Sandra, too. And Amy wasn't at all opposed to an epidural. Her doctor had assured her the baby wouldn't be adversely affected and explained that avoiding some of the pains of labor didn't make her any less a woman or a bad mother. She thought Dean might have laughed at her question, but instead it made him pensive and he led her to understand he was not at all happy that she was going to experience even a second of discomfort. Like he'd have any control over it. *That* was going to kill him.

If she was in denial about anything, it was about Dean's confidence in his ability to pull off being undercover, closer to a Donnie Briscoe than anything else. He absolutely wasn't a white knight—tarnished would be a far better way to describe him—but there was nothing to be done about it until everything shook down. A lot of time seemed to have passed since he'd indicated he thought things were coming to a head, but she left it to him, trusted him to take care of it. Amy recognized her impotence. Her role would come afterwards—when Dean would extricate himself and live life on the right side of the law. She forecast some significant adjustment issues, and she wasn't going to allow them to affect what they shared, or their child. And worst of all, she was going to have to do without Sandra.

She'd driven the cursed mommy-van over to her friend's after the lingerie purchase, for an impromptu iced tea, Sandra working the evening shift that day. Amy had a pressing the need to be with her. Just thinking about her moving on made her nose draw up and tears prickle at the back of her eyes.

"Amy? Are you thinking about me leaving?" Her best friend must be a mind reader.

"Why would you think that?" she managed, controlling her voice.

"Because you've been past the weepy stage for a while, and unless Dean is screwing up again, it's me you're crying about."

True. She didn't want to lay any guilt on Sandra, wanted her friend to do what she needed to do for her peace of mind. Amy also wanted to meddle. She saw how conflicted Sandra was, and in her own present happy state with Dean, fancied that Enrico might make Sandra equally happy. It really bothered her not to share Dean's secret with her friend, but she wouldn't betray his confidence, and it wasn't something she wanted to burden Sandra with. Sandra would worry even more.

"I'm gonna miss you so much."

"We'll keep in touch and visit. We will, Amy. Moving is something I have to do."

"So you haven't changed your mind." She sounded like a wistful little kid, and Sandra's eyes warmed as she hugged Amy.

"I'll be here until you get organized after the baby comes. I promised you that, and I will."

Sucking in a big breath, Amy pasted on a big smile, certain it would fool nobody, but determined not to weep. "Well, that'll be in about six or seven weeks and I'm thinking it can't be too soon. My back aches all the time."

Laughing, Sandra said, "You'll be whining really loudly when you go past your due date. First babies are notoriously late!"

"Wonderful." Amy knew that from her extensive research, but she'd successfully distracted both Sandra and herself from becoming maudlin. "Well, you're gonna need to get ready for work and I should get home before it gets much later."

"Suzy Homemaker?" Sandra teased.

"Yup. Trying out a new recipe tonight. And Mike probably wants to turn me over to the next shift. Olsen." Amy felt her lip curl. That man was such a creep in ways she didn't want to list. She hadn't forgotten his little speech at the July Fourth party, and he had a tendency to look at a person with sleaze in his eyes. Not to mention how the stench of tar and nicotine preceded him, and how yellow his teeth were.

"You've adjusted to your pseudo-bodyguards."

Shrugging, Amy got up in preparation to leave. "It was that or moving in with you, or going to stay with the Bowers."

"You're welcome here, Amy. Anytime."

"I want to be with Dean." *And if shit comes down, I don't want to drop you in it, too.*

"I get it. Call me tomorrow."

Another emphatic hug and Amy was out the door, watching her step as she made her way to the mommy-van. Mike was parked across the street. She saw his shades turn her way and he sketched her a casual salute. She was still annoyed with him for tattling on her about the Audi, but she smiled anyhow. He was a good kid, despite his chosen profession. And maybe he didn't think he had a lot of choices.

She led their little procession right to her driveway, and Mike peeled off with a hit to his horn as she pulled into the garage. Olsen was nowhere in sight so she figured he'd be inside the house.

He was waiting for her in the shadows of the garage, hidden in the corner, and Amy, her head elsewhere, tired and wanting to rest her back, didn't see him until she exited the car, locking the door behind her, giving herself no options. She actually smelled him, and felt him before she saw him. The stench of stale nicotine and second-hand smoke permeated her nostrils, the bruising grip of his hand on her biceps telegraphing nefarious intent. Adrenaline kicked in and her brain went into overdrive, searching for a way out. The overhead door rattled to a close, sealing them inside together.

Turning, she squinted at Olsen. What the hell was he doing skulking in the garage? She'd told Dean the man was like a weasel.

Pushing her hard against the side of the van, foul breath fanning past her ear, Olsen spoke quietly, the determination in his voice unmistakable. "You fight me and I'll hurt you, no contest, bitch. Mess you up. He told me to get you there, not the condition to deliver you in."

Overcoming the shock of her bodyguard being one of the bad guys, Amy didn't believe his threats. Olsen was taking reasonable care. He could have punched her, knocked her out. Whatever was planned for her wasn't going to be at the hands of this pathetic excuse for a man. She could feel his erection pressing up against her and that scared her more than anything. He'd fuck her if he thought he could get away with it. Gone were the days when she could endure such a thing and somehow move on. She wanted one man only, forever

"I won't fight you." Did he know Dean's secret? Her blood ran cold within her veins, her heart fighting to pump the suddenly sluggish fluid. She wasn't worth much as a bargaining chip if Olsen's boss knew—no one would side with Dean if they found out he wasn't really a criminal, except maybe Randy, and he had a wife to consider. She decided not to believe the worst.

Her purse was yanked from her unresisting hand and she heard the rattle of keys as he withdrew them. The bag sailed into the far corner of the garage, her phone inside. Olsen pulled her arm forward, adjusting his grip, bruising her again, and slammed the keys on the roof of the van in order to take hold of her other arm. Handcuffs closed around either wrist. Amy pressed her hands against her abdomen in an involuntary gesture.

Olsen sneered at her, his yellowing teeth like a feral animal's in the gloom. He gestured to her swollen belly. "Carrying his brat. Too bad."

And her heart turned to ice.

Stabbing the keys into the lock, Olsen wrestled the side door open, racheting it back on its hinges. He shoved her inside. She fell sideways across the seat, pulling in her legs to check her forward motion as Olsen slammed shut the door.

*Never get in the vehicle…*

Squirming into a sitting position, she heard the child proof locks engage and winced at the irony. A mommy-van, complete with safety locks and attachments for car seats, room for lots of baby paraphernalia, and a dog. The inane thoughts tumbled through her head but couldn't totally distract her from her plight. Tears pricked and her nose drew up. Amy fought it back and tried to think, prepare for anything. Olsen hit the remote and the garage door creaked upward. She prayed for it to take a huge amount of time. Maybe someone in the complex would be coming home, or going, and see Olsen driving her van, her behind him. That wouldn't look right, even though they'd know Olsen was supposed to be watching her back.

The vehicle shot backwards, tires chirping on the concrete, and he executed a quick three point turn to screech off towards the freeway. She caught a glimpse of a green jeep veering toward the sidewalk before the other car was past and they were speeding away from all hope of an immediate rescue. She sucked in deep breaths and struggled against the nausea of despair, fear for her baby and for Dean.

****

Pulling his fist from the hole he'd punched in the sheetrock, Dean contemplated his split and bleeding knuckles, pulling the beast back inside, getting his temper under control. When he turned to face Randy and Enrico, he knew none of his terror showed, drawing hard on past experience not to give a hint of anything other than competence. How long he could maintain his game face was anyone's guess.

He was tormented by visions of Amy being brutalized, assaulted and held in a dank, filthy room somewhere, or bound and tossed into the trunk of a car. Cold sweat pooled at the base of his spine as he thought of their baby, defenceless as its mother was subjected to what was meant for him. He was going to rip Olsen's throat out.

"So it's been Olsen all along." Cold and efficient, the machine he could be when necessary, he slipped into the role of crime boss. It took everything he had to remain calm, but finding Amy depended upon marshalling all of his talents, and losing it now wouldn't help her.

Randy nodded. "It makes sense now. Always the hanger on, making himself available, doing all the scut work. Never missing an opportunity to ingratiate. I ran another, deeper background check and his wife's stepfather's name is Burnett. He never adopted her, so it didn't show up earlier. Fuck."

Dean gestured, his injured right hand vaguely aching.

Enrico abruptly turned and left the room, his cell at his ear.

"Water under the bridge." Dean lowered his voice. "What's your take on Burnett knowing it all?"

"Who knows but you and me and Amy? You think your handler would…"

"No. He doesn't even keep a file, nothing. He emails from a library or internet café, never the same place twice, and it's nothing anyone would read anyhow. Hits my spam folder." Dean didn't share how he conveyed the information back. Randy didn't need to know because it wouldn't change anything. It wasn't like his second in command could call for reinforcements if Dean went down. There was a price to pay for being so incognito.

"Then you got your answer. He took her to force you out, trade her for the business." Dean fucking well hoped that was it. Teaching him a lesson, or even taking revenge on him were the other options—and neither bore thinking about.

Enrico came back into the room, carrying a first aid kit. Dean took a seat on the couch and allowed the young man to clean his hand, slap a bandage on the worst of the cuts. He nodded his thanks—no point in bleeding all over the office. The mundane would offset the adrenaline and let him think.

"I have called Sandra. I wish her to be safe. She will stay at the hospital. She is very upset and will want to know the news." Enrico's English became more stilted under pressure.

Dean doubted Amy's friend was in any danger, but who knew how Burnett's mind worked? He nodded. "You can keep her informed, 'Rico. Tell the rest of the crew to button up their women. You too, Randy. Have them go visit their mothers or something. And then set up a place to meet. Not here."

Striding into the den, he opened a cupboard set into the wall. The gun safe combination was stored nowhere but in his brain and he had the safe open and his favorite weapons out in a few smooth moves. Then he took the time to send his handler an email, taking the chance, the circumstances warranting the breach of protocol. It was the only time he'd spare to alert the man, because for Dean, shadow man was no longer the priority.

If Enrico hadn't seen the van, Olsen driving and nearly sideswiping him, they might never have known who had taken her, or maybe even that she *had* been taken. He would have worked himself up into a lather because she was late, probably never checking the surveillance tapes. At least not right away. A bout of uncontrollable shivering overtook him and he fumbled for the back of the chair, using the support to stay on his feet. *Amy.*

With a monumental effort, he composed himself, drywashing his face and pushing his abject terror away yet again. Dean headed back to the living room. Randy was still on his phone, Enrico shutting his.

"We have reached everyone, boss. And we set the meet at Grand Masters. Burnett will never think we'd use a legitimate business."

The complex was now eerily silent, and he knew the other men had moved their women, or shouted out to them, and then had scattered. Dean had faith they would make their way to Masters without being tailed. Mike was going to be in the fallback position, the most vulnerable one. Dean knew the other man had turned Amy over as per the usual procedure but everyone wondered if Mike could have headed this off, if he'd only gone inside the garage with Amy… But Dean could accept it would have only forced Olsen to either act out against Mike and put Amy in the line of fire, literally, or just caused Olsen to take a few more minutes to make his play. And then, Enrico wouldn't have seen the kidnapping. Mike wanted to make amends though, so took fallback, and Dean allowed it.

Dean had to have additional faith Olsen was the only bad apple. He was going to kill the man, right after he killed Burnett.

****

"We've identified a couple of places where they might be holding Amy." Randy laid the city map flat on the table in one of the back rooms of Grand Masters. It was low tech, but they had cobbled this together quickly, and the paper map was the only way they could all get the lay of the land. The decadently decorated room, shades of red predominating, was a strange back drop to their task. There was no hint of sex and passion, but rather the lust for revenge and payback—his crew took Amy's kidnapping personally. Dean was struck, not for the first time, at the loyalty and familial atmosphere evidenced by his crew. They huddled around to view the two small Xs marked in red on the map.

"Got a tip that someone closely resembling Burnett was here." He stabbed the X to the north with his pen, the ink making little blots across the paper. Dean thought they looked like blood drops and sweat popped out on his brow and his hands fisted as he again fought the fear, fear that would cripple his decision making. He thought hard.

"Any chance he's decoying?"

"Could be." Randy didn't say it—he didn't have to. It was what they had.

Enrico spoke up. "The other place. He would stand out like a sore thumb there. It is primarily a Hispanic neighborhood and there is no word that a white man is moving in to assume our action. I would have heard."

The youngest member of his crew was turning out to be priceless, Dean mused. He nodded. "Do we know if it's Burnett for sure and not some other usurper?"

"He became known after the thing with Amy, boss. Those pictures kinda blew his cover and they were circulated—not of Amy, just him. We provide protection for two businesses in that area, and the woman who owns one of them saw him. She doesn't miss much."

It pained Dean to think about how part of those businesses' profits went to pay his crew's salaries. He made certain to divert much of it back into the communities it came from, kind of like taxes for infrastructure, but it still rankled. That was the price of business, however, and he took some comfort in knowing he was a far kinder and benevolent crime boss than his predecessor.

"And no sign of any influx of soldiers."

Randy shook his head. "Nothing. A really low profile. If the competition is who we anticipate, then that's probably the best plan. If it was Unez, there would be movement and noise on the street."

And Amy would probably be dead. He couldn't quite stifle the shudder that ran through him. At least he was dealing with a professional—teaching lessons and retribution weren't likely to be high on the agenda, although he'd initially fallen prey to imagining those very things perpetrated against his wife and unborn child.

Shadow-man wanted his business, but wasn't yet willing to cause a bloodbath to get it, although Dean had no doubt he would if ransoming didn't work. Well, that unnamed man would drown in blood today. Dean was taking the war right to the fucker's doorstep. *Keep your shit together. Cool, calm and collected is going to get her back.*

For a moment he wondered if his crew would willingly trade their "jobs" for Amy, then dismissed the question. It didn't matter. He didn't have time to think about that now, or test each of them on varying degrees of loyalty. He was going to get Amy back. Then he and Randy could take their women and work the legal side of the business, or move and set up elsewhere. Dean had no call to spend a penny of his legitimate salary, living large on the money the business garnered, keeping up his image. So his investments had built up very nicely over the years and he was pretty comfortable. Randy was no slouch in that regard, either. And Dean had a flair for running a variety of businesses or putting people in place to do it in his stead. Regardless, he was out of this as soon as Amy came home.

Dropping his head, he took a deep breath through his nose, closing his eyes to focus. Even if shadow-man wasn't caught, he was out of this. Enough. Amy deserved better. Randy caught his eyes as they opened, and the message was clear—Randy was out, too. Dean nodded, a quick and silent agreement. Now they just had to deal.

The plan was solid after a few tweaks and considerable discussion. His crew slipped out the various exits and went to take their positions. If he was wrong, and Amy was being held elsewhere, they were fucked. But he felt in his gut that his luck was going to hold this time around. It had to.

"Dean?" Randy was folding up the map, ramming it into the pocket of his jacket.

"What?"

"He has no call to hurt her. But if he wants to trade…"

"I'll make my call if and when that happens. If our guy is coming to make the push himself, then we'll see. If not, Burnett goes away. Forever. But Amy's coming home, and then I'll take care of what needs to get taken care of."

"And if one of the crew wants to take your place?"

Dean shrugged. "He can try. No need for anyone to know about me, or that you knew."

"Men like you don't retire, Dean. Not from this. So they won't believe it."

"First time for everything, Randy. We don't have to stay here. Lots of other places to live."

Soberly, Randy nodded, then reached to the small of his back to pull out his weapon, transferring it to his pocket. There was no need for further talk—show time. They moved as one toward the door.

## Chapter Seventeen

"Get your ass in there, cunt." Olsen shoved her hard, hand in the small of her back. Amy was ready for it, setting her feet the instant he dragged her from the van. He casually kicked her when she resisted. She managed to stay upright. With her hands cuffed she wouldn't be able to easily break her fall and somehow had to protect the baby. Olsen snarled and moved around her, slapping her face. Her head snapped sideways with the force of the blow.

"Olsen!" A vaguely familiar voice pierced the air like the crack of a whip.

She had the satisfaction of seeing her captor's face pale before he stepped out of her line of vision.

"What the fuck are you doing?" Saul Burrows, Burnett, strode forward.

"You didn't have to listen to her bullshit all the way here," Olsen blustered. "She's got a fucking mouth on her and an attitude that rubs me the wrong way. Thinks she's so fucking special."

"You were told to bring her here, not to harm her. She's wearing cuffs, for fuck's sake."

Olsen shrugged. "I'm gonna park this piece of shit somewhere a long distance away. If you don't need me for some other fucking little thing."

"You do that. And come back. We're expecting that someone and I want everyone here. We're shorthanded, what with how quick this was put together."

"Yes, Sir!" The insubordination was evident to Burnett, judging by the look on his face, but he didn't respond. Instead he turned to her.

"Come inside, Amy. I heard you were pregnant, but didn't know how far along you were?"

She didn't respond to the implied question, or his attempt to establish some kind of chummy connection. "Why am I here?"

"Come inside and we'll talk about it. I'll get those cuffs off." He looked much the same to her now jaundiced eye, middle aged, soft around the middle, pale skin, unremarkable features. Despite the circumstances, he still didn't feel like he was dangerous, which was probably why he'd fooled her in the first place. She allowed him to take her elbow in one clammy hand and escort her through the door, wondering if she'd ever pass through it again alive. Terror roiled in her chest and she fought tears—for her baby. And for Dean.

They walked down a long hallway, before turning into a small room equipped with a cot and a chair, and to her horror, she saw a chemical toilet tucked into the far corner. Burnett urged her forward and stepped around her to fuss with the cuffs. The rigid circles of the metal dropped away from her wrists. She instantly rubbed the flesh marked by the confinement, then placed both hands on her belly, hunching slightly forward as she did so. Burnett backed away and was out the door, the sound of the lock being thrown making her spirits sink even further.

Having a choice between the cot and the chair, she chose the chair, moving to set it against the wall so she could watch the door, pretending her knees weren't weak. Her quick initial glance ascertained the lack of a window, so this was either a storage closet or a room built within a room. She suspected the former, because the overhead light was a light bulb screwed into a ceramic base and the light switch was nowhere to be seen. She wasn't a super spy or a television actor, so wouldn't be finding a magical way out of here. And they were clearly planning to keep her awhile, if that toilet meant anything. There was no running water, only a box of wipes set on the lid. The chair was uncomfortable, and the cot appeared to have just a blanket and a small pillow. It was like a jail cell, only without the cacophony of sound. At that moment she would have welcomed the noise to distract her.

Time passed slowly and checking her watch every couple of seconds didn't make it pass any quicker. Her lower back twinged and she couldn't sit any longer. Regrouping, she got up and walked around the room, carefully examining the walls, running her fingers over the ragged seams. It still felt like a closet. Her next thought was in regard to a camera—depending on how long they'd been planning this they might have installed a microphone, too.

Nearly an hour went by before she was convinced there was no one watching, her neck cricked from studying every inch of the ceiling and walls. It was both a relief and kind of depressing. They weren't interested in spying on her, but neither were they worried about her breaking out. Her belly rumbled and her back ached dully. With no sustenance in sight Amy slipped off her shoes and lay on her side on the cot, placing the blanket across her feet. She felt totally crappy, but she kept her mind focused on Dean finding her and taking her home without a segue into that mind numbing terror.

Movement outside the door had her sitting upright and feeling around with her toes for her shoes. It swung open and another man stood there, a paper sack under one arm and a piece of dark fabric in the other. She stared at him, trying to commit his face to memory but was stymied. Were all the new bad guys like Burnett? Vague and non memorable? A heavy gold ring adorned the middle finger of his right hand so she took note of that.

Without a word, ring man advanced into the little room and squatted to set the sack on the floor. He draped the cloth over the top of it, a black, closely woven something. He never took his eyes off her the whole time, but she couldn't read anything in his face except caution. When he spoke she flinched.

"When I return, I'll knock and you put the hood over your head—"

"Why?" Probably it wasn't a good idea to interrupt, for the caution was replaced by faint annoyance, although ring man kept talking as though she hadn't spoken.

"Someone will come to speak with you. If you see him you will never leave this place. The hood, Miss Copeland. He hasn't made war on women, especially pregnant women, but you'd better not see his face."

Motherfucker. Okay, then. "I'll put on the hood," she said immediately. "You'll knock first."

Pale lips twitching, ring man nodded. "That I will. You will remain seated on the bed. Speak when spoken to."

Shades of paternalism. Amy nodded, adding, "I understand."

His hand reached into his pocket and in spite of herself she flinched again. He pulled out a phone and almost casually took a picture of her and then another. Then he scanned her, impersonally. "Give me the bracelet," he ordered.

Hesitating, but only because it felt like she was giving up her last connection to Dean, Amy calmed herself. Her connection to Dean resided below her heart and swelled her belly. Ring man narrowed his eyes just a trifle and morphed from looking bland and unassuming to terrifying. She fumbled with the catch and stood with the links of gold dangling from her finger tips.

"Set it on the bed and move to the corner." He obviously was good at this kidnapping thing, so Amy did as she was told, watching him advance to snatch up her bracelet as she retreated.

Gesturing to the paper sack he turned on his heel and left the room, the door shutting quietly but firmly behind him, the lock engaging.

Moving back to the bed, Amy slipped her shoes on and went to the bag, eying it with caution. She first tucked the hood under her shirt, shoving a corner under the waistband of her pants—she didn't want it across the room when the knock came. A quick look inside determined the sack held a bottle of water and an apple. She decided to use the facilities, such as they were, then eat before the unknown man arrived. She figured she'd need all of her concentration and energy at that time.

****

As he swung into his truck, Dean's phone signalled an email and he yanked it out. Few people had this address. It was from an anonymous sender, but the subject line read *Amy*, and he impatiently waited for the two attachments to download. Randy's cell rang and his lieutenant answered it. Dean tried to focus on that conversation as the vision of Amy sitting on a narrow cot filled his phone screen, hands folded on her lap, staring at whomever was taking the picture. She looked tense but not terrified—whoever marked her face was going to pay dearly. Dean knew she was holding it together but his bowels turned to water even as his heart promised murder.

"Okay. No point in staying back. Message delivered. Go to…" Randy rattled off an address then concluded the conversation with a grunt. He put away his phone and looked at Dean.

"Somebody tossed a parcel on your steps, Dean. Mike didn't get a look at the driver, but did get a license plate." He pulled his laptop out and hit some keys. "Searching now. Still connected to wifi. Good thing."

Knowing his voice came from somewhere around his boots, Dean asked, "What the fuck was in the parcel, Randy?"

"It was an envelope with a gun in it. And Amy's bracelet. I don't figure the gun was just to give it heft." The other man didn't look at him, keeping his eyes glued on his computer screen.

A message—we have her and we will kill her unless... Dean swallowed and nodded. The bracelet was on Amy's wrist in both the cell phone pics, proof they had her. "What've you got?"

"It's a rental. License picture loading now. Fuck me. Fucking Olsen."

Dean thought hard again. "Burnett and Olsen. Why just the two of them? No way should they have put Olsen back in the spotlight again. Too visible."

Randy shrugged. "It doesn't make sense," he admitted.

Dean came to a conclusion. "They moved before they were ready. I have no clue why—but it forced Olsen's hand."

With a nod, Randy carried on with Dean's assumption. "So they took her prematurely and are undermanned. But something's coming down right quick if they sent you that email."

"You figure it's our guy?"

"Has to be. So that means he's not ready, either. But he'll bring people with."

Dean thought it through. "Maybe not. If they're scrambling, he's not ready. We go now."

"We should wait on the crews' take, buddy."

"They'll have to surveil in the time it takes us to get there."

"You may not get our guy if—"

"Doesn't matter." Dean cut him off and turned the engine over, pulling out into the street with a squeal of tires. "We miss him, tough shit. She's worth more to me. Time I put her first—more than time."

Randy was silent.

There really wasn't anything more to say.

****

A sharp rap on the door had Amy fumbling the hood over her head, the cloying fabric enveloping her with ominous ease, clinging to her mouth and nose. She was panicked, and struggling to sit upright on the edge of the bed, while being robbed of sight made her nauseous. Her back screamed with pain and a sudden cramp took her breath. She suffered through it and tried to identify the number of people in the room with her.

"Miss Copeland." A deep, smooth voice sounded directly in front of her and she heard what had to be the chair dragging across the floor. She made herself nod, her mouth suddenly dry as yet another cramp rippled near her groin. *Shit*. Braxton Hicks? She'd memorized such weird trivia from reading those pregnancy books.

"Amy?" The new guy was trying to get her attention.

Nodding again, she punctuated it with a raspy, "I'm Amy Copeland."

"She's Chambray's woman." Ring man's voice alerted her to his presence. "She doesn't seem to know anything. I—"

"So, you were Dean Chambray's woman?" The new guy spoke right over ring man.

Ice formed around her heart. Was that past tense? God. "I am." Her voice sounded really loud in her ears, yet muffled at the same time. Sweat formed around her temples and she longed to yank the stifling fabric off. Her hands twitched and she impulsively tucked them under her thighs. A cramp rolled across her lower belly, that one a little stronger.

In a conversational tone, new guy said, "Does he talk to you about his business?"

"No."

"But you know what it is he does."

"Generalities only." God, she felt terrible, her head pounding like a sledgehammer. Perspiration trickled down her spine. This was more than a reaction to being kidnapped and held for whatever.

"No matter. If he wants you back in one piece, he'll fold his tent."

Despite her preoccupation with her physical state, she thought the man was educated, to judge by his turn of phrase and careful speech. She didn't reply to his threat. Dean would come for her.

"I want you to call him and instruct him. I will tell you what to say."

"Sir?" Burnett's oily voice interrupted. "Sorry, but—"

"What is it?" New guy was obviously the boss, if his cold, nasty tone was anything to go by.

"There's activity in the area and one of your men hasn't checked in."

Another cramp distracted her and she involuntarily leaned forward, a sharp gasp escaping her. A hard hand grasped her shoulder. "What is wrong?" Ring man, she thought, his hand strangely comforting.

"Cramps," she managed.

A hand was placed on her other shoulder and she was urged backwards then turned and placed on her side. The blind movement disoriented her and she struggled not to vomit. Staggering rips of agony shot through her abdomen and red light sparked behind her eyes. She moaned. There was a brief dialogue of male voices but she couldn't concentrate. Then footsteps sounded and the door shut hard.

The hood was eased off and ring man set it aside. She looked up at him, barely able to fill her lungs. He glanced at the door and then back at her. An object was placed in her hand and her fingers pressed closed around it. "If you can, lock the door behind me. Don't open it to anyone. It won't stand up to a determined assault—they might shoot the lock—but it'll buy you some time."

Against the escalating cramping, she gritted her teeth to ask, "Who are you?"

"Not your enemy. Burnett hasn't figured out I wasn't sent by his boss, and the boss thinks I'm with Burnett, but if they talk, they'll figure it out quick. You hang on. Dean should be here soon." A little smile flitted over his features, making him suddenly approachable, despite her focus on her painful state, although she wasn't able to sort through his comments. "I, uh, pushed him a little. I expect the pictures and your jewellery hit a nerve. I can't get you out of here, but—"

His head came up and she heard it too—distant cracks, hollow and flat—it had to be gunfire.

"Shit. Dean *is* here. Lock up behind me." He squeezed her hand and hustled to the door, opening it cautiously before slipping through without a backward glance. It shut with a click. With one hand on her belly, clutching the key in the other, Amy got to her feet, only to double over again.

Falling to her knees, she raised her head and locked her eyes on that door—she had to get there, put a barrier between her and the bad guys. It took an eternity and by the time it came within reach she was weeping with the exertion, primarily because of the misery in her belly. It sucked her energy and the accompanying fear was so overwhelming she could barely force the key into the lock. It turned beneath her shaking fingers and she sank the rest of the way to the floor.

As if on cue something thudded against the door and the knob rattled. A foul curse permeated the wood and she rolled away instinctively to one side, a gush of heat christening her thighs as she did so. It was too much effort to do more than draw her knees up and curl over her belly. Her baby was coming—or dying. And it was Olsen outside that door. Amy sank into darkness.

****

Dean raced down the hallway, prepared for anything. Burnett lay in a heap behind him, having given up Amy's location within an instant of being *encouraged* to do so. Dean's fists still throbbed with satisfaction. Enrico stayed with the asshole in order to bind him. They'd met minimal resistance initially, only two men guarding the perimeter, but the three situated at the choke points were better trained and shots had been exchanged. Fortunately, none of his crew were injured aside from Lee, who caught a ricochet that tore a hunk out of his thigh. He'd been helped back to a vehicle and the rest of Dean's men infiltrated the building and worked their way through it with military precision. Burnett had been found huddling in the garage, obviously trying to liberate a vehicle.

Rounding the corner he saw two men locked in a struggle—Olsen was one of them. Dean closed the distance and took an opening, tearing Olsen free. He punched the smaller man directly in the face with every ounce of his terror and rage, feeling his nose crunch satisfyingly as his eyes crossed. Hurling him next into the opposite wall, Olsen hit with a thud and slid down it. The man he'd been struggling with stared and fucking *smiled.* Dean had to blink to keep his eyes in his head. His handler? What the fuck?

"Deal with that fucker quick, Dean," the man advised as he raised both hands, showing they were empty. "Amy's in there." He tipped his head at the door. "She's hurting. I have a bigger asshole to fry."

Randy appeared at his shoulder but Dean's focus was on the door.

"I'll follow whoever that was. You get Amy."

"Okay, but he's one of us. Help him, Randy." His lieutenant took off running, weapon held slightly ahead and to the side.

The door was locked—a deadbolt by the look of it. He rattled the knob and pounded on the panels, calling out her name, but Amy didn't reply. Not daring to fire at the lock he set his boot directly beneath it in a blistering kick. It took three solid hits but the frame splintered and he forced his way through. A quick scan of the room found Amy curled up on the floor to the right of the door in a pool of her own blood. He went to his knees and touched her face, breathing her name as his heart ruptured in his chest.

"Amy."

Her eyes fluttered and her pale lips parted a fraction. "I knew you'd come." And then she drifted away. He fucking saw her go.

Heart stopping dread froze him for only a moment. He had her scooped into his arms without another thought and strode out of the room to make his way to his truck, praying his men had cleared the place. Enrico gaped at him, still kneeling beside Burnett's worse-for-wear body. His bronze skin paled as his mouth thinned and then he was up, setting a scorching pace in front of Dean, running point. They made it to the vehicle without incident and Dean climbed in the back with Amy. He managed to dig his keys from his pocket and toss them to Enrico.

'Rico maybe thought he was driving a sports car the way he threw the truck around corners, accelerating to insane speeds on the straightaway, but Dean willed him to go faster. Amy was as white as snow, her breasts barely rising with her shallow breaths, and he could see faint evidence of a pulse in her throat. He didn't need to check her to know she was losing their baby and probably dying—he was soaked with her lifeblood already. He wanted to die in her stead and for the first time in forever, prayed, promising anything if only she would live. The litany and chant of his Catholic schooling came back without effort.

Vaguely aware of Enrico speaking into the phone, he pressed his lips to Amy's forehead. She felt so cold. *Please. I'll do anything.*

An eternity later they pulled into the emergency drive of the hospital and Sandra hauled the back door of the truck open, her face nearly as pale as Amy's. "We have a gurney. They want to hang blood now."

He was out of the vehicle with his precious burden in the next breath to lay her on the stretcher. True to her word, Sandra had Amy's arm exposed and was searching for a vein before he stepped back. He winced as the large bore needle slipped in but Amy didn't stir. At least she was spared her phobia.

He followed the stretcher, never taking his eyes off her beautiful face, imagining he could see some color creeping into her skin. He tried to touch her whenever the medical personnel weren't in his way. They all crowded onto the elevator, Amy on her rolling cot, Sandra and two beefy attendants, another nurse who looked askance at him. He supposed he was a mess and was relieved to remember tucking his weapon under the seat. There was medical jargon bandied about but he couldn't process.

Disembarking, their little huddle hurried to a door near the end of the corridor.

The strange nurse shook her head at him and peeled off, crooking a finger. He halted and looked at Sandra who also shook her head. "She's going into surgery right now, Dean. Dr. Wyatt assessed her on the fly." She pointed at one of the beefy guys, who nodded to him.

"It was desperate, sir. But she's stabilizing some with the transfusion. We couldn't get a pressure but now we can—she's a fighter. There's lots of hope, but we must take the baby."

The walls closed in and he stood numbly while Amy disappeared behind the absurdly normal-appearing green doors. The nurse swam into his vision. "You need to change and then you can go in with her."

Having a purpose galvanized him, and he followed her petite, white-garbed figure into a room not far from where Amy had disappeared. The nurse handed him scrubs and told him to strip down and change into them. "Put your clothes in one of those bags. I doubt you'll get all that blood out of them so you can put them in the bio trash it you like."

Eyes rounding, apparently replaying her comment, she raised one hand, then retreated. "When you're done wait outside the surgery door. Someone will come for you."

He fumbled with the scrubs. His hands were bruised and swollen, but they weren't the impediment. He needed to get in there with her and their soon-to-be-born child, yet he couldn't make his body obey. The pain emblazoned on Amy's face even in her unconscious state now unmanned him. How had he dared to put her in such a position? What the fuck had been going on in his head? What if the doctor was wrong and things didn't turn out for either her or the baby—or both? The damn material flexed beneath his hands, but he couldn't pull it on. He sat slumped in the chair, wearing only his shorts.

A slender form invaded his space and he automatically defended against it, belatedly realizing it was Sandra, clad in the very outfit he needed to don. He barely avoided decking her. She plucked the scrubs from his unresisting hands, clucking over the state of them and efficiently yanked the shirt over his head. Somehow his arms sought and found the armholes and slid down the sleeves, big wrists protruding at the cuff. Kneeling, Sandra inserted first his left, then his right foot into the pants and tugged them up to his knees before pulling some weird booties over his feet.

When she rose to her feet again, he felt her hands at his head and wished for a benediction, then realized she was pulling a cap over his hair.

"Get up, Dean. They've administered the epidural and will soon be taking the baby. She's awake, sort of." Her brisk, no nonsense tone gave him something to hang onto and he stood to pull the bottoms of the scrubs up the rest of the way.

Taking his wrist and shepherding him to the door, Sandra swiped at his hand with something wet and cold on a bundle of gauze. It stung like the fires of hell and he came back to himself, offering her the other bloody hand. By the time they reached the doors at the end of the hall designated as the operating room he was operating as himself, the Dean Chambray Amy needed.

Entering the room in Sandra's wake, he vaguely registered the presence of several gowned and masked individuals, but his attention was taken by Amy, lying on a narrow table, a piece of fabric tented over a frame nearly covering her torso. A thumping sound filled the room, two thumping sounds, one at a quicker rate than the other. He could barely see her face and he hastened his gait. He took his place at her side, down on one knee by her shoulder. Her hand fluttered up and he clasped it in his own, using the other to trace a fingertip down her cheek. She looked absolutely beautiful, no longer hurting so badly, and as her eyes locked with his she appeared to become almost sleepy.

"Are you okay?" he asked, like it wasn't the stupidest question of the century.

"I am now," she whispered back, and his gut clenched, as his heart swelled.

She was festooned with wires, and pads peeked out from her hospital gown. He realized the band on her arm was a blood pressure cuff, and that they were also monitoring her heart. And so the quicker beat must be the baby's. He made himself breathe and show nothing but calm.

The surgeon spoke as if from a great distance to tell them he was going to begin and at that moment the baby's heart beat stopped. Sandra spoke directly from the other side of Amy's head. "They removed the fetal monitor. It's fine."

Dean breathed again, but kept his hopefully calm gaze on Amy. She simply stared back, and he realized she'd put her trust in him, no matter that it wasn't him in the medical role—her whispered words when he burst into that fucking room they'd held her in would haunt him forever, and he'd spend the rest of his life proving she was right and that he was worthy of her. *I knew you'd come…*

Ignoring the sounds of metal instruments clanking against metal and other disparate sounds that were familiar but something he didn't want to identify, he crouched beside Amy and willed everything to turn out. Moments later there was a flurry of motion and a baby's thin wail filled the room, nearly drowning out the sudden roaring in his head. Amy's face turned and lit up from within, and her lips parted.

"May I—" Her eyes filled with yearning.

Sandra's capable hands reached to take the squirming, bloody, little form and lower it to Amy's chest. Amy's free hand hovered before resting on the downy head, tiny and blond and she smiled, an expression so full of emotion that he stared to emblazon it in his brain.

"She's beautiful, Amy." Sandra's voice was thready with tears. Dean blinked hard against his own. A girl. Two girls to fill his life. Forever.

## Epilogue

"She's finally asleep." Dean thought he'd wear a path right through the damn hardwood before Emma conceded defeat. His little girl had a cold and was fretful, not that it slowed the toddler down any significant amount. Then she'd become overtired and couldn't settle. Walking with her and rocking her usually worked, and tonight had been no different, except it took a whole lot longer. The evening hours with Amy were precious, because he rarely saw her during the day. He had a real job and she was preoccupied with Emma, having become one of the best mothers in existence, and he had the worst one to compare to. His mother had passed and aside from seeing to it that she was buried with some semblance of dignity, he didn't give her another thought. His life was within the four walls of the home he and Amy chose to raise Emma in—Emma and the little creature due to make its appearance in two months time.

Dragging him to parenting courses hadn't really been an effort—he'd have done anything for his now wife and child. And he had to admit he learned a lot and thought he'd turned out to be, if not dad of the year, a not too far off runner-up. Emma might have him wrapped around her little finger, but he still did what was in her best interest, and sometimes that meant saying no and thwarting her. That turned his thoughts to Amy. He hadn't thought another child was in *her* best interest, but her way of convincing him undermined his resistance.

Reaching out a slender hand to him, she raised a golden brow. "Heavy thoughts, babe?"

"No." He settled beside her on the couch and she leaned into him, pulling her legs up. The swell of her belly elicited a wave of possessiveness and he laid his hand on it. "Just thinking how fucking lucky I am."

"Dean!"

"What?" He gently rubbed her belly.

"You can't swear."

"Emma's asleep and this little guy can't talk yet."

"Little girl."

He groaned, he couldn't help it. He was so whipped. Surely cleaning up his act meant they'd have a boy this time… Amy laughed and he stared into her beautiful face. "I don't care about the gender, sweetheart. I just want you and him—or her—to be okay."

"It'll be fine, Dean." She was serene Amy, earth mother, although last night the languor had lifted and she'd blown his mind in their bed. Pregnant or not, she was like no other woman in his experience and he couldn't imagine life without her.

Walking away from his so-called life in Sacramento had been a no brainer. No one determined his undercover status to his knowledge, and his handler took his abdication with aplomb. After all, he wasn't on the "books" anywhere.

The man had done an end run on him out of necessity. Olsen had overheard talk of moving Amy to a safer location and panicked, fearing the plan would fizzle, and alerted Burnett. Learning from another source of the planned kidnap attempt too late, Dean's handler managed to arrive before shadow-man and pose as one of his "staff"—then took down the elusive crime lord himself, albeit with Randy's help. Dean supposed his handler had ears everywhere, and he'd actually felt no proprietal interest in bringing down his elusive prey. His priorities had shifted.

Regrettably, the evidence was sketchy and while they now had the identity of shadow man, the charges didn't stick—Burnett and Olsen were slapped with kidnapping and holding Amy against her will, presumably well-remunerated for taking the fall. Dean's handler had to settle for that lack of anonymity in return for covering up the impromptu gun battle, but Joshua Frye Corbett was now squarely in the eye of law enforcement. He could hardly run his empire without someone watching, so Dean supposed some good had come from Amy's ordeal.

He'd arranged for their condo to be packed up immediately after Emma's birth and stored until Amy could participate in a discussion about where she might want to live. Eugene, Oregon became their new home, and finding a suitable abode took one flying trip on his part—Amy fell in love with the older three bedroom, two bath house in the established neighborhood just from the pictures he sent. He'd paid careful attention to what she wanted, determined to meet her each and every need at all times.

Dean was just glad to move out of Sandra's home. Amy's friend was immensely helpful with the baby and Amy's aftercare. Amy had a stay in hospital until the personnel were certain she was out of danger and her blood levels and such were okay, and then Sandra took them in. But he was selfish. He wanted his wife and child under his roof and his care. Amy refused a big wedding, so they were married as soon as she was mobile, by a justice of the peace. He got his way with a ring—she just wanted her bracelet—and the enormous diamond above the matching band worn on the appropriate finger of her left hand both comforted and aroused him each and every time he saw it. His woman, his wife, in his bed and his life, always.

Now running a security consultant business based in Portland, far enough away to keep his home life quite separate—he'd learned that lesson well—yet close enough to make it an easy commute, he adjusted easily.

Most of his crew had scattered to the four winds, some to make their way legitimately, others not. The ones who took him up on his offer to go legit were working out well, assuming the mantle of keeping the law almost as easily as breaking it. Dean presumed it was because protection was protection in their eyes, and he didn't doubt his leadership had something to do with it. Providing security, acting as bodyguards and installing and monitoring high-tech security systems perhaps wasn't as challenging as their former lives, but it paid equally well and one didn't have to look over one's shoulder constantly. He never thought about who might assumed his role back in Sacramento.

"I've invited Sandra and Enrico for dinner on Saturday." Amy snuggled closer, her eyes shut. Dean had been correct about Enrico. The man was well established in Dean's business and had managed to convince Sandra to move to Eugene, although they weren't living together. There was more going on in that relationship than he was privy to, but he figured to stay out of it. Amy meddled enough for the both of them.

"What about Randy and Andrea?" His lieutenant was as indispensible as always. Dean gave him his head and his own portion of the security business, but they still worked closely together.

Violet eyes blinked open and studied him. "Andrea finally convinced that man to take some time off. They're going camping. Really camping. No flush toilets. Andrea wants to try it before she has the baby. I can't imagine."

He laughed. It felt good to just laugh at mundane things. It felt better not to have to guard his thoughts and hide how he felt. He remembered Randy talking about going back to nature, but hadn't felt the need to pay such close attention to detail as he had in his past life. Another blessing.

Baby number two hitched under his hand, pressing upwards as though seeking his touch. Fucking lucky. He could *think it* because it was true.

"I gotta crash, Dean. I'm pretty much done in." Amy stretched, her arms now above her head and he feasted his eyes on her curves. Maybe she'd have some energy once she was undressed and prone in their bed…

"You go ahead, sweetheart. I'll do a walk through." He hadn't gotten soft even if his life was vastly different. It was his job to keep his family safe. "And I'll check on Emma."

Rising to her feet with a little assistance Amy gifted him with her smile. She still wore her hair long, although braided it or left it in a ponytail as often as not. And he still loved to weave his hands through it, annoying the hell out of her when he freed it from its confinement.

Walking her down the hallway leading to the stairs, looping an arm around her shoulders, he reveled in her warmth and her scent, marveled yet again at his fucking luck. Dean Chambray sincerely hoped Amy Chambray had her forever, because he was definitely living his.

The End

**www.allysonyoung.com**

Evernight Publishing

www.evernightpublishing.com

www.ingramcontent.com/pod-product-compliance
Lightning Source LLC
Chambersburg PA
CBHW021447240626
47153CB00001B/328
*9781771309233*